Der.

Spies
on Bikes

Spies on Bikes

Typeset in Minion Pro

Editing, design, typesetting and publishing by UK Book Publishing

www.ukbookpublishing.com

ISBN: 978-1-912183-85-2

In memory of
Elizabeth Forster née Gray
(1944-2018)

Tuesday 29th August 1939

1

Sir Charles took the call in his study.

'Are you free to punt the pill?' asked the familiar voice.

'Give me time to check the weather.'

What did London want? To find out Sir Charles pressed a red button.

'You can blab away now, Freddy, I'm on the scrambler.'

'We need to use our eyes and ears in the North and that's you, Charlie, my darling.'

'Bit inconvenient that, don't you know, it's the shooting season. If I'm not out with the guns the dogs will sulk.'

'Don't play the mossback with me. This is a national emergency. I'm offering you the chance to hunt Germans. Better sport than shooting pheasants, what? And if you catch any, Germans I mean, you can set your dogs on 'em for all I care.'

'I've taken the fly; explain.'

'Last week a Focke-Wulf Condor belonging to Danish Air Lines, flying from Croydon to Copenhagen, took a circuitous route home. Before crossing the North Sea it flew up the coast to your part of the world. The pilot was German. We know his name, have his biography, have seen his flight log. He is claiming temporary instrument failure. A cock and bull story if ever there was one. He is a fervent Nazi. He was spying.'

'You think he's seen the masts?'

'That is exactly what I think. Jerry is a nosey fellow. He will want to know more, which brings me to why I might be going to spoil your shooting. Tomorrow a German steamer called the Nord docks at Newcastle's Corporation Quay; your neck of the woods, what? Her passengers include a posse of Hitler Youth.'

'Why, at this time of crises, is a German steamer bringing young Nazis to England?'

'Hitler doesn't think it will come to war. You and I have had lots of conversations with that pompous ass Ribbentrop … he doesn't think England has the stomach for another war … and that's what he keeps telling his boss … and his boss believes him. In the meantime, everyone's pretending there's not a black cloud in the sky … that it's business as usual while preparing for the worst. I don't know about you, Charlie, but I don't like these new gas masks … the young Nazis claim to be coming here for a cycling holiday. I think they are coming to spy. If war does break out I can't see them sitting back, drinking tea … they'll go down fighting.'

'Sabotage?'

'Anything's possible … if they cycle north our worst suspicions will be realised. The Daily Herald calls them 'Spyclists'.'

'Freddy, I only read The Times.'

'Ditto. I only know the word because a low ranker used it in a report. Despite its origins I thought it apt. I'll bet my last sovereign that these fellows are on a clandestine reconnaissance mission. Byker-Harrison is undercover on the boat. He spotted 'em boarding at Hamburg. He's a fox hunting man … how he manages to ride when he only has one arm I'll never know but he does, and, like his hounds, he knows when he's on to something. When he asked permission to follow 'em … do a spot of low grade intelligence gathering, I told him 'tallyho'. It is my experience that a sea voyage makes people think they are on holiday, makes 'em loosen up, makes 'em talk more, say things they'd never say in the office. He's a brave chap. Once saw him jump a six foot wall to get a fox. Not for the first time he's put himself in a bit of a tricky situation. It's a German ship, you see, so there's no one on board in authority he can take into his confidence.

'Charlie, you are one of the small number of people who know the purpose of the masts. They are the visible sign of England's secret weapon. If the boffins are right, we'll be able to see Hitler's Luftwaffe as flickering blobs of light on something like a very tiny cinema screen. It will give us precious minutes to scramble our fighters. We'll know when and where to post him our reply. If this technology works, we'll not be caught with our pants down. The Nazis will find that bombing England is not the piece of cake they found Guernica. If those cyclists on the Nord should decide to head your way I want you to flush 'em out. Set the beaters on them.'

'And when they break cover?'

'That is the problem. One would like to shoot 'em but they are not pheasants. Shooting pheasants is sport. Shooting people is murder.'

'And we are not murderers?'

'No, we are not. Some of the reports I'm receiving from Germany make me ashamed to be a human being. Anyone who opposes Hitler is taken away and shot. And as for the Jews, their crime is simply being Jewish. Terrible. Appalling. Which reminds me, how is your refugee, Jacob Schonfeld doing?'

'Elizabeth and Cook spoil him and Mike and Margaret have all but adopted him. He's quite a character, insists on being called Jack Field … says he wants to be English. He hates the Germans.'

'If those 'spyclists' do head north best keep him out of their way. The Nazis murdered his mother and father.'

'So I believe.'

'After all he has seen and had done to him I can't think of a better sanctuary for him than your estate in Northumberland. Believe me, I wish I could join you. London's too full of men digging trenches and filling bags with sand. I saw two soldiers making sand pies … Charlie, I don't think people realise the seriousness of the situation. All the titles are up north with their Purdy's. And that's where I'd be if it wasn't for Hitler … damn envious of the hospitality you'll be giving your American guests. When do you expect 'em?'

'The next few days … Elizabeth is flapping.'

'I don't need to remind you, but I'm going to anyway, to give the red carpet treatment to Professor Striker. She may be young and female but she is close to the President. She's spent the last month touring Germany as his unofficial eyes and ears. I have it on good authority that when she gets back to the States she will be sending him a report on everything she's seen. By all accounts she's very good looking … not at all the bluestocking. Woo her, Charlie; treat her like one of your gun dogs. If it comes to war we must have America on our side. Too many Americans are isolationists. Any influence we can bring to bear to make that great democracy our ally will have the most tremendous consequences. Blow the dust off your box of diplomatic conjuring tricks; see if you can pull a few rabbits out of the mess that is Europe. In the meantime, missing you terribly. Your cook might be a dragon but her soufflés are out of this world. Charlie, this is an order … stay close to the phone. I have a funny feeling on this one. I think your country is going to need you. All my love to Elizabeth.'

Beneath the green shaded lamp on his desk a cat purred. Sir Charles chucked its chin. Though it was summer, rain and gusting wind made it seem more like winter. He ordered a fire to be lit. The play of flickering flames on leather bound volumes and a collection of porcelain chamber pots soothed his anxiety. Yet, no doubt about it, Freddy's phone call had made the unseasonal bleakness worse. The cat stretched out its head begging for more. He absentmindedly obliged, all his thoughts being on the deteriorating international situation … American isolationism, German aggression, the British guarantee of Polish 'independence'. If Hitler did invade that country and Britain kept her word then the unthinkable would happen … Britain would once again be at war with Germany. In his left arm he had a piece of shrapnel from the war meant to end all wars. He put his hand down the sleeve of his tweed jacket. When it was damp, like today, it rose to the surface. And on top of all that, England was under attack from the IRA. In July one of their bombs had exploded in the King's Cross left luggage office. One man had been killed and two counter assistants seriously injured. In Coventry, department stores had been wrecked. Another bomb had devastated Victoria Station. It was all too depressing. He added coal to the fire. When the world seemed on the brink of falling to pieces a chap needed warmth.

2

Vomit sloshed in the Nord's stairwells. On a spray swept deck a less than stalwart member of the Hitler Youth asked a seaman if they were going to sink. In the vessel's lounge bar a waiter slopped water onto a table cloth.

'To stop the drinks go fall,' he explained to the young woman sitting at the table. 'Same again?'

'Why not.'

'That is ja?'

'Yes, Gunther, that is ja.'

'While you're here,' the middle aged man with one arm at the next table butted in, 'mine's a double Johnny Walker … none of your foreign rubbish, mind … with a splash of soda and I mean a splash … not half of what's rattling this ship's steel plates.' He addressed the young woman. 'It's alright for a pretty young fraulein like yourself … you attract waiters … me? They ignore. As far as young Lohengrin's concerned I could die of thirst. Byker-Harrison.' He held out his one and only hand. 'Odd shaking hands with your left hand … still can't get used to it … the Somme.'

'Marigold Striker … is it Byker-Harrison with a hyphen?'

'Actually, yes.'

'It makes you sound aristocratic … Byker-Harrison, how very English.'

'American?'

'Yes. I suppose if you were a German you'd be a 'von something'. I wonder if there are any 'vons' over there?' She gestured towards the group of Hitler Youth drinking at the bar. 'You know, when those guys start 'sieg heiling' and clicking their heels I just want to laugh … it's so comical, like watching an operetta set in Ruritania … the Boy Scout uniforms … I mean, are they for real?'

Men like Byker-Harrison liked to talk and expected women to listen. She often reflected that if ears increased in seize according to the amount of work they did then hers would be as large as an African elephant's. She knew four categories of men: Oglers … Gropers … those who made a girl feel patronised and those who, for unfathomable reasons, a girl fell in love with … even if they were Oglers, Gropers and Patronisers. She prepared to be lectured.

'Are they for real? I'm afraid they are, my dear. A few years ago, no one took the Nazis seriously, they were a joke, an extreme right-wing group that sane people thought had no hope of gaining power … now look where we are … on the brink of war. The master race is on the march and the rest of us had better keep out of their way. If we don't wave 'em through to wherever they want to go, expect trouble.'

'Will Britain "wave 'em through" if they attack Poland?'

'Au contraire, my dear, the British Lion will roar.'

'To defeat Germany in any future conflict I rather think the British lion will need the help of the American eagle.'

'Your ambassador to the United Kingdom is an isolationist.'

'Mr Kennedy wants to be president. He thinks Americans don't want any part of a second war between Germany and the United Kingdom. He thinks being an isolationist is his ticket to the White House.'

'You sound very well informed.'

'In Boston the Strikers and Kennedys are neighbours. Daddy has done lots of business deals with Mr Kennedy.'

'And very well connected.'

'Plug me in and I'll light up Manhattan … and you, Mr Byker-Harrison, could you light up Mayfair? And why are you carrying a gun?'

'What sharp eyes you have.'

'That's what Little Red Riding Hood said to the Big Bad Wolf. When you leaned over to hector the waiter I caught the hint of a shoulder holster.'

'I'm a policeman.'

'British cops don't carry guns.'

'They do when their job is to protect the British ambassador in Berlin.'

'You say you are a bodyguard but, excuse me, you only have one arm. Would it not be better for a bodyguard to have two arms? Mr Byker-Harrison … I do not believe you. You're as phoney as the salt dough cookies dime stores put in their windows to advertise their wares … they look the real thing but eating them will break your teeth. I think you are what you Brits call "top drawer". Cops crawl out of bottom drawers. Cops don't have hyphens. I know a well-tailored suit when I see one … that's not a rag you have on your back … that's Savile Row. Daddy has one just like it and he's a millionaire.'

'Your Bloody Mary, fraulein.'

'Thanks, Gunther, and keep the change.'

'Danke. Your Johnny, sir.'

'I beg your pardon.'

'The Johnny Walker you ordered, sir … your whisky splash.'

'And bring me the change … that's a British pound note.'

'Mr Byker-Harrison, has it ever occurred to you that waiters ignore you, not because you ain't sexy but because you are mean? Try tipping. No wonder India wants independence. Now, if you'll excuse me, I'm going to dress for dinner.'

3

'Are you free to punt the pill?'

'Give me time to check the weather.' Sir Charles pressed the red button. 'Go ahead.'

'Since our last parley-vous,' began Lord Frederick, 'I've been making enquiries … turned over a few stones you might say. A chap never ceases to be surprised. You know how it is, there you are enjoying a nice mouthful of juicy grouse, giblet gravy and all, when a molar breaks on a piece of shot. The amazing news is that thanks to the Boy Scouts … I mean thanks to the Boy Scouts of all people … we now have the Spyclists' itinerary. Baden-Powell's changing their nappies, don't you know … arranging campsites for the blighters through his Scout movement. BP's a nice chap, heart in the right place and all that, but like so many in the first echelon of our society, a dupe. He left my den this pm a chastened man. I bowled him a few home truths. He boasted that he'd met von Ribbentrop. I said, "Hasn't everyone?" He thought the German "charming". He's been hoodwinked into thinking the Hitler Youth is an organisation similar to his own. Are the Nazis mesmerists? What a load of tosh!'

'Boy Scouts do not murder Jews.'

'Quite … if these bastards stick to their schedule they will be spending tomorrow in Newcastle. Then, and this is where you come in, Charlie, they are planning to travel north. They have expressed a wish to go bird watching on the Farne Islands. I've checked the map. If they take the coastal route, which I'm certain they'll want to, they'll pass close to the masts. And when they do they'll use their Leicas like machine guns. Click. Click. Click. The Scouts have been instructed … now they know the score they are batting on our side … to point them in the direction of your estate … make their campsite where you can keep an eye on them. I want them where they can be stalked. Get your man Bert involved.'

'Freddy, Bert's my butler. I think you mean Mike. Mike's my gamekeeper.'

'Sorry, Old Thing, never very good with names. It is my view that when a chap rises to the rank of butler he should be obliged by law to change his name to Butler, unless of course he's already called Butler; same with gamekeepers, they should all be called Partridge, that way the lower orders know their place and yours truly doesn't get confused; not good for HMG when the head of MI5 is made to look an ass. As I was saying, Bert or Mike, or whatever he's called has a spot-on eye for the lie of the land. Without his help last year I'd never have bagged that five-pointer … damn proud of that shot. The Vicarage will also come in handy … lots of our men there if they should be needed … lots of expertise. Never thought we'd be using that facility so soon … and the war hasn't even started. I'm no voyeur, Charlie … take no pleasure in snooping, but the spooks tell me that if it comes to war and we put wounded Nazis into Ward Nine of your cottage hospital our men in the Vicarage will be able to hear them taking a pee, scratching their what's it ... and other things. I mean we can't say to their wounded we're not going to give you medical help unless you tell us your secrets, can we? That would be against the Geneva Convention. And we are British, aren't we? So, we listen to them farting on their bed pans telling each other how they never expected to be treated with such kindness, oh, and by the way, our secret weapon that Tommy knows nothing about is ... Charlie, fill your twelve bore with black powder and when you see 'em ... let 'em have it ... turn 'em into chimney sweeps. I have a meeting in ten minutes with Mr Churchill. He may not be in the government but he's got lots of influence. If he bumped into your Nazi campers he'd use real ammunition on them. Please give my love to Elizabeth. I'm missing the moors something rotten.'

The barometer began to rise. Better weather was on its way. Through rain streaked windows Sir Charles observed drooping delphiniums and lopsided lupines. He enjoyed summer rain. It refreshed the land. The downpour had been needed.

His dear wife, Elizabeth, did not share his empathy with storms. As soon as rain blighted an English summer's day she told him, 'That is why we should holiday in France.' Tonight he had little sympathy with such a point of view. Riviera sunshine was out of keeping with his mood. If he'd been in the National Gallery he'd have ignored the Impressionists and made straight for the Constables; especially the latter's sketches of brooding English skies.

The prospect of another war with Germany made him so melancholy that, for the first time in many years, he did not dress for dinner. His wife, who considered herself an expert on his moods, told him, 'It's Freddy, phoning from London ... I know it is. What will the servants think?'

After the fish course he confessed, 'I'm not hungry. If you'll excuse me, my dear, I'm off to the study. I have work to do. If it comes to war, we must be prepared.'

'Have you measured the back of the Rolls to see if it will take a stretcher?'

'Not yet.'

'Do you want me to do it?'

'No ... but if, God forbid, it comes to total war you may have to go down a coal mine.'

'To be safe from Hitler's bombers?'

'To be a coal miner.'

'You are joking?'

'I don't know. If it comes to war anything is possible.'

'Charles, I'm the daughter of a duke.'

'Mike's putting the Hitler Youth in the Meadow Field ... a good place for us to keep an eye on them. Freddy's men will be around as well.'

'From the Vicarage?'

'Yes.'

'I wish you'd tell me what's going on in there, you know I like to know. I am as discreet as anyone in Box One Hundred or whatever it is you boys call the organisation you work for.'

'MI5's its new name and as for what goes on in the Vicarage … that's top secret … only those who need to know, know.'

'Charles, sometimes you can be a real meanie … you could tell me if you wanted to, no one would know.'

'Suppose, just suppose German paratroopers suddenly fell out of the sky and landed right on top of The Hall and you were taken prisoner. They put you up against a wall. "Vat is going on in zee Vicarage?" If you don't know you can't tell them.'

'Don't be silly, Germans don't talk like that … they speak German. You have fluent German. They would speak to you in German. And what if they put you up against a brick wall?'

'I'd shoot myself before I blabbed.'

'Don't be so dramatic … you know perfectly well you wouldn't shoot yourself … I wouldn't let you … if you weren't here I'd have no one to boss.'

'The servants?'

'Not the same.'

'By the way, I think it would be a good idea for you to tell Jack that the Hitler Youth are coming … prepare the ground, so to speak. I don't want him thinking England's been invaded. The poor chap's already had too many shocks. These are the people who murdered his mother and father. It will be an unpleasant experience for him to come face to face with them again. Don't of course tell him that we think they are here to spy … that information we keep to ourselves. Outwardly we must make these young Germans as welcome as possible. We must seem to welcome them as warmly as we are sincerely planning to welcome our American guests. That way we will not arouse their suspicions … hospitality, my dear, is a subtle weapon.'

4

On board the Nord, Marigold found the force eight exhilarating. She empathised with its violence. Unlike many of her fellow passengers, she did not suffer from sea sickness. Uppermost on her mind as she returned to her cabin was what to wear for dinner. A gown was out of the question. The Nord was not the Queen Mary. On the latter vessel the American colleagues she was scheduled to meet up with at Sir Charles's residence in Northumberland would no doubt be whooping it up … champagne and caviar, paid for by the King of England, or something like that. She, on the other hand, had the dreary prospect of dining too close to that bumptious Englishman with one arm and the double-barrelled name.

She settled on a two-piece tweed suit. The jacket's lapels would allow her to show off one of her favourite pieces of jewellery, a diamond brooch in the shape of a dollar sign. Its diamonds were large and real. To reduce the risk of losing it, she pinned it in place with its own pin and a hatpin.

She put on lipstick. She checked her seams. It was while twisting round to do this that she noticed an envelope sticking out from under the cabin's door. Before she'd a chance to pick it up, it disappeared. What the prairie oyster was going on? To find out she opened the door.

The man holding the envelope was vomiting, otherwise he'd have been off.

'That's mine,' she said, plucking it out of his hand.

She watched him stagger off. Mal de mer. Tut. Tut. Some guys just weren't cut out to be sailors.

In the dining room she propped the envelope up against her clutch bag. Gunther came to take her order.

'You look very smart,' she complimented him.

'Danke.' He bowed. 'It is my service silver uniform. It is, how do you say, made by the Fuhrer.'

'Designed … by the Fuhrer?'

'Ja, that is it … designed by the Fuhrer.'

'I know Herr Hitler is an artist and a great leader, that the Third Reich is going to last for thousands of years but, forgive my ignorance, it's the first time I've heard he's a fashion designer. It seems to me that your boss man is a jack of all trades. He didn't by any chance write Hamlet, did he?'

'The Fuhrer can do anything.'

'Who says so?'

'Everyone says so … Herr Himmler, Herr Goering … everyone.'

'But you believe it?'

'Ja.'

'Why?'

'Warum?'

'Yes, warum?'

He fluttered a napkin onto her lap. 'It is best always to say only good things about the Fuhrer. The Englishman with one arm is Kaput.'

'What did you say?'

He looked scared. How many times had she seen that look on the faces of black Americans in Alabama?

'The Englishman with one arm is kaput. He swims with fishes. I have good ears. The men I hear talk said you were this man's friend. Fraulein, you are in danger … I know … the halibut mousse … an excellent choice.'

Joining in the charade she pointed at the menu. 'Do you not like the Nazis?'

'Nein … there will be no bones in the mousse.'

'Why?'

'Wine?' He picked up the wine list and, with a trembling finger, drew her attention to an expensive hock. 'My grandmother is a Jew.'

Poor Gunther. Why did the Nazis so hate the Jews? And who was posting mail under her cabin door? To find out she opened the envelope.

Dear Miss Striker,

If I fail to appear for dinner this evening you must assume my death, murdered, more than likely, by an Irishman by the name of Doyle. He will have been aided and abetted by the Hitler Youth. I am being hunted by fanatical Nazis and by at least one fanatical Irishman. I don't stand a chance. Or do I? By the way, Doyle is easy to recognise: sticking out from his left ear's outer rim he has an abnormality – looks like a marble covered in skin. He often fiddles with it. He is dangerous – VERY.

Your sharp eyes noticed that I carry what you Americans, I believe, call a 'piece'. If they attack me I will of course defend myself. However, there are many of them. I do not know where, when or how they will strike. The only thing I am certain of is that they will. You see, Miss Striker – I have taken the liberty of addressing you thus, as, during our little chat, I observed no wedding ring – I know too much. If I do join the angels – it's fifty-fifty – I beg you, on docking, ring Westminster 397. It's an exclusive number. England's enemies would give their right hand – no pun intended regarding my own disability – to know it is the private number of the head of the United Kingdom's Secret Service; ask for Lord Frederick. You will be put straight through. Tell Freddy, that is, Lord Frederick, that Byker-Harrison has uncovered an unholy alliance between the Nazis and the Irish Republican Movement. What infernal schemes of mayhem this duo of fanatics may be concocting, I know not. It is my knowledge of their alliance that has put a price on my head.

Let me help you understand my predicament by giving you an example from your own culture. This is in no way meant to be patronising. I do it merely to drive home my point; to hit the nail on the head, to make you 'feel' the seriousness of my situation. If we were in the Wild West, instead of on a storm-tossed ship, my picture would now be nailed to every hitching post in every one-horse town with tumbleweed blowing down its main street. 'Byker-Harrison Wanted Dead or Alive. And the 'alive' part would be window dressing. Do you understand?

I am painfully aware that in making you privy to this information I have, ipso facto, put your life in danger. For this, I apologise. My excuse is that England's safety comes first. It is imperative that London knows of the alliance between the Nazis and the fanatics of Southern Ireland.

But, let us look on the bright side. I am not yet dead. I survived the Somme. At least most of me did. So, if I do appear in the dining room this evening, please acknowledge me – a little smile perhaps. We are in this together now. You will surmise from the jaunty tone of this epistle that I don't really expect the blighters to get me. It's just that, well, if they do, you are my insurance policy. The American eagle may have to fly sooner than it thinks to rescue the British lion.

Finally, my apologies for the gauche way I introduced myself in the lounge bar. I am not the loudmouth you must think me. My only purpose was to make myself known. The only way this old soldier could think of achieving that aim was to be rather loud and, dare I say it, to play the role of the worst kind of English chauvinist.

Will I or will I not see you in the dining room? I could spin a coin. Once again I apologise for making you my carrier pigeon. By the way, Gunther can be trusted. Over the last few months I've tipped him monstrous amounts for information. So, you see, I do know about tipping. In anticipation of your co-operation,

Yours sincerely,

Byker-Harrison

PS Do not try to warn London by telegram from the ship. The radio operator will smile, take your message but not send it. I've tried; that's how I know I've been rumbled. The radio operator clicks his heels and shouts 'Sieg Heil', the man's an automaton, a fanatic of the first water. Apart from

Gunther, regard everyone on board as an enemy. And you were right; I'm not a policeman. I'm what the penny shockers call a secret agent.

The American embassy in Berlin had warned her to be on the look-out for Doyle. Rumours were circulating he had connections with one of the Americans she'd be meeting up with at The Hall.

'You can't miss this guy,' she'd been told. 'He has a funny ear. A word of warning, don't give yourself away by going around looking at ears.' (The advice desk operatives gave front line agents never ceased to amaze her.) 'You don't have to do anything. All we're asking is you keep your eyes and ears open. Your cover is one hundred per cent. He has no reason to suspect an American is on to him.'

But, now, thanks to Byker-Harrison, he had. Why couldn't the Brits fight their own wars?

Byker-Harrison did not appear in the dining room. And where was Gunther?

'Excuse me,' she asked a passing waiter, 'where is Gunther?'

'He has had a terrible accident. I do not think he will live.'

5

'Master Jack, milady.'

'Thank you, Bert.'

'Jack, come and sit beside me.'

'Why?'

'Because I have something to tell you.'

'What?'

'Shall I stay, milady?'

'No, Bert, I do not need a chaperone. Now then, Jack, for once in your life do as you are told, come and sit beside your Aunt Elizabeth. I promise not to hug you.'

'You are not my aunt.'

'I am trying to make you feel part of the family.'

'I am not.'

'I want you to feel at home at The Hall … you do like being here, don't you?'

'Yes.'

'Good, do come and sit down.'

'I'm dirty.'

'Yes, you are. Where did you sleep last night?'

'In my den on the moors.'

'Help yourself to a chocolate.'

'Thank you.'

'I hope you like the flavour; it is not to everyone's taste. Well, if you won't sit down you will have to hear my news standing up.' She cleared her throat. 'Soon, it is possible that members of the Hitler Youth will be camping in the Meadow Field. When you see them you are not to be scared. This is England, not Germany … they can do you no harm. England has policemen … Sir Charles is a force in the land.'

'Bert said you wanted to see me in the drawing room. Why is it called a 'drawing room'?'

'You've not listened to a word I've said, have you?'

'"The Germans are coming but I've not to be scared." If it's a drawing room where are the pencils and paper to draw on?'

'It's where Sir Charles and I like to take afternoon tea.'

'You 'take' tea? I 'drink' tea. Which is right please?' He took out his notebook. She explained.

'Why do you not call it the tea room?'

'Because we don't.'

'Why?'

'I don't know why.'

'You don't know everything?'

'No.'

'Mike says you do. He says, "Lady Elizabeth knows everything".'

'He said that?'

'Yes.'

'When?'

'Can't remember.'

'You think Mike was praising me?'

'Yes.'

'Is that why you told me?'

'Yes.'

'Because you thought he was praising me?'

'Was he not … how do you say in English, giving you a pat on the head?'

'No.'

She could hear Mike saying – 'She knows everything'. The tone of voice. The implied criticism. He needed to be reminded of his position, that he was a servant. How she would enjoy seeing him fall into a cesspit. To clear her head, she sniffed from a bottle of Sal volatile she'd taken to keeping within reach ever since Hitler had marched into Czechoslovakia.

'Have I made you sniff your bottle? Mike makes faces like that when he has his first whisky.'

'And what time would that be?'

'Six o'clock.'

'It is my opinion, Jack, that you are sorely in need of the company of boys of your own age. The day after tomorrow our grandson is coming to stay. He is called George. You and he are the same age … more or less. I'm sure you'll like him. We all love him to bits. He's the 'apple' of his grandfather's eye … that's one of our silly English expressions, it means … '

'I know what it means … I'm the 'apple' of Phyllis's eye.'

'You are?'

'Yes.'

'Well, don't forget Cook is also fond of George. She's known our grandson a lot longer than she's known you. And the good thing about George coming is that he'll be able to show you all the secret places on the estate my husband tells me you boys like to explore when you play Cowboys and Indians.'

'There's no secret places I don't know. I'll bet I know a place George doesn't know. Even Uncle Mike didn't know this place … it's my den, until I showed him.'

'Maybe that's true and maybe it isn't … and if dear, dear George doesn't know the whereabouts of your den it's because he's not as agile as you are. We can't all climb trees like monkeys, you know. George, you see, has problems.'

She explained their nature. What she told him made him think that this 'apple' of The Hall's 'eye' was not going to be much of a rival.

'Do you think Uncle Mike knew where my secret den was before I told him?'

'He's like me, he knows everything.'

'He told me he didn't.'

'He might have been telling a white lie.'

'What's that?'

'It's when you tell a lie so as not to hurt someone's feelings. Maybe Mike saw how proud you were of your secret den and did not want you to think it's not as secret as you thought. You are not eating your chocolate … do you not like it?'

'It is nice.'

'But? I can tell there is a 'but'. Are you perhaps not telling me the truth because you do not wish to hurt my feelings?'

'It is nice, but ginger is not my favourite.'

'Jack Field, what a fibber you are. You've told a white lie. I think you really, really hate ginger.'

He nodded. 'Do you think Uncle Mike knew about the den?'

'I don't know.'

'Are there any other colours of lies in English?'

'No, just white … all the rest we describe by size … big lies, little lies or the very tiny ones we call fibs.'

'Hitler tells lies.'

'He tells whoppers.'

'Whoppers, are they big lies?'

'Yes, the biggest there are.'

'When are the Americans coming?'

'How do you know about them?'

'I want to go to America.'

'I know you do. Believe me, Sir Charles and I are making every effort to trace your American relatives.'

'You are leaving no stone unturned?'

'Yes, Jack, we are leaving no stone unturned.'

'Are all Americans rich?'

'No.'

'The ones coming … are they rich?'

'Yes, rich and powerful.'

'Will they help Britain fight the Nazis?'

'Whatever put that idea into your head?'

'That's what Sir Charles says … I heard him telling you.'

'Did you indeed.'

'Yes, I was up a tree.'

'Eavesdropping?'

'No, climbing a tree looking for Moses.'

'Your pet ferret.'

'Moses is my best friend.'

'Sir Charles is my best friend.'

'Do you kiss him? I kiss Moses.'

'Jack, you do not ask English ladies such questions.'

'Have I put my foot in it?'

'Both feet … where are you sleeping tonight?'

'In my den.'

'Are you not scared outside on the moors, alone, in the dark, at night?'

'I am not alone … Moses is with me. He is my company. The moors are my friend … they do not want to kill me because I am a Jew, like the Nazis.'

6

Sir Charles and Lady Elizabeth's double bed allowed intimacy or estrangement. During their long married life together they'd used both facilities. Tonight they lay close together.

'Charles, you've been at the garlic, when?'

'Phyllis made me a cheese and garlic sandwich for supper … had it in the study.'

'You should have eaten your dinner. I don't approve of snacking. You smell like a Frenchman. I know you are fond of the stuff, but it makes sleeping with you something of a trial. Why do wedding vows make no mention of garlic?'

'Write to the Archbishop of Canterbury.'

'What are you reading?'

'Mein Kampf.'

'I object to sharing my bed with Hitler … he'll put you in a bad mood. I'm certain the man has bad breath. I don't know why I should think that, do you? It's just that when I see him on the newsreels I always think, "I'll bet he has bad breath". You've met him, haven't you? Does he?'

'What?'

'Have bad breath?'

'In the sense that the man has soured Anglo-German relations I suppose, yes, he does.'

'Will he attack Poland?'

'Probably.'

'And Neville will stand by England's promise to protect Poland if she is attacked?'

'Yes.'

'What will the Americans do?'

'Sit on the fence unless we push them off.'

'Which is why we are to play host to these Americans?'

'Yes.'

'Do Americans like garlic? If they don't you will have to talk to them from afar, through a megaphone.'

'Or issue them with a gas mask.'

'The staff are looking forward to them coming. They think Americans are glamorous … especially Bert.'

'I know, he likes Americans.'

'Do you?'

'It matters not a jot whether I do or don't. My job is to get them to spout pro-British propaganda. You will find them a varied lot. Weinberger is an oil baron … very rich, lots of influence with Congress.'

'Weinberger … sounds German.'

'His grandfather came from Bavaria.'

'If war breaks out will he not side with the Germans?'

'He was born in America. Germany, I'm sure, means nothing to him. He owes everything to the greatest democracy the world has ever known.'

'I thought our English Parliament was the great exemplar of that form of government?'

'I know it is, you know it is, everyone knows it is except the Americans. My hyperbole was, in a manner of speaking, a rehearsal. It is a phrase I intend to use on our guests … flattery, my dear, is an important diplomatic weapon. Mario Mancini is a professor of economics.'

'He sounds Italian.'

'The family come from Florence … his father sells ice cream.'

'His family is in trade? I shall arrange for him to be given the smallest bedroom.'

'His father has sold rather a lot of ice cream. He is a millionaire. He could buy The Hall many times over. Then there's O'Neil and Macdonald. They are bankers.'

'An Irishman and a Scot by the sound of their names.'

'America is a country of immigrants.'

'Are there no Anglo-Saxons in the party?'

'Professor Striker … Marigold Striker.'

'A woman?'

'She's a history professor … quite a gal by all accounts, only met her once, a face across a room. I'm told she's a good shot. Her hobby is big game hunting. She can trace her family's arrival in America back to the Mayflower. For the past few months she's been touring Germany as the President's unofficial eyes and ears. Before she joins us, she's giving a lecture at Durham University.'

'She's not on the Queen Mary with the others?'

'No, she's an independent traveller. I've no idea how she's getting here … probably by air. Americans use aeroplanes the way we use taxis. She knows the group's itinerary and has written to tell me she will ring from Durham as soon as she is free. She is by far the most important member of the group. When you are talking to her you are talking to the President. She goes right to the top.'

'You are well informed about our American guests. It would not surprise me if you knew Professor Mancini's favourite flavour of ice cream.'

'Chocolate.'

'How do you know these things? After all the years I've been married to you, Charles, I'm never sure when you are pulling my leg.'

'Our ambassador in Washington informs the FO, who tells Freddy, who tells me.'

'Chinese Whispers is a dangerous game to play when the stakes are so high.'

'Which is why Harry is visiting us tomorrow.'

Sir Charles and Lady Elizabeth had two daughters but no sons. For this reason they rather doted on their nephew Harry. Sir Charles loved the young man just enough not to be blind to his faults. Lady Elizabeth, on the other hand, had no such reservations. She thought him 'dishy' and a splendid catch for any female on the look-out for a husband. Sadly the blood link was too close for her to think of him as a prospective son-in-law.

'I thought his visit was social? He's coming to stay because he needs a base from which to go into town. Pruney's having a birthday party at the Assembly Rooms.'

'So he is, but he is also bringing me information, in the shape of a letter, from one of his American relatives … a lady who is privy to conversations beyond the detective powers of even His Majesty's American Ambassador.'

'About our American guests?'

'Yes.'

'You have turned the 'boy' into a spy. Charles, how could you?'

'He is not a 'boy', he is a young man. At his age I was in the trenches.'

'Don't remind me.'

'Intelligence gathering, my dear, is akin to throwing a fishing net into a fast-flowing river. Sometimes you use a fine mesh, sometimes a large, depending upon what you want to catch. The mesh in the American net I am hauling in, with the help of Harry, is of the finest mesh. It catches the give-away 'sour look', the 'raised eyebrow', the 'indiscreet remark' when someone, for a moment, drops their guard.'

They switched off their bedside lights. They kissed goodnight.

'I'm looking forward to meeting Marigold,' said Lady Elizabeth. 'It will be nice having another woman around. Does she have children?'

'She's not married.'

'I do hope she's not one of those women who dislike children. I'd be surprised if she didn't like George … everyone likes George.'

'He is our grandson. We are prejudiced.'

'You've not forgotten he's coming to stay with us? At the moment you have so much on your mind.'

'Of course not.'

'What you will be like if war is declared, I dread to think. What about Jack? We'd better keep him away from the Americans. You find his practical jokes amusing … they make me anxious. I never know what might happen next. He doesn't understand that some people are scared of snakes.'

'They were only grass snakes.'

'What if they'd been adders?'

'But they weren't … you told him about the Hitler Youth?'

'Yes.'

'Good'

'You know where he is sleeping tonight?'

'His den.'

'How did you know that?'

'By your tone of disapproval. When I was his age I used to sleep out on the moors all summer … Mike and I together, it did us no harm.'

'Mike is too familiar.'

'Goodnight.'

'What if Jack puts a frog in the Americans' coffee?'

'If Professor Striker is as good a shot as our file on her states she might shoot him with his own pea shooter.'

'Does he have a pea shooter?'

'I don't know … I'd be surprised if he didn't. When I was his age I had one.'

'Do you think George will get on with Jack?'

'I don't know. I'm not a sage … go to sleep.'

'The day after tomorrow will be a busy day … George is coming, the Americans will be arriving and in the Meadow Field the Hitler Youth will be camping. I will tell Phyllis to make chocolate ice cream for Professor Mancini … do you think that would be a good idea? Charles … are you asleep?'

'Yes.'

7

In her cabin Marigold re-read Byker-Harrison's note. What she knew of the Irish Republican Movement she knew from friends of Irish descent. Irish Americans disliked, even hated, England. In support of their 'cause', meaning an independent Ireland, these Anglophobes were forever organising fundraising events; innocent sounding events like coffee and cake mornings and, for a dollar, guess the number of plastic shamrocks hidden in a jar of sweets. The money raised they handed over to the hard men of the Republican Movement. She recalled an article she'd read in the New York Times that Republicans had begun a new campaign of violence in England. They'd blown up some building or other in London. As sure as eggs made omelettes England and Germany were preparing for war. In any coming conflict the Southern Irish would side with the Nazis. The Leprechaun would not be able to resist tweaking the Lion's Tail. An alliance between Germany and Eire made sense.

And where, if he wasn't already at the bottom of the sea, was Byker-Harrison? It worried her that he'd not showed up for dinner. Even in America, nice, innocent people did not carry a '45 or whatever it was he had in his holster. If the CIA hadn't told her to keep an eye open for this man Doyle she'd have put money on the Englishman's note being a hoax. The stratagems men were capable of concocting to get themselves into her knickers never ceased to amaze her. And some of the old guys were the worst.

The knock on the door made her jump.

'What do you want?'

'The storm is getting worse,' said the steward. 'All port holes must be made secure. It is an order.'

Storm or no storm she only let him in after she'd checked his ears. On his way out she asked him for the cabin number of the Englishman with one arm. When he claimed not to know she waggled a high value Deutschmark note under his nose and suggested he might like to find out.

'Fraulein,' he said, 'Gunther is sick. I do not wish to be sick like Gunther.'

8

Jack stood close to his den's entrance, but not too close. Birds never flew straight to their nests.

After the storm every branch and twig dripped water. A blanket of humid air hung over the darkening fields.

Aunt Elizabeth, as she liked to be called, had given him much to think about. Sleeping in his den would help him chew over what she'd told him. His attic bedroom in The Hall gave him nightmares. On nights when he relived the murder of his mother and father, its sloping ceiling threatened him like SS men wielding batons. When this happened, he controlled his mind by learning English words and proverbs from a book given him by Sir Charles. He liked the proverb, 'A bird in the hand is worth two in the bush'. To help him understand its meaning he'd changed it to, 'Better to kill a Nazi in your gun sight than wait for an opportunity to kill more'.

Only when he was certain no one was watching did he duck down and disappear under a clump of gorse. Rainwater trapped in its prickly canopy soaked his neck … the first water in many days to touch any part of his body, washing not being one of his priorities.

After much wriggling on his stomach and elbows he stood up in a cave lit by light coming in through a fissure made when the house size boulders making the outcrop had crashed together millions of years ago.

To make the cave 'homely' he'd tied miniature besoms of rosemary and thyme to the roots of plants growing through the cave's sandy ceiling.

They reminded him of a flower shop in Berlin, a Jewish shop whose owner, because he was a relative, gave his mother a discount. 'Put it in Jacob's money box,' the Ashkenazi would say; 'use it to buy the boy an umbrella for a rainy day.'

He fed Moses. For his meeting with Aunt Elizabeth in the room called the drawing room but which was not used for drawing, he'd left the ferret tied to a root. Aunt Elizabeth would have screamed if he'd taken his best pal into the house, maybe even fainted. Moses liked disappearing up women's skirts.

And Phyllis wasn't much fonder of his pet, either. 'Let me make myself clear, young Jack, I don't mind feeding the little brute but don't bring him into my kitchen. I'll give him board but not lodging.'

In the fading light he watched Moses tuck into a meal of chicken scraps provided by Phyllis. Phyllis's bark was worse than her bite. An English expression. English was a funny language.

He worried about taking away Moses's freedom. He knew he wouldn't like to be kept on a leash. Moses only struggled when you gave him too many kisses.

Jack's bed for the night was a wooden pallet strewn with heather. He'd made it himself. Mike had given him the wood. He'd brought it into the cave in pieces.

In the cave he kept a diary of the animals he saw through the fissure … badgers, foxes, squirrels and the big stag. He recorded how they behaved. When he grew up he'd a vague idea that he'd like to work with animals. The big stag was the one Mike wanted to shoot.

With his bow and arrow he liked to think of himself as a hunter. At the same time he did not want to kill the stag. He did not want Mike to kill it. He wanted it to be left alone. From his den he'd seen it many times but had never told Mike. If such a beautiful animal were shot from his den he'd never sleep in the den again. He'd made up his mind about that.

Shooting Nazis from the den was different. Through the fissure he could see the Meadow Field. Out of his fingers he made a pretend gun. In the direction of the Nazis' proposed campsite he fired many shots.

Wednesday 30th August 1939

1

The sun was shining. Water vapour, as visible as breath on a frosty day, rose in wisps from the sodden ground, evaporating away yesterday's downpour.

Over breakfast Sir Charles told his wife, 'Wonderful, don't you think, Nature's ability to recover? I mean after yesterday's battering who'd have thought our gladioli would ever stand up straight again? But they have. Wonderful, quite wonderful. Today is going to be a scorcher, mark my words; if I'm wrong I'll grow a Hitler moustache.' He cocked an ear at an open French window. 'Listen … you can hear the grass growing … it's that sort of day. Take my word for it. Pass the marmalade. I'll warrant my melons will be growing faster than the pointers on a watch move. If it's like this tonight we might dine al fresco.'

'I don't think so.'

'I do.'

'Be a dear and pour me another cup of tea.'

'You always just have one cup.'

'This morning, if it's alright with you, Charles, I am going to have a second cup … it's the heat … it's making me thirsty.'

'I think I'll join you.'

Lady Elizabeth's mind was on gazpacho. For dinner she wanted a chilled soup like she had when she stayed with Freddy and Dot at their villa in Cannes. Would Phyllis have a recipe? She so hoped Freddy would not be ringing her husband. The scrambler meant she couldn't listen in. Freddy's official calls invariably meant trouble. Freddy was making it difficult for her to forget the storm clouds gathering over Europe.

Sir Charles tried, unsuccessfully, to stop thinking about Hitler by thinking about melons.

In the 'melon house' he chatted with Tom, his head gardener; should they increase the depth of the hot beds?

In a conversational lull the gardener asked, 'Will it come to war, sir?'

Sir Charles was thinking how to answer the question on everyone's mind when he spotted not one but three snails on a melon. He unstuck them from their breakfast.

'I've never seen that before, Tom.'

'The little bugger's done it again,' exploded the embarrassed gardener. 'He'll get me the sack, he will. It's the refugee lad, sir. It's his sense of humour. He puts them on the melons to tease me. If I catch him I'll put the hosepipe on him.'

'I suspect he'd rather like that.'

'He'll be watching us.'

'No doubt waiting for us to shout and scream … best pretend we've not noticed his devilment. If we don't react he'll get bored … stop doing it.'

'He'll not stop until I have no melons for her Ladyship's dinner parties …
snails and melons don't go together, sir; lamb and mint sauce do, sir, but snails
and melons don't.'

'Nor do shoes and dead mice.'

'You've lost me, sir.'

'You are not the only victim of Jack's practical jokes. I fear he is what the
Germans call an 'elf king' … a mischievous spirit. We'd call him 'Puck'. Last
week I found a dead mouse in one of my brogues. Bert was upset, rather thought
he'd let the side down … hadn't been doing his job properly. Do you like the lad?'

'He has a way with him, sir … heaven help the women when he's older.'

'When he played one of his practical jokes on Phyllis … she laughed.'

'I'm not calling you a liar, sir, but I find that difficult to believe … if you take
my meaning, sir.'

'I do, Tom, I do, but, you said yourself, 'he has a way with him'. It has been my
experience of public life, Tom, that if people like you, well, you can get away with
murder. And boys will be boys, don't you think? Now to answer your question,
"Will it come to war?".' He pointed at the snails in his palm. 'They're like Hitler,
don't you think? Wherever they go they leave a trail of slime. Hitler's trail is
strewn with brutal murders … the snails with damaged melons. It's no good
telling them to stop eating melons and eat weeds, is it?'

'Snails don't have ears, or if they do they're full of wax … that's my experience
of snails, sir.'

'In that case my answer to your question is, yes, it will come to war.'

'Let me do the honours, sir.'

Sir Charles dropped the snails into the gardener's calloused palm.

'It's like cracking walnuts, sir, shell against shell, it's easy.'

'Now, let's have some fun,' said Sir Charles. 'Where do you think young Jack
might be hiding?'

'I know exactly where the little blighter is … behind the rhododendron bush
over there. He thinks he knows all the hiding places but so do I.'

'Do you think we should water the rhododendron?'

'I'll get the hosepipe.'

Jack knew he'd been rumbled. There was nothing to water in the direction
that Egg Head (Sir Charles had a bald head) and Tom were heading. He had to
be the target. Also, they were both whistling as if they'd not a care in the world.
They had a lot to learn. On the streets of Berlin they would be dead ducks.

When spray battered the rhododendron's leaves he was in Phyllis's kitchen
tucking into a bowl of strawberries and cream.

2

Harry, Sir Charles and Lady Elizabeth's nephew, flew the Puss Moth he owned to an aerodrome some fifteen miles from The Hall. The three-seater de Havilland monoplane had a good turn of speed. His ownership of it made him the envy of all but the richest of his fellow undergraduates. It was his good luck that his father, one of Sir Charles's younger brothers, had married an American heiress. The plane was a gift from an aunt on the other side of the pond. She thought his English accent the best thing since buttermilk came in tins. In any coming conflict he intended to be a fighter pilot. As a privileged young man he'd already logged ten hours on 'Spits', the abbreviation used by his clique when they talked about the Spitfire, the RAF's most up to date fighter. He loved the sense of power it gave him. It never crossed his mind that in a real conflict he might get hurt.

Mike met him at the aerodrome. For as long as Harry could remember the big gamekeeper had been as much a part of his uncle's estate as its lakes and trees. In his youth he'd been won over by the man's easy going ways. Now that he was older he found him too familiar. It rankled that he kept calling him 'Young Harry'. Damn it, he was nineteen. The fellow's 'hale fellow well met' pats on the back were blows. They made one bristle. More to the point they were out of place coming from a servant.

At Oxford there was talk about a new-fangled idea called the 'Unconscious'. An altogether unsettling idea because it said a chap did things for reasons he knew nothing about. You married a brunette because your mother was a brunette, that sort of thing. 'Impulses' and 'drives' the psychoanalysts called them, laid down in early life. On the drive to The Hall in the Rolls he pondered the question … to what extent was his attitude towards Mike the product of the 'Shooting Party' incident?

At the age of thirteen he'd dropped his gun in the Hall's lake. It never occurred to him that a servant wouldn't get it out. Mike had told him, in no uncertain terms, 'You dropped it in the water, you get it out.' How stern Uncle Charles had looked, so changed from the kind Uncle Charles who'd given him piggy-back rides.

'It's for your own good,' said Mike. Snow was falling. He was told to strip to his underpants. The water was brown. It came up to his waist. He located the gun with his feet. To get hold of it he had to go right under. It took him three tries. Afterwards he remembered how well he'd been looked after, each man in the party volunteering an item of clothing. He was ordered to swig from a hip flask. 'Warm you better than a hot water bottle,' said Mike. 'And here's my ulster.' It was an hour's walk back to The Hall.

Now that he was older he knew why they'd made him do it. And, while it was true that on subsequent shoots he'd never again dropped his gun, he thought making him responsible for correcting his carelessness had not made him more careful. He also thought a servant should have gone into the water. Further, and this was something he tried to push to the back of his mind, he did not like to think his uncle and Mike had seen his fear … all in all he did not care for the unconscious mind.

The journey to The Hall usually took forty minutes. They arrived in thirty.

'There you are, Young Harry, didn't I tell you I'd have you here before you could say, Jack Robinson … hop out and don't forget your bag.'

'You drive too fast.'

'I thought you air force chaps were used to speed.'

'A Rolls-Royce is not an aeroplane.'

'I told Charlie I'd get you here in time for lunch and I have.'

'I take it, by "Charlie" you mean my uncle, Sir Charles?'

'You're not in uniform, Harry and I'm not on parade. Hop out, there's a good lad and don't forget your bag.'

'Lovely to see you, sir,' said Bert, coming out of The Hall's front door to bid him welcome the way a servant should. Harry liked Bert. Bert knew his place.

'Thank you, Bert.'

'Allow me.' He took Harry's bag. 'The family are in the library, sir.'

Uncle Charles greeted him with a firm handshake, Aunt Elizabeth with kisses and a hug that made him aware of the pneumatic qualities of her ample bosom.

'And you are in time for lunch,' said Sir Charles. 'Mike said he would get you here on time. A good man, Mike …one of the best.'

3

In the Tyne estuary the Nord stopped rocking; passengers who'd spent the voyage vomiting into sick bags began to feel that, maybe after all, they were not going to die.

The appearance on deck of these convalescents led Marigold to ponder the recuperative powers of the man who'd tried to steal Byker-Harrison's note. Doyle? If the crossing had been a calm one would she now be dead? More than likely dumped over the side. Which of the Hitler Youth were the Irishman's accomplices? She made a point of not standing too close to railings, to look around before she descended stairs, to be always with other passengers. She spent a lot of time looking at men's ears.

They docked within sight of Newcastle's iconic Tyne Bridge. Having been to Australia and seen the Sydney Harbour Bridge she thought this version a dinky toy replica. She was, however, much taken with the castle. Its position at the top of a steep bank made it appear to grow out of the roofs of properties built lower down, while those in turn appeared to grow out of the roofs of properties even lower down. In other words, a bricks and mortar version of the English class system. She'd jump off the Brooklyn Bridge if the properties at the bottom weren't slums.

There were lots of bridges, all offering different engineering solutions to the problem of getting people, cars, and trains over a river flowing between high banks. Ships hooted, kittiwakes shrieked. The air tasted of smoke. A stink of rotten eggs. A paddlewheel tugboat, cumulus clouds of smoke belching from its stack, thrashed its way seawards. A place of rude energy. It reminded her of New York. She liked it.

In a surge of emotion, all defiance against a pervasive sense of threat, she gave in to the 'feeling' that the city was bidding her welcome, that here, no matter what, she'd be safe. Her great grandmother hailed from the area. Family stories related how, for hundreds of years, the Greys – her great-grandmother's maiden name – had controlled, in the names of various English monarchs, a swath of east Northumberland. They were a reiver family, one of the 'names' living on the border between Scotland and England. She believed Sir Charles, whose guest she'd be in a few days' time, to be a distant relative.

While she waited for a porter to collect her bags she crossed her fingers, hoping she might see Byker-Harrison. Her gut instinct was that she wouldn't. She didn't. OK, so the guy was feeding the fishes. The Germans had taken his arm off him, the Irish Republicans, his life, or so it would seem.

At the first opportunity she'd phone the American embassy in London and tell them his story. What they did with the information was up to them.

In the meantime, she did her best to rein in her understandable desire to look at men's ears in too obvious a way. She wished she were wearing something summery. Newcastle was hot. She watched the Hitler Youth disembark.

Each young Nazi pushed a bicycle. Panniers behind the bicycles' seats carried what looked like bedding wrapped in a waterproof sheet. They were singing. She liked the way they used their bicycle bells as percussion. Their master in Berlin would be proud of them.

'Taxi, miss?'

'That would be great.'

'You sound American?'

'That's because I am.'

'Around here they call me the Pied Piper … you'll be wanting to know why? When I tell my customers, 'follow me', they always do, that's why.'

A stocky, broad shouldered man, he carried her bags down the gangway as if they were baubles. She knew about the Tyneside accent from family fireside stories …how the natives said 'hyem' for 'home' and 'ganin' for 'going', how it had similarities with modern Norwegian, how all Geordies thought they were Vikings. From the porter's few words she guessed he wasn't local.

On the quayside a man was holding a piece of cardboard with her name on it. Durham University had sent her a taxi.

'Here you are, Cinderella, this will take you to the Ball, 'said the Pied Piper.

'My taxi is over there.'

'No, Miss, this is your taxi. Let me tell you something, the Pied Piper is never wrong. Now, be a good colleen and sit your bum on that seat. You wouldn't be wanting your blood on the cobbles, would you?'

The Irish accent, the hint that he had a gun in his pocket, the firm grip he'd taken of her arm, left her no alternative but to do as she was told. His intimacy was intolerable. The man in the driver's seat had a funny ear. She began to struggle.

'Let go of my arm.'

'We've a fighting filly here, Mr Doyle.'

'What about my bags? You can't leave them on the quayside.'

'Darling, you won't be needing them where you're going.'

The blarney from the ape gripping her arm left her unimpressed. There was a Boston Brahmin she knew who talked just like that. He'd tried to grope her. To hide the black eye she'd given him he'd worn dark glasses for six months.

Railway trucks, horse drawn wagons and warehouses spewing cargo made it impossible for her kidnappers to do, what in the movies is called 'a quick getaway'. Now the Hitler Youth blocked their way.

Goddamit, she was the daughter of a millionaire. Back home a servant ran her bath, checked the water temperature before she stepped in, hot towels awaited her exit. She was an American citizen. She was a professor. She'd lectured at Yale and

Harvard. She was a confidante of the President of the United States of America. Her sense of invulnerability took a lot of denting.

'Do you men know who I am? And you, take your hands off me … goddam Irish ape.'

'Shut her up,' ordered Doyle.

The blow made her bite her lip so hard she tasted blood.

She was vaguely aware that Doyle was greeting the Hitler Youth, as if they were old friends.

'Heil Hitler! It is you, Herr Doyle.'

They were speaking German but, though a fluent speaker of that language, panic left her incapable of eavesdropping.

Without conscious thought her hand flew to the hat pin she used as an ancillary fastening for her dollar shaped diamond brooch. She took hold of its pearl head as if it were a dagger, eased it free, and, with all her strength, plunged it, as if it WERE a dagger, into the Pied Piper's crotch.

She left the car with the Irish thug looking between his spread legs as if he couldn't believe what had happened. Nice girls weren't supposed to do things like that.

Which way to run? A horse and cart blocked one route, the Hitler Youth another and then, of course, there was the river. She'd no wish to escape by jumping into that water. She took the only option available to her. She ran down the quayside towards the Tyne Bridge.

4

'I give cook ten out of ten for the salmon and minted new potatoes,' Sir Charles told his wife at the end of lunch. 'Phyllis may be a dragon … you know how she cooks, Harry? She breathes fire … never uses the gas. Only one complaint, my dear, on a day like today we should have eaten outside on the terrace.'

'Charles, Northumberland is not the south of France.'

'It is today.'

'There's always a breeze. You know the flies bother me. Why they attack me and leave you alone I will never understand.'

'India, my dear, turned my skin to leather. At least let's have coffee on the terrace. What do you say, Harry? Or tea, I always have tea.'

'Sounds spot on to me.'

'In that case I'll leave you gentlemen to talk. I know you have much to discuss. I've no doubt you'll want to smoke. In the house, Harry, I sometimes think your uncle's pipe should have its own chimney … a dirty masculine habit.'

In the garden Sir Charles sniffed a rose. 'It's all this talk about war, you know,' he explained to his nephew, 'it's making your aunt, well, tetchy. She worries about what I'm getting up to.'

'How much does she know?'

'She is my confidante, but I don't tell her everything. No point in worrying the dear thing unnecessarily.'

'Does she know my visit here is more than social?'

'Yes and I suspect that is another reason why she was complaining about my pipe. Your presence here has reminded her of the nasty things happening in Europe. If Elizabeth had her way she'd build the highest of high walls round the estate. She likes to think she can shut out Hitler with a few bricks. Of course she knows she can't but, on a day like today, I do sympathise with her point of view.'

'What do you make of Hitler, Uncle Charles? My view is that the man's a thug … look what he did to Rohm and his followers.'

'The Night of the Long Knives?'

'Cold blooded murder. You can't talk to a man like that. If he does that to his fellow Germans, what might he do to us?'

'Make us wear lederhosen.'

'It's not funny, Uncle Charles. The situation is grave. How can you joke about it?'

'In the Great War I used to say my tin hat protected my head, but my sense of humour kept me sane … take the advice of an old man.'

'You're not that old.'

'As far as soldiering goes I am. If the worst happens and, God forbid, we are again at war with Germany, His Majesty's Government will not be asking me to bear arms.'

'You are still active in the TA.'

'The Territorial Army is full of old officers like me. If war is declared we will have to be got rid of … at the very least put behind desks. Oh, yes, we mean well, our hearts are made of oak and all that silly nonsense, but we are weekend soldiers. We are amateurs. The German army is a professional army. The amateur is no match for the professional. Take my watercolours … they please me but they can never be hung on the same wall as Turner's.'

'They say Hitler paints?'

'When I was in Berlin I saw some of his work … very mediocre.'

'Are yours better?'

'Much …not like me to blow my own trumpet so you can guess how bad I thought them.'

'Have you met Hitler?'

'Twice, first time was at an embassy party … didn't take to him at all … sort of chap who uses his knife to shovel peas into his mouth. Second time was at a Reichstag party to celebrate his forty-sixth birthday. The champagne was excellent. He gave Anthony and Sir John a public lecture … more of a screaming rant, actually … on why the Versailles Treaty had humiliated Germany.'

'Will it come to war?'

'Yes.'

'That's an unambiguous answer for a diplomat.'

'My answer is unambiguous because I have seen at first hand the spell he has cast over the German people. They see him as a kind of Messiah.'

'He's certainly not the Jews' messiah.'

'His treatment of the Jews is appalling. Yet the German people treat him in ways one can imagine the Jews treating their messiah should he ever materialise. The fervour and passion he arouses is difficult for an Englishman to grasp. Of course, not every German is a fan. Those who are open in their criticism are sent to concentration camps or taken away in the middle of the night and shot. I've heard terrible stories. Tea? It's Darjeeling … the prince of teas, don't you know.'

'Coffee, if you don't mind, Uncle Charles.'

'You are in danger of becoming a European, Harry … Englishmen drink tea.'

'Not after lunch.'

'I do.'

'You belong to a different generation, Uncle. These stories, coming out of Germany … you think they are true?'

'Yes … dear me, I am being unambiguous today. By the way I'm stocking up on Darjeeling. If there is a war we'll be reusing tea leaves the way we reupholster chairs. Only in times of peace can tea be transported half way around the world.'

'I've been told I'm going to a Spitfire squadron.'

'I'm scared for you, Harry. In war men die. I don't want to lose you. I want no man to do what I did, to see the things I saw. War is hell. The Great War killed too many of my friends. It left me feeling lonely. You are one of the few people who know about my nightmares. A grown man frightened of the dark. I jump when water gurgles in pipes.'

'To your old regiment you are a hero. Clarkson-Ball is always asking after you.'

'And still a major, after all these years.'

'Believe it or not CB wants war, or so I've heard on the grapevine.'

'His daughter, Pruney, tell you?'

'As a matter of fact, yes. Her mother's death has left her feeling pretty low … being a widower has hit CB hard. He thinks a war will take his mind off his bereavement. I have a sneaking suspicion he wants to be a hero. He's always on about your VC … how your winning it was very good for the regiment.'

'CB is a pompous twit. I once tried telling him a joke. Waste of time. Life in the trenches opened my eyes. Some of the men were much cleverer than me. "Full many a flower is born to blush unseen/And waste its sweetness on the desert air." I'm surprised CB is still talking to me. He's not pleased that I'm a member of the Labour Party. Behind my back he calls me a communist. At last year's Hunt Ball I said to him, "You think I'm the Red under the Bed, don't you? The squire on fire?" I'd had too many whiskies.'

'CB does have a point. What about your class? You are not some common working man … like Mike.'

'Did he upset you this morning?'

'He kept calling me, "Young Harry".'

'That's because he's fond of you. I seem to remember that when he was teaching you to fish and shoot you thought he was God.'

'I'm older now and I don't like it … he's a servant. He should call me "Sir".'

'He calls me "Charlie" but only when we are alone. He knows the rules.'

'He made me carry my bag. He winked at Bert.'

'Oh dear, he really has ruffled your feathers.'

'Aunt Elizabeth thinks you are too friendly with him. He is not your equal. He is your servant. You employ him. You pay him to do what he does. Without your patronage he would be nothing. You should not let him use your Christian name. He should use your title. You are a knight of the realm. You own a country house and many acres. Aunt Elizabeth is the daughter of a duke.'

'She is the third daughter of a third rate duke. Everything in England has its pecking order. Mike and I played together as boys. His father taught me all I know about fishing and stalking. His father was my father's gamekeeper; now he is mine. We are from the same village. I live in the big house everyone calls The Hall, he lives in a cottage belonging to me. He has two bedrooms, I have twenty.

He was my batman in Flanders. You learn a lot about a man – and yourself come to that – when you are under fire. We played together as children, we fought together as men.'

'No matter what you say, Uncle, you know and I know, he is not one of us.'

'Not one of us … not human, you mean? Neanderthal perhaps? Should he show me deference with a Hitler salute? Or, what about making him swear an oath of allegiance to me … the way every German soldier does to Hitler? "I swear by God this sacred oath that I will render unconditional obedience to Sir Charles, the Fuhrer of The Hall and will be ready as a brave gamekeeper to risk my life at any time for this oath." He'd fall about laughing and so would I. Can you imagine the British people addressing Mr Chamberlain as "My leader"? Poor Neville wouldn't know where to look … and all our Members of Parliament snapping up their arms at him like railway signals … terrible, not at all our way of doing things. What poor Neville doesn't understand is that Hitler is not a gentleman.'

'Mike is not a gentleman.'

'I suspect that judgement is based on the fact that my gamekeeper did not go to Eton and Balliol. If only everyone who went to those wonderful institutions was a gentleman, what a wonderful place our England would be. Mike is a gentleman. I will tell you why. He keeps his word. He said he would have you here for lunch and he did. When a chap's in trouble he puts his shoulder to the wheel. In this coming war England will need men like Mike. I prophesy that you may well end up under the command of a man whose father is a gamekeeper. If you do you will have a better than average chance of coming through. Such a man will have achieved his position on merit, not because he was born like you and me with a silver spoon in his mouth. He will know what he is doing.'

'There is already talk of sergeant pilots. The chaps I know don't want to mix with them. We certainly have no intention of messing with them. They'll probably eat with their fingers.'

'That is a Nineteen-Twenty attitude … whether we like it or not the Great War shook our class system to its foundations. A second war will almost certainly finish off what the first started. In the coming conflict our dear England will have to put into a cockpit every man who has the brains to fly … and courage. The country will not have a choice. Any fool can be an infantryman. Can you imagine CB flying a Spitfire? Do try to be more like your mother's side of the family. Americans are so much more relaxed about class.'

'Uncle Charles, I do believe Aunt Elizabeth is right … you've gone native. You need to get out of Northumberland more.'

'And you are too much under her influence … and your father's. I know my dear wife means well but she is living in the past. Your father should set you a better example. He knows the Great War changed everything. Mark my words, Hitler is not a gentleman. What the man with the funny moustache says does not square with what he does. It's what people do, my boy, that counts, not what they promise. He's torn up the Versailles Treaty.'

'Mr Greenwood, the deputy leader of your Labour Party, says Hitler is sincere.'

'It is not "my Labour Party".'

'Greenwood says Hitler is holding out an olive branch, that he is sincere in wanting peace.'

'The only branch Hitler is holding out, he's taken from a holly bush. More tea? It's Darjeeling.'

'I know, Uncle, you've told me. In case you've forgotten, I'm drinking coffee.'

5

Marigold paused for breath under the Tyne Bridge. Its huge girders increased her sense of insecurity; made her feel she was having one of those dreams where everything is bigger than oneself.

The Pied Piper was giving chase; such was his urgency to get to her he was knocking over big men like skittles. Why didn't those guys do something? Were Geordies soft? If he'd spun a guy round like that in Chicago the Irish ape would now be lying flat on his back in a pool of his own blood. How she wished she were armed. One shot, that's all she would need. Any injury she'd done him had not slowed him down.

She ran close to the quay's edge. One slip and she'd be in the stinking water. She didn't care. She had nothing to lose. She was fleeing for her life. She hurdled mooring rings, coils of rope, burst open crates of oranges; nothing was going to stop her escaping. She heard wolf whistles, was subliminally aware that people were looking at her.

She ran up steps and found herself on a bridge. For some reason its traffic wasn't moving. The pedestrians on its sidewalks were standing still. The Brits were weird. She'd heard about their love affair with queuing but this was ridiculous. A ship in the middle of the river blew three long blasts on its hooter. Like the cars and pedestrians it too seemed in limbo. Why didn't the cars find an alternative route? The pedestrians swim? By American standards the river was barely wide enough to be a named tributary of the Mississippi. And these people were in charge of an Empire!

In between breathing in gulps of air, in an attempt to get her breath back, she watched the taxi driven by Doyle join the line of cars waiting to cross the bridge. Looking over the bridge's parapet she saw the Pied Piper charging down the quayside like an angry orang-utan.

At the front of the traffic jam she spotted a man leaning against a red and white striped pole suspended at waist height across the road. She assumed him to be somehow responsible for bringing everything to a standstill and now to be in charge of the ensuing stasis. She ran towards him.

'Excuse me?'

The man in charge of the barrier knew he was attractive to women. It was one of those things, wasn't it? Some blokes had it, some didn't. It was like keeping your own teeth. Some of his mates had dentures, he didn't. To show he knew he was talking to a lady, he removed his cap.

'What can I dee for yuh, pet?'

'Why are the cars not moving? Why can't I cross? You see, it's important that I cross now.'

The expression on his face changed to one she'd seen many times on the faces of her brothers when she'd not known something they thought everyone but an idiot must know … like the probability of getting a full house in poker was six-hundred and ninety-three to one. By way of explanation she added, 'I'm American.'

He found it 'thrilling' that he was talking to a native of the country that made 'cowboy pictures'. Here was someone from the land of milk and honey. He'd never met an American before. And she was good looking. What a pair of legs. She looked posh. He sniffed expensive perfume. She might have met Walt Disney, shaken John Wayne's hand … and he knew something she didn't … well, well, well.

'It's a swing bridge, yuh see,' he explained, 'so that big fella doon there (pointing at the ship which had hooted three times) can gan up to the staithes at Dunston. If I didn't put the barrier doon the cars would fall in the watta … and if I didn't shut the gates folk would fall in the watta … and we wouldn't want that, would we? It'll be moving soon. It's like my missus, it takes a while to get gannin.'

'You have an important job.'

'Aye, I suppose I do … it's the biggest swing bridge in the world, yuh nar. Lord Armstrong, a local lad made good, built it … hydraulics do the work … eighteen-seventy-six and still going strong, opens and shuts like … aye, well, never mind that.'

He'd bet a monkey the man she kept looking at over her shoulder was a boyfriend. He'd never had a 'domestic' on the bridge … first time for everything though, wasn't there?

'It's moving,' he told her.

'Where?'

'Come on the road, if you want, you'll see better from there.'

'Can I?'

'Climb over the girder, howay, give's your hand.'

'Would that not be dangerous?'

'Not when you are with me.'

If saving her life meant showing this lecherous artisan the colour of her pantyhose, then, he had a deal. At the 'flash' he grinned like a waiter receiving a large tip.

Wonder of wonders the road was indeed moving. It reminded her of the earthquake she'd once experienced in Kathmandu, six on the Richter scale, only now there was no shaking; everything being smooth and controlled. Also the kittiwakes were still screaming. In the real thing the birds had gone quiet.

'The miracle of the moving road,' said her ad hoc guide, puffing out his chest. She did her best to look impressed. Nothing touchier than local pride. She knew from bitter experience that you never told a mother her baby was ugly. She needed this oaf's protection. With him around the Pied Piper wouldn't dare try anything.

The fellow was tall and wiry, an oil stained version of Gary Cooper. To let him know she was mightily impressed by the 'miracle of the moving road' she shot him a 'come-on' smile. The grin he shot back showed brown teeth.

He could tell she liked him. He knew a lot about women. Emboldened by his assessment of the way their relationship was developing he winked, nodded his head in the direction of the Pied Piper, all to let her know he knew there was something going on between them.

The real Pied Piper had attracted children and rats – well, she was neither. She was an American. Americans were a 'can-do' people. When a wheel fell off a wagon they put it back on.

A yard from where she was standing, on the other side of the red and white pole, she watched the moving bridge reveal more and more of the River Tyne's stinking, black water. Every second she dithered there was less road for her to jump onto.

'Look out!' she said, pointing at an imaginary 'something' behind the Geordie's back.

As soon as he turned to look, she ducked under the red and white pole and walked onto the moving part of the road as easily as if stepping onto an escalator at Macy's.

'Hoy! You can't do that.'

For the moment she was safe.

In four hours' time she was due to give a lecture to the great and good of Durham University on 'Anglo-American Relations 1861-1865'. Present circumstances made this as likely as the United States begging to be made part of the British Empire.

From too much running in the wrong type of shoes her feet hurt. Her Boston chiropodist would be appalled. She watched with awe the steamer – for which the bridge had swung – sail through the opened channel. In ballast it towered as high above her as a New York skyscraper, or gave that impression. Its proximity made it seem to be moving faster than it was.

All too soon the apparent movement of the castle, a fixed point, made her aware the bridge was closing. In minutes it would be open to traffic. To put as much distance as possible between herself and her pursuers she walked to its opposite side.

The man in charge on the Gateshead side shook his head. He'd had his eye on her for quite a while. This happened about twice a year. The daft things folk did.

'Where've you come from then, bonnie lass? You're not a mermaid, are yuh?'

'I'm an American.'

A head poking out of a car shouted, 'Lift the bloody barrier, will you. I don't want to be here when the war starts.'

This side of the river was less busy, its narrow lanes offering plenty of cover to slit her throat. The thought of ending up in a gutter next to a used condom made her shudder. Stairs zigzagging up a grassy escarpment caught her eye. They led to the underbelly of another bridge. Its bottom span supported a road, its top a railway. She took them two at a time.

Half way up she paused for breath. The smoky air made her cough. Looking down onto the road below, she saw the Pied Piper jump out of the taxi driven by Doyle.

She'd learnt the skill of pitching a baseball from her brothers. They'd taught her every trick they knew. At the time she'd thought it a chore, something she had to do to stop them pulling her pigtails. Now she began to think it the most useful skill she'd ever mastered, better than her perfect German or esoteric knowledge of the battles of the American Civil War.

Looking around she saw lots of ammunition for what she had in mind. On a landing, where the steps changed direction, she began collecting pieces of broken brick as close as possible in weight and shape to a baseball. The Pied Piper had made her bite her tongue; she was going to make him bite the dirt. Her skewering of his privates, it would seem, had done little damage. How far would he be able to run if she took his head off? Decapitated chickens managed no more than a couple of yards.

Her arsenal complete, she looked down the stairs to the landing below where the Pied Piper had stopped for breath. When he looked up, she gave him a 'come and get me' gesture.

What in the name of Jesus Christ Our Saviour was she doing? He'd never seen an American baseball match, had no idea of the stance a pitcher adopts prior to delivery. He did not understand the theatrical arm swinging, the important part played by the leading leg and the way the body twists, all in one smooth action, before letting the ball, in this case a lump of brick, fly.

The improvised baseball hit him between his eyes.

It was with a sense of relief and righteous justification that – as if a great weight had been taken off her shoulders – she watched him fall onto his knees, as if in prayer.

Ever so slowly her breathing began to return to normal. She was safe. At the top of the stairs she walked through a dripping tunnel.

In its walls were niches, bolt holes for pedestrians when vehicles passed. It was from one of these that Doyle watched her pass. He crossed himself for his cause was a holy one. He raised the Luger, a present from his German friends, a much better weapon than the Webley carried by the late Byker-Harrison.

6

'Let's take a stroll, Harry, but not too far, Freddy's told me to stay close to the phone.'

'Freddy? Lord Frederick?'

'The very same.'

'But he's in charge of MI5.'

'I know.'

'Who are you?'

'I'm your Uncle Charles, His Majesty's eyes and ears in the North. Now, about that letter you gave me from your American aunt, the one who bought you the Puss Moth. I've given it the once over. The information she's given me about the American guests I'm expecting is most helpful. Does this aunt talk a lot?'

'Rather.'

'In that case she writes the same way as she talks. She's written pages. It will take me time to separate the wheat from the chaff. She likes gossip?'

'Of course, she's a woman.'

'Don't say that to your Aunt Elizabeth. Is she a mischief maker?'

'Definitely not.'

'She tells it as she sees it?'

'Yes … Uncle Charles, she's a good woman. You asked her to help and she's done her best.'

'You are prejudiced. She bought you an aeroplane.'

'She is from Boston. Her family landed with the Pilgrim Fathers. Whatever it is she's written that's making you question her integrity, believe me, it will be true or she will, hand on heart, believe it to be true.'

'Sorry to raise your hackles, Harry, I wanted to know more about my source, that's all. Before I share my suspicions with London I must be certain that the information she's given me is bona fide.'

'My American aunt is kind, generous and pro-British. She has two cats. One is called Nelson, the other, Wellington.'

'I'm convinced … no cat lover would name her cats after people she disliked.'

'Are you going to share your suspicions with me?'

'Better not.'

'She's my aunt, dash it.'

'When you meet my guests and know my suspicions about one of them you will give the game away. You will be hostile to the suspect.'

'I will not … I'm as good a patriot as the next man.'

'But you are not an actor. When you can hide your dislike of Mike then you will be ready for diplomacy. Your American aunt has given me the key to a door I'd hitherto not thought of opening. For that you must thank her. In diplomacy it is always an advantage to know what the other side is thinking – some people are such good liars.'

'Are you?'

'I like to think I am. When a diplomat knows a truthful answer is 'yes' he must learn, with absolute conviction, to answer 'no' if that is the answer the security of his country demands. I will not give you a written answer to your aunt's letter. If one has a choice, never put anything in writing. A letter falling into the wrong hands can leave a chap up the Limpopo without a paddle. There are too many Americans who'd like to have evidence that people close to the President are keen to embroil their country in another European war. I would, however, like you to make certain that she knows of my gratitude.'

'Where are your American guests now?'

'All are on the Queen Mary, except for Marigold Striker. She's a professor of history. She's coming to join us from somewhere in Germany. I'll have you know she's the President's eyes and ears.'

'A female professor?'

'Women do have brains, you know. Before joining us, she's giving a lecture at Durham University. She's clever and rich. Your American aunt knows all about her. In her letter she hints that it would be ever so nice if you and the professor were to become an item.'

'I say, Uncle Charles, steady on.'

'On the QM I've arranged for the Americans to dine in the Veranda Grill.'

'A class better than first class. You are spoiling them.'

'His Majesty's Government is paying.'

'Does that mean the visit is official?'

'No, officially the visit is unofficial. They are coming to The Hall as my guests for a shooting holiday.'

'And when they are here?'

'To call a spade a spade we will discuss how to involve America in any conflict that might arise between Great Britain and Germany. All my guests are sympathetic to that aim, or at least I thought they were. Your aunt's letter has suggested that I may have to watch my back. All have influence in their country. Professor Striker will inform President Roosevelt of all we say ... that part of our get-together, at least, is official. So difficult to believe, standing here, looking at Northumberland's rolling hills, everything so peaceful, that, in a civilised country like Germany, the home of Goethe and Beethoven, you can be beaten to death because you are a Jew. When I ponder what the coming months might bring, I experience the feeling I had when I went over the top at the Somme. It is one of bowel emptying resignation. It is not like the fear of making your first speech in the House. I see the sky above our heads full of aeroplanes daubed with swastikas. Hitler will try to bomb us into submission. In the coming conflict there will be no civilians. Everyone who lives in this green and pleasant land of ours will be a target. HMG has commissioned a study to find out how long it will take the Luftwaffe to destroy London – many, many years apparently. Thank goodness our capital is vast. To obliterate London the Bohemian Corporal will need an air force too big even for him to build. I suppose that's one piece of good news. By the way, while you are here, there's a favour Elizabeth and I want to ask. It concerns our refugee. He has relatives in America – can you help us find them?'

'You want me to use my family contacts?'

'Yes, get your aunt involved. Once they are located he'll be off our hands.'

'You make him sound less than desirable. Is he a handful?'

'Shall we say, boys will be "boys". It was the Countess of Reading who persuaded myself and Elizabeth to do our bit and take in a Jewish child. Stella can be very persuasive. We are all very fond of the lad. The rabbis are the problem. They are concerned about Jewish children been placed in non-Jewish homes.'

'Are they frightened he might eat a bacon sandwich?'

'When you have seen your mother and father bludgeoned to death I suspect the fear of eating a taboo food becomes somewhat irrelevant. The lad knows the rules of his religion. When I asked him about them he told me he wanted to be treated like an English boy. He calls me Uncle Charles. "Uncle Charles," he told me, "do not tell me what I am eating. If I like it, I will eat it." I took the same view in the trenches. We all did. Once Mike presented me with a plate of stew. When I asked him what it was he said, "Don't ask." He knew that I knew it was rat, but we all played this game. Silly, really, but there you are. We were all so hungry. It was hot and meaty. We gobbled it down by telling ourselves we were eating beef. It helped us survive. When the Germans attacked we were full of protein. That was the day I won my VC. If I hadn't eaten rat I wouldn't have had the strength to run across no-man's land and take out that German machine gun.

To keep the rabbis happy he goes to a Jewish school in Newcastle. He's never keen to go, much prefers roaming the moors. He's gaining confidence now that he knows he's not going to be attacked because he is a Jew. He takes himself off into the heather for days at a time. He is quite the loner. Mike has taught him how to hunt rabbits with a longbow. He has the great gift of making people like him, no matter what he does. Elizabeth calls him her "Ray of Noisy Sunshine". It helps us remember the time when our girls, your dear cousins, were pushing dolls' prams round the house … how they used to argue.'

'They still do.'

'I know … I'm growing old, Harry. I'm in danger of forgetting just how much patience it takes to handle children. This morning I nearly lost my temper when I found Jack had been teasing Tom by putting snails on the melons.'

'Does the lad not know how passionate you are about growing the perfect melon?'

'I think not. Last week he upset Cook. The little devil hardboiled the eggs she'd set aside for breakfast. Phyllis couldn't understand why they wouldn't crack. He was watching her, I was told, giggling under a table. In the end both thought it funny. Phyllis now says that every time she thinks about it she gets a fit of the giggles.'

'He made Phyllis laugh?'

'Yes … I told you the blighter had a way with him. She spoils him and so does Elizabeth. I think my dear wife misses not having a son.'

'You have a grandson. How is George? He's joining us tomorrow, I gather.'

'Yes, that at least is something to look forward to. Elizabeth tells me that when George is here I'm much easier to live with.'

'His health?'

'The doctors have advised that the iron on his leg be removed. The poor chap will have to accept that for the rest of his life he will have a limp. Polio is a terrible thing. Yet, he's been lucky. He has survived. He is still with us and for that I thank God.'

'And what of his hearing?'

'He has a partial loss. Meningitis and polio … the poor chap has had his share of misfortune. Elizabeth and I love him to bits. He'll be spending what's left of his summer holidays with us. We've told him that this year he'll have someone to play with.'

'Will he get on with Jack?'

'I hope so … in their different ways both have had their share of bad luck. Both are tough characters. They are survivors. George is nowhere near as disabled as someone reading his medical history might imagine. He's a crack shot. His limp never stops him walking miles over the moors. He can drive a tractor and manoeuvre it and its trailer into the tightest of spots. When they meet I think it might be like watching two stags during the rut. I would not bet on the winner. A good job they've not started thinking about, you know, the opposite sex. At least I don't think they have. But it won't be long before they do. At twelve they are no longer children.'

'How is Jack's English?'

'Coming on in leaps and bounds. Like many Jews he has a gift for languages. In his youthful way he is quite the scholar. He keeps a notebook in which he writes rules of grammar, new words … use a word he's not heard before and he's at you like a dog at a bone … wants to know what it means, how to use it, how to spell it. "So I'll not forget," he says when he's at his jottings. A few days ago he told me he'd been "fucking" a pheasant with Mike. I said, "You mean plucking a pheasant?" He looked me straight in the eye and said, "I pluck a pheasant, I do not fuck a pheasant?" "Yes," I said, looking at him hard, "that's right … pluck. We don't use the other word. Make sure you write that down in your book." I gave him the benefit of the doubt, but I do think he had a twinkle in his eye.'

'Mike is a bad influence.'

'Mike is like army rations, Harry, an acquired taste. You are prejudiced. He's good for the lad. Mike and his wife have all but adopted him. Jack says he has four homes … Germany, The Hall, Mike's cottage and his 'erdgeist lager', his earth-spirit home. It's a kind of den he's made for himself at the top of the Meadow Hill. When Mike and I were boys it was our den. Latterly he's taken to sleeping there. He says being close to Mother Earth makes him feel safe. I fear the Nazis have traumatised him. Elizabeth fusses about him being out all night. She wants to wrap him in cotton wool. When I was his age I loved sleeping under the stars. I refuse to hem the lad in. He's seen too much of the beast in man. I am giving him the medicine that helps me live with my memories of the Somme.' He gestured towards the fields which, because of a ha-ha, rolled like a wave of uninterrupted green on to the terrace. He sniffed the air like a dog.

'The champagne air of Northumberland,' suggested Harry.

'Yes, and the good news is he is drinking it up in goblets. Mike is teaching him all the things he taught you. He's had him out stalking … tells me the lad is a natural, says he uses the lie of the land without having to be told … never forgets which way the wind is blowing. You know what noses deer have on them. The slightest whiff of human and they're off.'

'Maybe he's a good hunter because he's been hunted. Don't they say a deer which has been shot at is twice as wary as one which has not?'

'That's why Mike is having trouble stalking that big stag. The first time he took a pot at him he missed by inches. I gather we'll not see you for dinner?'

'I'm off to Pruney's birthday party.'

'CB's daughter?'

'Yes.'

'I've heard she's nothing like her father, rather a good looking girl by all accounts.'

'Rather.'

'She must take after her mother. CB's wife was an attractive woman … sad she died so young. I could never understand her marrying CB. Women are funny creatures, don't you think? Where's the party?'

'Assembly Rooms.'

'Take the MG. Mother told me she married Father because he drove a phaeton. Let's see what an MG does for your chances with Pruney. I'll tell Bert to leave you a cold supper. I won't expect you back until the early hours. Your aunt and I will be tucked up in bed. If war breaks out people will be going to parties to help them forget rather than for pleasure. Harry … go and enjoy yourself. At your age I was in the trenches.'

7

To avoid the rat, Marigold lurched to one side. A sound like a bee in a hurry passed close to her head. Waves of sound broke against the tunnel's walls. She turned, saw Doyle and ran.

At the end of the tunnel, chest heaving, sucking in lungful after lungful of smoky air, she ran towards a group of men unloading a lorry. A rotund man, with red cheeks and a shock of white hair, appeared to be in charge. Every time a sheaf of poles was unloaded he sucked a pencil and made a note on a clipboard. She ran at him like a sprinter who, knowing his competitors are hard on his heels, throws himself over the finishing line.

'What's the matter, pet? Is the polis after yuh?'

'You bet.'

Her shortness of breath made her whisper 'you' while her American accent boomed out 'bet'. Because he was expecting a 'runner' (someone who broke the law by taking betting money to a bookie) and he was very keen that his bet be placed, 'cos it was a dead cert', he was more than half way to believing that that was what she was.

'Are you the new runner?'

When she nodded her head, not to answer his question but because she was out of breath, well, that was good enough for him.

'We've never had a woman 'runner' before. I saw a cloud this morning that looked like a horse. I've got sixpence each way on Geordie Black. Do's a favour pet, to bring me luck, touch my clipboard. McPherson keeps the money … ask for Eddy … in you go … follow the shunting poles. You can get out the back way …over the railway lines. I'll take care of the polis … plain clothes man, is he? Leave him to me.'

A notice warned, 'Trespassers will be prosecuted. London and North-East Railways, Supplies and Contracts Dept'. The warehouse was cold, like a larder. There was a smell of dampness, a dungeon smell, also the smell of carbolic soap and wood resin, the aroma of the hardware store. One bay she passed was piled high with extra-long broom handles, shunting poles, she guessed; poles designed to make light work, through leverage, of lifting the steel couplings joining one railway wagon to another. Another bay held tottering stacks of galvanised buckets; another, untidy heaps of mop heads, thrown in, she got the impression, any old how, as the butchers of the French Revolution might have piled the guillotined heads of their aristocratic victims. If Doyle and the Pied Piper caught her, would they chop off her head, cut her up into little pieces and, mafia style, feed her to the fishes? Nearly tripping over a cardboard box smelling of soap she cautioned herself to concentrate, to curb her flights of fancy. She was alive and had every intention of staying that way.

The place was a maze. A spiral staircase corkscrewed to an upper floor. A glass booth seemed to be some kind of office; through its grimy windows she glimpsed dockets filled with rolls of paper. Above its closed door, a crude sign, 'Eddy's'. The money man? What odds would Eddy give on her not being murdered by Doyle? Ahead she saw railway signals and daylight.

Breathing heavily, gasping for air, she found herself on a loading dock where a shunting engine was beginning to move a short train of closed wagons. She jumped into the last wagon because its sliding door was slightly open. On its side, scrawled in chalk, 'Kielder'; which she misread as 'kill her', such was her state of mind.

She found her bolt hole to be full of shunting poles and galvanised buckets. Like the warehouse, it smelled of soap.

By the time Doyle appeared at the door the train had gathered speed. His splayed arms and legs struggled to get a hold on the moving wagon. The advantage was all hers. She went at him with the hooked end of a shunting pole, like an English pike man attacking a Frenchman at Agincourt. To avoid disembowelment he jumped off, disappearing through floating feathers of steam.

All too soon the train stopped. She wanted not one mile but hundreds of miles between herself and Doyle. In case he should reappear, she held the shunting pole in a way that showed she was ready for a fight. She heard voices … Geordie voices, a man whistling … someone happy at his work … someone talking about football … Newcastle were playing Arsenal … the door slid shut.

At first the wagon moved in fits and starts. Its unpredictable jolts left her no choice but to sit on its dirty floor. She found the noise and constant jolting exhausting.

Later, the lights of passing stations appeared and disappeared through cracks in the wagon's ill-fitting door. Her discomfort was worse than anything she'd endured during last night's stormy crossing of the North Sea. She made a pillow out of mop heads. At midnight, with great reluctance, but compelled by necessity, she relieved herself in a galvanised bucket.

8

In preparation for afternoon tea, Lady Elizabeth instructed Bert to open the French Windows.

'My aim, Bert,' she told the butler, 'is to make Sir Charles 'think' he is al fresco. He is a perfect fiend for wanting to share his food with the elements and, since his spell in the trenches, with the poor as well. I sometimes think he's mad.'

'You sit there, dear,' she told her husband, 'then you'll think you are sitting outside … and why are you not wearing a tie?'

'Because I'm hot.'

'That is why I instructed Bert to open the French Windows … all of them. There is quite a breeze coming in.'

'If there is, I can't feel it.'

Afternoon tea in the library was an established part of their routine. What was novel about this occasion was the utilitarian crockery. Before commenting, Sir Charles cast a wry glance at a cabinet full of fine porcelain. In particular he eyed a teacup, the sort that made anyone sipping from it splay out his or her fingers like a cockatoo's crest.

'I know what you are thinking, Charles, but in my opinion it is never too early to fly the flag.'

'The last time I drank out of a tin mug was in nineteen-seventeen. I was in a trench up to my knees in mud. What's wrong with the Crown Derby?'

'Hitler might break it.'

'We are not at war … yet.'

'Your napkin, please use it … the heat is making the strawberry jam runny. If you must know I am setting a good example. At a WVS meeting Clarkson-Ball told us that if we go to war with Germany we can expect to be bombed.'

'CB is a windbag.'

'If Harry marries his daughter he will be family. I know you don't hold him in high regard, but it seemed to me he spoke a lot of sense. Do you know a bomb dropped half a mile away will bring down our ceilings?'

'And break the Crown Derby?'

'Yes.'

'What about the Worcester?'

'I am making plans to have that stored in the cellar. Charles, we must be prepared. Cook was telling me that you have started stockpiling Darjeeling. I don't see why you should take umbrage at my precautionary measures when you are doing the same. And do stop nodding your head like that; it might fall off. If you agree with me, say so … watercress or cucumber?'

'Ask me if I want ham.'

'Your habit of asking for something not on the table … in that roundabout way, I find most annoying. I know you like ham sandwiches. I have been married to you for forty years.'

'With mustard … ask me if I want mustard on the ham.'

'You know as well as I do that we agreed to veto ham to help Jack. We don't want him turning into a gentile, do we? We must respect the boy's religion. That is what we will be fighting for. The right of each individual to live their life as he or she chooses.'

'I'm confused … as far as I'm aware Jack is not taking tea with us. I know he's good at hiding … perhaps I should look under the carpet.'

'What if he pops in?'

'He's probably collecting slugs to put on my melons … actually he's down at Mike's practising the longbow.'

'That child needs all the love we can give him. I don't want him feeling awkward having to refuse food we've prepared for him.'

'A slice of pig won't hurt him.'

'It will not make him a good Jew.'

'I think Jack will say a good Jew is a Jew who kills Germans. According to Mike, he likes nothing better than a bacon sandwich. In the trenches I once ate rat.'

'Not that story again.'

'Mike knows what he's doing. He's good at looking after fledglings … that's why we have so many pheasants to shoot.'

'You are surely not comparing the raising of game birds to looking after a child?'

'I am pointing out that Mike is trustworthy and reliable. He and Margaret have all but adopted the lad. Mike tells me his wife is quite besotted with him. And so, my dear, I think are you.'

'Rubbish!'

'What else can explain the absence of ham sandwiches? Until Jack came on the scene we always had ham sandwiches for tea … with mustard.'

'Charles, if you mention ham sandwiches once more I will scream.'

'It would be better if you rang the bell and told Cook to make me some. And another thing … an aesthetic point, dainty triangles filled with cucumber do not look right on tin plates. It's … it's as out of place as riding to hounds in Oxford bags.'

'I blame Freddy.'

'What for?'

'Making you grumpy … thank goodness George is coming, he always puts you in a good mood. My efforts to do so have singularly failed. I thought taking tea at the French window would have put a smile on your face … clearly, I was wrong. Charles … I do try to please.'

'I know you do, my darling and it is much appreciated.'

'Please do not call me "darling". You only do that when you are being facetious.'

'Sorry.'

'And don't apologise.'

'Give me your hand. Let's not argue. For dinner tonight let's do something romantic. If Mr Hitler oversteps the mark it may be our last chance to do carefree things for many years to come. I told Harry to take the MG. Goodness knows what time he'll be back. Do you really think he's sweet on Pruney? Let's not hide behind French doors, even if they are open. Tell Bert to set a table on the terrace. We'll toast sunset with a bottle of something nice. Such a warm evening is not to be taken for granted …it is to be enjoyed. If the midges bother you wear a hat with a veil.'

At dinner, after a second glass of wine, Lady Elizabeth patted her husband's hand. 'Charles, it is as warm as Cannes. It was a good idea. You are not often right but this time you are … you were right and I was wrong.'

'What about the midges?'

'Your pipe and my perfume have scared them off.'

She wished the evening would go on forever. The long shadows of evening, the bird song, the sheer green lusciousness of England made her forget that horrid Adolf Hitler. She was happy. Manicured lawns, flower beds and, in the distance, the rolling acres of her husband's estate held her gaze like a hypnotist's pendulum.

'So still, so still,' she chanted. 'The fields are green swimming pools. They are like Dot's pool at Cannes, first thing in the morning … before swimmers make ripples.'

'And here comes someone who, I rather fancy, is going to make a bomb splash … you know, like Freddy does, diluting our martinis with spray.'

Both craned forward to get a better view of Bert hurdling over a bed of red-hot pokers.

'For goodness sake, Bert, what is it?' asked Lady Elizabeth.

'My apologies, Milady, but London is on the phone for Sir Charles. It is urgent.'

'Freddy?'

'Yes, sir.'

'We were just talking about him … that's a coincidence, don't you think?'

'Lord Frederick left me no choice, sir, but to interrupt your meal … Cook is furious.'

'The lemon soufflés?'

'They are ready to serve, sir. When I told Phyllis to put them on hold she became agitated. An airborne rolling pin forced me to exit the kitchen through the garden door, hence my gallop across the lawn.'

'Soufflés and Freddy: one goes flat if it is kept waiting … the other explodes.'

'I've taken the liberty of putting the call through to the study, sir. Lord Frederick's agitation suggests the special phone will be needed.'

9

'Go ahead, Freddy, I'm on the scrambler.'

'Bad news, I'm afraid. The captain of the Nord has notified the local police that he's lost a man overboard.'

'Byker-Harrison?'

'Yes. The Germans have witnesses … two members of the crew …all Nazis of course … victims of indoctrination … they'd swear to anything. Why they've reported the incident, I don't know.'

'Germans love filling in forms … doing things by the book.'

'Perhaps the filling in of a few forms makes them feel that bumping off an Englishman is an OK thing to do.'

'What's their story?'

'They claim B-H was drunk and jumped. Rubbish, of course. B-H could drink a bottle of whisky and still thread a needle. I've told the inspector looking into the matter not to make too much of a fuss. I don't want HMG involved in a diplomatic row – there's already more than enough trouble between Germany and England. No need to put cream on that trifle.'

'That sounds like appeasement. I thought that phase of our foreign policy was finished.'

'Appeasement is a badly shot buck, Charlie. Before it falls, it staggers. My suspicion is that one of the 'spyclists' is a murderer. When he is caught and found guilty he will hang. That is justice, not appeasement. Tonight these thugs are camping on Newcastle's Town Moor. A bit like London's Hampstead Heath, I've been told.'

'It's acres of grassland to the north of the city. If you are a freeman of the city you have grazing rights.'

'As from tonight it would seem a gang of Nazis has been given 'camping rights'. I've been told that when they cycled through the 'toon', as I believe the locals call their city, these vermin sang the Horst Wessel … can you believe it? Worse, the chief constable has informed me that they were applauded. You Geordies are too hospitable.'

'What the good people of Newcastle were responding to was, I suspect, a kind of mini Hitler rally. Freddy, we may not like these people, but they are impressive. They are motivated in a way we are not. A Hitler rally is like drinking champagne. It goes to the head. I speak from experience. I tell you frankly, at Nuremberg the waves of emotion which swept through the stadium almost had me shouting, 'Sieg Heil'.'

'But you didn't?'

'No, I did not.'

'I would have refused to believe any other answer.'

'All I am saying is, the man in the street should not be blamed for aping his betters. Too many of our politicians are ambivalent about Hitler. If Londonderry had been in the crowd he'd have offered to oil the blighters' bicycle chains.'

'Winston wouldn't, he's raging about these 'spyclists'. He wants to shoot them. When Winston is on your side, doors don't so much open as fall down. He's adamant that we are given carte blanche. He may not be in the government, but he has tremendous influence. Charles, we can't let him down. When these thugs head your way, I want the people in your neck of the woods to be vigilant to a man. We'll make our HQ the Vicarage. Lots of resources there and, by God, we'll use them. In the meantime, the local constabulary will be keeping an eye on them. If they split up, we'll have our work cut out. Instead of following them individually our plan is to put men in areas where we've a good idea they'll want to go snooping … the Tyne's many bridges, Armstrong's tank and gun factory. Any Nazis seen taking photographs there will be dealt with. I've been told it's on Scotswood Road … a rough area?'

'Very, more public houses per square mile than any other street in England.'

'Fights often break out?'

'Yes.'

'If any Nazi gets too nosey we'll dish out to them a taste of what they are giving the Jews. Charlie, you are on standby. By the by, what's the weather like up there?'

'Warm and sunny.'

'Pity, I was hoping it might be cold and wet. I do hope our German visitors are not finding it too warm sleeping under canvas.'

'Freddy, that's schadenfreude.'

'I know … what sort of people are they to need a word to describe one's malicious joy at another's misfortune? I shall ponder that in my bath … my love to Elizabeth.'

Lady Elizabeth was at her husband as soon as he came out of the study.

'Where are you going?'

'Walking the dogs.'

'You never walk them at this time.'

'I'm off to see Mike.'

'Because of Freddy's phone call?'

'Yes.'

'Can I help?'

'Things have turned nasty. One of our agents is missing.'

'Murdered?'

'Probably.'

'By whom?'

'The Hitler Youth.'

'Do we have to have them?'

'England Expects … did the scrambler work by the way?'

'You knew I was trying to listen in?'

'Did it work?'

'Yes … I found it most frustrating not being able to eavesdrop. Someone sensible has to know what you are up to. Charles, you are no longer young. You need looking after.'

'In that case why can't I have ham sandwiches … with mustard?'

Before going their separate ways, they embraced with a passion more in keeping with a bedroom than a public place.

In the snug privacy of the gamekeeper's potting shed Sir Charles repeated to Mike everything London had told him.

'After all these years I'm going to be hunting Germans again – that can't be a bad thing, can it? And one of them might be a murderer, that's even better. If they want to fight rough and dirty, that suits me fine. If they want to give out bloody noses they'd better be ready to receive them. This calls for a glass.'

'In anticipation of your reaction I packed my hip flask.'

'Rusty Nail?'

'How did you guess? Of course, I didn't tell Elizabeth. If she had her way I'd be on carrot juice all day and every day.'

By the time the two friends, master and servant, had finalised their plans, they were feeling rather merry.

10

Close to midnight Bert roused Sir Charles from his slumbers.

'It's Lord Frederick, sir. I told him you were in bed, but he said if I didn't wake you he'd shoot me. I don't think his Lordship meant it … just his way of telling me it was urgent. I've put the call through to the study, sir … on the scrambler.'

In his rush to get out of bed Sir Charles knocked over a lamp. Lady Elizabeth seethed.

'I've told you before not to drink with Mike,' she told her husband. 'He leads you astray. He has a strong head … you don't. Do you know what you are doing?'

'Yes.'

'Do you want me to take the call?'

'No.'

'Bert, bring Sir Charles a glass of water … he needs rehydrating.'

'Go ahead, Freddy, I'm on the scrambler.'

'It's about Professor Striker. Her bags have been found. She was a passenger on the Nord – did you know that?'

'No. Where is she now?'

'She's disappeared.'

'Not another "man overboard"?'

'We don't think so.'

'Did she disembark?'

'We're not sure … lots of rumours flying around … witnesses say they saw a woman running down the quayside. She was been chased by a man who more than one witness has described as a "gorilla" … there's been a shooting in a railway warehouse on the other side of the river, a guy with a split head's in hospital … we think he might be involved. Charlie, we have to find her. She's the eyes and ears of the president of the United States.'

Back in bed Sir Charles and Lady Elizabeth discussed what might have happened to Professor Striker.

'It seems to me,' said Sir Charles, 'that the Nord is a singularly ill-fated ship. One passenger falls overboard and another goes missing … and neither of them are Germans.'

'How much did you have to drink with Mike?'

'I'm perfectly sober.'

'You do realise the lamp you knocked over is broken?'

'I'm sorry, it won't happen again.'

'It will.'

'It won't.'

'It will.'

'I agree … you are right … it will happen again … happy?'

A couple of hours later, both sleeping as far apart as the bed allowed, Bert coughed to wake them up.

'What now?' grumbled Sir Charles.

'It's Mr Harry, sir, he has bad news.'

'Charles, what is it?'

'It's Harry.'

'Hitler?'

'No, Harry … something to do with Harry. Where is he?'

'The library, sir.'

'We'll be straight down.'

'Have you been down a coalmine, Harry?' said Lady Elizabeth. 'You look like one of those coalminers I saw on Pathe News. Your dinner jacket is missing a sleeve. Whatever have you been doing? I know you've been partying but really … in my day we did have standards.'

In his time at the Front Sir Charles had seen many men in shock. 'What is it, Harry? What's happened? A car accident?' Harry shook his head. 'Sit down, my boy.'

'Pruney's dead.'

'What?'

'They've blown up the Assembly Rooms.'

'Who has?' said Lady Elizabeth.

'The Irish Republicans … they've had a go at London and Manchester; tonight it was Newcastle's turn. Is this what war is like, Uncle Charles?'

'Yes, I'm afraid it is.'

'I don't want any part of it.'

'Bert?'

'Like we used to do, sir?'

Sir Charles nodded. 'Now, Harry, tell us what happened … Bert's bringing tea.'

Bert served the tea in the enamelled mugs he'd been told to use for afternoon tea. 'Trench mugs, sir … a little something extra for Mr Harry … two sugars, I'd recommend.'

'Don't forget the brandy.'

'No fear of that, sir.'

'And I'll have the same.'

'Charles, you've already had too much to drink.'

The 'look' he gave his wife made it clear to that good lady that this was not the time for a lecture.

'And one for yourself, Bert.'

'Thank you, sir.'

After a few sips of his 'medicine', Harry did his best to explain what had happened.

'I was at the bar buying drinks when the bomb went off … if I hadn't I'd be dead. You know what happened to Pruney? They blew her head off. I found it under a table. I don't know where my sleeve is. I did look for it, but I couldn't find it.'

'Bert?'

'Milady?'

'I need a drink. The same as you gave yourself and Sir Charles.'

Thursday 31st August 1939

1

'Leave your bow and arrows outside,' Phyllis told Jack. 'I don't want arrowheads in my pies, nor snails, either. I've a busy day ahead of me. The Americans are coming, I have to put on a show and so do you. Go and wash, I've seen cleaner chimney sweeps … and no tricks when the guests are here, agreed?'

'Why are they coming?'

'For a holiday … people at the top of the tree lead busy lives, they need to have a rest.'

'When do you go on holiday?'

'I don't.'

'Why?'

'Two facts for your notebook, young Jack … yeast makes bread rise and cooks in posh country houses don't get holidays.'

'I know why the Americans are coming.'

'Do you indeed?'

'Yes.'

'Have you been listening at keyholes?'

'Do you want to know?'

'No, I do not … it's none of my business.'

'Are you in a bad mood?'

'No, but I am busy. And even if I was in a bad mood you'd still be my bonnie bairn. Here's your eggs, soft boiled … plenty of butter on your bread, mind … you need fattening up. Where did you sleep last night?'

'In my den.'

'What did you see?'

'Two rabbits and a badger … what have the Irish done?'

'How'd you know about that? You've the sharpest eyes and ears of any bairn I know. Mister Harry is upset … we all are. I'd heard talk that he was sweet on the young lady that they killed … it's a wicked thing the Irish have done.'

'It might have been the Hitler Youth … they were in Newcastle last night … Aunt Elizabeth told me they are coming here. Nazis will kill anyone.'

'Not in England they wouldn't … they wouldn't dare. No, the bomb was the work of the Irish.'

'What's George like?'

'Your new friend?'

'He's not my friend. I've never met him. I'm sick of everyone going on about him all the time …how wonderful he is.'

'Now who's in a bad mood? You mentioned George, not me.'

'What if he doesn't like Jews?'

'So, that's what's troubling you … George is not a Nazi. Now, if you don't mind, I've work to do.'

2

'No time for a shave this morning?' Sir Charles asked his nephew. 'It will take hard scrubbing to get the muck from the bomb out of your pores. You'd feel better if you shaved. In the army we shaved everyday … no matter what. Come and join us for breakfast. I'm having the kedgeree; tuck in. If there's any left Phyllis will think we don't like it … then we'll all be in trouble. Cook has a lot to do today.'

'If you don't mind my saying so, Uncle, your enthusiasm for food at a time like this shows a lack of feeling. I know you're not a big fan of CB but, dash it all, the poor chap has lost a wife and now a daughter … and that's all before this bloody war we all keep talking about has even started. If CB doesn't deserve sympathy, I don't know who does … and I've lost Pruney. Do you wonder that I might not be hungry? I don't think I'll ever eat again after what I saw last night.'

'In which case when the time comes for retribution you will be too starved to strike a blow. I, on the other hand, will be a hearty fellow, able to wield a club. Pruney's death is one terrible blow.'

'Murder, you mean … she was murdered, blown up by cowards. The Irish need to be taught a lesson.'

'As much as we may wish it otherwise, what has happened cannot be undone. You must put the atrocity behind you.'

'Stiff upper lip?'

'Yes … if it comes to war you will have to get used to people being killed … though of course one never does … be a good chap and drive into town and pick up George. He's on the Flying Scotsman. I'd go myself, but I have to be here to greet the Americans … they'd not think much of an absent host.'

'Why can't Mike go?'

'He's busy preparing for the arrival of the Hitler Youth … don't you feel up to driving?'

'No.'

'I thought as much … that's why I want you to go.'

'Are you ordering me?'

'I do not have that authority.'

'But if you had?'

'Yes, I'd order you. When you fall off a horse you have to get back on. Pruney's death – all right, murder – was a blow … a terrible blow. Only if you allow it to fester will it be fatal to your good self. To please your uncle, be a good chap, get back on your horse … go pick up George. He looks up to you, you know … we all do – flying a fighter plane would scare the hell out of me.'

'It's like the time you made me dive for my shotgun, isn't it?'

'Harry, I don't know what you are talking about … be a good chap and pass the marmalade. George will be thrilled to see you. The Flying Scotsman is never late but you will be if you don't get a move on.'

Harry shaved but gave breakfast a miss. He supposed he'd have to pick up George.

'Is it wrong for a chap to want time to grieve?' he asked his aunt.

'No.'

'Uncle Charles was right, though, wasn't he? He's always right.'

'I wouldn't say that.'

After they'd seen their nephew off Sir Charles said to his wife, 'You think I was hard on the boy?'

'At breakfast you sounded like the colonel you once were, admonishing a junior officer.'

'I didn't raise my voice.'

'When you are in that mood you don't have to … it's your tone, the look that could sink a thousand ships.'

'If it comes to war he will be an officer. Officers must show leadership, set an example.'

'He's so young.'

'If he's lucky Jerry might give him time to learn … that storm we had, how it knocked the plants flat on their backs … next day, sunshine … up they popped. He's resilient … he'll pop up again … he's spoilt.'

'I find it interesting he's not forgotten you made him retrieve his gun from the lake. I seem to remember we had words. I wonder what Freud would make of him remembering?'

'My own view is that the medicine worked.'

'Why did you pretend not to remember?'

'Didn't want to embarrass him.'

'Charles, you do have a soft centre after all.'

'I know.'

'Which is why I love you.'

'I know.'

3

Jack watched the Hitler Youth through Mike's binoculars.

Mike had told him: 'I took them off a German officer in 1917 ... spoils of war. You'll not get better. Use them to keep an eye on the blighters. You are not scared of them, I hope? They can't hurt you here.'

Scared of them? What should have scared him was his desire for revenge. He'd never forgive them for what they'd done ... what he'd seen them do with his own eyes. His knowledge of their evil was first hand. But it didn't seem right wanting to kill people in England.

Back home in Germany it was also not right to kill people but, in Germany, there was no law. If you said bad things about the Nazis ... Jew or gentile, it made no difference, you were taken away, at first in the middle of the night but later, when the thugs were more confident, at any time of day. Sometimes the bodies of the brave people who'd stood up for what they knew to be right were found dead. Sometimes they just disappeared as if they'd never existed. The difference between the gentile and the Jew in Germany was that for the Jew to be murdered or made to disappear he did not have to criticise the Nazis; his crime was being a Jew.

He thought the English did not always believe his stories of Nazi atrocities. They thought he exaggerated. He knew they did. They didn't call him a liar – that, he was learning, was not the English way ... they just looked at him and smiled, smug and superior in their Englishness, comfy in the knowledge that through their Empire they ruled half the world, that their battleships made them invincible.

Yet, he understood why they might doubt him. They lived on an island, a beautiful green island. Living on an island had made them insular and snooty. To them, Europeans were foreigners; foreigners spoke 'funny'. They didn't eat beef. They were lazy.

Mike's orders were 'keep an eye on the blighters'. He'd do more than that. He'd observe them like a naturalist. The more you knew about your enemy, the greater your chance of killing him without him killing you.

The Nazi campsite was like a beehive: so much activity, so much coming and going. They'd corralled their bicycles in groups of three. That was the way the baker in Berlin had arranged his apfelstrudel.

They'd put up their tents, not in a haphazard way, but in rows. If their camp was a beehive, then Hitler, far away in Berlin, was the queen bee. Though many hundreds of miles away they were doing his bidding. What long arms he must have, what influence; it was in his name, in the name of National Socialism, they'd murdered his mother and father. If he'd had a machine gun he'd have killed all of them.

How could they be responsible for such crimes and look so, as the English would say, run of the mill? If Jews had to wear a yellow star in Germany, these people should be made to paint their faces red. They were devils, so they should look like devils … not like Boy Scouts. The English had not seen them do the things he had … smashing the windows of Jewish shops, humiliating a rabbi by making him clean a doorstep with a toothbrush.

Already they were plundering. Had Uncle Charles given them permission to chop a branch off a tree? He'd not like them making a flagpole out of it. He knew he wouldn't. Nor would Mike.

To mark their territory animals defecate. By hoisting the Nazi flag, the Hitler Youth were saying, 'This part of England is mine'.

Was it by chance they'd used a branch lobbed off an oak tree for their flagpole? Oak trees were as English as bowler hats. The Nazis loved their symbols and badges. Were they sending the English a message? He'd read Treasure Island. Were they giving England the 'black spot'?

In a Berlin art gallery his father had drawn his attention to a painting. Its artist had used glossy oils to show a hotchpotch of mortals looking up in awe at a host of angels surrounding the risen Christ. His father had whispered, 'That is how the people of Germany think of Herr Hitler. They think he has come to save them from the Versailles Treaty. Look at the cobbler's face. You see the same look of rapture on the faces of Germans at a Hitler rally.'

When the Hitler Youth saluted the Nazi flag, Jack, looking through binoculars, saw 'rapture' on their faces.

4

The front door of The Hall – a massive piece of English oak hanging on hinges cast from French cannon captured at Waterloo by one of Sir Charles's ancestors – swung open. From out of this imposing frame stepped Bert, pulling down his waistcoat points and slicking his hair with fingers moistened by his own saliva.

When the Americans arrived he wanted to look his best. In Flanders an American had given him a bar of chocolate. He'd never forgotten the kindness. At the time he'd been in quite a bad way. It was his private opinion that the Hershey Bar had saved his life. He was therefore keen that the Americans receive the very best service that he and the other members of The Hall's staff were capable of providing.

Things were going to plan in so much as the local stationmaster had telephoned to say, as he'd put it, 'The cigars and Stetsons are on their way'. Bert knew the man, recently appointed to the job, a stranger to the area, to be a radical.

From long experience he also knew the time it took a car to travel from the railway station to The Hall. He was therefore not surprised when he spied, in the middle distance, a Rolls-Royce, followed by a horse drawn phaeton.

At once he set in motion The Hall's well-rehearsed procedure for receiving VIPs.

According to character and their status within The Hall's hierarchy, chauffeurs, footmen, maids, cook and domestics ambled and shuffled into a line of 'welcome' that would have been given five out of ten by an RSM of a Guard's regiment.

Bert inspected them for smartness and cheerfulness. He told the boot boy, a dour fourteen year old who resented authority, 'Smile, lad, smile … take my word for it, no smile is too big for an American. It's the prairies you know … big skies, big smiles.'

He informed Sir Charles and Lady Elizabeth, 'The Americans have crossed the bridge, sir.'

'Is anyone in the phaeton?' said Sir Charles.

'A little too far away for me to tell, sir, that is for certain, but I think so.'

'I hope so … a nice touch, I thought, sending the phaeton … arriving at The Hall in a horse drawn vehicle will give them a sense of history … remind them, if it does come to war, what we'll be fighting for.'

'They might also think we've not heard of the internal combustion engine,' said Lady Elizabeth.

'That's why I also sent the Rolls. I will be able to tell much about their characters from their choice of conveyance.'

'You have set them a test?'

'Yes.'

'Freud?'

'Yes.'

'Harry doesn't like Freud's ideas.'

'I know.'

'If it were raining I'd sit in the Rolls … if it was warm and sunny, like today, I'd sit in the phaeton.'

'I know you would, my dear. You are practical, that's why I married you. No family should have more than one romantic under its roof.'

'Who will be found wanting, the Roll's riders or the phaeton fresh air fiends? Knowing your penchant for al fresco, I've no doubt the former. People are becoming bores the way they talk about Freud. Do you remember at Cannes when we played the Freud game? "I'm going to say a word," said Freddy, "then I want you to say the first word that pops into your head".'

'And Freddy said, "Beelzebub" and you said, "Mike".'

'And you all fell about laughing … I don't know why, I don't think Mike is the devil. But I do think he is a bad influence.'

'Have we ice, Bert?' said Sir Charles.

'Sufficient to build an igloo, sir.'

'And Phyllis?'

'Cook now accepts that for the purpose of my obtaining ice for the Americans' drinks – and for that purpose only – I may enter her kitchen and remove ice from HER new American ice-box.'

'The ice-house was easier?'

'Yes, sir, but the new machine is cleaner.'

'No bits of unspecified black bits in the ice cubes?'

'Yes, sir.'

'We wouldn't want the Americans to think we were trying to poison them. Americans, Bert, are foreigners … think of them as Hottentots or Bushmen and you won't be going far wrong. Because they speak our language we think they are the same as us; they are not. They have strange habits. They are not too fond of tea and they love iced water. If we run short of ice they will think us backward. Now, my dear, England expects.' He gave her his arm. 'This visit is important. We must treat them like royalty. In their own country they have influence. We need them to spread the gospel that if it comes to war with Germany, England will need the help of America.'

'So, I'm to be a missionary?'

'Of a sort, my dear, yes.'

'I'm to convert them to the British point of view?'

'Yes, but baptism will not be necessary. They are all anglophiles, or at least I think they are.'

'You are not certain?'

'I am certain that they are all patriots. In any coming conflict they will put America first. When the chips are down we will be like a dog begging … our job is to persuade them to throw us a bone.'

'You make them sound quite horrid. Yet you invite them to sleep under our roof … Charles, we might be murdered in our beds.'

'I am prepared for that eventuality … show her ladyship the gun, Bert.'

'It's stuck, sir.'

'Let me help, turn round.'

Sir Charles parted the butler's tailed coat to reveal a service revolver dangling from a snake-clasp belt.

'I think you are both quite mad.'

'It's for the parachutists, my dear,' explained Sir Charles. 'If it comes to war and Hitler invades he might well use paratroopers. If he does, we are ready for them. Bert's a good shot with a Webley.'

'Thank you, sir.'

'You know,' said Sir Charles, coming over all thoughtful, 'I do believe you could hide a sheep under a tailed coat and never know it was there.'

5

George was pleased to see Harry but would have preferred to have been met by Mike. Harry could be thoughtless. He forgot a chap was a bit deaf.

'Where's Mike? Grandfather always sends Mike … pick me up.'

Harry explained.

'Nazis, at The Hall!' said George.

'If war breaks out they might shoot us,' said Harry.

'Will Mike shoot them?'

'Yes.'

'Really?'

'Joking … on the other hand your grandfather's gamekeeper is a law unto himself. In my view he needs putting in his place. He picked me up from the airfield … drove like a maniac … made me carry my own bag.'

'You're in your aeroplane?'

'Yes.'

'Will you take me up?'

'One day.'

'I missed that … what?'

So that George was able to lip read Harry turned from looking at a woman who'd caught his eye. 'One day,' he repeated.

'Don't shout.'

'Are you peckish? I am … missed breakfast. Hotel across the road. Give me your bag. How's the leg?'

'Better without the iron. I can do a hundred in twenty-five.'

Harry ordered two cheese sandwiches, a lemonade and a half of bitter. He tried but failed not to ogle the barmaid's cleavage. The way she stroked the Cock O' the North pump made him ache.

'Me hand's still shaking,' she said.

'Pardon?'

'Yuh nar … from the bomb last neet. A thought the war had started. I blame them Hitler Youth. They marched through the toon pushing their bicycles bold as brass, singing and whistling and ringing their bells … every one of them a one man band … lovely legs … they were wearing short trousers, you see.'

'Lederhosen.'

'Is that what they're called? I never knew that. Mind you, I don't think they'd suit my Albert. They'd suit you. I have this thing about legs … they turn me on, if you know what I mean? They were all good looking lads … bit like yourself, if you don't mind my saying … by, aren't you the thirsty one, you've drank that quick … and I've not poured the lemonade yet … have another, on the house.'

'That's very kind.'

'You can buy me one, next time you're in … when you're on your own. You're a flyer, aren't you?'

'How did you know that?'

'I'm perspicacious … have I said it right? That's what my friend calls me … Miss Perspicacious … he's at the bar.'

Harry looked round.

'No, silly, he's a lawyer.'

Harry picked a table which would give him a good view of Miss Perspicacious pulling pints of Cock o' the North.

'Harry, do look at me when you are talking,' said George. 'I need clues from your lips to help me understand what you are saying. I don't think you want me here … I'm in the way. The barmaid is blowing me kisses. This is embarrassing.'

'They are for me … you are too young to be attractive to women.'

'At school one of the chaps has this book … it says things I don't believe … what men do to women, you know, to have babies … what's it like?'

'What is what like?'

'Fucking, if you've done it you should know. I don't want to do it, but the older boys say I will when I'm old enough to wear long trousers. What's it like? You have done it, I suppose?'

'Would you like me to take you up?'

'In your plane?'

'Yes.'

'Rather … when?'

'Now.'

6

Bert stood to attention, head back, nose in the air, hairy nostrils flared. 'The Americans will be here in thirty seconds, sar.'

'Bert,' said Lady Elizabeth, 'please do not say "sar" … do please try to forget that you were once an RSM. The Hall's drive is not a parade ground.'

'Begging your ladyship's pardon, it's the Americans.'

'How are they to blame?'

'They make me think of the Great War, milady.'

'Freud,' said Sir Charles, 'association … Beelzebub …Mike.'

As protocol demanded, Sir Charles and Lady Elizabeth positioned themselves just far enough away from the servants to show they belonged to a different group. For their part the servants acknowledged the arrival of their employers by standing that bit more upright.

Both groups were tense. Sir Charles was, to all intents and purposes, receiving a diplomatic mission. The fact that it was unofficial and a wee bit cloak and dagger made him uneasy. He kept reminding himself of HMG's aims; what it hoped to achieve from this gathering of five powerful, rich, influential Americans. No formal meetings would take place. There was to be no agenda, no secretaries to take minutes. Views on the developing situation in Germany would be discussed ad hoc over five course meals and sundry other pleasant ways of passing the time. To preserve anonymity each guest would sign the visitors' book using a nom de guerre.

As an experienced diplomat he well knew how surroundings could be used to exert influence. In the game of twisting arms, The Hall was a major player. A shoot had been organised. If one of his guests went home with a pair of antlers to hang on a wall, so much the better. But, where was Professor Striker? Losing a guest was bad form.

For her part Lady Elizabeth feared for her life. All this talk of war and the Irish bombers blowing up the Assembly Rooms made her anxious. She worried that the servants were not up to scratch. She fretted about the Webley under Bert's coat tails. Ridiculous! What if the thing went off? As soon as the Americans were settled in their rooms she planned to visit CB. He needed a hand to hold.

For the servants, the Americans were a lucky dip. In the coming days these unknown quantities might treat a lowly lad or lass like a human being or like muck. They might complain about everything done to make them comfortable, or they might praise. They might borrow money off you or tip lavishly. When you were at the bottom of the pile you just never knew. You kept your fingers crossed and hoped for the best.

Lady Elizabeth cupped an ear. 'Can you hear music, Charles?'

Sir Charles shook his head. His focus was on the approaching cavalcade … the Rolls in front, the phaeton behind. He saw that three of his guests, brave souls, had opted for the phaeton. He hoped they were not regretting their decision. The springs on the old coach did seem to be rather lacking in bounce.

Did this mean that three of his guests were romantics? We'll support England at any cost – and the other a hard headed pragmatist? Would that life was so simple. Did the togetherness of the three in the phaeton auger bonding? He doubted that as well. All these men had large egos. They were team players only up to a point. Oh dear, the romantics did seem to be on the receiving end of a fair bit of jolting. The 'brilliant' idea of offering one's guest's transport from a bygone era was not without its drawbacks.

'Can you hear singing, Bert?' said Lady Elizabeth.

The butler waggled his pinnas – he was one of those gifted people who could do that – and, after a moment's reflection explained, 'It's the Hitler Youth, milady.'

'Singing?'

'They are comrades in arms, milady … perhaps they are hauling on ropes, putting up their tents … altogether, one, two, three, that sort of thing.'

'Like sailors singing a shanty?'

'Yes, milady. I have it on good authority that when they cycled through the village they were at it like a Welsh male voice choir.'

'Song birds should be kept in cages, Bert, don't you think?'

'I do, milady, but Mr Chamberlain will have to make a strong cage if he's to keep those birds locked up; that is my opinion, milady.'

'Here they come,' said Sir Charles, 'best foot forward, my dear.'

The aeroplane was too low. A chimney sweep's brush sticking out of one of The Hall's chimneys would have scratched its undercarriage. Lady Elizabeth knew a Puss-Moth when she saw one. Why was everyone lying on the ground? If Harry was flying it one had no need to worry. He was a wonderful pilot.

When the horses reared up Bert ran forward to steady them.

7

In the aeroplane George put the finishing touches to a parachute he'd made from his pocket handkerchief and a bulldog clip.

'What shall I write?'

Harry felt at home flying an aeroplane. He might still be a virgin, but he bloody well did know how to fly.

'What about … home in time for dinner. Love Harry and George … hang on, I'm turning. If I was doing this in a Spitfire your eyes would be popping out of your head.'

'Like yours were at that barmaid?'

'Don't be cheeky.'

8

'It's Harry,' said Lady Elizabeth, 'in his Puss-Moth. I'd know it anywhere. I do believe he's turning to come back. He's going to give us an encore. That's just like him; generous to a fault. He's just the most brilliant pilot, don't you think? Someone's waving … it's George … George is in the aeroplane.'

Lady Elizabeth clapped. This was as exciting as the time she'd won first prize at the Hexham gymkhana.

'He's coming around again,' said Sir Charles.

'He's one helluva fly-boy,' said one of the Americans.

'Weinberger,' said Sir Charles, 'lovely to see you. You are looking well.'

'Sea air and good food on the QM.'

'Look,' said Lady Elizabeth, 'a parachute.'

'Where?' said Bert.

'Bert, do not draw the Webley. It is not a Hitler parachute. I think it is a Harry parachute.'

'Mancini, welcome,' said Sir Charles.

'Mancini, I said to myself, is this North-Humber-Land or the Wild West? Last time I took a ride in a horse drawn carriage I was ten years old and selling ice cream with my grandfather in good 'ol Philly … nice to see you, Sir Charles … lovely place you got here, nobody told me you lived on an airfield.'

'Macdonald, welcome.'

'Back in the carriage … '

'It's a phaeton,' said Lady Elizabeth.

Sir Charles introduced his wife.

'Pleased to meet you, Lady Elizabeth … back there in the phaeton there was a moment when I was pleased I'd taken out life insurance. If those horses had bolted who knows what might have happened … think of the headlines, Sir Charles: "American banker killed in runaway phaeton". That would have blown our cover. I'm relieved to be out of the phaeton and have my "feet on" the ground.'

'He's a fool, that pilot,' said the American who'd travelled in the Rolls.

'Pleased to meet you, O'Neil,' said Sir Charles.

'May I take your golf bag, sir?' said Bert.

'No, you may not. You know the idiot flying the airplane?'

'My nephew is the pilot,' said Sir Charles.

'You can tell him from me, I don't mind him killing himself but I ain't in no suicide pact with him.'

'You can tell him yourself,' said Lady Elizabeth, 'he's stopping at The Hall. Where's the parachute? I think this is exciting. Bert, retrieve the parachute.'

'Don't you have dogs to do that?' said O'Neil.

'Dogs don't do parachutes, dogs do pheasants … and do be a sensible American and give Bert your golf bag. That's what Bert is for. Look, it's coming down near the river, how absolutely thrilling. It has to be darling Harry … it's his very own Puss-Moth, you know. Don't you think he's just the most brilliant pilot?'

'It will be like looking for a needle in a haystack,' said Sir Charles. 'It could be anywhere.'

'My God, he's coming back to have another go at us,' said O'Neil.

'Bert,' said Sir Charles, 'never mind the parachute, back to the horses.'

9

Jack was awestruck by the low flying plane. It made him forget the Hitler Youth. The noise of the thing, how it swooped down as if going to land, then, at the last minute, how it clawed its way back up into the sky was thrilling. A boy in the aeroplane had waved to him; he'd waved back.

10

'Will they get our message?' said George.

'They will if they find the parachute. Did you see the Nazis?'

'No.'

'If you want to be a fighter pilot you've to miss nothing … have eyes in the back of your head … in your arse as well. Let's see how tight this kite will turn … hang on. I'm going to give those Nazis the fright of their lives.'

Harry, tight lipped and with a look of determination that would have surprised his uncle, dived the Puss-Moth down onto the Hitler Youth's campsite. 'Look at them run … rabbits … dagga, dagga, dagga,' he shouted as he fired imaginary guns.

'Harry?'

'What?'

'I think I'm going to be sick.'

11

Sir Charles picked up the Visitors' Book and took it to his study. As agreed each guest had used a nom de guerre. He smiled as he read, 'Charles Earl Grey', 'Mickey Mouse', 'Gelato' and 'Count Rushmore'. He rang Freddy.

'Are you free to punt the pill?'

'Give me time to check the weather. Shoot.'

'I have the nom de guerre of each of my American guests.' He reeled off the fictitious names.

'Mount Rushmore?'

'No, Count Rushmore, as in Dracula.'

'I wonder what the pun will tell Professor Freud about the American who picked the name.'

'Freddy, what is espionage coming to when we employ, what do you call them?'

'Psychoanalysts. Now he's living in London, the Professor is keen to help HMG. Information, from whoppers to tit-bits that we pass on to him about people we are interested in, he uses to interpret their deepest motives … the aim, to find the bad apple in the barrel. He wants to psychoanalyse the PM. For the life of me I can't see Neville lying on a couch blabbing for two hours about his sex life. Dashed un-British telling a chap about your dreams and other things.'

'We had no secrets at Eton … remember those pictures we got hold of from Paris?'

'Chaps one went to school with are different … tell me which nom de guerre belongs to which guest.'

'I can't.'

'What?'

'When they were signing I was distracted. Bert saw to the business … sorry to have let the side down. When you shoot me I don't want a blindfold.'

'Don't be silly, one doesn't shoot chaps one went to school with … if, however, you wish to shoot yourself, Ha! Ha! Well, that's a different matter. Reminds me of a story Dot told me. You'll remember she volunteered for a spot of auxiliary nursing in seventeen … first day wearing the white starch, matron told her to clean the men's false teeth … full of enthusiasm she put them en masse in a bedpan … redistribution was a nightmare. Instead of a bedpan full of disenfranchised false teeth I have a list of nom de guerre doing what nom de guerre are supposed to do … protect their owners' identities.'

'What about "Mickey Mouse"?'

'Find out which of your guests is a fan of Walt Disney.'

'"Gelato" has to be Mancini.'

'Agreed.'

'O'Neil looks a bit like, Count Dracula. I'd link him to "Count Rushmore".'

'I've been told I look like Bing Crosby, but, I don't sing and I'm head of MI5.'

'Point taken.'

'It's an extra problem for Professor Freud.'

'Is he getting paid?'

'As much as a Permanent Secretary.'

'There's money in psychoanalyses?'

'Yes, not my idea to employ the fellow … out of my hands. Why use 'Charles Earl Grey' as a nom de guerre?'

'Ask Freud.'

'What do you think he might say?'

'Look for an American who drinks Earl Grey tea?'

'Earl Grey, he's the Lord responsible for giving the plebs the vote, 1832 Reform Bill and all that stuff. What makes it interesting, Charlie, is the reforming earl was from your neck of the woods.'

'He's my cousin three times removed. In the centre of Newcastle we have a monument to him … it looks a bit like Nelson's column.'

'I know you have, I have a photograph of it in front of me.'

'Freddy, do cut to the quick.'

'At Eton you were always better at Algebra than me so it is with a certain smug pleasure that I now occupy the "knowing" ground. The local police are linking Professor Striker to the shooting incident in Gateshead. Where she is now, dead or alive, no one knows. The interesting development is the unconscious male found on stairs close to where the Professor was last seen alive.'

'A drunk?'

'No, though he was "stoned", not with alcohol, but in the Biblical sense of "stoned to death". A lump of brick lathered with part of his skull was found close by. At the moment he's unconscious in a local hospital. He's an Irishman by the name of DeVelera. He was armed with a Webley. Its serial number shows it to be the weapon we signed out to Byker-Harrison. We have a file on him. He's an active member of the IRA. The local police have put in a lot of leg work. It would seem that our unconscious Irishman met someone off the Nord.'

'Who?'

'To find the answer to that question they are checking the Nord's passenger list. DeVelera is employed by Newcastle City Council as a rat catcher. He's also caretaker of Grey's Monument.'

'It is open to the public. Inside its column is a spiral staircase. At the top you come out onto a narrow platform. It lets you walk round the plinth upon which the statue of the great man stands. I've been up myself. It offers splendid views of the city.'

'A good place for an IRA man to view possible targets?'

'Yes. What about the man this fellow probably picked up off the Nord? I think we may assume he was IRA. Do we know where he is or who he is?'

'No, and like Professor Striker he's disappeared.'

'A mystery man and a missing American Professor.'

'Only she's not just any old American Professor, she's the eyes and ears of the President of the United States of America.'

'I know, Freddy, I know. What a toxic cargo the Nord has brought to Tyneside … the Hitler Youth and, more than likely, Irish Republican fanatics. And Byker-Harrison's gun in the hands of an IRA man.'

'We are fighting on three fronts, Charlie: the Hitler Youth, the IRA and the Americans.'

'We are not fighting the Americans.'

'We are fighting for their goodwill.'

'Put like that I, of course, agree.'

'How are they doing? Have you put the central heating on?'

'You know we lack that luxury at The Hall.'

'To an American, Charlie, central heating is not a luxury, it's a necessity … they'll freeze.'

'We are having an Indian summer. If it turns cold hot water bottles and whisky will keep them warm.'

'I'm jealous … London's hot and stuffy. Everyone is anxious. Passing Buckingham Palace, I had to tell my driver to stop … couldn't believe my peepers. The Palace guards were wearing khaki … what have we come to? Would their ceremonial uniforms have made them targets? Is HMG expecting Nazi snipers in Whitehall? Ever heard the name Sean Roy?'

'No.'

'It was written on the inside of a cigarette packet taken from DeVelera.'

'When you submit the nom de guerre to the Professor, tell him that only one of my guests did not ride in the phaeton.'

'And that was?'

'O'Neil.'

'And it wasn't raining?'

'No. Freddy, I do believe you are more into this this than you admit.'

12

Who was ringing now? Where was Bert? Bert was in charge of the telephone. He was in danger of neglecting his American guests.

'Yes?' said Sir Charles.

'To whom am I speaking?'

'Sir Charles … who is it? What do you want?'

'Sergeant Belt, sir, Kielder Police Station, North Northumberland, thirty miles north of the Wall.'

'I know where Kielder is, get on with it, man.'

'Of course you would, sir, I was forgetting … it's the railway. I always said it would bring trouble and it has.'

'Elaborate.'

'What was that?'

'What kind of trouble?'

'It's a woman, sir … trespassing with intent … in a goods wagon. The station master thinks she was after the Brown Windsor.'

'Soap?'

'Yes, you see, sir, it's a supply train … comes once a month full of buckets and mops and other useful stuff …if the station runs short of Brown Windsor it might have to close.'

'That would be a tragedy.'

'I can see, sir, our minds run on similar lines … cleanliness been next to godliness, a station without soap would be full of sin.'

'What has this to do with me?'

'The person I've charged claims to know you, sir … says she's been invited to stay at The Hall. She spins a good yarn, I'll give her that. She wanted me to phone London … says she has vital information for His Majesty's Secret Service. In my time I've heard all sorts of excuses …. "It wasn't me what stole the bread, officer, it was my identical twin" … then, if that wasn't enough to swallow … tells me she's a professor. I told her, "Madam, if you are a professor, I'm Harry Lauder." She doesn't look like a professor to me … she smells. She told me I'd smell if I'd been locked up all night in a railway wagon. She said, I have it in my wee notebook … "A railway goods wagon, sergeant, does not have a powder room." To hide my embarrassment because I think I knew at what she was hinting, I fiddled with my pipe. She said, "Don't even think about it." I said, "Madam, the day I smoke in front of a lady without asking permission will be the day Britain no longer has an Empire." She said, "If you don't telephone London that's just what will happen." Comments like that set my fingers a-tapping. When she saw I wasn't for budging, well, sir, that's when she poured a mug of tea over my head. It never pays to be nice to prisoners. I broke my rule and I paid the price. A lesson learnt.

She's so violent I've had to lock her up. I only have the one cell. It was fortunate it was not in use. As I said before, sir, the constabulary at Kielder is a long way from what we, in 1914, called the front line ... to tell the truth, sir, it's the first time the cell's been used. I'm sick of her banging and shouting. If she'd been a bloke I'd have belted her one ... that always shuts them up. She said if I wouldn't call London, would I call you ... so I have. When I eat my steak and kidney I want to hear the birds singing not her thumping and screaming.'

'For God's sake, sergeant, cut to the quick, tell me the woman's name.'

'Striker, sir ... Marigold Striker ... Professor Striker, she says.'

'Where is she now?'

'In the cell, doing what my steak and kidney's doing ... cooling down.'

'Put her on the phone.'

'You know her?'

'Yes, she is everything she says she is and more. Put her on the phone, that's an order.'

13

Marigold talked. Sir Charles listened. When she'd told him everything Sir Charles said, 'I'll arrange for Mike to pick you up, he's my gamekeeper. You'll be safe with him.'

'I don't need a "minder", I need a "bath".'

Talk of female hygiene made Sir Charles feel out of his depth. At a loss as to how he should reply, he pressed on with his original offer of well-intentioned help.

'What I mean is, Mike's "a good man with whom to go to the well"; an American expression, I believe?'

'Tell him to "Tallyho" … isn't that what you Brits scream when you are hunting Mr Fox? In other words, step on the gas and get me out of this place. Until I ended up here I thought the Keystone Cops were fiction … are you still there? Sir Charles?'

'Yes, I'm still here. I was pondering. I will cut to the quick. What do you know about O'Neil? Don't answer. I wish to give you time to mull. I would confide in you on this line but for the fact that, if I did, the whole of Northumberland would be privy in an hour to what I wish to keep secret. Mike will appraise you of my interest in the gentleman, Professor Striker.'

'Call me Marigold.'

'Call me Charlie. My gamekeeper does.'

'Should he do that?'

'No.'

'He sounds naughty.'

'He is.'

'In that case he and I will rub along just fine. I'm not a fan of conformists.'

'Marigold, what Mike tells you will, I fear, put you in a compromising situation.'

'Charlie, you Brits and your confidences are beginning to scare the hell out of me. Byker-Harrison's confidence near got me murdered. What's so scary is your politeness … "I do apologise but what I'm going to tell you might get you killed".'

14

'Mike,' said Sir Charles, bounding into Mike's cottage, 'I have a job for you.'

'So,' said Bert, having allowed Sir Charles to blab uninterrupted for ten minutes, 'I'm to persuade this American woman to spy on her own people?'

'Not persuade … from all I've heard of her she's unpersuadable … tell her about the letter from Harry's aunt. How she decides to play the game will be up to her. I'm off to phone London.'

15

'Nazis and the Irish,' mused Lord Frederick, 'in cahoots. I am surprised, but, on reflection, I shouldn't be. We've no intelligence on such a coalition, that's the prob. No coincidence they were all passengers on the Nord … a crucible of saboteurs and spies, that ship. In our line of work, Charlie, a coincidence is so often a clue. Years ago I kept bumping into Dot outside my club. First time it happened I said, "Freddy, is this a coincidence?" When it kept happening, that's when the penny dropped; that's when I twigged Dot was after changing my status from bachelor to married man …never mentioned I'd rumbled her ruse, pointless … she'd have denied it. B-H was right when he thought he was on to something … nose like a blood hound, that man. I will of course recommend him for a gong … pity it will have to be posthumous.' He paused. 'I heard about CB's daughter … tragic. How's he coping?'

'Elizabeth's gone to visit … see what she can do.'

'Good filly, your Elizabeth.'

'She makes me eat an orange a day.'

'A bit of fruit keeps the bowels open. You were always constipated at Eton. Matron's syrup of figs opened me up like a can of beans … never seemed to move you.'

'Loose talk costs lives.'

'Touché. Americans don't take kindly to foreigners telling them they might have a bad apple in the barrel.'

'Harry's aunt is a reliable source. She has two cats. Their names are Nelson and Wellington.'

'That's good enough for me. I have contacts in the CIA, trouble is, they are miserly about sharing intelligence. For us, Charlie, it would seem the war has started early.'

16

Over a buffet al fresco lunch Sir Charles apologised to his American guests for his wife's absence. 'She's visiting an old friend. The chap's daughter was blown up last night by Irish bombers. My nephew was with her. Harry is lucky not to be with the angels.'

'He the idiot flying the tree cutter?' said O'Neil.

'As a matter of fact, yes.'

'How many lives does he think he has to lose?'

'We heard about the atrocity,' said Mancini, 'terrible, terrible.'

'You call it an "atrocity",' said O'Neil, pausing to suck an oyster from its shell. 'I think the people responsible will call it giving the oppressors a poke in the eye. Ireland should belong to the Irish. India should belong to the Indians.'

'There he goes again,' said Mancini. 'Give it a rest, O'Neil, remember our host. The British Empire paid for the champagne you are drinking.'

'I'm drinking iced water. The views I've expressed are not mine.' He grinned. 'I'm putting myself in the shoes of the IRA.'

'They seem a remarkably good fit,' said Sir Charles.

'If you drank champagne you might be more affable,' said Mancini. 'You going to lock him up in the Tower of London, Sir Charles?'

'I might try the stocks.'

'Lay a finger on me, Sir Charles and I'll kill you.'

'Are you sure you won't join us in a glass of champagne?'

'I'm teetotal. I made a pledge ... until Ireland is free of the British, I won't touch a drop. I'm joking! Can't you guys take a joke?'

'Anyone for toppers?'

Mancini raised a hand.

'That's your fourth glass,' said O'Neil.

'O'Neil, you ain't my mom.'

'You asking me if the sun is hot?' said Macdonald. 'Of course I'll have more champagne.'

'Champagne,' said Weinberger, 'fizzy lemonade with a kick like a mule ... just the ticket for such a hot day; gee, I never knew England could be so hot.'

'Bert, toppers all round. Iced water for Mr O'Neil who has declared an unshakable preference for that beverage.'

'Ireland for the Irish?' said Weinberger. 'What about Texas for the Texans? Let Texas leave the Union Ha! Ha! Ha! The GOP would just love that.'

'And Scotland for the Scots,' said Macdonald; 'take the cross of St Andrew out of the Union Jack.'

'If that happened,' said Sir Charles, 'Newcastle will once again be a border city. My ancestors were reivers, border bandits, neither Scots nor English, a law unto themselves. Part of The Hall … that bit over there, started life as a Pele Tower, its walls are ten feet thick. In times of trouble my distant ancestors locked themselves in there … sheep and cattle downstairs, people on the top floor.'

'It won't protect you from Hitler's Stukas,' said Mancini. 'Look what they did to Guernica … terrible … terrible.'

'Ireland will make England weep,' said O'Neil. 'That's what I'm hearing, not my view, just repeating what everyone knows.'

'Bert?'

'Sir?'

'Crack open two more bottles.'

'Don't forget the bucket of hail, Bert,' said Mancini.

'I beg your pardon, sir?'

'The ice bucket … you do have more ice?'

'Enough to make an igloo, sir.'

'Bert, I like you.'

'Thank you, sir.'

'By the by,' said Sir Charles, 'I've had a phone call from Professor Striker. She'll be joining us later this afternoon. My man has gone to pick her up. She'd have been here earlier, but she boarded the wrong train.'

It would be up to the Professor to decide how much she told her fellow Americans of her recent adventures. If O'Neil was involved with the IRA it seemed a wise move not to let him know of Marigold's run-in with that organisation. He was looking forward to meeting the woman who'd poured a mug of tea over a police sergeant's head. She sounded the sort of spirited filly who'd enjoy a water pistol fight in the shrubbery.

'Marigold will have been shopping,' said O'Neil, 'that's what women do on business trips, go shopping … women should stay at home and look after the kids.'

'You wouldn't say that if Marigold was here,' said Mancini. 'I'm frightened of three women: my mother, my wife and Marigold. I'm surprised she got on the wrong train. Newcastle Central is not New York.'

'The Prof lost or something?' said Weinberger. 'This smoked salmon … best I've tasted, local?'

'The Tweed … you fish?' said Sir Charles.

'I don't have the patience. Oilmen are proactive. If I was fishing this River Tweed … that where the Harris Tweed comes from, Sir Charles?'

'No, that comes from the Isle of Harris, way up north in Scotland.'

'If I was fishing this River Tweed I'd use dynamite … Boom! Boom!'

Macdonald flicked a flake of salmon off his forehead.

'Begging your pardon, Mac, Texans have big mouths but even we shouldn't talk with 'em full of food … Mother would not be proud of her first-born.'

'A gentleman would never use dynamite,' said Sir Charles.

'Hitler uses dynamite when he goes fishing for Lebensraum,' said Macdonald.

'Sir Charles,' said Weinberger, 'if it comes to war you Brits are going to have to learn that shouting, "I say, that's not fair play" is pissing in the wind. You are going to have to learn to be brutal. If Hitler was in charge of India, Mr Gandhi would be dead.'

'But he's not in charge of India,' said Sir Charles, 'the British are, and that's a fact. I've served there, I know the country well.'

'Bet you don't have any Indian friends?' said O'Neil.

'On behalf of my fellow guests, Sir Charles, I apologise,' said Macdonald. 'O'Neil, you are out of line. It is not Sir Charles' fault Britain has an Empire.'

'Empires come and go,' said Mancini. 'Look at the Roman Empire, how many more ice creams the Mancini family would have sold if Rome still ruled the world … Coliseum Cornets … Senator Sorbets … here's an angle … whatever flavour it said on the wrapper would be a lie. You buy a chocolate Senator Sorbet, don't expect chocolate … expect anything but chocolate. If you do buy a Chocolate Senator Sorbet and get chocolate then you win a prize … you've found a senator who tells the truth.'

'You remind me of why I signed the pledge,' said O'Neil.

'What would the O'Neil flavour be? Sour Grapes?'

'Give it to him,' said Weinberger. 'Always good sport watching a Wop fight a Mick.'

'Gentlemen,' said Sir Charles, 'I do fear that in vino veritas we are in danger of becoming too boisterous. Before deck chairs are broken over heads may I suggest a tour of The Hall's grounds?'

'Will we be going off piste?' said Mancini.

'Wellingtons and sticks will be provided.'

'Count me in.'

'Me too,' said Macdonald.

'When do we get to shoot something?' said Weinberger.

'My gamekeeper's organised a shoot for tomorrow. He's a big stag lined up for someone.'

'I know where I'm going to hang the head … you got seize thirteen wellingtons? If you do you'll be the first host who's kitted out Jasper Weinberger with the right size footwear, ever.'

'Sir Charles knows all our foot sizes,' said Macdonald. 'The British Secret Service tipped my valet on the Mary, only I tipped the guy more to find out why he was writing down my personal details … right, Sir Charles?'

'To be a good host I have found it indispensable to know the shoe sizes of my guests.'

'You take any more measurements?' said O'Neil.

'If any of you gentlemen should require a new suit while you are at The Hall, for whatever reason … falling into a ditch, an accident at the dinner table … my tailor has your measurements. From memory, Jasper, you have a thirty-four inch inside leg and a thirty-nine inch waist … you dress on the left side.'

'Never knew that about you,' said Mancini. He looked at the Texan's crotch. 'You sure?'

'Big oil wells, big gonads, that's what we say in Texas and my oil wells are big, don't you ever go forgetting that … big.'

'I'm afraid, O'Neil, I don't have your particulars – your valet was incorruptible. He was Irish, I believe.'

'Is it a crime to be Irish?'

'Bribery, it would seem has brought us the possibility of gratis boots and suits,' said Mancini.

'But does the end justify the means?' said Macdonald.

'If Grandfather hadn't bribed a bank manager with free ice cream there'd have been no bank loan … without the loan he wouldn't have been able to expand, without the expansion I wouldn't have gone to Harvard … if I hadn't gone to Harvard I wouldn't be here … I'd be selling ice cream.'

'That's one of the best arguments against bribery I've heard,' said O'Neil; 'no bribes, no Mancini. And count me out of this jaunt. You got a golf course, Sir Charles?'

'I have a putting green.'

'How many holes?'

'Nine the last time I counted but we are having trouble with rabbits.'

'Golf helps me unwind. After that plane scalped me I need to relax.'

'Never knew you were a golfer,' said Macdonald.

'When you get the bug the only place you can be happy is on a golf course.'

'And you have this bug?'

'Smitten.'

'Typhus is a bug,' said Mancini. 'Why didn't you get the typhus bug? Sir Charles, I believe you are wanted.'

Sir Charles, looking over his shoulder, saw his head gardener.

'Tom, come and join us … gentlemen, may I introduce you to Tom, my head gardener.'

'I've brought you the parachute, sir, what her ladyship was looking for.'

Sir Charles read its message out loud.

'"Home in time for dinner, Love Harry and George."'

'That the air mail from the suicide pilot?' said O'Neil.

'My nephew had a fright last night.'

'Not as big as the one he gave me.'

'I think he was blowing off steam.'

'If he wants to relax he should get the golf bug … it's safer than diving airplanes damn near into the ground.'

'I think the boy has guts,' said Weinberger.

'Fine, fine … so the boy's the new Richthofen … fine, he has guts … I just don't want them spilled down my suit.'

'When I heard on the grapevine, sir, that her ladyship was keen to find the parachute, well, as soon as I found it, I brought it here after, that is, I made sure I knew where, You Know Who was.'

'Where is Jack?'

'He is spying on us, sir.'

'Who is spying on us?' said O'Neil. 'I thought our visit to The Hall was private?'

'It's the grapevine,' said Mancini, 'the gardener's telephone … sorry, couldn't resist …'

'Booze, women and puns, anything else you can't resist?' said O'Neil.

'Yeah, punching you on the nose.'

17

On her way back to The Hall Marigold asked Mike, 'Do they have running hot water?'

'Only on Thursdays.'

'So, it's my lucky day.'

'Yes.'

'What happens the other days?'

'There's a pump in the courtyard or you can bathe in one of the lakes. Sir Charles thinks lake bathing is best when the lake is skimmed with ice.'

'Have I asked the wrong question?'

'We Brits do not like to be thought of as we think of the French.'

'Backward?'

'Their toilets are holes in the ground.'

'You have flush toilets?'

'Yes.'

'And running hot water?'

'Of course.'

'And central heating?'

'No.'

'I've heard stories about English country houses.'

'If it turns cold Sir Charles will order a fire lit in your room. You won't have to ask. There'll be a hot water bottle in your bed. He looks after his guests. Are you going to go along with his plan?'

'I'm thinking about it. Why are we turning off the road?'

'Trust me.'

'Why should I?'

'Local knowledge.'

The off-road track took them deep into a forest of densely planted fir trees. The sun disappeared. They'd entered a green cave.

Back home in the States her nanny would have rolled her eyes and said, 'Miss Marigold, this ain't a good place to dry your ball gown.'

'We are being followed,' said Mike. 'This is Sir Charles's county, nothing goes on that he and I don't know about. When I stopped for gas …'

'I thought you Brits called it "petrol"?'

'I was trying to make you feel at home.'

'For a tough guy you are very thoughtful.'

'When I stopped for petrol on the way here I was told a man with an Irish accent had been asking the way to Kielder. In a side road near the railway station I spotted a Newcastle taxi; that's like seeing a penguin at the North Pole. They don't belong to this part of the world.'

'Local knowledge?'

'Yes.'

'He's following us.'

'Is that why you were driving fast?'

'I always drive fast.'

'The men who tried to kidnap me were in a taxi. Kielder was chalked on the side of the railway wagon in which I escaped. Do you think he has come all this way to kill me, to stop me talking? He must have worked it out that his liaison with the Hitler Youth is no longer a secret … that I've been rescued and will have spilled the beans.'

'You have caused him a lot of bother.'

'I have caused HIM "bother" … do you know what he and his pal did to me? If it is them, I wonder which one it is, Doyle or the Pied Piper? I'd be disappointed if it was the Pied Piper. The lump of brick with which I hit that ape should have given him more than a headache.'

'Perhaps this gentleman is in the area because of the Hitler Youth. They are camped close to The Hall.'

'And I'm unfinished business?'

'Last night the IRA bombed the Newcastle Assembly Rooms. Anyone with an Irish accent is now regarded with suspicion. When a man with that accent asks if he is on the right road to Kielder, phones are picked up. He's been tracked ever since he opened his mouth. Let's stretch our legs; watch out for adders.'

'So typical of you Brits to have a snake that can only kill babies. In the States we have rattlesnakes. Now, that's a real snake. Have you eaten rattlesnake? I have … what you doing?' She watched him unload a wicker basket. 'Are we going to have a picnic? How very English to sit on the grass and drink tepid tea while being stalked by a murderer. You guys just love your tradition of the gentleman amateur. If it comes to war, take my advice: forget that Drake played bowls before he sailed to duff up the Spanish Armada. What I've seen in Germany leads me to believe the Nazis won't give you time to say, "Christopher Columbus".'

When Mike took a shotgun and a bandolier of cartridges out of the basket she shut up.

'You Brits are as unpredictable as your weather. I suppose I should apologise … sorry.'

Some fifty yards from them a stag crossed the firebreak they were in at speed.

'Get down … he's picked up a scent … it's not ours, we're downwind … someone's out there.'

The crack of a rifle being fired and Mike falling backwards on top of her were, to Marigold, simultaneous happenings.

'You're squashing me … oh, my God, you've been hit.'

She studied the splinter of wood sticking out of the gamekeeper's thigh. Around its point of entry his trousers were showing a spreading stain of dark red. The big man had gone white. Was he going to pass out?

'Have you got a knife?'

From a jacket pocket he produced a clasp knife.

'Is it sharp?'

'Of course it's bloody sharp.'

'Try not to move.'

The second shot bounced the Rolls up and down.

'Lie on your back, put your feet up on the running board. I'm going to cut your pants. I have to see how bad this is.'

She saw blood pumping out of an arterial wound.

'Take off your belt … you're not going to pass out, I hope? I'm going to make a tourniquet.'

'That's tight enough.'

'One more notch … a tourniquet, Mr Mike, is not a bandana.'

A third shot, passing through one of the Rolls' windows, showered them with glass; shards as sharp as razors nicked their faces, making them look a lot more badly injured than they were.

'Give me the gun.'

'Do you know how to use it?'

'I'm an American.'

'You a good shot?'

'Daddy says I'm a natural.'

Without saying another word she hunkered off into the forest.

The tap she gave him on the shoulder when she returned from the opposite direction almost opened his bowels.

'Indian medicine … Comanche.'

She packed the moss she'd foraged round his wound.

'Press hard down on it and you'll live.'

'The Comanche taught you their medicine?'

'Don't be dumb, back home in the States Comanche are as rare as hens' teeth. If we hadn't killed them all we wouldn't have had Colorado or Texas. I saw a Comanche use moss on a wound in a movie. It saved John Wayne's life.'

From her next foray she brought a long pole with a piece of flexible material, a little larger than a spade's blade, tied to its end.

'It's a fire beater.'

'I know what it is.'

'Take hold of it. When I give you the signal stick it up over the car's roof. I'm betting that from a distance it will look like a human head. If someone takes a pot shot at it they will give themselves away; that's when I get a chance to get even.'

She smeared her face with mud.

'You hear a stone hit the car, that's when you stick up the fire beater.'

She disappeared humming the Battle Hymn of the Republic. A stone hit the car. Mike raised the fire beater, at first tentatively, as if someone might be trying to peep without showing too much of themselves. When nothing happened he raised it all the way. The shot knocked it out of his hands, then all hell broke loose. Shotgun fire. Rifle fire. How quick could she reload? What rifle was the Irishman using? At times the shotgun sounded like an automatic. How many cartridges did she have?

18

In the shrubbery Jack was hearing everything Egghead and his American guests were saying. He was armed with a pea shooter and a bag of barley. When he'd called it a "barley shooter" Phyllis had laughed and wagged her fat cook's finger at him. 'If you don't want people to laugh at you call it a "pea shooter", that's what we call it in England and you want to be English, don't you?' His school boy's cap was pierced with twigs, his cheeks smeared with mud.

'Ouch!' said O'Neil.

Sir Charles and Tom exchanged glances.

'Ouch!'

'It's the Northumberland Nettle Fly,' said Mancini. 'If it bites you three times you die or, in your case, O'Neil, it knocks that chip off your shoulder.'

'Gentlemen,' said Sir Charles, 'it is now my turn to apologise. We are not under attack from the Northumberland Nettle Fly, if indeed such an insect exists.'

'Ouch!' said O'Neil. 'Why am I the only one getting stung? You guys bribed the insect?'

'I fear we are under attack from a young man armed with that most deadly of school boy weapons, the pea shooter.'

'If I catch him, I'll take my belt to him.'

'That will not be necessary, indeed it will not be allowed,' said Sir Charles.

'A Jewish refugee,' said Mancini, all thoughtful after having listened to Sir Charles' précis of what the Nazis had done to Jack. 'The Mancinis love Jews, you know why? They have big families, like the Italians, and they all eat ice cream. They are good for business. Leave this to me. I have seven children. I know how kids think. Jack is playing a game with us, all we have to do is join in. Everyone put up their hands and shout, "surrender". O'Neil, get your hands up. Jack, come on out, we surrender. We know where you are.'

'How long do we give him?' said Weinberger.

'For as long as it takes … it's like cutting a deal, give the guy time.'

'Spare the rod and spoil the child,' said O'Neil. 'The teachers who taught me were Jesuits.'

'That explains a lot,' said Mancini.

'And what's that supposed to mean?'

'Never mind, just put up your hands. It's your fault he's not coming out. You haven't surrendered?'

'Gentlemen,' said Sir Charles, 'I think we have stood here looking foolish for quite long enough. I suggest we leave the field of battle.' He looked at his watch. 'May I suggest we all meet in the gunroom … say, in an hour? Bert will show you the way.'

'Then it's off-piste and into the cow pats,' said Weinberger. 'You sure you got size thirteen boots?'

19

Lady Elizabeth called the Baby Austin, Bashful. When she accelerated she told it, 'walk on'. Once she'd driven it to a garage and filled it with petrol all by herself with not a servant in sight. She'd asked the garage man, 'How many carrots do I give it?' Among her 'set' it was the 'thing' to self-drive short distances.

Visiting CB made her feel she was doing 'good'. The poor, dear man had lost a wife and now a daughter. It took courage to visit the afflicted. At her side a Dundee cake bounced in a cardboard box. She'd show her sympathy with a gift of food; going empty handed was out of the question.

The taxi coming towards her was on the wrong side of the road. Its driver, going so fast, he'd no option but to take the tight corner racing driver style.

Because she and Sir Charles owned the road Lady Elizabeth saw no reason to obey that silly rule which said you must drive on the left. It was HER road. On this occasion her aristocratic arrogance saved her life.

The fleeting glimpse she had of the taxi led her to believe it had been in a fight; one of those dreadful bare knuckle fights she'd read about in history books. Its madman driver had been looking at her through a porthole of broken glass. She picked the Dundee cake off the floor, where the near-miss had jolted it and tucked it back into its box. CB would be too full of grief to notice the dog hairs sticking to it.

20

Sir Charles looked round the kitchen. 'Where is he?'

Phyllis knew from the look on Sir Charles' face that he meant business. On the other hand, Master was a good actor. She'd worked for him since leaving school. She knew his moods. Only when he winked did she relax. Jack was not in for a scorching after all.

'He's in the pantry, sir. He saw you coming. A rat couldn't have moved quicker. What's the bairn done now?'

'Shooting barley at the Americans. Phyllis, make a pot of tea, please, and three mugs.' He raised his voice. 'Jack is fond of tea, aren't you, Jack?'

'You should have been an actor, sir.'

'I was, Phyllis. For three years I played the British Embassy in Berlin, trouble was I only had walk on parts. Hitler was always top of the bill. Jack, come out, drinking tea will make you English. Jack, do please come out, I want to talk to you.' He played his ace. 'Egghead wants to talk to you. I know you are peeking … look, my flag of surrender.'

He waved George's makeshift parachute. Jack peeped round the door.

'How'd you know I call you Egghead?'

'Because I've been around a long time. It's my job to know what's going on … do come out and join our tea party. Phyllis, you be mum. How many sugars, Jack?'

Egghead was a clever cove. He knew how to get his own way. He asked easy questions that a chap didn't mind answering … before a chap knew it, a chap was having a conversation as if nothing had happened.

'Jack, how many sugars?'

'Three.'

'Heaped spoons or level?'

'Heaped.'

'We are waiting.'

Jack took his time.

'Sit here,' said Sir Charles, 'here's your tea.'

'Can I not have lemonade?'

'On a hot day like today tea is refreshing, better than cold lemonade. It is the English way … and you want to be English, don't you, Jack?'

'Yes, or American.'

'When you answer Sir Charles,' said Phyllis, 'do try and smile. You're not sucking a gooseberry, are you? You are not going to get told off, is he, Sir Charles?'

'No … I'm just going to shoot him.'

'Nazi!' Jack ran to the door.

'Jack, the door is bolted. I anticipated you might do a runner. As I told you before, I've been around a long time. You know I'm not a Nazi. You know I'm not going to shoot you.'

'Mr O'Neil would.'

'Indeed he might. He has cause. Do come and sit down. I want to talk to you about country house etiquette.'

'What's that?'

'Come and sit down and I'll tell you.'

'Has he upset the Americans, sir?' said Phyllis.

'If it comes to war he may well have stopped America coming to our rescue. One of my guests has a bump on his head as big as one of those gobstoppers I used to suck when I was Jack's age. What was your ammunition, Jack? Golf balls?'

'Barley.'

'I always used rice but I think you are a better shot than I ever was. You are angry because you do not wish to admit that what you did was wrong. By all means unbolt the kitchen door and run off, but, always remember, you cannot run away from your conscience.'

'Come and sit down,' said Phyllis, 'and listen to what Sir Charles has to say. It seems to me that Sir Charles has a lot more to be angry about than you.'

'Let's play the Anger Game,' said Sir Charles. 'I am going to put my hand, palm outwards, against the wall. When I do so I want you to hit it. You can be gentle or vicious … striking out will dissipate your anger. It's like smashing plates and saucers.'

'Dissipate?'

'You will feel less angry.'

'Sir Charles, he'll hurt your hand.'

'Before you lash out, Jack, I must warn you that at the last moment I may remove my hand. If you punch hard and I am quicker at removing my hand than you are at punching you will hurt your hand. Do you want to play?'

Jack grinned.

'You've made him smile,' said Phyllis.

'But can I make his knuckles bleed? How angry are you, Jack? You look pretty bloody minded to me. You know the rules?' Jack nodded. 'Who will be quickest? I'm ready if you are?'

Jack clenched a fist. He fancied his chances. He liked games like this. He'd have to be careful, though. When Egghead and Mike had been teaching him to play cricket Egghead had made an impressive number of difficult catches. When he had to, or wanted to, Egghead could move fast.

This was man against man, old age against youth, experience against youthful reflexes. They were duellists. Egghead had thrown down the gauntlet, he'd picked it up. He was in no mood to back down.

They exchanged looks, each trying to read the other's mind. Sir Charles's look said, 'Come on, do your worst. Best man wins.' Jack's look said, 'I know you are going to move your hand. You are tempting me to lash out. I know you are, but, I am not going to be tempted. I'm not.'

No way was he going to put all his weight behind his first blow. You only dived into water when you knew its depth. First, a few pretend blows to test Egghead's reactions, to see how fast he'd move his hand. How close would Egghead let him get?

He threw a feint. Sir Charles pulled away his hand. He pantomimed more feints, grinning each time he made the target hand flinch. Changing tactics, he landed a light blow, then another. Not a twitch from Egghead's hand. Another feint then, Wham! He lashed out. His punch hit home. What a pity he'd not used all his force. Ha! Ha! He couldn't stop grinning. He'd been quicker than Egghead; he'd won.

'Sir Charles,' said Phyllis, 'he'll hurt your hand. I'm getting ice ready for whoever has sore knuckles. I never thought the new freezer would be a medicine cabinet, but it is … life's full of surprises and it's all the fault of that Adolph Hitler.' She bustled off, shaking her head.

Moderate success made Jack think he could hit the jackpot. Part of him, though, was still cautious. He pondered how to fool Egghead into thinking he was making a feint when really he was launching an all-out attack.

'Think of the Nazis,' said Sir Charles.

Jack's knuckles slammed into the wall. Ouch! The pain made him angry. It was a stupid game. He lashed out a kick at Sir Charles' shin.

'You knew the rules when you started to play,' said Phyllis, pushing him into a chair. 'You're a bad loser, Jack Field. Put your hand in this basin of iced water. It's a good job Phyllis is here to look after you, that's all I can say. And don't you go taking out your temper on Sir Charles. You played the game and lost. You'd have been like a rooster saying good morning if you'd won. It was a silly game to play.'

'I wasn't shooting barley at the American guests,' said Jack. 'I was shooting barley at one American guest.'

'O'Neil?'

'He doesn't like you and you don't like him.'

'You were sticking up for me? That was very kind of you, but I think it best, I really do, that I'm allowed to fight my own battles.'

'I know from what I saw in Berlin when someone is up to no good. Soon after he arrived that American went for a walk. He kept looking to see if he was being followed. When he thought no one was watching he hid behind a bush. He did not wish to be seen. I know. He smoked many cigarettes. Sometimes he took only two or three puffs, then threw the cigarette away. My father did that when he did not know what to do … when the Nazis were burning our synagogues. But in all other ways this man is not like my father.'

'Perhaps O'Neil is of a nervous disposition. The aeroplane that flew over The Hall gave him the most awful fright … did you see it?'

'Yes, a boy was flying it. He waved to me.'

'That was my grandson, George. You'll meet him soon. He should be here later this afternoon. And, though I'm sure George would love to fly an aeroplane, on this occasion he was a passenger. The pilot was Harry. He arrived to stay yesterday, which I'm sure you know. You miss nothing – when you are older I'll get you a job with MI5.'

'What's that?'

'The British Secret Service.'

'Would I have a gun?'

Sir Charles nodded.

'And use invisible ink to send messages?'

'Do you know how to make invisible ink?'

'You use lemon juice.'

'Would you like Harry to take you up?'

'Take me up, where?'

'In his aeroplane, would you like that?'

Jack nodded.

'Of course there will be conditions.'

'I'm not giving you my pea shooter.'

'You may keep your weapon.'

'But you don't want me to use it on the American?'

'Is that a deal?'

'Put it in writing about the aeroplane.'

'Jack,' said Phyllis, 'Sir Charles' promise would be good enough for me. Sir Charles is an English gentleman.'

'What if we just shake hands?' said Sir Charles.

'We have a deal. Phyllis, you will bear witness.'

As they shook hands Sir Charles, solemn and serious, said, 'I, Sir Charles of The Hall promise one Jack Field that I will persuade my nephew Harry, to take the said Jack Field up for a flight in an aeroplane on condition that the said Jack Field does not use his pea shooter on any of my American guests.'

'I promise,' said Jack. 'Can I use it on other people?'

'No.'

'If I tell you what Mr O'Neil did can I use it on other people?'

'What did he do?'

'What's the deal?'

'I agree to your terms.'

'Swear?'

'I swear.'

'On the graves of your ancestors?'

'I swear on the graves of my ancestors.'

'He went into the telephone box beside the bridge.'

'Did he make a call?'

'Yes.'

'Phyllis, let Jack have anything he wants.'

'I like ice cream,' said Jack.

'If I am His Majesty's Eyes and Ears in the North, Jack, then you are The Hall's Eyes and Ears. Raise your right hand and say after me, 'I promise to be the Eyes and Ears of The Hall. If I break this oath I will have to give Phyllis a kiss every morning at eight o'clock when she is at her busiest making breakfast for everyone and is in no mood to be interrupted.'

'I'd always find time to give Jack a kiss,' said Phyllis.

'Jack, you are now working for MI5. Here's a shilling.'

He knew they were joking but you could never tell with adults. He didn't fancy kissing Phyllis. She was fat and had a moustache.

21

She kissed him on both cheeks.

'Lovely to see you, CB,' said Lady Elizabeth.

'That's a French habit. I don't like the French.'

'To cheer you up I've brought you a Dundee cake.'

'The only thing that'll cheer me up is a war with Germany, can't wait for the show to start, hope the Nazis shoot me right here–' tapping his forehead – 'best way to go, won't feel a thing. When the war starts I won't have time to brood.'

'Don't be ghoulish, you have everything to live for.'

'No, I don't and you know I don't. What was all that shooting about? Upset the horses. I won't have that, had to go down and give Ginger a carrot. Has Mike organised a shoot? Why wasn't I invited?'

'Mike's gone to pick up one of our American guests ... Professor Marigold Striker.'

'Striker, name rings a bell ... Striker. I sold a stallion to a Striker last year. Come along in, we'll talk about funerals ... funny business that shooting, shotguns and rifles, unusual. Who the hell is that?'

His question related to the figure he'd spotted some two hundred yards off in Ginger's paddock.

'The blighter's riding Ginger. It's a woman, one of those gypsy types. What's she up to? Christ! She's jumped the wall. She knows how to ride, I'll say that for her ... bare back, takes some doing. Hoy! Bloody gypsies. She's stolen Ginger. Elizabeth, the keys to your car.'

'Are you giving chase?'

'Of course I'm giving chase. Do you know how much that horse cost? Your keys, Elizabeth.'

'It may be your horse, CB, but it's my car.'

'I can drive faster than you.'

'Bashful doesn't like being manhandled.'

'Bashful?'

'It's my name for the Austen.'

'What about Ginger? If we don't catch him he could be horse meat by sunset.'

'CB, I don't often remind you of this, but I am the daughter of a duke – do be a good peasant and sit your bum in the passenger seat. Bashful and I will do you proud. Don't dither, man, or Ginger won't be just horsemeat he'll be a stock cube.'

22

The 'eyes and ears' of The Hall watched from the cover of bracken. They couldn't see him but he could see them. What were the soldiers doing? They'd arrived in an army lorry. Why were they digging up the signpost? There were three of them. The short one with a big belly had three stripes on his arm.

'Make your minds up, lads. I don't mind if Hexham points to Screw My Arse, just so long as it's pointing the wrong way. Our task is to spread confusion to the enemy. As I said last year when I put on a blindfold and went into that brothel in Cairo, I'm not fussy. I'll bet King George never keeps the Queen waiting … just put your shoulders to the wheel for once in your bloody lives. I've not had a woman since seven o'clock this morning and my wife's not a patient woman.'

The three stripe man reminded Jack of the Nazis. He had a mean face. In Berlin there were lots of little fat Nazis.

When they'd gone he left his hideout to study the signpost close to. Its new alignment had turned the world upside down. Take the Newcastle road and you'd end up in Scotland. At the sound of an approaching car he ran back into the bracken.

The open-topped two-seater passed the signpost at speed, reversed back at speed.

'I say,' said Harry, 'it's telling pork pies.'

'What is?' said George.

'The signpost. Someone's made it point the wrong way.'

'The Hitler Youth?'

'Could be. If a stranger comes with an urgent message for Uncle Charles, the poor fellow might end up in Berwick. If it comes to war, despatch riders will be up and down this road seven days a week. Uncle Charles is an important man.'

'Grandfather is retired.'

'Your grandfather is the eyes and ears of His Majesty's Government in Northumberland. If the Nazis invade it will be his job to organise the fightback.'

Ginger had visited The Hall's stables many times. At The Hall's stables there was this soppy boss woman. Nuzzle her and she gave you a carrot. His rider might not know where she was going but he, most certainly, did.

With flared nostrils he jumped the MG without missing a stride. The five barred gates he'd jumped on the hunting field made the motor car easy. He put on a spurt. No point hanging around when you were this close to bran.

Ginger's acceleration jolted Marigold from an astride riding position to a clinging crouch. She wondered for how much longer she could hang on. For Mike's sake she had to. He needed help and she wasn't going to let him down.

'What a pair of legs,' said Harry.

'Is that why women should ride side saddle … for their modesty?' said George.

'Yes, George, for their modesty … only some of them aren't very modest.'

'You know a lot about women.'

'More than you … get in, let's see if we can catch up with the mad gypsy woman.'

'She wasn't a gypsy.'

'How do you know?'

'Why do you think she was?'

'She was riding bare back … her skin was a dark colour.'

'That was mud on her face.'

'You sure?'

'If you hadn't been looking at her legs you'd have seen.'

'I can't wait until you reach puberty.'

'Where's that?'

'The nine o'clock train takes you there.'

'Is it near Newcastle?'

'Cockermouth.'

'I know where that is … why should I want to go there?'

'Believe me, you'll like it when you get there. Come on, back in the car. Something's afoot and I for one want to know what it is.'

From his hideout in the bracken, Jack pondered all he'd seen … soldiers pointing signposts in the wrong direction … a horse jumping over a car.

The boy in the MG had to be George. He looked to be what the English called a 'decent chap'.

Not another car? He'd never known the road so busy.

He recognised it. Once Lady Elizabeth had driven him to the village in it to buy sweets. While reversing she'd put its back wheels into a ditch. She'd kept apologising, not to him, but to the car, 'Bashful, I do apologise. I really do.' The English were mad. Today they seemed madder than ever. Perhaps it was the heat. They weren't used to it. When it had been hot in Berlin his uncles had closed their shops and taken a siesta. Maybe the English needed to be taught the benefits of an afternoon nap.

At the signpost the car did what driving instructors call an emergency stop.

'Ginger went that way,' said CB. 'I can smell him. If I'd been driving, we'd have caught him by now.'

'There's something wrong,' said Lady Elizabeth.

'Yes, there is, someone's stolen my horse. I know you are the daughter of a duke, Elizabeth but my father was a bishop.'

'The signpost's telling me the wrong way to The Hall.'

'I don't care.'

'CB, please do stop kicking my car's door. It's not Bashful's fault your horse has been stolen. If you dent the door I will send you the bill.'

'I want my horse back. It's my horse and I want him back.'

Sir Charles drove the open-top Bentley like a gun-dog looking for a shot pheasant. In its front passenger seat a swaying Bert was removing his collar and tie. The Webley, the one he kept under his coat tails, now, for all to see, on his lap; also a shotgun. A bandolier of cartridges hung round his neck like a horse's collar.

The Bentley had a good turn of speed. When he saw Bashful Sir Charles had his foot to the floor. The emergency stop he executed skidded him to a halt within a cat's whisker of putting a dent into the front mudguard of his wife's pride and joy.

'CB,' shouted Sir Charles, 'the very man we need; climb aboard, I'll explain later.'

'What's wrong?' said Lady Elizabeth.

'I'll tell you what's wrong,' said CB, 'someone's stolen Ginger.'

'Shut up, CB. What's happening, Charles?'

'No time to explain. CB, get in, that's an order. Bert?'

'Sah?'

'Give CB the shotgun.'

'Sah!'

'Elizabeth, you look after the Americans … oh, and by the way, George is here … Mike's been hurt … watch out, here comes the cavalry.'

The MG, driven by Harry with Marigold at his side, passed Bashful and the Bentley without stopping.

'She's the one who stole Ginger,' said CB.

'Ginger is safe,' said Sir Charles. 'You wanted war, CB, well, you've got one. Hang on.'

23

The blow from behind pushed George to the ground.

'Why do you not answer when I speak?' said the German.

'Because I did not hear you. I am deaf.'

'Why do you spy on us?'

'I am not spying on you. I am picking mushrooms for Phyllis. She's our cook. Can't you see, my trug, it is full of mushrooms. If I am deaf maybe you are blind.'

'We have seen you many times. We call you "The Fox". When we do not see you we know you are there. You are a spy. We do not like spies. In Germany we tie spies to a post and shoot them.'

'It wasn't me you saw. I've just arrived.'

'When you think you are going to be shot you blame … someone else. When the war starts you English will blame … someone else. When you lose the war you will blame … someone else. You are a coward.'

'I am not. Grandfather has the Victoria Cross. I have better things to do than spy on men wearing short trousers.'

'Lederhosen is the German national costume. You do not wear the kilt?'

'I am not a Scot. I am a Northumbrian.'

'You wear the short trousers … you wear the English lederhosen. The Fuhrer wears the lederhosen in all the weathers.'

'I'm wearing short trousers because I'm on my hols. At school I wear long trousers. Mother says I'll soon be allowed to wear Oxford Bags.'

'You trespass, this is the Hitler Youth campsite.'

'I beg your pardon. This is my grandfather's land. I have every right to be here. You are the trespasser. And, another thing, pick up the mushrooms you made me spill, that's what a decent chap would do.'

'I like mushrooms, maybe I take them for my supper.'

'No, you will not. You have taken Alsace-Lorraine and the Rhineland, but you will not take my ink caps.'

'Who is going to stop me? You bristle like the hedgehog. You have a limp. You tell me you are deaf. You are not the perfect specimen. The Fuhrer would not let you have children.'

'I don't want children. I don't like girls and I'm never going to get married. Hitler doesn't scare me.'

'Ach, you are so young. Give me the mushrooms and I will let you go.'

'Get off, bully.'

The German made an easy target. Jack regretted his arrows' tips were only sharpened wood, not proper arrow heads. Mike had said that arrows fired from English longbows at Agincourt had gone straight through the breastplates of the French knights. What might such an arrow do to lederhosen? Better still, he wished he'd a gun.

His opportunity to fire came when the German pushed George to the ground.

When he saw that the arrow he'd fired had stuck in the German's arm he whooped a war-cry. He'd done right to pick the arrow with the sharpest point. His skill with a penknife had paid off. Mike would be proud of him.

George saw the arrow, but, where was the archer?

Less than six paces from him, what looked like a 'bush', was waving a bow at him. His rescuer was not only a good shot with a bow and arrow, he was also expert in the art of camouflage.

Without further bidding he followed his rescuer through a chicane of rhododendron and azalea. His limp slowed him down. He could not hurdle fallen tree trunks the way the 'bush' could. He had to climb over them. His deafness stopped him hearing that the German was close behind. Jack, however, was well aware of the danger. Through signs he made it clear to George that they needed to get a move on.

Once out of sight of the German, they hid behind the trunk of a fallen tree. In this place of temporary safety they shook hands. Then, to George's amazement, his new friend stood up and walked into the clearing in front of the fallen tree.

'Over here, Fritz!' shouted Jack. 'Fritz, I'm here. Come and get me.'

You'd have thought a threshing machine was making its way through the shrubbery. Boy, was the German angry!

'Over here, Fritz.'

Jack hoped he was very angry. Angry people did not think straight, they were like, as the English saying said, 'a bull in a china shop'.

When they saw each other, Jack gestured that the German should come and get him.

'Come on, Fritz, what are you waiting for?'

To provoke the German, in the same way 'Egghead' had provoked him in their silly game, he shouted in German, 'Hitler is a piece of shit'. When the German took the bait and charged, he pretended to flee.

As soon as he heard the German fall into the pit he'd dug he ran back, whooping all the way.

The German was arse up in the pit. For weeks he'd tried to get Egghead and Mike to walk over its flimsy roof of twigs and leaves but they knew his game.

With his bow pulled back as far as he could manage he aimed at one of the German's fleshy thighs.

'Das ist fur mein mudda.'

'Have you killed him?' said George.

'Nein. The pit is not deep. He will soon be out.'

24

George thought the den 'smashing'. He'd a memory of the hunt losing a fox near this outcrop of rock. Maybe this had been its den. Enough light entered to make out jam jars on a rock shelf. When something moved he jumped.

'That's Moses,' said Jack.

'Does he bite?' said George.

'He is my friend. I have told him you are my friend. He will not bite.'

George found his head touching a ceiling of rock and soil. The roots of plants combed his hair. Jack hung up his bow and quiver of arrows on a root shaped like a hook.

I am George.'

'I know who you are.'

'Pardon?'

'I … know … who … you … are.'

'Do not shout and do not talk "funny" … talking like that makes it harder for me to understand.'

'I know who you are. You were in the aeroplane, you waved to me. You were with Harry when the horse jumped over the car.'

'You spy on the Germans?'

'Yes. I work for the British Secret Service.'

'Are you the "Fox"?'

'That is what they call me. I am good at camouflage. Do you like my den?'

'Rather!'

'It is my erdgeist lager. You do not know German?' George shook his head. 'It is my earth-spirit camp. I share it with my friend Moses … now I will share it with you. Here, I feel safe. I have lemonade and biscuits. We share. The German will tire of looking, I will know when.' He handed over a pair of binoculars. 'Mike's.'

George focussed on the tents he could see through the fissure. The view was marred by out of focus tufts of grass; nevertheless a chap had a pretty good view.

'My turn now,' said Jack, taking the binoculars. 'Fritz is back. He is the German who tried to steal your mushrooms.'

'What did you shout at him? You made him angry.'

'I was giving a red rag to the bull and pulling the tiger's tail.'

'You were lucky he didn't catch you.'

'Not getting caught was part of my plan.'

'What did you shout at him?'

'"Hitler is a piece of shit".'

'He shouldn't have stolen my mushrooms. I'm glad you upset him. You know the names of all the Germans?'

'I know Heinrich. I know Fritz. I know Gunther. They are the leaders. They are up to something, I know. We are safe. I am sorry I do not have tea. I am learning your English ways. Punch me in the tummy … go on.'

'Why?'

'To show you I am tough. Go on, I'm ready. The secret is to be ready.'

'I don't want to.'

'If you don't want to I won't make you. Do you know how babies are made?'

'One of the boys at school showed me a book.'

'Did it have pictures?'

'Well … drawings.'

'I've seen a book like that. Do you think it's true?'

'If it's in a book it must be true.'

'You have not lived in Nazi Germany. The books the Nazis write are full of lies. Do you like jokes? I do. Please sit. I will pretend to be Bert. "Would sir like his lemonade fizzy? Would sir like a biscuit?" Moses wants one, don't you Moses? Moses is a greedy ferret.'

'Grandfather likes jokes.'

'I call your grandfather Egghead.'

'So do I … behind his back. When I was younger and would not eat my breakfast boiled egg he'd put a handkerchief over his face so all I could see of him was the top of his baldhead. "I'm an egg," he'd say. "If you don't eat me, I'll cry".'

'I like very much your grandfather.'

'Do you have grandparents?'

'They are dead.'

'Sorry.'

'I remember one grandfather. He told me the same story many times. Mama called him "The Gramophone Record". She would say, "Father, Jacob has heard that before." It did not stop him. Once he was wound up he went on and on.'

'Is your real name Jacob?'

'Jack is my English name. It is my disguise to keep me safe. I feel safe when I think I am English. Jack is a good English name.'

'When I think about it, I suppose Egghead's a bit of a record player. Every birthday he asks me, "Who are your heroes?" He says it is his way of finding out the kind of person I am. This year I told him, Charlie Chaplin. My answer must have pleased him because he gave me half-a-crown.'

'If I told him my hero was Adolf Hitler, he would think me not a nice people?'

'Not a nice "person".'

'I will not again make that mistake.'

'I wish I could speak German.'

'You do not get the practice. I speak French and German because until I was nine we lived in Alsace. My Italian is good because of holidays with Uncle

Solomon in Verona. You English think everyone should speak English. You are not part of Europe. You have your Empire. You have webbed feet.'

'We do not.'

'A joke … a Swiss friend told me it rains so much in England the English have webbed feet. I have been reading Darwin. I think, maybe, you have adapted to your climate … like the lizards that eat seaweed. You are not offended?'

'I think it is funny. I will tell Grandfather. It will make him laugh.'

'He will give you another half-a-crown? I will tell you the truth. If I was English I would not bother to speak another language. But I am not. I am Jewish. We are a people without a home. We are the Diaspora.'

'What does that mean?'

'You do not know? Now, I am teaching you English. That is funny. My head is swelling. It means we are a scattered people. There are Jews all over the world. We survive because we have learnt to adapt. In France we speak French. In Germany we speak German. In the synagogue we speak Hebrew. Uncle Solomon speaks Hindi. He translates for the English and makes lots of money.'

'You are like the chameleon who can change his colour.'

'That is why I am good at camouflage … but I am still a Jew. I am proud to be a Jew.'

'I am a Northumbrian … would you eat a bacon sandwich?'

'I answered that question on Reichskristallnacht. That is another word you do not know, yes? In English … "Crystal Night". It was the night the Nazis killed Papa and Mama … the night the Nazis' hatred of us Jews exploded. The night they attacked all things Jewish. All over Germany our synagogues were looted and burned. They broke the window of any shop belonging to a Jew. The pavements were covered with broken glass. I do not think broken glass looks like crystal. Thugs make up nice names for their crimes.'

'What happened?'

'When they came to our apartment Papa told me to go upstairs to the attic. His last words to me were, "Get out onto the roof. If they get you they will kill you. Jacob, go! I love you".'

'What an adventure.'

'You do not understand … it was not an adventure.'

'Were you not frightened you might fall off the roof?'

'I was more frightened of been captured by the Nazis. You English are fond of your fox hunting. I have watched the men in red coats many times. Mike has told me about them. It makes me feel sorry for the fox. I know what it is like to be the fox. To escape I took great risks. I jumped between buildings. In the streets below, I saw Jews being kicked to death. Fires were everywhere. They were burning our sacred books. My ladders down were drainpipes. I did not know where to go. I was like the fox caught out in the open. Which way to run? It doesn't know. That's when I bought a bratwurst. If that is something else you do not know I tell you it is a German sausage full of pig meat. I made a big show of eating it. It was my camouflage. The SS men who passed me ruffled my hair and laughed. "He's not what we're after. No Jew would eat a good German bratwurst".'

'The Nazis are not your heroes?'

'That is irony, ja? I like the English irony. It is like Papa's jokes. If Egghead asks me who my heroes are I will say, Moses and Julius Caesar. You are thinking, Moses I can understand but why Caesar? I will tell you. When he was captured by pirates he told them he would fetch a good ransom, that he was worth more to them alive than dead. His ransom was paid. In Rome he raised an army, went back to the pirates' camp and killed them. I will show the Nazis no mercy. The bratwurst saved my life. To stay alive I will eat anything. A dead Jew can't kill Nazis.'

'In the last war Grandfather ate rat.'

'Biscuits and lemonade are better.'

'Rather!'

'I check on the enemy … they are up to something. I know this because they are Nazis. Nazis are always up to something.'

They argued.

'Newcastle is a small city.'

'No, it isn't.'

'Yes, it is.'

'It is not.'

'It is not big like Berlin.'

'We have London.'

'London is a great city.'

'We agree?'

'Yes.'

'We are still friends?'

'Yes.'

'I show you my Erdgeist diary.'

From a wooden box Jack took out an exercise book.

'I wish I could draw like that,' said George. 'I recognise the stag. It is the one Mike has been hunting.'

'One day in my den I watch him for a long time. He did not know I was here. Now that the Nazis are here he will not come, I know. They have chased him away.'

'The way they chased you out of Germany?'

'Yes … before they come I write down and draw all the animals I see. I watch how the pheasants talk to each other. When I grow up I will be a naturalist. Now, I write down all that the Nazis do. Where they go, who is the boss?'

'The Nazi who tried to steal my mushrooms was right, you are a spy. He said they shoot spies.'

'This is not Germany … here they do not have power.'

'Will you make me some camouflage, so I can help you spy on the Germans? I know my limp slows me down, but I can teach you to talk with your hands. We can talk together without making a noise. Real spies use secret signs. This is the sign for toilet. I'm bursting for a piss.'

'You piss in that.' Jack pointed to a piece of drainpipe. 'It takes your piss outside, clever?'

'Rather.'

'If you want a shit … that's the problem.'

While he was pissing George said, 'At boarding school a chap has to learn to stick up for himself. That German who tried to steal my mushrooms was a bully. I don't like bullies. I think he should be taught a lesson. You hate the Nazis?'

'You know I do.'

'Now, I hate them. Fritz should not have stolen my mushrooms. That story about Julius Caesar, tell me it again.'

25

Sir Charles, Lady Elizabeth, Marigold, Harry, CB and Bert were in Sir Charles' study. On a silver tray Bert had brought in tea and biscuits.

'Close the door, Bert,' said Sir Charles. 'Elizabeth, what are the Americans doing? They must think me awfully bad mannered dashing off the way I did.'

'I told them that something had happened to your gamekeeper ... some kind of accident, which, indeed, was all I knew at the time. You were responding to an emergency. As far as I'm aware all of them are having a siesta. The tour of the estate rather tired them. From what I've heard they are drunk.'

'Who told you that?'

'Jack. Mr O'Neil appears to be the only one sober. Such a nice man ... not one of those people who want to talk about themselves all the time. He wanted to know all about the area. Where is the nearest golf course? Is there a quick way to walk to the railway station, through the fields, perhaps? He said he just loves our little railway station ... said it was "cute".'

'Where is he now?'

'Charles, I am not the man's keeper. Most of the time I don't know where you are, let alone a guest. Why don't you ask the Eyes and Ears of The Hall?'

'Jack has been spilling the beans?'

'Don't talk American. Now, tell me again what happened. You might all have been killed.'

'But we weren't. Bert, you must join us, I insist, come and sit down ... Elizabeth will be mum.'

'So,' said Lady Elizabeth, uncomfortable at pouring tea for her own butler, 'Mike was not that badly wounded?'

'He's safe and well, tucked up in bed in the Cottage Hospital. Crozier's looking after him. He's in good hands.'

'Nice Mr Crozier, the nautical surgeon. If he's as good with flesh wounds as he was with your haemorrhoids, Charles, you are right, Mike is in good hands.'

'He passed out because he can't stand the sight of blood,' said Marigold.

'The man's a gamekeeper,' said CB, 'he must be used to seeing blood.'

'Not his own.'

'I always thought him such a tough fellow as well.'

'He's still a good man with whom to go to the well ... an American expression, CB. If he hadn't spotted we were being followed I'd be doing be-bops with the angels.'

'Well, I'm so glad you are not doing whatever it was you said with the angels,' said Lady Elizabeth. 'Professor Striker, welcome to The Hall.' They shook hands. 'Your unusual arrival has made me forget my manners. Events have robbed me of the opportunity of making you formally welcome. So few of our guests arrive half naked riding a stolen horse bare back.'

'Where is Ginger?' said CB.

'He is being well looked after,' said Lady Elizabeth. 'What about a ginger snap? Bert, hand round the biscuits. You may dunk if you wish.'

'I don't want a ginger snap. I want Ginger. You, young lady, gave me quite a fright stealing my horse. In America I believe they shoot horse thieves.'

'In the movies they do.'

'You are a fine horse woman, Professor. I invite you to ride to hounds … but you shouldn't have stolen Ginger, bad form, that.'

'It was expedient. I saved Mike,' said Marigold. 'I thought he'd fainted through loss of blood, not a phobia.'

'You did what a woman should always do, Professor,' said Lady Elizabeth, 'you took charge.'

'Call me Marigold.'

'I'm Elizabeth.'

'I have a pal back home in the States called Elizabeth, I call her "Lizzie". OK if I call you that?'

'How delightfully informal. Yes, call me, Lizzie … I rather like it.'

'You can call me CB,' said CB; 'everyone else does. They seem to forget I'm a major.'

'I suppose I'll still be Harry,' said Harry.

'Prince Hal,' said Marigold, 'you drove the MG like a racing driver. You were wonderful.'

Harry blushed.

'Stay for dinner, CB,' said Sir Charles.

'I'm dressed for the trenches, not dinner … nothing to change into.'

'If it comes to war, I rather think dressing for dinner will not be a priority. A chap will be too busy trying to stay alive.'

'Very kind, I'm sure, but I have to get back. The undertaker's calling to talk about Pruney's funeral. I do hope I haven't missed the fellow. At times like this tradesmen take advantage. They tell you a time that is convenient for them … know you are too down to argue. He'll put the price up, I know he will. He'll charge me more because I'm a major … thinks I have money because I breed horses.'

'CB,' said Lady Elizabeth, 'I apologise … all that has been happening has made us forget dear Pruney.'

'Some of us more than others.' He looked at Harry. 'She was in love with you, you know?'

'If the dear girl had lived we might have become relatives. Charles and I would have liked that very much, wouldn't we, Charles?'

'Yes … yes, if there's anything we can do to help, just say the word.'

'Put a saddle on Ginger. I'll ride home.'

'Let me give you a hug,' said Marigold. 'Am I forgiven for stealing Ginger?'

'You did not steal, you borrowed. I'm a widower, you know. You ride like an angel. That's what made me fall in love with my wife. When she rode to hounds she'd no fear of jumping a five-barred gate. She used to tell me, "CB, you are a good jumper, but I'm better." I didn't mind her saying that … it was true, you see.'

'I'm pretty good on a horse,' said Harry. 'Isn't that so, Uncle Charles?'

'Of course you are, my dear,' said Lady Elizabeth. 'CB, when are you going to measure our Rolls-Royces to see if they can be used as ambulances?'

'I'm giving a talk tonight at the Institute on that very subject. "How to make Extraordinary use of the Ordinary." I don't feel like giving a talk, I can tell you … personal circumstances being what they are, but my country needs me, so I will. In peacetime who'd ever think of using a Rolls-Royce as an ambulance? Perhaps, Marigold, you might be interested in attending? Front row seat … won't miss a word of what I have to say.'

'That's very kind, CB, but if you don't mind I won't commit myself. I have letters to write to the President.'

'Of which organisation?'

'The United States of America.'

'Oh, that President. I fear the good Lord has dealt me a bad hand. I can't compete with Roosevelt. Bert, take me to Ginger. He at least will be pleased to see me. Sir Charles, Lady Elizabeth, Harry, Marigold, I bid you all good afternoon. Please don't show me out. I know you have matters of great import to discuss. If I'm to catch the undertaker I'll have to give Ginger the spur. With your permission, Charles, I'll take the short cut over the top field.'

'Of course, anything … anything we can do to help.'

'Elizabeth, where's my Dundee cake?'

'I don't know. Let me think … you know I do believe I put it on Bashful's roof … you know, when we saw Marigold, though of course at the time we didn't know it was Marigold, stealing, I mean, borrowing Ginger. It will have fallen off the roof. When you get home look in the grass beside your front door.'

'If the coffin filler finds it first he'll keep it. I know this fellow, had dealings with him when my wife died.'

'No time to lose then, is there?' said Sir Charles.

26

As soon as CB and Bert had left Lady Elizabeth said, 'Charles, you were naughty to make me pour tea for my own butler.'

'Lizzie,' said Marigold, 'think of it as practice for how things will change if war does break out.'

'I'm assuming, Marigold,' said Sir Charles, 'that before the incident of the shooting, Mike appraised you of my suspicions?'

'You mean before he fainted at the sight of his own blood?' said Lady Elizabeth.

'He did.'

'And?'

'I am prepared to go along with your plan. The shooting removed my last doubts.'

'The story we will concoct may make you seem less than a model of efficiency. I suspect your compatriots may take advantage.'

'Will someone please tell me what's going on?' said Harry. 'I'm nineteen and when this war starts I will be fighting for my king and country … so, if it's not too much trouble …'

'Shall we?' said Sir Charles.

'I'm not sure,' said Marigold, 'he could be a security risk.'

'Stop teasing.'

'Harry,' said Lady Elizabeth, 'I know just how you feel … no one ever tells me anything.'

'It's O'Neil,' said Sir Charles.

'Is he the one my aunt made you think was not a full shilling?'

'Your dear, kind, generous aunt was the first to lift the stone; since then discreet enquiries have been made. A picture is emerging. The British Embassy in Washington has been working overtime. At dinner, please do not sit and stare at him. He may not be the ogre we think. When you skimmed our rooftops this morning he thought you were trying to kill him. He was not amused by your daredevil antics.'

'I thought you were wonderful, Harry. I knew it was you,' said Lady Elizabeth. 'Marigold, he was so low … Harry has his very own aeroplane. People were frightened he would crash. I wasn't … he is such a wonderful pilot.'

'What's your crate?' said Marigold.

'I beg your pardon?'

'What kind of plane do you own?'

'It's a Puss Moth.'

'Mine's a Tiger Moth.'

'You fly?'

115

'Got my aviator's licence before I got my driver's licence.'

'Wow!'

'How very American,' said Lady Elizabeth.

'The scare you gave O'Neil, Harry,' said Sir Charles, 'made him cuddle his golf bag the way you used to cuddle Pumpkin. Do you remember that game we used to play? If The Hall was on fire and you could only save one thing, what would you pick? You, Harry, always said you'd save Pumpkin. I wonder … would O'Neil save his golf bag? And if so, why? He's very attached to it.'

'Pumpkin is my teddy bear,' explained Harry. 'I still have him. He's my mascot, now. All the chaps in the squadron have mascots.'

'I have a stuffed rattlesnake,' said Marigold. 'I killed it when I was ten. Daddy had it stuffed for me.'

'Fathers will do anything for their daughters,' said Lady Elizabeth. 'He must love you very much.'

'O'Neil,' said Sir Charles, 'is not a member of the Anglo-American club. Further, I now know he pulled strings to be my guest. He arrives on Tyneside at the same time as the Irish bombers. Your aunt tells me he is anti-British and back home is a known supporter of Ireland for the Irish Movement. What is he doing here drinking … I was going to say, "My champagne" but the fellow's one of those odd bod teetotallers … drinking my tap water? Do you know him, Marigold?'

'I know he doesn't play golf.'

'Perhaps it's a new passion,' said Lady Elizabeth. 'Charles once had a passion for stamp collecting, didn't you, Charles? It lasted a whole year. It sort of flared up and then burnt itself out. Mr O'Neil came across to me as a very nice man.'

'Even if O'Neil is not connected to the Irish bombers,' said Sir Charles, 'the question Lord Frederick and I have been asking is, why are the Nazis and the Irish Republicans fraternising? What's their game? Marigold has agreed to keep her run-in with the latter sub judice. If O'Neil should be playing a double game I think it a sensible precaution not to let him know, Marigold, that you are able to identify his possible contacts.'

'I agree.'

'I say,' said Harry, 'if O'Neil is sharing a bed with these … Republicans, he's involved in Pruney's murder. If it's ever proven you'll have to tie my hands behind my back. I'm telling you, if I get my hands on him, I'll punch him on the nose.'

'Not a good idea, Harry, he's bigger than you. If an involvement is proven, we'll let the law decide his fate. Now, what's our story going to be? First of all there was no shooting this afternoon. Mike is in hospital because he ran the Rolls off the road. Marigold borrowed Ginger to tell us Mike needed help. When one lies one should stick as close to the truth as possible,' said Sir Charles.

'And,' said Marigold, 'how did I find myself in a railway station as remote as a cavalry fort in Wyoming?'

'You got lost.'

'Because I'm a silly woman and that's what women do, get lost?'

'Yes.'

'I do not like to be made to look foolish but if Mike is to be made an incompetent driver and all for the sake of saving the British Empire, then, count me in.'

'Thank you, Marigold. If it comes to war I hope your President will be as helpful. Now, I suggest we disperse. I am missing my afternoon nap.'

'Charles must have his nap,' said Lady Elizabeth. 'Without his nap he is quite useless.'

'Dinner is at seven-thirty. Snifters will be served on the terrace at seven. Listen for the gong.'

'Excuse me,' said Marigold, 'but what am I going to wear?'

'Ah, the small matter of your missing luggage.'

'It's not a small matter to me.'

'My dear,' said Lady Elizabeth, 'my dresser is a wizard with a needle. I assure you, at dinner, you will look stunning.'

'On a practical note,' said Sir Charles, 'it would be helpful if no one bathed in a full bath of hot water. The boiler is limited. Now, I suggest we don't all leave together. We don't want to give the impression of a meeting breaking up, do we? Harry, you go first.'

'Shall I whistle?'

'Good idea … nonchalance … not a care in the world.'

27

Sir Charles lay on top of the bed, eyes shut. As his wife kept reminding him he was no longer a young man. He thanked the Good Lord that Mike was in no danger. His prayer was born of deep personal conviction. Life was not pointless. In the trenches he'd seen atheists pray.

The Americans were all younger than himself. Was that why they were so full of energy? Or, were they like that because they were Americans? They had thought the largest of his fields, "kinda like a model of the real thing".

'Your brandy and soda, sir.'

He opened his eyes. 'Where am I?'

'In bed, sir.'

'Bert, you know I don't drink this early. You have made a mistake. Not at all like you.'

'It's my cover, sir.'

'I beg your pardon?'

'It's my cover, sir, my excuse for disturbing you, sir. It concerns the American in the Blue Room. He gave me this.'

From a pocket Bert pulled out a five pound note.

'That's a handsome tip.'

'It's not a tip, sir. It is, "Bert, keep your mouth shut money." He thinks I know something he doesn't want me to know.'

'And do you?'

'What I seen was odd, sir, that's all. Such times as these makes even easy going men like me suspicious.'

'He's the gentleman who doesn't drink?'

'That's right, sir. Mr O'Neil.'

'Prefers golf to shooting?'

'That's him, sir.'

'Never trust a man who doesn't take a dram, Bert. Hitler's a teetotaller, don't you know? If you had come to me with suspicions about any other guest but this fellow, I'd have been sceptical … sit yourself down.'

'Thank you, sir.'

'Let's share the brandy.'

Another glass was found.

'It's his golf clubs, sir … his Mashie-Niblick is not as long as it should be.'

28

'Charles, what are these two glasses doing in here?' said Lady Elizabeth. 'May I remind you, Charles … this is a bedroom? Why one balloon and one tumbler?' She sniffed the tumbler. 'Brandy … why is it here and not in the bathroom? And please don't tell me it has legs and walked in here by itself. Tumblers, as both you and I know, Charles, do not have legs.'

'It tumbled.'

'Don't be clever. You never drink in the bedroom unless you have a head cold. You're not ill, are you? If Mike hadn't been in hospital I'd have suspected him of leading you astray. Who is the guilty party this time … one of the Americans? They are all high consumers, except of course, O'Neil.'

'He is the guilty party.'

'He's one of those, is he … says he's teetotal but knocks it back in private.'

'Bert was my drinking companion, O'Neil was its cause.'

'Bert? Our butler has enjoyed a meteoric rise in status this afternoon. I, mistress of The Hall, pour out his tea when he is paid to pour out mine … and now I find he is your secret drinking companion. You should not have asked me to pour, Charles … you really shouldn't. What I found shocking was the fact that our butler did not appear to be in the least fazed … took to being waited on like a duck to water. What Marigold must have thought, I do not know … the mistress of an English country house pouring her butler a cup of tea.'

'She will have thought you enlightened. Americans love informality. May I now tell you why Bert served me a drink in our bedroom?'

'Will we be murdered in our beds?' said Lady Elizabeth after digesting her husband's explanation.

'Highly unlikely.'

'I wish Mike was here.'

'Because he's a good man with whom to go to the well?'

'Yes.'

'You know, my dear, Mike can't win. You accuse him of overfamiliarity, then, as soon as he's out of action you want him sleeping outside our bedroom door with a shotgun.'

'I wouldn't give him a pillow but he could have a chair.'

'You are too hard on the poor fellow.'

'Not after what Jack told me.'

'What's our little Puck been up to now?'

'He says … Mike says, "I know everything".'

'Is that not a compliment?'

'You know as well as I do the tone of voice in which Mike would have made the remark … "that woman, she knows everything".'

'What a good impersonation … can you do a cuckoo?'

'Charles, you may find it amusing … I do not.'

'I can hear him saying it.'

'So can I … that's what makes it so annoying. You should have him horse whipped.'

'But you'd still like him on guard?'

'Yes.'

'You'd trust him with your life?'

'Yes.'

'And, so would I. Jack is a mischief-maker. For his age he is too knowing. He has an old head on young shoulders. Now that I've employed him as the Eyes and Ears of The Hall he'll not have time for tittle-tattle. Without his vigilance I'd not have known of O'Neil's trip to the telephone box. If the fellow had nothing to hide he'd have used The Hall's telephone.'

'I do hope George gets on with Jack.'

'Since dashing off to rescue Mike I've not seen my grandson. I suppose they'll bump into each other, sooner or later. Having someone the same age to play with will be good for both of them … keep them out of mischief.'

'They should not be allowed to run wild.'

'I did at their age, it's done me no harm.'

'It's made you eccentric. Freddy and Dot think you're eccentric.'

'Freddy has a train set.'

'Because of your melon infatuation we've missed Ascot twice. Our set think us … standoffish. Do you know it's a year since we were in London?'

'Have you been discussing me with Harry?'

'I don't have to. Harry and I think the same. You are in grave danger of forgetting your class. You were not born in a pigsty … no matter how much you might like to think you were, you were not. However hard you try, you will always prefer claret to beer. Your tailor in London makes your cloth caps.'

'Is my socialism the reason I'm thought eccentric?'

'We must be the only titled family in England with an armed butler.'

'The Webley is not loaded.'

'After recent events I think it should be. It seems to me, Charles, that it is time to stop playing games.'

'Dressing for dinner is playing a game … as outmoded as burning heretics.'

'I disagree. I do hope you've not encouraged the Americans to dine without jackets?'

'Showing off their braces?'

'Charles, please, do not tease.'

'To make our guests feel at home I told them it was their choice to dress or not to dress for dinner. They are forever telling me how free and easy they are in the New World.'

'But, Charles, we always dress for dinner. What will the servants think waiting on men in lounge suits?'

'Bert will love it. He has socialist leanings.'

'Well, I don't.'

'The good news is … the Americans insist on dressing for dinner.'

'I am not surprised. It is my experience that Americans have good manners.'

'I think it shows their imperialist streak. They copy what they profess to despise. The eagle is a predatory bird. Their capital buildings are modelled on those of Ancient Rome. They have senators. We all know how ambitious Rome was. They can't wait to take over our Empire? When they do, Bombay will be full of fast food shops selling hamburgers. One informality I have agreed with them is that we call each other by our familiar names. From now on, you are Elizabeth and I am Charles. I do think Marigold went too far calling you Lizzie.'

'Funnily enough I don't mind. It makes me feel liberated. The Americans, they have sensible English names? If I have to call Weinberger, Texas … Mancini, Mississippi, I will smirk.'

'Weinberger is Jasper. Mancini is Mario. O'Neil is Bob and Macdonald is Angus.'

'Jasper, Mario, Bob and Angus … JMBA, are you coming out to play? Reminds me of a skipping song Nanny taught me.'

'Have you been able to provide Marigold with something nice to wear?'

'Even as we speak needles are at work. What agonies she must have suffered in that railway wagon. I think she will look quite stunning this evening. Harry had better watch out.'

'Do you think he is smitten?'

'He can't stop blushing.'

'I think she likes Harry. If she does maybe he can persuade her to persuade the President to come in on our side if war breaks out. We must not forget, Elizabeth, in the hurly-burly of events, the Americans are here to have their wallets emptied.'

29

In the butler's pantry Sir Charles and Bert spoke in whispers.

'Bert, after you've organised drinks and hors d'oeuvres on the terrace I want you to disappear. I'll do the pouring.'

'Are you sure, sir?'

'Why, don't you think I'm up to mixing a cocktail?'

'It's Lady Elizabeth, sir.'

'What about her?'

'This afternoon, sir, when she was playing mum in the study, I don't think she liked it, you know, pouring tea for a servant. When she sees you serving, sir, when it's my job … I'm not being eased out, sir, am I?'

'Fret not, Bert. When you should be serving you will not be unemployed.'

'Special mission is it, sir?'

'As soon as O'Neil comes down for his orange juice or whatever it is teetotallers drink, go to his room.'

'The golf bag, sir?'

'Yes, give it the once over. I read in Time magazine that President Roosevelt makes his own cocktails. The Americans will think I'm copying their leader. It will make them think I'm the sort of chap who'd be happy to hand over India to Mr Gandhi. Full works on the terrace, mind you, Bert; red carpet, wheelbarrow seats, deck chairs and cushions on the steps.'

30

The terrace radiated heat. To carry out his duties as a 'stand-in' butler Sir Charles stood beside the make-shift bar – a pony trap filled with booze and red geraniums – as ready for action as a chap who'd never boiled an egg in his life could be. His confidence was high. He'd already mixed and poured, with suitable flourishes, Martinis for Macdonald, Mancini and Weinberger. No complaints, except he was finding it difficult to keep up with their rate of consumption. They were like the Rolls – to keep her going you had to keep filling her up.

It irritated him that, while he worked like a sapper, they were lounging in his deck chairs. He longed to join them. His legs were aching. Wonderful evening though.

He did not expect Elizabeth for another ten minutes. She was always late. More than likely she'd be fussing over Marigold. Harry was young and silly and had probably lost a shoe. But, where was O'Neil? On the other side of the Ha-Ha, sheep and cattle slept in the shade of an oak.

'Is it always this hot in Northumberland, Charles?' said Mancini.

'Sadly, no.'

'The peace before the storm?' suggested Macdonald.

'You refer of course to the European situation?'

'I do.'

'What will happen?'

'If it comes to war?'

'Yes.'

'As an oil man,' said Weinberger, 'I'll make a lot of money. I'll be like your Prime Minister Stanley Baldwin. His family made a fortune out of the last war.'

'Stanley did indeed do well financially,' said Sir Charles. 'It is to his credit that he returned much of his profit to His Majesty's Exchequer.'

'Stanley … you on intimate terms with Baldwin?'

'A distant relative.'

'I'd speculate that war with Germany will bankrupt England,' said Macdonald.

'We have an Empire.'

'Will the Indians fight for you?'

'Will America?'

'I'm an anglophile … you know my thoughts on the matter. If Hitler is allowed carte blanche in Europe where will his ambition end? It is not in the long-term interests of the greatest democracy the world has ever known to sit back and let the Old World be taken over by a bunch of thugs.'

'You will use your influence?'

'Charles, with all my heart and soul I will put the case for intervention to my fellow citizens … but I am not the commander-in-chief.'

'Speaking of whom,' said Mancini, 'here comes his surrogate, or so I'm led to believe.' He stood up. 'Marigold, great to see you.'

'Mario, give me a hug … Angus … Jasper … it seems a lifetime since I heard American English.'

'You've missed your wood-notes wild?' said Macdonald.

'After a month in Germany my head is spinning with, "Sieg Heil! Sieg Heil!".'

'Gentlemen, my nephew, Harry,' said Sir Charles. 'What with all the hurly-burly of rescuing my man Mike from his motor-car accident I don't think you have had the pleasure of being introduced.'

'We've met his aeroplane,' said Mancini. 'Pleased to meet you, Harry.'

'Hi! You the flier who parted my hair?' said Weinberger. 'Pleased to meet you, Harry – never met a flying barber before.'

'You don't need a barber, Jasper, you need a wig … pleased to meet you, Harry,' said Macdonald.

'Drink?' said Sir Charles to Marigold and Harry. 'May I recommend the house cocktail? It's called The President.'

'I'll take Marigold's,' said Harry. 'Marigold, your drink. Uncle tells me it's President Roosevelt's recipe.'

'Watch him, Marigold, he's a fly-boy,' said Mancini.

'Actually, I'm in the RAF. If war breaks out I'll be flying Spits.'

'What's a "Spit"?' said Macdonald.

'It's a fighter plane … a Spitfire.'

'You ever get lost?' said Weinberger.

'When I'm flying? Not so far …in bad weather a chap follows his instruments.'

'Marigold gets lost, don't you, Marigold?'

'How'd you get lost in little ol' England, Marigold?' said Mancini.

'I didn't.'

'Sir Charles said you did, didn't you, Charles?'

'Ok, Ok, I got lost … I got on the wrong train, I'm embarrassed.'

'You get lost in Germany?' said Weinberger.

'All the time, I'm a woman, what do you expect?'

'You said that, not me.'

'But that's what you were thinking. Jasper, I know you too well.'

'Sorry, Marigold, white flag.' He waved a napkin.

'If Marigold did get lost,' said Mancini, 'it's because she's used to having a chauffeur. When she wants to go some-place … she clicks her fingers.'

'You saying I'm some kind of spoilt rich kid? I'll have you know, Mario, I've been through hell in the last twenty-four hours. I'm lucky to be here.'

'The car crash was that bad?'

'It was the porter who put Marigold on the wrong train,' said Harry. 'Some of those fellows will tell a chap anything. They leave school unable to read and write. No one should have the vote unless they can read and write.'

'You are not a socialist, Harry?' said Mancini.

'No, he is not,' said Lady Elizabeth, joining the group, 'and that is something I applaud. And for goodness sake, all of you, stop picking on my dear friend Marigold. You are worse than a pack of wolves … but nice American wolves who, if it comes to war, will bite the Germans, I hope. We don't want another war… war makes men brutal. When Charles came home from the front in seventeen he'd forgotten that one used keys to open doors.'

'My crime, I seem to remember, was putting my shoulder to a door and breaking it,' said Sir Charles.

'All you had to do was turn its handle.'

'It was stiff.'

'And you put a milk bottle on the table.'

'Did I?'

'Phyllis – she's our cook – was shocked. Bert was still away in the trenches. Where is Bert? Why is he not serving?'

'I told him to delegate.'

'To whom?'

'Me … if the President of the United States makes his guests cocktails, why can't I?'

'I don't approve. Bert is paid to serve. The thought of running The Hall short-staffed because of another war keeps me awake at night. I hate Hitler. Marigold, I implore you, when you get home tell the President Lady Elizabeth begs him to be on our side. If it will help, tell him, we'll give India to that fellow who goes around half naked.'

'I say, Aunt Elizabeth,' said Harry, 'steady on.'

'The views you have expressed, Lizzie,' said Marigold, 'are eminently sensible … if we lived in a rational world, but we don't … sadly, Utopia does not exist.'

'Stopping Utopia getting built,' said Weinberger, 'is an animal called "Democracy". It ties the President's hands.'

'Surely Americans would never vote to let England be defeated by Germany?' said Harry.

'Some would.'

'My American aunt has never been anything but generous to me. I thought all Americans loved England.'

'Let me tell you something … you call us "Yanks", we call you "Limeys". In Washington they've got a new name for you … "Olivers".'

'Oh dear, you think we'll always be asking for more?' said Sir Charles.

'Yes.'

'You won't pull our chestnuts out of the fire?'

'If we do my hunch is Uncle Sam will charge you for every chestnut he saves. Your companies with real estate in the US will have to be sold. There'll be fire sales. The money raised will pay for your war.'

'Our war?'

'Yes, your war, not America's … Courtauld's, Lever Brothers, Dunlop, all your companies with assets in the States will have a gun put to their heads, they'll be sold cheap. I'll be sniffing around. I'm a capitalist. I like making money. You know what? Making money makes me feel good.'

'Charles, do not offer Jasper another drink, 'said Lady Elizabeth.

'I'm telling you the way things are, not the way I'd like them to be.'

'You will have to sell your gold reserves,' said Mancini. 'England will not be a good place to sell ice cream – no one will have money.'

'What happens when we've sold everything?' said Harry.

'That's when people like Jasper start eating the corpse.'

'I don't much like the sound of that. Why can't you just write us a cheque and we'll give you an IOU? After all, dash it, Mr Chamberlain and his ministers are gentlemen.'

'I'm sure they are, Harry. The problem is that American businessmen are not gentlemen.'

'Wolves, howling wolves,' said Lady Elizabeth.

'In any coming conflict Mr Hare will be the businessman and Mr Tortoise the Good Samaritan.'

'Well, that at least is a consolation,' said Sir Charles. 'We all know that the tortoise won in the end. Who's for toppers?'

31

Everyone wanted a 'topper'.

'It's like being in a green sauna,' said Macdonald.

'What's a sauna?' said Harry.

Macdonald explained.

'Men and women together … no clothes on … naked … Finland,' repeated Harry in a trance.

'Hot as Texas, Northumberland,' said Weinberger, 'and no rattlesnakes to worry about … never told this to anyone before but I don't like them.'

'You mean you are scared of them?' said Mancini.

'Me? No … what the hell, yes, I'm scared of them.'

'I don't like midges,' said Lady Elizabeth.

'If you walk down to the river you will see lots of rattlesnakes,' said Sir Charles. 'They wear short trousers and look like Boy Scouts.'

'The Hitler Youth?' said Marigold. 'In my travels through Germany I have seen them commit crimes that I refuse to talk about on such a beautiful evening … be grateful you are not a Jew living in Nazi Germany. Mario, how is Maria? How many children do you have now?'

'Seven.'

'Last time we met you had six.'

'Maria's insatiable.'

'Are there women like that?' said Harry.

'She wears me out.'

'Try birth control,' said Marigold.

'I'm a Catholic.'

'The Pope won't know if you don't tell him. I'd recommend the diaphragm and spermicidal gel method, better than the Pro-Race Cap.'

'Call me old fashioned,' said Lady Elizabeth, 'but I don't believe birth control should be discussed in mixed company. We all know about these things, so there's no need to talk about them, is there?'

'I don't know about them,' said Harry.

'I should think you shouldn't. Dear me, Harry, you have made your aunt blush, shame on you.'

'I do believe O'Neil is at last coming to join us,' said Sir Charles.

All heads turned to the figure, coming to join them on the patio.

'He told me he needed to stretch his legs,' said Mancini. 'If he doesn't keep in shape his golf will suffer, that's what he told me. The guy's a looney.'

'On the Queen Mary he was never out of the gym,' said Weinberger.

'That's because the guy in charge was Irish,' said Mancini; 'they used to talk to each other in Gaelic.'

'Exercise can be a drug,' said Macdonald, 'once you start doing it, you gotta keep doing it. If you don't you get withdrawal symptoms. You think you're going to die.'

'You are speaking from experience?' said Sir Charles.

'If you substitute "champagne" for "exercise" I will plead guilty to speaking from "experience".'

'Let me fill your glass.'

'Thank you, Charles … your hospitality, the beautiful surroundings … everything is so green, is something I for one will never forget.'

'But is it worth fighting for?'

'Charles, take your foot off the pedal. I'm on your side but I'm not the President.'

32

'Bob O'Neil,' said Marigold. They shook hands. 'You golfers and your need to keep fit.'

'Who's been talking about me?'

'I have,' said Mancini. 'When you told me you liked to keep in shape for your golf I didn't know I'd signed the Official Secrets Act.'

'If you were a banker you'd be more discreet … and drink less. And,' turning to Harry, 'who are you? If you are who I think you are then I have something to say to you.'

'He's the low flyer who cut your hair,' said Weinberger, 'we call him, "Harry the Barber". If it comes to war we're going to need guys like him to give Hitler a short back and sides.'

'Young man, you nearly killed me, have you nothing to say?'

'Would you like a drink?'

'The bar's this way,' said Lady Elizabeth. 'Marigold, let us escort Mr O'Neil.' The women linked him. 'Bert, you are back on duty?'

'Yes, my lady.'

Sir Charles had noted his butler's return shortly after O'Neil's spectre-like emergence from the gloaming. What his 'man' had found out about O'Neil's golf clubs would have to wait. He knew from years of experience at diplomatic functions that any knowing looks they exchanged would be spotted. For this reason he avoided looking at his butler; difficult though, like trying not to scratch an itch.

'What are you going to have, Bob? I may call you Bob?' said Lady Elizabeth.

'I'd recommend the Roosevelt Martini,' said Marigold.

'I don't drink.'

'You used to.'

'Well, now I don't.'

'We think you should, don't we, Lizzie?'

'Tell you what,' said Lady Elizabeth, 'you have a Roosevelt and you can call me Lizzie and I'll call you Bob.'

'Only a boor would turn down an offer like that and you're not a boor, are you, Bob? Bert, a Roosevelt for Mr O'Neil,' said Marigold.

'I've told you, I don't drink.'

'With your Ladyship's permission,' said Bert, 'I think sir is a candidate for a "special".'

With a certain amount of je ne sais quoi, to drum into his audience the 'specialness' of what he was about to serve, Bert produced from behind a red geranium, a bottle of Coca-Cola.

'What's that?' said Lady Elizabeth.

'An American drink, milady; specially imported by Mr Harry for the American guests.'

O'Neil scrutinised the butler. The tip he'd given him when he'd spotted the truncated Mashie-Niblick had been money well spent.

'Thank you, Bert.'

'Now you can call me, Lizzie,' said Lady Elizabeth. 'And don't go upsetting my nephew – he's a fine pilot, knows exactly what he's doing.'

'Lizzie, show me the Ha-Ha,' said Marigold.

33

'What is it, Bert?'

'A delicate matter, sir.'

'Excuse me, gentlemen.'

'A gentleman of the road is asking to see you, sir.'

'A tramp?'

'Yes and no, sir. He's in the kitchen.'

'Phyllis is feeding the poor fellow?'

'Yes, sir.'

'Good. You know my policy on tramps. The fellow's down on his luck. More than likely a victim of the war. If he wants he can sleep in the potting shed. Bacon and eggs for breakfast.'

'The gentleman said, "Are you free to punt the pill?", sir.'

'He did, did he?'

'Yes, sir.'

'Tell Lord Frederick, "Give me time to check the weather". I'll meet him in the potting shed ASAP.'

'I knew it was him, sir. He fooled Phyllis but he didn't fool me. I hadn't the heart to tell his Lordship he'd been rumbled. He insisted on pretending to be a tramp. "I'm a tramp, sir," he kept saying. The number of times he pulled his forelock was embarrassing; talk about amateur theatricals. I will say this for his Lordship, he puts his heart and soul into his act. If I'd told Lord Frederick I knew it was him, I'd have spoilt his day … and I'd never do that. His Lordship's been kind to me in the past.'

'How'd you rumble him?'

'Tramps don't have clean fingernails, sir … nor do they smell of aftershave.'

'You're sharp, Bert, very sharp.'

'Thank you, sir.'

'O'Neil's golf clubs?'

'I've searched his room, sir, like you said I was to do but can't find them. A wardrobe is locked. I assume they are in there.'

'And he has the key?'

'It's not in the keyhole, sir.'

'You looked under the bed? Yes, of course you would. Sorry. By the by, what's O'Neil drinking?'

'Coca-Cola, sir.'

'Never heard of it.'

'Mr Harry brought it, sir, courtesy of his American aunt.'

'You'll never guess what,' said Marigold, sauntering up to them and smiling. 'Harry's fallen into the Ha-Ha and O'Neil's shouting, "Ha-Ha" at him.'

'Bert ...'
'Sir?'
'Bang the gong.'

34

'Before you sit down to dinner, Harry,' said Sir Charles, 'you need dusting down, that bruise on your forehead … looks nasty. Elizabeth, be a dear and show our guests into the dining room. I'll look after Harry.'

'He pushed me,' said Harry.

'Who did?'

'O'Neil.'

'When you flew low over The Hall this morning he thought you were trying to kill him. O'Neil is an Old Testament American; an eye for an eye, that sort of thing.'

In the kitchen Phyllis refused to provide meat for a poultice.

'What you need is this. Sit down, Mr Harry, this'll sting.'

'Ouch!'

'Harry, I'm sending you on a mission,' said Sir Charles. 'When we finish dinner I want you to excuse yourself. Use the bump on your head as an excuse.'

'If I do that everyone will think I'm a wimp.'

'You will be in good company. May I remind you that Marigold is acting the part of a dumb blonde unable to read a railway timetable and Mike, though he does not yet know it, is going to have to play the part of a reckless driver.'

'That won't be difficult for him. I don't like the idea of Marigold thinking I'm a wimp.'

'She is privy to all our subterfuges. When we tell her why, she will think you a hero. I want you and Freddy …'

'Lord Frederick is here?'

'In the potting shed dressed as a tramp. He's working under cover. When you make your excuse I want you to go to the potting shed and tell Freddy that you and he are to break into the wardrobe in O'Neil's room. If England's top spy can't use a hatpin on a wardrobe lock, the country's done for.'

'What are we looking for?'

'Golf clubs which are too small with which to play golf. By the by, how is my grandson?'

'The ride I gave him in the Puss Moth made him sick.'

'Did it indeed? What with all the afternoon's shenanigans I've not had a chance to have a proper chat with him. I wonder if he's met Jack.'

'If he has, we'd better watch out.'

35

At the end of dinner Sir Charles suggested that the women be allowed to join the men for port and cigars.

'It's a break with tradition, I know, but I think it important that Marigold is included in all our discussions, however informal.'

'I agree,' said Mancini. 'We all know she is closest to the President.'

'Charles,' said Lady Elizabeth, 'this may come as a shock, but Marigold and I are not available for port and cigars. We are off to the railway station to collect Marigold's bags. We have been informed they are awaiting collection.'

'Why can't one of the servants go?'

'I have a letter to post to the President,' said Marigold. 'It goes registered mail.'

'The post office will be closed.'

'Lizzie knows the post mistress.'

'Emily will open up for me. A registered letter to the American Embassy in London for the President of the United States of America will give her something to gossip about. Clothes may not be important to you, Charles, but they are to us women. Marigold is young. She wants to look her best. Tell your guests about your melons. My husband is a keen melon grower, Marigold. In fact, talk about anything but Hitler, but of course, that is what you will talk about. I'm sick and tired of hearing about Hitler.'

36

After one glass of port Harry asked to be excused.

'You chasing after the women?' said Mancini.

'You took a nasty tumble when you fell into the Ha-Ha,' said Weinberger.

'Too many cocktails?' said Macdonald.

'I was pushed.'

'Who are you accusing?' said O'Neil.

'Chaps don't tell tales.'

'Ah, the British stiff upper lip,' said Macdonald. 'Hitler has a toothbrush moustache on his stiff upper lip.'

'Will the American eagle peck it off?' said Sir Charles.

'Charles, in days of old when knights were bold, all roads led to Rome. In your case it is becoming increasingly obvious that all conversation now leads to discussing American intervention in Europe.'

'Ha!' said Mancini. 'Let each of us talk about something and see how long it takes Charles to reintroduce the subject of American involvement in a second war with Germany. Butterflies.'

'I'd suggest that American intervention is at the pupa stage,' said Sir Charles.

'Good night,' said Harry.

'If that bump on your head swells to an egg, I'll have it for breakfast,' said Weinberger.

'Scrambled or sunny side up?'

'Harry … you're cracking me up.'

'Touché. Good night, gentlemen.'

37

'I hope the boy doesn't give in so easily when he has a 109 on his tail,' said Weinberger. 'You shouldn't have pushed him, Bob.'

'I didn't, he slipped.'

'What would you say if I said I saw you push him?'

'It's lucky any of us are alive after the way the young idiot flew his plane so low. He might have taken us all to Kingdom come … if he wants to play hard ball that's fine by me. There's nothing wrong with his appetite … he's Ok.'

'He won't be able to leave a combat zone as easily as he's left us to our port and cigars, that's for sure. "Excuse me, Mr German Fighter Pilot but I've a headache, may we resume hostilities tomorrow?" What do you say, Charles?'

'My nephew is a good pilot – that is why he did not crash when he flew low over The Hall. If it comes to war and he finds a 109 is chasing him, he will not give in.'

'How'd you know?'

'I, of course, don't, not for certain. It is my experience that a chap does not know how he will react under fire until he is put to the test.'

'In the trenches,' said Macdonald, 'I was never sure if my diarrhoea was due to dysentery or fear.'

'But our fear did not stop us doing our duty,' said Sir Charles. 'How did you find the war, Bob?'

'I've not so far had the experience of fighting for my life.'

'Combat makes you scared,' said Weinberger, 'then it makes you angry. You don't want to get killed so you start fighting back.'

'If Germany takes over Europe will America feel "scared", then "threatened", then "fight back"?'

'Charles, you've done it again,' said Mancini, 'all roads lead to Rome.'

38

'There's a murderer in the potting shed,' said George, bursting unannounced into the Smoking Room. 'We've locked him in.'

'We don't know that he's a murderer, not for certain,' said Jack, 'but he was acting suspicious.'

'He didn't see us because of our camouflage.'

'I knocked him out with a brick.'

'I apologise for the intrusion, sir,' said Bert, hard on the heels of the gate-crashers, 'but Master Jack put Moses up my trouser leg.'

''Moses?' said Mancini.

'The young gentleman's pet ferret, sir. It was while I was struggling to stop it reaching my vital parts that the young gentlemen, taking advantage of my predicament, gained entry to the port and cigars. I fear, sir, that the gentleman they have incapacitated is the tramp I told you about.'

Sir Charles lit his pipe.

'Boys, do you know the meaning of the term "Friendly fire"?'

'Have we done something wrong?' said George.

'Sometimes, chaps think they are doing the right thing when, actually, they are rather putting their foot in it.'

'Is he not a murderer?'

'Probably not if he is who Bert and I think he is. Better go and check, Bert.'

'Sah!'

'I'm afraid the gentleman you have hit on the head is probably a policeman. His Majesty's Government, you see, have doubts about the Hitler Youth.'

'What do you mean "doubts"?' said O'Neil.

'We think they are here to spy. The area around The Hall is under surveillance. If you see a postman riding a bike and his mail sack looks empty, assume he's a policeman. If you see workmen digging a hole in the road, assume they are policemen.'

'I knew they weren't workmen,' said Jack. 'They kept sweeping the road over and over again in the same place.'

'What do you think of the Nazis, Jack?' said Macdonald. 'Charles has told us of your brush with the regime.'

'I hate them. They murdered my father and mother.'

'You sure you're not making that up?' said O'Neil. 'Who said they did?'

'I saw them do it.'

'You're the sniper with the peashooter, aren't you? If I had my way I'd take my belt to you.'

'Boys,' said Sir Charles, 'I think it best that you wait outside. I'll decide what to do when Bert reports back.'

'Where's the ferret?' said Mancini.

'He your friend?' said Macdonald.

'He is my best friend.'

'Sometimes, in some situations an animal is the best friend you can have,' said Weinberger. 'You gonna let us see your friend?'

Jack brought out Moses. Everyone stroked him except O'Neil.

'Bert?'

'It's who we thought it was, sir.'

'Badly injured?'

'Nasty cut on his head, sir.'

'If you will excuse me, gentlemen. Bert will look after your every need. Boys, follow me.'

39

Sir Charles walked fast. George and Jack followed like dogs with drooping tails. What had they done wrong? They'd never seen Egghead so determined. At the potting shed they met Harry.

'How is he?' said Sir Charles.

'Bert told you what happened?'

'Yes.'

'Bloody … a head wound, they always bleed a lot. He's confused. God, how I hate the Irish. First it was Pruney, now this, the head of MI5 No time for a peek inside the wardrobe, Uncle Charles. When I found his Lordship he was already out of action. He's lucky to be alive. I wonder why they didn't kill him.'

'The IRA didn't kill him because they weren't responsible. Jack and George are the culprits.'

40

Harry's torch showed a stubble faced tramp holding a blood soaked handkerchief to a head wound.

'Newspaper,' said Sir Charles.

From a pile kept in the potting shed for the purpose of stuffing inside upturned plant pots to catch creepy crawlies, Sir Charles made a poultice.

'Did this many times in the war.'

He dipped the folded paper into a tank of water.

'Freddy, hold this over the wound. Five sheets of the Times is better than a bandage.'

'Where am I?'

'You are at The Hall.'

'At a ball?'

'No, The Hall.'

'Is that you, Charlie?'

'Yes. I'm taking you to hospital.'

'Don't want to see a vet. What happened?'

'Someone hit you on the head with a brick.'

'Is the brick alright? Ha, ha!'

'It's broken and so is your head.'

'Who hit me? They must have been professionals … '

'We'll talk about that later. Can you walk?'

'Of course I can bloody talk. What do you think I'm doing now? Where's the brick? I want to see the weapon. Find the weapon, I always say, and you are well on the way to making an arrest. Bloody Irish or was it the Hitler Youth?'

'Friendly fire.'

'Kindly hire … what are you talking about? I don't want to hire anything. I want the brick. Where's the bloody brick?'

Sir Charles picked up a brick. 'As requested, Freddy, the brick with which you were hit.'

'That's not the one. It's not cracked. You said the blow that cracked my head, cracked the brick.'

'This is the one,' said Jack.

'This is the one, Freddy.'

'That's better. Now that I have evidence I shall take a nap.'

'Not a good idea, Freddy. Harry, keep him awake. I'm going to get the Rolls. We've got to get him to hospital. Boys, you come with me.'

41

'He's on our side, isn't he?' said George. 'I am sorry, Grandfather. But why is Lord Frederick dressed as a tramp?'

'He is working undercover.'

'Pardon, I missed that.'

Sir Charles moved to a moonlit part of the path.

'Lord Frederick,' he repeated, 'is working undercover.'

'Being a tramp is his camouflage?'

'Yes.'

'Where are we going?'

'To the garage to get a car. We've got to get Freddy to hospital. Run on ahead, get the garage doors open.'

'Come on, Jack.'

At the garage Sir Charles told the boys, 'When I'm away at the hospital I want you to keep your eyes and ears open. And do be careful. This afternoon Mike and the American guest he was chauffeuring to The Hall were attacked. They are lucky to be alive. We think the fellow who tried to kill them was an Irishman.'

'Did he blow up the Assembly Rooms?' said Jack.

'We don't know. But he is dangerous. We think he is friends with the Hitler Youth. The car in which he escaped was badly damaged. He has a funny ear. If you see a man like that tell Bert.'

'Where is this man now, Uncle Charles?'

'We don't know. He's disappeared.'

42

'What a lovely little station,' said Marigold.

'It is, isn't it? Sir Charles' father had it built. "If I have to have trains puffing across my land," he always said, "then I want my own railway station".'

'How olde-worlde.'

'Bags?' repeated the railwayman through the ticket window grill, sounding as if he'd said 'sins' like an irritable priest taking confession.

'Yes,' said Marigold, 'bags.'

'You don't want tickets?'

'No.'

'This window is for tickets.'

'You rang The Hall to say my bags were here.'

'Not tickets?'

'I can see them. The two green cases beside the golf bag.'

'Hang on a tick.'

'I'd like to hang him,' said Lady Elizabeth. 'Does he have to repeat every question we ask? I once had a maid like that. I'd say, "Tea, Gladys" – she was called, Gladys – and she'd say, "Tea?" as if she expected me to reply, "No, I want a nice lamb chop" ... good manners are in short supply these days. If it comes to war Charles says everything will be in short supply. He's started stockpiling Darjeeling. Where's the fellow gone? Coo-ee!'

'If you'd come through, ladies,' said the railwayman, poking his head round the door next to the ticket office.

'That's them,' said Marigold.

'Name?' said the railwayman.

'Striker.'

'That's not what it says on the tags.'

'Those are my cases.'

He looked at the tags. 'It says, "Professor Striker", you a Professor?'

'Of course she's a professor,' said Lady Elizabeth.

'In that case they must be yours, mustn't they? You were right and I was wrong.'

'I'm always right.'

'Is that because you're gentry or because you're a woman?'

'Don't be flippant. You are new here?'

'Two weeks a station master, in charge of myself and half a porter when he's not lying in bed picking his nose. You one of the Stetsons?'

'If you are asking in your vulgar way if Professor Striker is an American,' said Lady Elizabeth, 'the answer is, yes. Though what it has to do with you is beyond me. I knew the old station master very well. He liked venison. Do you like venison? What's your name?'

'Sean.'

'Sean, what?'

'Roy.'

'Well, Roy, until we know each other better you will not be receiving free venison from The Hall.'

'It must be difficult for you to call me Roy when my surname could be a Christian name … makes us sound as if we know each other really well, doesn't it?'

'I assure you, young man, that it is extremely unlikely that I will ever know you … really well. Pigs will fly before I do. You have the look of a poacher. I will tell my gamekeeper to keep a sharp eye open for a poacher wearing a railwayman's uniform. My car is outside.'

'Your car?'

'Yes.'

'Why?'

'Why, what?'

'Why are you telling me your car is outside?'

'I wish you to know where to carry the cases.'

'To the car?'

'Yes, and you will not be receiving a tip … and make sure to water the geraniums in the horse trough. Norman, the old station master, made the station quite botanical. His horticultural efforts made my using public transport almost bearable. The man with green fingers will be a hard act to follow.'

'I have no intention of following Norman.'

'Oh?'

'Norman is dead.'

'Natural causes?'

'Venison poisoning.'

'Get on with it and be grateful I will not be writing a letter of complaint.'

'Yes, my lady.'

'Next stop, Marigold, the Post Office. Emily, the post mistress, will be pleased to see us. When you tell her who your letter is for she will faint. She is Bert's sister. Since her husband died she lives alone. She doesn't like me and I don't like her. What makes her tolerable is her gossip. I would never admit this to Charles but I do like to know what's going on in the village. She likes to talk to me because of who I am. She is a snob. The difference between us is that I know I'm a snob, she thinks she isn't.'

'Will she curtsey?'

'She is a socialist.'

'Like Sir Charles?'

'Unfortunately, yes.'

43

Mr Crozier's white coat was bloody.

'Some days, Sir Charles, patients bleed, some days they don't. One of life's little mysteries, I'm thinking. So, the wee chap with the head wound I've been stitching up is important?'

'Yes.'

'A battleship, not a frigate.'

'Let me put it to you this way, Crozier … if this was Trafalgar you'd be dealing with Lord Nelson.'

'I was there, you know.'

'Trafalgar?'

'Yes.'

'You have mentioned that before.'

'It worries you?'

'One of my chauffeurs has a penchant for wearing odd socks. I find his eccentricity amusing. When my surgeon believes in reincarnation, it makes me thoughtful.'

'Your haemorrhoids OK?'

'No longer a problem.'

'I did a good job?'

'You did.'

'You know why? Practice. I did my first haemorrhoidectomy in fifty-seven BC. You might have heard of my patient … Julius Caesar. The man with the hook nose as the Swan of Avon called him. Julius was in a lot of pain during the Gallic wars. Without my expertise he might have lost those campaigns.'

'Is it true that he only had one ball?'

'Sir Charles, you should know better than that. A medical man is never allowed to divulge a patient's details.'

'You told me Caesar had haemorrhoids. Is that not a breach of the rules governing the doctor-patient relationship?'

'I mentioned the great man's affliction to give you confidence in my skill as a surgeon. Despite the bleeding, your chap will be fine. A three stitch wound, hardly worth a needle and thread. He's a little confused but, then again, these days, aren't we all? He's right at the top of the ladder you say, a gold braid and epaulettes man, but you can't say more?'

'You have correctly read my signal flags.'

'England expects?'

'Yes.'

'You can rely on me, Sir Charles.'

'And how is Leading Seaman Mike?'

'I'll no repeat what the big fellow said when I asked him if he wanted cross stitch or satin. When you brought him in he was the Victory after Trafalgar. He's ready to sail. He's asking for shore leave. I'll be glad to see him disembark. He's drinking all my grog. Last time I had a patient like that was in 1066; terrible boozers the Normans … that's why they wore those helmets with nose guards, you know, to hide their red noses. Don't look so worried, Sir Charles, I made that up to scare you. But I did help William the Conqueror with an ingrown toenail, now, that is true. Dinna look so worried, man, or I'll be putting you into bed next. One of the nice new beds in Ward Nine with its newly painted walls. I've never seen so much new plastering in a hospital.'

'You should not have told me about the Conqueror's ingrown toenail … doctor-patient confidentiality, what?'

'And you will not tell me the secret of Ward Nine?'

'Official Secrets Act.'

44

Mike limped to the Rolls.

'You need a stick?' said Sir Charles.

'I need a drink.'

'The glove compartment.'

'Blended or malt?'

'Rusty Nail.'

'My God, I needed that. He's mad, isn't he?'

'Crozier been telling you his stories? Which one was it? Caesar's haemorrhoids or William the Conqueror's ingrown toenail?'

'He says he operated on Samuel Pepys for the stone.'

'That's a new one. How did you react?'

'I looked at him as if I thought he'd gone mad.'

'What did he do?'

'He stuck a needle in me, next thing I woke up in bed with this bloody bandage on.'

'It was his way of testing you. He was tickling your grey cells with a tall story. He wanted to know if you were compos mentis. If you hadn't looked alarmed when he told you that cock and bull story about Samuel Pepys he might well have thought you were off your rocker.'

'How many people know I fainted at the sight of my own blood?'

'Marigold's not been discreet.'

'Damn.'

'Some women like vulnerability in a man, don't you know, brings out their motherly instincts. If she had her way she'd award you a Purple Heart.'

'What about Harry? I suppose in his eyes I'm some kind of coward?'

'He's much too busy making eyes at Marigold.'

'Really?'

'The boy's smitten.'

Sir Charles parked outside the village post office.

'Isn't that Lady Elizabeth's car?'

'It is. That's why I stopped. Let's join the ladies.'

'Ladies?'

'Marigold and Elizabeth. Marigold's posting a letter to the President.'

45

'Charles, thank goodness you are here,' said Lady Elizabeth.

'Mike,' said Marigold, 'how's the leg?'

'Sore.'

'Sit down, take my chair, I insist.'

'I hear you fainted at the sight of your own blood,' said Lady Elizabeth, 'and you've been drinking. Only you could turn a hospital into a public house. Pure alcohol, was it? From the dispensary? And why are you here?'

'I'm with Sir Charles, my lady.'

'I know that. What I meant was … why is he here? Why are you here, Charles? Don't bother to answer. I'm weary of hearing cock and bull stories. Charles, you have authority.'

'Do I?'

Lady Elizabeth loved her husband to the moon and back but sometimes, quite often in fact, she found him infuriating. On this occasion she ignored his feigned modesty and, rather like a distant third cousin who'd perished in the Charge of the Light Brigade, pressed on regardless.

'I want you to use your authority to make Emily here break the rules and tell us what she heard when she broke the rules and listened in to a certain conversation she's been hinting at telling us about. Emily, appraise Sir Charles of the situation.'

'Beg pardon?'

'Tell Sir Charles what's been going on.'

Emily, a little woman with small eyes that sparkled like diamonds, swivelled on her telephonist's chair. The switchboard she was sitting in front of, reminded Sir Charles of the coat stand in The Hall's vestibule, the one used for hanging up dog leads and horse whips.

'It was the call from the telephone box at the crossroads,' said Emily. She paused. All these rich, powerful people hanging on her every word. Lovely. She looked at Marigold. She'd never met an American before. She'd met one Frenchman, two Italians and a German weightlifter when she'd been a high kicking dancer (two Christmas seasons in the chorus line at Newcastle's Empire Theatre) but never an American, and her a professor as well. She looked too young to be a professor. Why, oh why, had she fallen in love with a postmaster who'd had to go and die? He'd left her a useful inheritance, that was true, but not a glamorous one. The only fun she had now was eavesdropping. 'Of course I never listen-in, that would be against GPO rules.'

'And you, being a Methodist, obey the rules?' said Lady Elizabeth.

'I'm C-of-E, Lady Elizabeth. I won't have religion coming between me and my glass of sherry. If you don't mind my saying, Lady Elizabeth, I know why you might be thinking I'm a Methodist. My speaking part in the pantomime last year was given me on merit. I can't deny Reverend Ponsonby wanted me to join his flock, but I wasn't for turning. Percy, that's the Reverend Ponsonby, respects my principles. He would have it no other way. After "flights of angels" took my Albert up to his eternal resting place, Percy was very good to me. His "goodness" upset a lot of people. It's a mystery to me how doing "good" can cause such a lot of upset … but there you are.'

'What's a pantomime?' said Marigold.

'If you're a professor, like her Ladyship said you were, I'm surprised, Lady Marigold, that you don't know what a pantomime is.'

'Marigold is not a "Lady",' said Lady Elizabeth, 'she is an American. Americans have money but not titles, nor do they have pantomimes … isn't that right, Marigold?'

'Ladies,' interrupted Sir Charles, 'may we for the moment put to one side an explanation of the British pantomime. While we digress I fear England's enemies are preparing to attack. Emily, cut to the quick and spill the beans.'

'Charles, British telephonists do not "spill the beans", they elucidate. Emily, elucidate.'

'I'd rather "spill the beans".'

46

'So,' said Sir Charles, 'if I may sum up all you have told us, Emily. It was when you were making sure that the American was connected to the railway station that you heard him speak "foreign". At first you thought there was something wrong with the connection and so continued listening. The person to whom the American was speaking was a man and this man answered in what sounded like the same language. As a high kicking dancer, front row of the chorus line, at Newcastle's Empire Theatre, you met people from France, Germany and Italy. Because of your contact with these foreigners you are familiar with how their languages sound, though not a fluent speaker of any. You have a suspicion that the American and the railwayman were speaking Gaelic … is that correct?'

'The more I think about it, Sir Charles, the more certain I am it was the Gaelic. Sergeant Belt, he's in charge of Kielder Police Station, you know, the village in North Northumberland.'

'I know where Kielder is, Emily.'

'Sergeant Belt hails from the Western Isles. The only time I heard him use the Gaelic was at the pantomime this year. When you've worked in the theatre like I've done you get an ear for the ways people speak. You see, Sir Charles, since my dear Albert passed away, I've been in demand.'

'In demand?'

'She has suitors, Charles,' said Lady Elizabeth.

'Ah.'

'Sergeant Belt fancies me. I know that for a fact. You can always tell, can't you?'

'Can you?'

'Of course you can.'

'Perhaps it's a gift, like being a clairvoyant.'

'Do you think so? When he gave me a bunch of flowers and spoke to me in a language I didn't understand and had never heard before, not even back stage at the Empire, that's when I knew. Though I didn't know what he was saying, I knew he was saying nice things, you could just tell … at least I could. I wonder if I am clairvoyant.'

'My dogs are like that. They know when you are telling them that you love them. It's your tone of voice.'

'Do you think Sergeant Belt was telling me he loved me?'

'Charles,' said Lady Elizabeth, 'you are not an agony aunt. Straighten your back and remember why we are here. England, our dear England, is under attack.'

'Quite right, my dear … and the only two words you recognised, you say were … "Mickey Mouse" and "Walt Disney"?'

'Excuse me, I have a customer.' A light was flashing on the switchboard. Emily plugged in a 'dog lead'. 'Operator speaking. How may I help you? Number please … I mean the number you are calling from. If you are in a public phone box you will find its number in the middle of the dial. Thank you … and the number you wish to call? That will be three pence. One moment please while I connect.'

'In America that switchboard would be in a museum,' said Marigold.

'Who is it?' said Lady Elizabeth.

'I've told you, milady, I work for the GPO and they have strict rules. It's more than my job's worth. You see, milady, I once saw this picture. It was at the Stoll in Newcastle if I remember right where a brave telephonist refused to let a private detective … I'll bet you've met private detectives, Lady Marigold, you being an American.'

'Marigold is not a Lady,' said Lady Elizabeth, 'how many times do I have to tell you?'

'Call me Marigold,' said Marigold. 'Tell me about the movie.'

'I love the way you Americans call the pictures, the "movies". I've been to the movies. It sounds more exciting than going to the pictures. Anyway, as I was saying, the brave telephonist refused to let the private detective listen to the caller because he didn't have a walnut.'

'You mean a warrant?' said Marigold.

'Is that what they are called? I was close though, wasn't I?'

'What happened to the telephonist?' said Sir Charles.

'The private detective shot her.'

'Well, Emily, I can assure you that no one here is going to shoot you though the person waiting to be connected may well wish to do so. Now, tell me, is the person waiting to be connected the Gaelic speaker?'

'Not sure … don't think so.'

'American?'

'Yes. He's calling from the telephone box at the crossroads near The Hall. The number of the telephone he gave me tells me that. I'm not clairvoyant, but I wish I was.'

'What number does he want?'

'It's a Newcastle number.'

'Not the railway station?'

'No.'

'Better connect him.'

'Sorry for keeping you waiting, sir … don't you talk to me like that, I said I was sorry … cheek! You are through now, sir.'

47

'He's speaking foreign,' said Emily, 'talking to a woman. Gina … she's called, Gina. She sounds pleased. I think they know each other.'

'Is he speaking Gaelic?' said Sir Charles.

'No, this is different. He keeps saying, "Bella Bella". There was a sword swallower at the Empire who kept saying that and he was Italian, couldn't keep his hands to himself. All the girls called him Bella the Octopus.'

'Give me the headphones,' said Marigold, 'I speak Italian. It's Mario.'

'Who's Mario?' said Emily.

'An American friend,' said Sir Charles, 'he's a guest at The Hall. Emily, is this the man you heard speaking what you thought was Gaelic?'

'No, this gentleman sounds sexy. I shouldn't say things like that, should I? But he does. I suppose that's because he's Italian. The other gentleman sounded bad tempered.'

'Men,' said Marigold. 'I knew Mario had an eye for the ladies but what he's saying to Gina, well, if my mother had been doing the eavesdropping she'd have been disgusted.'

'I wish I could speak Italian,' said Emily. 'Italians are passionate, aren't they?'

'Emily,' said Lady Elizabeth, 'we are in mixed company.'

'I wonder if Maurice, that's Sergeant Belt when he's not in uniform, has Italian blood. You never know, do you? Him telling me he loved me in the Gaelic was romantic, wasn't it?'

'You don't know what he was saying. He might have been saying, "Have you found my handcuffs?".'

'I didn't know he'd lost his handcuffs. When did he do that?'

'What would you say, Emily,' said Sir Charles, 'if I told you I am thinking of ordering Sergeant Belt to work under you here at the Post Office?'

'Under me?'

'If our American friend calls again and you are right about him speaking the Gaelic then we need an interpreter. From what you have told us it would seem that Belt's our man … and he's a policeman, an officer of the law, not a private detective. Listening in with a policeman I would say makes eavesdropping lawful, wouldn't you agree? He'd have to lodge with you. It would mean being on duty twenty-four hours a day.'

'Working with Maurice under me, that would be nice. Where would he sleep?'

'I'm sure you'll think of something.'

48

'Where have you been?' said Lady Elizabeth. 'You left the Post Office before me so you should have been home before me. Bashful is not as powerful as the Rolls. Marigold and I were worried about you.'

'I took Mike home,' said Sir Charles.

'I thought that's where you'd be … fainting at the sight of his own blood, who'd ever have thought it? You've not been drinking, I hope?'

'No, I have not, though I was offered. Where are the Americans?'

'Mooching. They are like sheep who've found a hole in a fence. They turn up in the most unexpected places. They think our home is a museum, one of those new-fangled museums where you are encouraged to touch the exhibits. Bert is rounding them up. I've told him to serve drinks in the Green Room.'

'To make O'Neil feel at home?'

'To tease, Charles, to tease. If you are not going completely gaga you must remember that over the fireplace in the Green Room there hangs a painting of your ancestor who owned fifty thousand acres of the Pale.'

'General Percival, whose ancestors fought with William of Orange at the Battle of the Boyne … dear me, Elizabeth, you are in a mood. Remember why the Americans are here.'

'I am not, as you put it "in a mood". O'Neil's presence in our home is ambiguous. While we are supposed to be using him, he might well be using us.'

49

'I know it's a warm day,' said Sir Charles, 'but I do like to see logs burning in a grate. A fire makes a room look cosy.'

'It's a vaccination against what's happening in the wicked world outside these four walls,' said Weinberger, 'gives us all a false sense of security, don't you think?'

'Whisky and a log fire,' said Macdonald, 'heaven on Earth. Has anyone heard of a guy called Hitler? I don't think so.'

'Charlie,' said Marigold, 'I do believe that under all that tweed there lies a Romantic. What's it like being married to a Romantic, Lizzie?'

'I don't get flowers on my birthday, if that's what you mean, I get melons. Charles thinks melons are Fabergé Eggs, don't you, Charles?'

'Marigold,' said Harry, 'would you like to see Uncle's Melon House? May I, Uncle? We'll take the dogs.'

'I'll get a wrap,' said Marigold.

'No need for that. My flying jacket's on a peg in the hall. You can borrow that.'

50

'Charles, be a dear and ring for Bert to draw the curtains,' said Lady Elizabeth.

'If it comes to war I fear we will be forced to spend too much time behind drawn blinds. There will have to be a black-out, you know. Any light will be a target for German bombers. Carpe diem. Let's enjoy watching the sun set by firelight for as long as we can. Something we take for granted may soon be a luxury.'

'Hitler wouldn't dare attack Poland. The Anglo-Polish Pact puts that quite out of the question. Only a madman would contemplate attacking the British Empire. We have battleships.'

'Lady Elizabeth,' said Weinberger with some solemnity, 'Herr Hitler *is* a madman.'

'Charles, be a dear, pour me a small sherry.'

'If it comes to war,' said Sir Charles, 'sherry may well become a luxury. Perhaps the rationing of sherry should start now.'

'Charles, stop teasing. What a mood you are in. What must our guests think?'

'We are all married,' said Macdonald.

'Charles, pour your good lady a sherry,' said Weinberger; 'if you don't, I'll tell Marigold to tell the President not to give you any battleships.'

'In that case I pour the sherry.'

'If it does come to war, Charles, what would England need?'

'Everything man can make and money can buy.'

'You Brits don't have the money to pay for a war,' said O'Neil.

'The telephone, sir,' said Bert.

'Who is it?'

'The Major, sir.'

'You wanted by the army, Charles?' said Mancini.

'If they want recruits as old as me, then I fear we are done for. Excuse me, my dear, gentlemen.'

'It's the phone in the study, sir.'

'Thank you, Bert. Oh and Bert, can you serve Mr O'Neil one of his "specials".'

'In the Great War,' said Lady Elizabeth, 'my husband won the VC. It makes the army think him indispensable. I sometimes think they forget he is no longer a young man. I know his limitations; they, on the other hand, think he can do anything.'

'After he'd finished David,' said Mancini, 'the Pope thought Michelangelo could do anything – that's what success does. On the East coast the Mancinis are famous for ice cream. People think we can make any flavour ice cream. They think, with ice cream, the Mancinis can do anything. Why? Because the

Mancinis are Italian and the entire world knows Italians make the best gelato. Think Italian and you think ice cream.'

'You believe in the idea that while a nation is made up of many individuals their membership of the same club gives them a common identity? All Englishmen wear bowler hats, that sort of thing? Italian men chase women?'

'All the Greeks I know,' said Macdonald, 'think they're philosophers.'

'Because they are Greek?'

'Yes.'

'Mother's milk?'

'The guy back home who shines my shoes, he's Greek. His birth name is Socrates. He wears a lucky Athena charm round his neck. It's on a gold chain. He wants you to know he's living the American dream. "Hi, look at me, a shoe-shine man with a gold chain." If you want good luck he lets you touch it, charges a dollar. Only from him can you get the Genuine Parthenon Marble Shine. An American but still so Greek … and he's third generation.'

'And you, Angus Macdonald … what a Scottish sounding name, just saying it makes one hear bagpipes… do you celebrate your ancestors?'

'I drink whisky: "To the whistle in the thistle and the weather in the heather, my love plays the pipes for me".'

'Burns?'

'Just made it up.'

'My ancestors were German,' said Weinberger. 'I guess that doesn't make me too popular at the moment.'

'The Green Room is called the "Green Room",' said Lady Elizabeth, 'in memory of an ancestor who owned estates in Ireland. That's him there, General Percival. He taught his tenants how to use a knife. Robert O'Neil, Bob, do you celebrate your heritage?'

'My allegiance is all to the Stars and Stripes.'

'The Irish believe in fairies.'

'Do you believe George killed a dragon?'

'You celebrate St Patrick's Day?'

'Of course, as do many thousands of Irish-Americans.'

'I find it interesting that you say "Irish-American" and not "American-Irish". Is your allegiance in that order?'

'I'm an American, Lady Elizabeth, and sometime soon your country will, more than likely, be asking my country for money.'

'Is that why you are here, to assess us like a bank manager to see if we are the right sort of people to be trusted with a loan?'

'It is clear to me, Lady Elizabeth, that in this family your husband is the diplomat. And, like all the best diplomats, he knows exactly when to make an entry.'

'Charles, I was telling Bob about General Percival,' said Lady Elizabeth on seeing her husband return from his phone call.

'Your wife would never make a diplomat, Charles,' said O'Neil.'

Sir Charles smiled. 'Elizabeth has been telling you about my ancestor with estates in the Pale? Bob, you must look upon my ancestor as Hitler looks upon the Jews. That was CB on the phone, wants to know when I'm going to fill in that government form asking to know how many cars and horses we have on the estate. I feel as if I've been talking to one of William the Conqueror's clerks doing an audit for the Doomsday Book. Who's for toppers?'

51

Before turning in for the night Sir Charles browsed the Visitors' Book. He wanted to check. And there it was: Mickey Mouse. Emily had recognised two words between the men she'd called the "Gaelic Speakers": Mickey Mouse and Walt Disney. The speaker who'd made the call was Mickey Mouse. She was certain of that because that was how he'd introduced himself, in English; "Mickey Mouse here", before switching to the foreign language she thought was Gaelic. Was "Mickey Mouse" O'Neil's nom de guerre? If it wasn't, then whose was it? And who was "Walt Disney"? Had "Mickey Mouse" been talking to "Walt Disney"? Or had "Mickey Mouse" been asking to speak to "Walt Disney"? Was "Walt Disney" at, or not at, the railway station? If he wasn't, was "Walt Disney" expecting him to be there? Was O'Neil using the nom de guerre he'd possibly used in the Visitors' Book as a code word for other, altogether darker purposes? He was a Gaelic speaker. It was not as if the world was full of Gaelic speakers. It had to be him. Sir Charles hoped that Sergeant Belt's designs on Emily would not take that good man's mind off his duties. Sex put more men out of action than enemy fire. In the last war venereal disease had reduced the fighting strength of some 'dirty' regiments by fifty per cent.

It was good to know that Freddy's men at the Vicarage were out and about. On the way back to The Hall from the Post Office he'd never seen so many night watchmen huddled over braziers, all pretending to be keeping an eye on wheelbarrows and spades. There was a gypsy caravan he'd never seen before as well. It had to be MI5. The tricks the young bloods in the service got up to.

'Making sure we've all signed in?' said O'Neil.

Damn the fellow. Where'd he come from? 'Are you Mickey Mouse?'

'I might be.'

'If you are you will have to tell Walt Disney.'

'The next time I'm in Hollywood, I'll do that. Good night, Sir Charles.'

52

'You know,' said Sir Charles, climbing into bed beside his wife, 'since the Americans arrived this is the only place I feel free to talk … and it's my house; they are everywhere.'

'Don't be theatrical, five people can't be everywhere. We don't live in a cottage. The Hall is large enough to accommodate an army of Americans.'

'It's so much easier being a diplomat in an embassy. I'm not used to bringing work home. All the time I'm thinking, how can I please the Americans? How can I get them on our side? I can't threaten them with the rack or bribe them with a knighthood. In the first instance they are too powerful and in the second you have to be a Brit or a member of the Commonwealth. All I can do is try and disguise my grovelling, make them think it's all just me trying to be a good host. It would make my ancestors puke. Ponsonby, who climbed the cliffs with Wolfe at Quebec, shook his head at me when I passed him in the vestibule; as if to say, "Dear Boy, to think it has come to this".'

'If you really think you saw Ponsonby's head move you should see Crozier.'

'Crozier's a surgeon, not a psychiatrist. Anyway, he's too busy looking after Freddy.'

'Dear Freddy, I do hope he pulls through. You say I shouldn't send him flowers?'

'He is supposed to be a tramp. The Lady of the Manor does not send a tramp flowers. It just isn't done. It would draw attention to who he really is.'

'Blow his cover?'

'In a manner of speaking, yes. Crozier knows Freddy's not a tramp, that he is top drawer but no more than that.'

'Not that he's head of MI5?'

'Good Lord, no. And keep your voice down.'

'Charles, there is no one under the bed.'

'What about listening through the keyhole?'

'Perhaps you should see a psychiatrist. Americans affect people in strange ways. Bert has started talking American. When he put a vase of sweet peas on the table he said, "Gee, don't they smell just great". He did apologise. Since the Americans arrived he's had a spring in his step. They must be tipping well.'

'Or, in the case of O'Neil, too well.'

'If we shouted fire do you think O'Neil would dash out with his golf clubs?'

'He is very attached to them; strange that he borrowed my putter for his knockabout.'

'Why didn't he use his own?'

'Good question.'

'I thought golfers preferred to play with their own clubs; you would.'

'Yet he brought his own clubs all the way from America. Bert said the club which fell out was too short to play with.'

'When I first met him, I thought him most pleasant. Now I've changed my mind.'

'A black cloud hangs over the fellow. Never trust a man who doesn't drink or shoot. The more I talk to these guys, I mean, men, the more it reinforces what I already know, that, though we speak the same language, we are different. The chip on their shoulders is that they can't forget we were once their owners.'

'Yet, a common language is such a bond. If Marigold had spoken only Chinese, Harry would have found it difficult to ask her if she wanted to see the Melon House. I wonder if the Chinese have a word for melon. Do they grow melons in China? You never got to the Far East, did you, dear? You know, it's just crossed my mind that Harry is going to be like his father … besotted with Americans. I wonder if Marigold is rich. Another heiress coming into the family wouldn't be at all a bad thing. Do you think the Americans would be more likely to help us if we gave Mr Gandhi India?'

'Elizabeth, I wish you would not keep talking about giving Mr Gandhi, India. It is not helpful. When the Americans hear an Englishwoman saying things like that it puts ideas into their heads. You heard what they had to say about intervention. They are businessmen. In the coming conflict if they give us a destroyer they will charge us for a battleship. That's what they did when they finally rolled up their sleeves and came into the last war.'

'But we didn't pay, did we?'

'No, and they have not forgotten. If it comes to war they will take the coats off our backs.'

'What if we gave India to Herr Hitler?'

'He'd take it and then, you know what he'd do? He'd shoot Mr Gandhi, then he'd blitz Bombay.'

'If he was busy doing that it might make him forget about Europe.'

'A treaty with the fellow is not worth the paper it is written on. He means what he says in that awful book of his. The trouble is people don't believe him. He hates Jews, he hates Communists. He wants land and lots of it. He has his sights on Russia. He's written it all down. To that extent he is not a hypocrite, just unbelievable.'

'I didn't like the Americans calling us "Olivers". Ugh! It makes me see green, pink and heliotrope.'

'I sometimes feel like bending their ears and reminding them of a few home truths. Who gave you democracy? We did, the Brits. Did we charge you for it? No, we did not. They are so pious. When they go on about our Empire they forget what they did to the Indians.'

'You tell them, Charles.'

'And as for slavery the least said about that the better.'

'You don't mention it?'

'Avoid it like the plague. It would rub them up the wrong way. In diplomacy you don't use sandpaper. The weapon of choice is baby oil. You see, my dear, we Brits must accept with good grace that the Americans are the rich relations we cannot afford to upset. If war is a licence to kill, then diplomacy is a licence to be a hypocrite. In the eyes of Americans, Great Britain is Oedipus. We are the father they want to kill.'

'Who told you that? It's not something you've read in Horse and Hound.'

'Harry. It's Freud. And the professor is working for MI5. He's been paid a prodigious sum to analyse our guests' nom de guerre.'

'What will he make of Marigold's nom de guerre?'

'She hasn't signed, has she?'

'No.'

'I suspect he will charge extra for an omission. By the by I've told Mike that when he feels up to it you want him sleeping outside our bedroom door with a shotgun, that is, for as long as the Americans are here.'

'You didn't?'

'Of course I didn't.'

'For that you do not get a goodnight kiss.'

'In that case I'll give you one.'

'Charles!'

53

A stub of candle stuck in a saucer lit the den.

'Have another pickled onion,' said Jack. 'I have three more jars. Moses, there is no more cheese, go to sleep.'

'Where do you get them from?' said George.

'Phyllis gives them to me.'

'I'll bet she doesn't. I bet you took them.'

'I did take them, but Phyllis knows I take them. She told me she turns a blind eye.'

'She doesn't mind?'

'She feels sorry for me. I feel sorry for her.'

'Why should anyone want to feel sorry for Phyllis? She is not a refugee.'

'She does not get a holiday.'

'I have never thought about that. I mean, she's Phyllis. She's always there. She's paid to be there. She's kind to everyone except Bert. She doesn't like Bert. When I go into the kitchen she gives me marzipan.'

'She's given me marzipan.'

'Do you like it?' Jack pulled a face. 'If she gives you some, you take it and give it to me. I love marzipan. What are the Nazis doing?'

Jack picked up the binoculars. He liked using them. They made him feel like a soldier.

'I can see their camp fire. They are eating.'

'My mushrooms?'

'Too far away to tell.'

'Jack, would you like to give the Nazis a pain in their tummies? That big Nazi who attacked me said he wanted my mushrooms. Why don't we pick him some?'

'I'm not picking mushrooms to give to Nazis.'

'What if they were poisonous mushrooms?'

'Why would they eat poisonous mushrooms?'

'We will make them want them.'

'The way they want Poland?'

'But how?' Jack listened. 'That is a wisdom of King Solomon plan. You must be Jewish.'

'No, I am Northumbrian. My ancestors were Reivers.'

54

In bed with her husband snuggled up beside her, Lady Elizabeth confided to the love of her life, 'Emily's performance was operatic, don't you think?'

'Operatic?' said Sir Charles.

'Her recitative, dear.'

'The length of time it takes an opera singer to die?'

'Yes, everyone knows Emily listens in to our conversations. Did you count the number of times she explained that she only knew about the American on the phone because she was making sure the connection was working?'

'No.'

'Four times.'

'Her recitative?'

'Yes, and you, Charles, know I do not like opera.'

Friday 1ˢᵗ September 1939

1

Sir Charles and Bert watched O'Neil from under the branches of an ancient yew. Sir Charles had his arms folded. Bert wanted to do the same but thought the stance unsuitable for a servant.

'He's filling in time,' said Sir Charles, 'but what's he up to? Why is he carrying a bag of golf clubs while at the same time using my putter for his knock around? What time's his taxi, Bert?'

'In an hour, sir.'

'He refused my offer of having one of The Hall's staff drive him to the golf course … said he liked trains, got quite huffy when I tried to insist. Refused point blank to join the shoot. Tell me again what happened when he gave you the tip.'

'It was when the golf bag he won't let anyone near fell over, sir. A club fell out.'

'A Mashie-Niblick?'

'Yes, sir. There was no length to its handle; looked to me more like a cricket stump than a golf club.'

'Too short to play with?'

'Definitely, sir. When he saw that I'd seen it he snapped sharp at me. "Don't ever touch my clubs," he said. He sounded as if he meant it, sir. Then he laughed and gave me the bribe.'

'What's his game, Bert?'

'I don't know, sir, but every time he's taken a swipe at that ball he's taken himself further away from The Hall. Now he's in the bushes. And, do you know what, sir? It wouldn't surprise me if he didn't come out. And I think I know where he's a heading.'

'So do I. Trail him, Bert.'

'Boo!' said Marigold. 'On whom are you spying?'

'We are bird watching,' said Sir Charles.

'Don't believe you.'

'You can't have rumbled me, I'm a retired diplomat – telling porkies was my profession.'

'Then you are out of practice. Isn't that right, Bert?'

'Yes, madam.'

'Carry on, Bert.'

'Sar!'

'Tell me, Charles,' said Marigold, as they watched Bert disappear, 'why does your 'man' sometimes call you, "sir" and sometimes, "sar!"?'

'When I told him to "carry on" he thought he and I were back in the army. "Carry on" is army jargon. It means something like, you are dismissed. Go away and get on with the job you've been told to do.'

'And what "job" has he been told to do?'

'He's keeping an eye on O'Neil. We think your compatriot is off to use the telephone box at the crossroads.'

'Before he goes off to play that game of golf he was mouthing off about over breakfast?'

Bert's speedy return told Sir Charles something was afoot.

'He's doing what we thought, sir.'

'He's telephoning?'

'He is now, sir but he's had to wait. When he got to the box a member of the Hitler Youth was using it. Both parties, sir, are what you might call agitated. There's something going on in the Nazi camp. They're running around like scalded cats. I don't speak German, sir, but the mouthful the young Nazi shouted at Mr O'Neil, well, it didn't sound as if he was asking Mr O'Neil if his father was keeping well.'

'Be a good chap, go and see what's happening. If O'Neil asks why you are prowling, tell him the truth. Something's up at the Nazi camp and you've been sent to investigate. Carry on, Bert.'

'Sar!'

'I never knew butlers could run,' said Marigold.

'In his youth Bert was the village's one hundred yard sprint champion.'

'Give me your arm, Charlie. Now, while you and me go "walkies" round this nice big garden of yours, let's talk. Jasper, Mario and Angus are out on the shoot?' Sir Charles nodded. 'What if, to encourage an exchange of ideas, I told you I know that Professor Freud is working for Freddy?'

'How did you know that?'

'I'm the President's eyes and ears. The Herr Professor is working for you Brits because we in the States are bowled over by his ideas. When I get round to signing The Hall's Visitor's Book, I'm using my real name.'

'The Americans made MI5 employ the professor?'

'Yes.'

'Freddy did mention that the Professor had been foisted on him.'

'America is a new country. We welcome new ideas. Ever played word association?'

'After Bridge it's my favourite game.'

'Cat?'

'Dog.'

'America?'

'Help.'

'Which of course is the reason I and my fellow Americans are here. Toasted muffin?'

'Are we still playing?'

'Yes, toasted muffin?'

'Afternoon tea.'

'You ask a Bostonian to word associate "toasted muffin" and eighty per cent of them will reply, "Burn the British".'

'They've not forgotten their Tea Party?'

'In a Boston diner you don't ask for a "toasted muffin", you ask for a "Burn the British". "Gimme two Burn the British," they say. Sometimes I think they enjoy saying it more than the muffins.'

'I understand what you are saying. A lot of Americans do not like the British.'

'That's the Kilimanjaro you have to climb. Trust me, Charlie. I will do my best to help your cause. I'm pro-British. My great-grandmother came from this part of the world.'

'I know, she was a Grey. One of her ancestors stands on top of a column in Newcastle.'

'You have done your homework. Or should I say MI5 has done it for you.'

'Was it by chance you were on the Nord with the Hitler Youth and an Irish fanatic or was the CIA involved?'

'Let's sit,' said Marigold.

She steered Sir Charles to a white garden seat with a wheel at one end and handles at the other.

'I love wheelbarrow seats,' said Marigold. 'I call them, follow the sun seats. If only life were like a wheelbarrow seat, Charlie. Every time something nasty was about to happen we could wheel ourselves out of harm's way. Bert's taking his time. Did he save your life in the war? Isn't that what happens when a master takes his servant to war?'

'No, he did not and nor did I save his. We relied on each other. We helped each other. If you must know sometimes both of us were so scared we forgot all about class. We wanted only one thing and that was to survive.'

'Which is why you do not want another war at any cost?'

'You will twist the President's arm?'

'Charlie, no one does that to President Roosevelt. He does the arm twisting. Here comes Bert. Over here, Bert.'

'Mr O'Neil's on the telephone, sir and the Nazis have been poisoned. They say the two boys who live here gave them poison mushrooms.'

'George and Jack?'

'It has to be them, sir. Some of the Nazis are hallucinating, some are terrible sick and one is dead. And you'll never guess what, sir. Someone's taken down their Nazi flag and hoisted the Star of David. They hadn't noticed till I pointed it out to them. That's when I had to run.'

'Uncle Charles! Uncle Charles! Thank goodness I've found you,' said Harry. 'The Germans have invaded Poland.'

2

The bad news chilled the sunshine filling the drawing room. Though it was a warm day Sir Charles could feel the piece of Great War shrapnel in his arm. It wasn't supposed to do that. That party trick it kept for damp days. Marigold doodled, finding consolation in giving words in The Times a three-dimensional look. Harry wandered; stopping at a window he studied the sky, the arena in which he might soon find himself fighting for his life. Which was the better plane? The Spitfire or the Messerschmitt?

'If we honour our treaty with Poland,' said Harry, looking out of the window, 'and declare war on Germany, the Hitler Youth will be our enemy. Damn them! Will we declare war on Germany, Uncle Charles?'

'I've been on to London. By all accounts Chamberlain and the Cabinet are dithering. They know the fox is in the chicken house but don't know what to do. A rumour's going round that Churchill's been offered a place in the Cabinet. Ah, Bert. Good man.'

'I thought under the circumstances, sir, tea and biscuits. I think you might also like to know, sir, that Mr O'Neil's off in the taxi I ordered for him.'

'I'd forgotten about him. With his golf bag?'

'Yes, sir.'

'No news from Emily and Sergeant Belt?'

'They've not rang, sir.'

'Perhaps our suspicions were unjustified.'

'Perhaps he has a friend, like Mario,' said Marigold.

'I doubt it. Does he know Germany has attacked Poland?'

'I don't think so, sir.'

'You didn't tell him?'

'No, sir. If I may make so bold, sir, this morning Mr O'Neil did not wish to be told anything.'

'He will, of course, be followed. Freddy's men will see to that.'

'The men that keep arriving at the Vicarage, sir?'

'The village drums have been beating, have they?'

'People talk, sir. The traffic between the mystery masts and the Vicarage has been noted.'

'But not understood?'

'Yes, sir. Lady Elizabeth told me, sir, to tell you she's taking a Dundee cake to Lord Frederick, but you are not to worry because she will not be delivering the cake in person. Phyllis will take the cake into the hospital. Her Ladyship is of the opinion that a cook taking a cake to a tramp will not arouse suspicions as to who the tramp really is. Her Ladyship explained your thoughts to me on the matter, sir.'

'You think it a sensible precaution?'

'I do, sir.'

'And Jack and George, do we know where they are?'

'No, sir. I suspect they will be in hiding.'

'I am beginning to think my grandson and Jack have stretched the expression "boys will be boys" to breaking point. First they nearly kill Freddy and now it would seem they've poisoned the Hitler Youth. Harry, would you mind terribly if I asked you to pop down to the Germans' campsite and find out what's going on.'

'I'll go with you, Harry. I speak German,' said Marigold.

'In the meantime, Bert and I will hold the fort here. I have a feeling London will be calling. Harry, I don't wish to sound alarmist but if I was you I'd be ready to leave at a moment's notice. You might be flying Spitfires in action rather sooner than you thought. Harry …'

'Uncle?'

'It is possible we may be living through the last days of peace – make the most of them.'

3

'What did you find out, Harry? You look grim. Bert, pour me a large whisky, the same for Harry. Marigold?'

'Whisky, large.'

'I've a feeling that what I'm about to hear requires a stiffener. Bert, if you feel the same as I do, help yourself.'

'Thank you, sir.'

'Well,' said Harry, 'at the last count two of the Hitler Youth are dead and three are in hospital with sickness and diarrhoea. Half a dozen others are hallucinating. I never thought I'd feel sorry for Germans, but I do now.'

'Do they not know mushrooms can be poisonous?'

'One member of the group I spoke to,' said Marigold, 'said two boys, I assume they were Jack and George, were cooking mushrooms and bacon on an open fire. He said the smell of the food cooking made everyone hungry. When some of his friends went to say hello, the boys ran away. Apparently there was trouble yesterday. One of the boys fired an arrow at one of the Hitler Youth.'

'Jack and George didn't give them the mushrooms?'

'No, the Germans helped themselves.'

'George knows which mushrooms to pick and which to leave alone. When he's here Phyllis has him out foraging for them. He's been collecting them for the pot for as long as I can remember.'

'Well, whoever did the collecting this time made a mistake,' said Harry.

'I am sorry for the Hitler Youth,' said Sir Charles, 'but I am also relieved that Jack and George did not eat them. I think we owe their lives to Nazi acquisitiveness.'

'You are assuming the boys were going to eat the mushrooms,' said Marigold. 'If they'd had trouble with the Nazis why build a camp fire close to the enemies' camp? Jack detests them.'

'I was thinking the same,' said Harry. 'Jack wouldn't give the Nazis eight half-a-crowns for a pound.'

'Would he give them poison?'

'Bert?' said Sir Charles.

'Master George knows his mushrooms, sir.'

'Whatever they were cooking or had prepared to cook,' said Harry, 'must have been a mixture of the deadly poisonous and what you, Uncle Charles, once told me you call "magic mushrooms". The ones that make you hallucinate.'

'I remember once, the whole village under their influence,' said Sir Charles, smiling at the happy memory, 'including the vicar; all of us looking for fairies under ferns.'

'Some of the hallucinating Nazis, Uncle Charles, are better to watch than Charlie Chaplin. They are giving Nazi salutes to oak trees. One was reading Mein Kampf to a cow.'

'The cheek of the fellow, indoctrinating one of my animals.'

'Others are wandering like lost souls,' said Marigold.

'Peripatetic Nazis,' said Sir Charles; 'if Hitler has his way he'll soon be sending them all over Europe. They'll make the plague look like chicken pox.'

'Charlie, this is serious. The ones who are not sick are convinced Jack and George are responsible for the deaths of their friends. They are in a pretty unforgiving mood. The Star of David flag flying over their campsite made their eyes pop.'

'That's just the sort of trick Jack would pull. Better than the frog he put in my shoe.'

'Charlie, these young Nazis are angry. I've seen at close quarters what they are capable of doing. If they get their hands on Jack and George, anything might happen.'

'Bert, the Webley, is it loaded?'

'It is, sir. I loaded it as soon as I heard Hitler had invaded Poland.'

'If a member of the Hitler Youth lays a finger on them, use it.'

'Charlie, before you start shooting, we have to find them. I think they need protecting. Where might they be?'

'Try what Jack calls his "Erdgeist Lager". Harry, you know where it is. It used to be your den. Dear Jack thinks he's the first one to have found the place but he's wrong. When I was his age it was my den. As a child my father played in it. If you are going hunting you will need weapons. Go to the gun room and help yourselves. If you do have to confront the Hitler Youth, the fact that you are armed may make them think twice. Off you go. Good luck.'

The phone rang. Bert answered. 'It's the Major, sir.'

'CB, how are you?'

'Have you heard the news?'

'Yes.'

'When will the war start?'

'I think the politicians are trying to work something out.'

'There's nothing to work out. We made the Poles a promise. If the Nazis don't pack their bags and get out of Poland we go in and chuck them out. And when we do, I want a piece of the action. You will put in a word for me, Charles? Charles, are you still on the line?'

'Yes.'

'Then why don't you answer my question? I've lost my wife, my daughter has been murdered by the Irish; a war will take my mind off things. Well?'

'I'll do my best.'

'I hope so. I've not mentioned this before but the last horse I sold your Elizabeth, well, I gave her a good discount. What I'm saying is, you scratch my back and I'll scratch yours. Charles, I'm desperate to go into action. What do you want me to do, beg?'

'Certainly not … what I do want you to do is to sit down with a glass of whisky and ask yourself a few questions.'

'Such as?'

'Your age.'

'I was out on Ginger this morning, rode ten miles. I'm as fit as a man half my age. Which brings me to the other reason I'm ringing. On my ride I found a Newcastle taxi. Its windows were shot out. I've informed the police. It had been driven off the road into bushes.'

'Where was it?' Sir Charles listened. 'That close to The Hall? If its driver was the man Marigold says is called Doyle, he'd have a long walk to find a safe haven.'

'You told me the Irishman came over on the same boat as the Hitler Youth, that they know each other. What safer haven than the Nazis' campsite?'

'CB, I do believe you have hit the nail on its head.'

'Charles, you will put in a word for me?'

4

'He won't take no for an answer, sir,' said Bert. 'He wants to see the Fuhrer and I for one don't think he'll be happy till he does.'

'And I'm the Fuhrer?'

'In a manner of speaking, yes, sir.'

'Discombobulated, is he?'

'He's been at the magic mushrooms, sir, no doubt about that; keeps pointing at the sun saying, "the moon is hot, ja?" When I left him in the hall, sir, he was looking for Jews behind the tapestries.'

'Fungal phantasies?'

'Put it this way, sir, if the "fungal phantasies" were measles he'd have more spots than the leopard.'

'Aggressive?'

'More like the weather we've been having in the last few days, sir. One minute wet and windy then all sunshine and blue sky. One minute he's affable and giggly, the next he's goose stepping through the red-hot pokers … which is where Phyllis spotted him and I was summoned to take control. Phyllis and I may not always see eye to eye, sir but she knows where to turn when she needs help. The Nazi has fair ruined the red-hot pokers.'

'They'll pop up again. They did after the storm.'

'The storm bent them, sir. The Nazi has broken them.'

'Nothing is irreparable, Bert. It's just that some repairs take longer than others. If the red-hot pokers are broken, we'll have to be patient and wait for 'em to pop up again next year. Hitler has stuffed this young man's head full of silly notions. When we marched off to war in 1914 … rather too full of ourselves I seem to remember, we had no idea what war was like … the damage a shell can do to a man …'

'Don't think about it, sir.'

'I'm forever telling myself to do just that but sometimes … '

'I know, sir.'

'If he's as under the influence as you say he is, I wonder how susceptible he is to suggestion. Any more dead?'

'Still two, sir; lots very sick and some of those in the hospital very close to getting harps.'

On a piece of paper Bert watched Sir Charles draw the 'mystery' masts. The people who worked there kept their mouths shut. They had their own NAAFI and didn't drink in the local pubs. Even his sister had not found out their purpose. All she knew was that they had their own telephone line and had no need to use her exchange, which she thought a shame. In the village men talked about them as much as they talked about football. According to one theory they were look-out towers. If it came to war some poor bugger would have to sit up there with a pair of binoculars and a cup of tea. Those who knew the force of the prevalent north-east wind said that the tea would be cold in thirty seconds.

'What do you think, Bert?'

Bert looked at the sketch. He did not care for his employer's artistic efforts – too often they did not look like the things they were supposed to look like. They were dark and gloomy. Lady Elizabeth was of the same opinion. She always spoke her mind. You knew where you stood with Lady Elizabeth … no knives in the back from her ladyship. She'd once been less than complimentary about one of her husband's 'efforts'. He'd never forgotten Sir Charles' look of dejection. Artists, Bert had concluded, were touchy about criticism.

'Come on, Bert, what do you think?'

'You want my opinion, sir?'

'I want you to tell me if you recognise what I've drawn.'

'The masts on top of the hill, sir.'

'Good man … now, watch this.' Sir Charles sketched zig-zag flashes of lightning round the masts he'd drawn. 'That will make them look like transmitters, don't you think?' In capital letters at the top of the paper he wrote, BBC World Service. 'What do you think they might be transmitting, Bert?'

'Mrs Dale's Diary, sir.'

'That's what we want the Nazi under the influence to think. What's his name?'

'Fritz, sir.'

'When you bring him in, I'll be watching to see if my drawing catches his eye. You know what they say, Bert, a eunuch can walk down a street full of pretty girls and yawn whereas your heterosexual male, well, think back to when we were both twenty.'

'The Hitler Youth are interested in the masts, sir? The mystery masts the folk in the village call them. Nobody knows what they are for.'

'They are indeed a mystery, Bert, but ours not to reason why, what? Wheel the fanatic in, Bert.'

5

'Fritz of the Hitler Youth, sir.'

'Welcome to The Hall,' said Sir Charles.

The young man was tall, fair haired and blue eyed. A ten out of ten Aryan. A much better example of the so-called master-race than Goebbels.

In an attempt to understand why he was plucking the air in front of him like a man trying to catch a fly, Sir Charles said, 'Have you caught it?'

'Ja.'

'What is it?'

'An edelweiss.'

'Does it smell nice?'

'Heil Hitler!'

'Very pleased to meet you. May I draw your attention to my collection of chamber pots? The provenance of each one you will find written on billy-do's tied to their handles. One example,' Sir Charles read out loud, 'Circa 48BC Excavated Pharsulus. Great Caesar might have pissed in this pot – no evidence, but I like to think he did.'

The proximity of these utilities to the collected works of Shakespeare, Fielding and Smollett amused Sir Charles. The works of Milton and the Lives of the Saints he kept in a bookcase in his wife's private drawing room.

'This one might interest you. It's Meisen, a real work of art, hand painted, no transfers. We call them Jerries.'

'Why do you not call them Tommies?'

'Because we don't.'

'Heil Hitler!'

'Absolutely.'

The German opened a violin case.

'Do you play?'

'I bang out the odd tune, you know, like Sherlock Holmes.'

'Ah, the great German detective.'

'Do you play?'

'I have the perfect pitch.'

There was something about the way Fritz tuned up, the way he held the fiddle under his chin, how he closed his eyes before bringing down the bow that made Sir Charles anticipate a virtuoso performance. He was not disappointed.

'The Blue Danube,' said Sir Charles. 'Fritz, you have made me feel twenty years younger. You have made me forget that your country has invaded Poland. Let me show you this.' He picked up a chamber pot, drew the young man's attention to the floral motif on its sides. 'You know what they are?'

'Mushrooms.'

'Shamrock, my boy, shamrock. Irish shamrock. What do you know about the Irish, Fritz? Chat to them on the Nord, did you?'

'If I tell you they will shoot me.'

'If you don't tell me, I'll shoot you.'

'I want only to play the fiddle. The man who taught me to play was a Jew. He was a good man. What have the Nazis done to him? I have heard rumours.'

'Sit down, my boy.'

'I play the fiddle. When I play I forget.'

'If you tell me and Bert about the Irish, we'll let you fiddle all the day long. Isn't that right, Bert?'

'Sah!'

'I play the fiddle.'

'No, you will not. It's my fiddle and I want it back. You've taken the Sudetenland, Austria and now Poland, but you are not taking my fiddle.'

'I play the fiddle.'

'First, you spill the beans.'

'I play the fiddle.'

'No, you will not.'

Fritz brought his face close to Sir Charles' and said, 'I vill.'

Sir Charles poked him in the eye.

'I vill! I vill!' he shouted.

Memories of guests at The Hall's New Year's Eve parties using chamber pots as hats gave Bert the idea.

'Here's a bowler hat for you, bonny lad,' said Bert.

To make the chamber fit Bert used force.

'A piss pot for an arsehole, sir.'

'I can't see,' said Fritz.

'A jerry on a Jerry,' said Sir Charles. 'Well done, Bert.'

6

Bert phoned for an ambulance.

'Not another one,' said the ambulance driver.

'The poorly Germans are keeping you busy?' said Sir Charles.

'I was meaning, sir, not another one with a pisspot stuck on his head. Last week it was Mrs Hall's son.'

'It is a common occurrence?'

'More common this time of year, don't ask me why. Now then, young man.'

'Me, Fritz. Fritz play the fiddle,' said Fritz.

'Your voice not half echoes, Fritz, sounds as if you're talking through a loud hailer.'

'I want fiddle.'

'If we don't get you to hospital and get that "gusunder" off your head you won't be able to see where you're piddling and then we'll all be paddling, won't we?'

'He's under the influence,' said Sir Charles.

'In that case there's nothing for it but Bertha.'

'I want fiddle.'

7

With the sense of a job well done, Sir Charles and Bert watched the ambulance set off down The Hall's drive.

'I wonder what the medic gave him,' said Sir Charles.

'I don't know, sir, but the needle looked big.'

'And to call it Bertha. Never liked needles myself. I've seen big men faint at the sight of one. It did the trick though, it got Fritz into the blood wagon. I do hope they won't have to break the chamber pot to get it off his head. It's not one of my more valuable collectables but, still, in many ways it's a niche item. I wonder if Crozier has done a chamberpotectomy before.'

'As we both know, sir, Mr Crozier has a long history of medical experience. When he removed half of my left testicle …'

'When you were hit by a cricket ball bowled by the Reverend Fraser?'

'Yes, sir, when Mr Crozier removed half of my, as he put it, starboard propeller and told me I'd still be able to do thirty knots, his stories of the other lives he's lived scared me. If the gas hadn't knocked me out quick as it did I'd have been off that operating table quicker than a slice of tripe. And, I do wonder, sir, if he was ever in the navy. It's my port testicle he had a go at. I did try to correct him but he'd none of it … insisted on calling it my starboard propeller.'

'Be grateful he was not amputating one of your legs.'

'If he was in charge of a ship, sir, he'd end up on rocks … getting his port and starboard muddled. What will happen to Fritz, sir?'

'Lord Frederick's men will find out what game he's playing.'

'The rack, sir? Thumb screw? Or one of them coffins with nails in its lid?'

'Au contraire, Bert … five star treatment in a nice room with his other sick pals. It's a funny old room because everything the Nazis say, we'll be able to hear. I'll tell you about it later. Now that war looks all but certain, I think it time your name was put on the list of people who need to know. I spy with my little eye, Bashful approaching at speed; watch out!'

To avoid been knocked down the two men retreated up steps.

8

Lady Elizabeth's driving made Phyllis, sitting beside her ladyship in Bashful's front passenger seat, think the dangers of the kitchen – things like spitting fat and hot pan handles – to be as harmless as fairy cakes. She prepared for the anticipated abrupt stop by placing the basket she was holding between her bosom and Bashful's dashboard.

Both women were curious about the ambulance they'd seen leaving The Hall.

'Who is poorly, Charles? Has there been an accident?'

'One of the Hitler Youth has a chamber pot stuck on his head.'

'What!'

'One of the Hitler Youth has a chamber pot stuck on his head.'

'I heard the first time. How?'

Sir Charles gave an abridged explanation. He did not mention George and Jack's probable involvement, a time and place for everything, what?

'And, by the way, have you heard … Germany's invaded Poland?'

'The world is going mad. Phyllis, tell Sir Charles what you saw in the hospital.'

'Lord Frederick, sir, has lost his marbles.'

'Freddy was singing – Charles, you'll never believe this – he was singing "Forty Years On".'

'What?'

'He was singing, Charles, the Harrow song.'

'But he went to Eton.'

'When he was singing it, sir, he winked at me,' said Phyllis, 'that is, when he thought no one was looking.'

'That knock on the head has certainly affected him. Did you see Mr Crozier, Phyllis?'

'The doctor? Yes, sir. He gave Lord Frederick tablets but his Lordship only pretended to take them. When Mr Crozier wasn't looking his Lordship gave them to me. I have them here.' She produced a handkerchief. 'They're a bit soggy because they've been in his Lordship's mouth.'

'And when I was waiting outside in Bashful, Charles, I saw an ambulance bring in poorly Hitler Youth. When I made enquiries I was told they were victims of mushroom poisoning. Whatever made them eat poisonous mushrooms? Don't they know anything?'

'Mr Crozier, sir,' said Phyllis, 'didn't like it when the Hitler Youth were taken to the new ward. He said he didn't like army doctors taking over his hospital.'

'I'm sure he doesn't but we are on the brink of war. When that happens those young Germans will be our enemy.'

'Mr Crozier, sir, kept asking me questions about the new ward.'

'Curious about it, was he?'

'Like a cat at a mousehole, sir. When I said to him, "Why do you think a cook should know something about your hospital that you don't know?" he said, "I thought you might have heard rumours at The Hall". I told him if I had I wouldn't tell him, but in any case, I hadn't.'

'Sir.'

'Yes, Bert?'

'A policeman on a bicycle is approaching at a wobble, sir.'

'Sergeant Belt, sir, Kielder Police Station, temporally on special duties.'

'Bert, please show the sergeant into the study.'

'Very wise, sir,' said Sergeant Belt, 'a public place is not for the likes of what I have to tell you.'

9

'Do have a seat, Sergeant.'

'I'd rather stand, sir, if you don't mind. Since my secondment to the post office I've been horizontal too much.'

'You need a change?'

'I need a rest, sir.'

'What about a drink? Tea or something stronger?' Sir Charles took the hint. 'Bert, a whisky for the Sergeant.'

'That's very kind, sir. Emily's a lovely woman but she takes a lot out of a man.'

'I must caution you, Sergeant.'

'Caution? I'm the one what does that, sir.'

'I didn't mean "caution" in the legal sense. Before you proceed with further revelations concerning Emily, I think it best you know that Bert here is her brother.'

'Your balls aching, Sergeant?' said Bert. 'I've given you a treble. My sister's a passionate woman. I love my sister but she's a terror for the men. It's my view "passion" killed her first husband, the Post Master. I well remember what he told me when I was in the post office buying one of those tubes of sherbet with a liquorice straw. I know they are for children, sir but I like them.'

'What did he tell you?' said Sergeant Belt.

'I remember his very words: "Bert, she's too much for me". Do you understand what I'm saying, Sergeant?'

'I do. I do. And I'll tell you this, riding a bicycle doesn't help.'

'You should have phoned,' said Sir Charles.

'I would have, sir, but it was for reasons of security that I wanted to tell you face to face what the Gaelic speaker said. And, if I'm honest, I wanted time away from Emily. Even in the police force you get a day off.'

'Are you sure you won't sit?'

'I think I will, sir, if you don't mind. I'm not standing for Parliament so I don't have to pretend I've had a change of mind. A soft seat, if you have one.'

'Another whisky?'

'I shouldn't, sir.'

'But you will?'

'Think of it as ointment,' said Bert. 'May I?'

'The Garlic speaker, sir … '

'The Gaelic speaker,' said Sir Charles.

'That's what I said, sir, the Gaelic speaker.'

'Emily was right then, he was speaking Gaelic?'

'Emily was right, sir. The mystery language he was speaking was Garlic.'

'Walt Disney was someone at the railway station?'

'Yes, sir. Mickey Mouse said,' – the Sergeant took out his note book – 'Mickey Mouse said, "I have Pluto with me." Walt Disney said, "Has Pluto brought feathers for Donald Duck's nest?" Mickey Mouse said, "The good news is he's brought enough feathers to make two nests." Walt Disney said, "When might Donald Duck expect the feathers?" Mickey Mouse said, "This morning." Walt Disney said, "Thank you, Mickey Mouse." Mickey Mouse said, "Thank you, Walt Disney." Then they laughed.'

'It has to be O'Neil, sir,' said Bert. 'I saw him in the phone box and the time fits. We've got him.'

'The Gaelic speaker was speaking from the call box at the crossroads?'

'Emily said he was, sir. How she knows which wires to plug into which holes beats me. She's an amazing woman.'

'Lord Frederick's men are keeping an eye on O'Neil. When they report we'll have a better idea of what's going on. Bert, take the good Sergeant to see Phyllis.'

'Phyllis?'

'The Hall's cook.'

'Is she married?'

'Don't you go being unfaithful to my Emily,' said Bert. 'She's a soft spot for you. You're a lucky man, you are.'

'Am I?' said the sergeant patting his uniform pockets.

'Lost something?' said Sir Charles.

'My handcuffs.'

'Left them locked on a bedpost, if I know Emily,' said Bert. 'I know what she likes and I know what she's like. Tut! Tut! And you a police sergeant. Your lot locks up folk for doing things like that. Don't blush, man, you're not a bairn.'

10

'We are condoning murder,' said Lady Elizabeth.

'It was a childish prank,' said Sir Charles.

'They knew what they were doing. My grandson is a murderer. It's all Hitler's fault.'

'I disagree. The boys are not killers.'

'Jack would kill Germans.'

'It is my view that they aimed to give the Nazis no more than an upset stomach, make them vomit for a few hours, that's all. From what Marigold said the Germans stole the mushrooms. Their greed may have saved our grandson's life and Jack's.'

'You and I both know that George knows which mushrooms to pick and which to leave alone.'

'He would not be the first mushroom picker to have made a mistake. Until we speak to the boys I am assuming they are innocent. Harry and Marigold will track them down. If it comes to war it will be legal to kill Germans.'

'You make it sound as if we should give them medals.'

'Nobody should be given a medal for killing another human being.'

'You were.'

'I accepted the VC because I'm a coward. Brave on the battlefield but terrified to upset the regiment's top brass by refusing the honour. If the law made it possible for me to relinquish my title I'd go into parliament as a Labour MP.'

'I wouldn't let you.'

11

'A member of the Hitler Youth is demanding to see you, sir,' said Bert. 'He's not under the influence. He says he's Fritz's brother. Name's Gunther.'

'I wonder if he plays the violin.'

'If he does, sir, it'll be Wagner.'

'A nasty Nazi, is he?'

'Straight out of the text book, sir.'

'Show the wee laddie in, Bert.'

'Heil Hitler,' said Gunther. 'Where is my brother?'

'In hospital.'

'My brother is going to die?'

'No.'

'He did not eat the poison mushrooms?'

'Just the magic ones that make a chap blab. When Bert and I put him in the ambulance he was sounding potty.'

'Potty?'

'Not talking sense … going on about all the Irish people he knows.'

'Fritz does not know any Irish.'

'Are you saying your brother was lying?'

'It is the magic mushrooms talking, not my brother. Two of my friends are dead. The Herr Doctor says some of those who are sick may die. You have poisoned us. You are murderers. The boys wanted us to take the mushrooms.'

'The boys?'

'The two boys who live here. They are watching us all the time. The first lot of mushrooms I was not meant to steal. The second lot of mushrooms I was meant to steal. I know this now.'

'Good God, man, how many mushrooms have you stolen? Can you not collect your own?'

'The boys were cooking the killer mushrooms to tempt us. They were not going to eat them. When my friends went to say, how do you do, they ran away.'

'So your pals helped themselves and, in so doing, fatally poisoned two of their friends and made others very sick. Thank God you stopped the boys eating them.'

'I tell you, they were not going to eat them. I know. They are murderers. They, how do you say, set us up?'

'Are you seriously suggesting that two English school boys outsmarted the Hitler Youth?'

'The one with the limp is a poor specimen. The Fuhrer would have him eliminated.'

'The young man you have referred to as a "poor specimen" is my grandson.'

'I know. He told me when I took the mushrooms I was not meant to take. His friend fired an arrow at me. Look! I have a scar. The Fuhrer says a good German stands up for himself. If he is attacked he fights back.'

'I've met Herr Hitler, you know.'

'You have met the Fuhrer?'

'Once had a cup of tea with the great man. Or, rather, I had tea and he had water.'

'The Fuhrer does not drink.'

'He drinks water.'

'He does not drink stimulating beverages … that is what I meant. He does not have the need. I have never met the Fuhrer. You were impressed?'

'Very, a most interesting human being. Never met anyone like him.'

'The Fuhrer is special, ja?'

'Oh, very, as I said, I've never met anyone like him.'

'You are one of the English who think Germany and England should be friends? You are not like Mr Churchill?'

'Absolutely. The last thing I want is for England and Germany to start knocking each other's blocks off.'

'I don't understand.'

'I want us to be friends. No more wars, eh? Now, about these nasty mushrooms your friends have been eating, I'm sure we can sort something out.'

'You can bring back the dead?'

'Sadly, no, but I do think before chaps go around accusing George and Jack of murder it would be a good idea to hear their side of the story.'

'You do not know where they are?'

'No.'

'When you find them, you will tell me?'

'Why?'

'I will make them eat the mushrooms they made my friends eat.'

'That would not be a good idea.'

'You will stop me?'

'Yes. This is England, Gunther. We have laws. By the by, do you know your country has invaded Poland?'

'I did not know, but I am not surprised. Poland belongs to Germany. Many Poles speak German. If you declare war on Germany, these,' picking up Sir Charles' drawing of the masts, 'will not help you. The Fuhrer knows all about England's secret weapon. The Fuhrer has many secret weapons. You will take me in one of your motor cars to the hospital to see my brother.'

'You have a bicycle: use it. See him off the premises, Bert.'

12

'Has he gone?'

'Yes, sir.'

'Do sit down, Bert, we need to talk. Tea, or something stronger?'

His question being rhetorical, Sir Charles set about mixing two Rusty Nails.

'That should help put Hitler in his place. You know, Bert, I'm always worried Lady Elizabeth leaves the Church of England and gets the Methodist bug.'

'Her ladyship would never do that, sir.'

'One never knows. Life is so unpredictable. I mean, who would have thought that after the war to end wars we are once again teetering on the brink; which brings me to what I want to talk to you about. You know that England is preparing for war?'

'Even the three wise monkeys knows something is up, sir, what with gas masks and the army all over the place. Everyone's waiting to see what happens.'

'We all are. What I'm about to tell you, it goes without saying, goes no further. Mum's the word, Bert.'

'Mum's the word, sir.'

'To what use do you think the army is putting the Vicarage?'

'I've been told, sir … the gossip, sir, is that the soldiers stationed there have been seen mucking around with the local signposts. Everything's pointing the wrong way.'

'It's to confuse the enemy.'

'Parachutists?'

'Yes, a fifth column, the IRA, who knows? Now, to the point. The Vicarage, Bert, is not army; it is MI5. The chap in charge is Colonel Eckford … not his real name, nor is he a real colonel. He's a rather eccentric boffin. When you're talking to him, he practises spin bowling. Loves his cricket. Drives around in an army staff car, lady driver; clever fellow. He doesn't shoot. I've heard he's a vegetarian.'

'What's one of them, sir?'

'He doesn't eat meat.'

'Well, I'm blow'd. Takes all sorts. I don't know why I should be surprised, after all the things I seen in the trenches, but I am. Doesn't eat meat, eh?'

'He's a wizz with radio and electrical bits and bobs. The more I hear about him the more pleased I am that he's on our side. When it comes to winning a war, Bert, brains are as important as bombs. Earlier this year I attended secret meetings in London. On the agenda, Bert … What does Britain need to win? To win, Bert, our country needs to know what the enemy is up to. Under the pretext of bringing our Cottage Hospital's electrical wiring into the twentieth century, Colonel Eckford and his men have installed listening devices in certain wards and rooms. I might add that the regular medical staff, including senior staff such as

Mr Crozier, are not privy to these installations. MI5 take the view that the fewer people who know about them, the better.'

'His Majesty's secrets are safe with me, sir.'

'I know they are, Bert.'

'I was wondering, sir, why money was been spent on our Cottage Hospital. No one's ever been keen to spend money on it before. And the Vicarage is next door to the hospital.'

'You catch on quick, Bert. In the event of war, the plan is to bring wounded German prisoners who we think might know things we want to know up North, patch them up, make them feel snug and safe and while they are tucked up in bed listen in to their bedtime stories.'

'The people doing the listening will be in the Vicarage?'

'Yes. Colonel Eckford tells me the system has been tried and tested. It works. The "special" ward is run by army medics. I have arranged for all the sick Germans to be transferred to this ward. When Gunther meets his brother, we will be able to eavesdrop on everything they say. A much more civilised way of finding out what the enemy is thinking, Bert, than using the rack, don't you think?'

'They'll be speaking German, sir.'

'Bert, Colonel Eckford's men speak German – that is their job. Your job will be to liaise between The Hall and the Vicarage. With Lord Frederick out of action, I'm taking charge of keeping an eye on the Hitler Youth.'

'And the Irish?'

'Them as well.'

'And the Americans?'

'Them too.'

'You are going to need lots of "eyes", sir.'

'And that's just what we have, Bert. Lord Frederick's men are all over the place.'

'The road diggers, sir?'

'Yes.'

'And the gypsy caravan?'

'Probably.'

'Lots of tramps around as well, sir. I spotted one cleaning a pair of binoculars.'

'That was careless. Let us hope that the Hitler Youth are not as eagle-eyed as your good self. When you were showing young Gunther out, I phoned the Vicarage. The boffins sounded excited at the prospect of doing the real thing.'

'Wouldn't it be interesting, sir if we heard the young Nazis say bad things about Hitler.'

'It would indeed, Bert. But I don't think that is very likely. I will be most interested to hear what Gunther has to say to his brother. If I have played my cards right, Gunther now suspects Fritz of blabbing to the enemy.'

13

'Boys,' said Lady Elizabeth, 'I'm so glad you are safe. If you have done horrid things to the Hitler Youth that does not give them the right to do horrid things to you. Two wrongs never did and never will make a right. Please remove your camouflage. When I am talking to you I wish to see your faces. It is disconcerting talking to foliage. You smell of the ditch. When did you last bathe? Charles, look at them.'

'Where did you find them?' said Sir Charles.

'They found us,' said Marigold.

'Gave me quite a fright,' said Harry.

'George,' said Lady Elizabeth,' sneaking up on people is not funny. And you, Jack, you are older than George, you should know better.'

'They were sneaking up on us,' said Jack.

'We were the better sneakers,' said George. 'That's all. We won.'

'And you, Harry,' continued Lady Elizabeth, 'your bags, at the knees, are dirty.'

'It's from crawling into the boys' den.'

'Why did you do that? You are not a school boy.'

'They wanted to show me these.'

From his pockets Harry took out two Lugers.

'We knew from watching that there was something different about this tent, didn't we, George?' said Jack.

'It was apart from all the other tents,' said George, 'under a tree. The Nazis would go to this tent and come out with bags of soil.'

'Not bags, exactly. They used blankets to carry the soil. Two of them to a blanket. They dumped the soil behind bushes. When they started to take poorly, that's when we got into the tent.'

'They were so busy vomiting, they never noticed us. That's when Jack took down their flag and put up the Star of David flag. We made it out of a pillow case. In the tent we found a hole.'

'It was big enough to bury a body.'

'It looked like a grave.'

'We know what they are doing.'

'They are burying guns and explosives.'

'The guns are wrapped in oilskin.'

'How many guns are in the hole?' said Sir Charles.

'Hundreds,' said George.

'I counted them,' said Jack; 'there are twenty.'

'There was more.'

'Twenty, I counted them.'

'You might have missed some. You had to count awful fast.'

'And explosives?' said Sir Charles.

'There were German hand grenades,' said Jack.

'They looked like tins of beans stuck on wooden handles,' said George. 'Jack said they were hand grenades.'

'They are hand grenades.'

'The handles,' said Sir Charles, 'allow them to be thrown a long way.'

'Farther than our hand grenades?' said George.

'Yes, much farther.'

'Why don't we put handles on our hand grenades?'

'Pride.'

'Who are the weapons for? Why are they burying them?'

'I suspect they are for the Irish bombers.'

'The people who blew up the Assembly Rooms?'

'If they are for the Irish nationalists,' said Marigold, 'what are the Irish giving the Germans?'

'The satisfaction of knowing,' said Harry, 'that if it comes to war they have armed a force hostile to HMG; imagine a sky full of German paratroopers. When they land the Irish will be armed and ready to help them. Good God, the country is done for. Uncle Charles, what are we going to do?'

'Questions, questions,' said Lady Elizabeth. 'The question I want the boys to ask is, "Where is the bathroom?".'

'We know where the bathroom is,' said Jack. 'Don't we, George?'

'Before you go and wash,' said Sir Charles, 'I want both of you to listen to what I have to say. Germany has invaded Poland. If His Majesty's Government honours its treaty with that country, then Britain will declare war on Germany. If that happens the young Nazis camping in the Meadow Field will be our enemies.'

'Will I be able to kill them?' said Jack.

'No, definitely not. They will become prisoners of war. CB will be in charge of locking them up. These fellows are in an ugly mood. Rightly or wrongly they think you poisoned them. You do realise that two of the Hitler Youth are dead?'

'Because of the mushrooms?' said George.

'Yes.'

'We only wanted to give them bad tummies.'

'When you were not looking, George,' said Jack, 'I picked a Death Cap. I chopped it small. I fried it with the bacon. I do not care if they die. I want them to die. I am glad they are dead.'

'You laid a trap for them?' said Sir Charles.

'It only worked because they were greedy.'

'What I am going to say next is an order, do you understand? You do not have a choice. You are to stay inside The Hall. If the Hitler Youth get their hands on you I fear for your lives. I do not think you understand the danger you are in. For the moment there will be no more sleeping out under the stars. You sleep inside. When Mike returns with the Americans I will tell him to keep an eye on you. This is not a game. So far in England we have been protected from Nazi atrocities. What you did, Jack, was wrong. I understand why you did it, but it was wrong.'

'When the Nazis drop bombs on The Hall you will not say that. You won't. I know you won't. Then you will want to kill Nazis as much as I do.'

'Jack,' said Lady Elizabeth, 'come here.'

In the sanctuary of her arms he revealed what for so long he'd been hiding behind a brave front.

'I want my mother! I want my mother!' he suddenly cried out in German.

His sobs reminded Sir Charles of his own tendency to 'bubble' when he thought of the friends he'd lost in the Great War.

To minimise his embarrassment, Lady Elizabeth took Jack out of the room.

'George, go and help your grandmother,' said Sir Charles, in a quivering voice. 'I think Jack needs you.'

14

'The Americans have returned from the shoot, sir,' said Bert.

Sir Charles met his guests in The Hall's foyer.

'Gentlemen, I have dire news. Germany has attacked Poland. The Luftwaffe is bombing Warsaw.'

'While we've been shooting pheasants,' said Weinberger, 'the Nazis have been shooting Poles. What's your government going to do, Charles?'

'Will you honour your pact with Poland?' said Mancini.

'What are the French doing?' said Macdonald.

'Dithering.'

'Is London keeping you informed?'

'From private contacts I am getting the impression that no one at the top knows what to do.'

'What a bloody awful end to a wonderful day. Thank you very much, Adolf Hitler,' said Mancini.

'Did the shoot go well?' said Sir Charles.

'Excellent sport,' said Macdonald, 'excellent. Your man Mike knows his stuff.'

'Showed me a superb stag,' said Weinberger, 'said we might go after him tomorrow. I wonder if by tomorrow your country will be at war, Charles.'

'The stag lives another day because tomorrow we will be too busy killing each other to kill him. How will it all end?' said Macdonald.

'I'm gonna make a lot of money,' said Weinberger, 'that's how it will end. Wars eat oil and gas.'

'And what's up with the Hitler Youth?' said Mancini. 'There were two walking the moors … ignored the beaters; wouldn't do as they were told … came damn close to getting shot.'

'There's been an incident,' said Sir Charles. He explained.

'Boys will be boys,' said Macdonald.

'Mushrooms that make you hallucinate, interesting,' said Mancini. 'That explains the Nazi I saw talking to a rabbit hole.'

'May I suggest, gentlemen, that when you have changed we meet on the terrace,' said Sir Charles. 'Hitler's invasion of Poland has put a gun to our heads. We have much to talk about.'

'If you hear me whistling Yankee Doodle Dandy in the bathroom, Charles,' said Mancini, 'it means I'm trying to cheer myself up. It's 1914 all over again.'

'I'm gonna fill the tub to the top,' said Weinberger. 'The shoot has made my legs ache and now Hitler's gone and made my head ache.'

'If we all fill our tubs to the top,' said Macdonald, 'there'll be no hot water for O'Neil. Is he back yet, Charles?'

'Not so far as I know.'

'He doesn't drink. He doesn't shoot,' said Mancini. 'The guy's a moron. What's he been doing all day?'

'Playing golf.'

'Pity Hitler didn't play golf, take his mind off Lebensraum. "Who are we going to attack today, Mein Fuhrer? Poland? Denmark?" "Nein. The ninth hole."'

'I never thought he'd do it?' said Weinberger.

'How hard do you push a guy before he fights back?' said Macdonald.

'That question, I fear, will be answered sooner rather than later,' said Sir Charles. 'I have it on good authority that Ribbentrop has informed Hitler that England will not fight … that we have no stomach for war.'

'And you think he is wrong?'

'Yes. I think that this time Mr Hitler has pushed too hard. What is it, Bert?

'A despatch from the Vicarage, sir.'

'Take it into the study, Bert.'

'Sah!'

'Gentlemen, if you'll excuse me … drinks on the terrace as soon as convenient. No fixed time. Herr Hitler's activities have put an end to cosy domestic timetables.'

15

The despatch was a letter from Colonel Eckford.

'Charles, apologies for sending the attached handwritten but considered speed of delivery more important than presentation. Know your German is fluent so no translation either. All saves time. What these Nazis might be up to makes my hair stand on end.

Tallyho, Reg.

PS The system works. Very excited. We heard them loud and clear.'

The 'handwritten' was a verbatim transcript, in German, of a conversation between Gunther and his brother Fritz. Sir Charles was not surprised that the latter was still feeling unwell. A medical orderly, a member of MI5, had given Fritz a sedative. His 'wide awake 'brother kept shouting at him not to go to sleep. How had he got his head stuck in a piss pot? What had he told the English milord about Doyle? He was a traitor. When they got back home, brother or no brother, he would report his treachery. How do we get what the Irishman Doyle has promised us? You were in charge of the mission. It is the reason we came. You prefer music to National Socialism. Tell me what to do and I will not report your treachery. Fritz, tell me. Soon we must go home. We have given the Irish weapons. We have kept our part of the bargain. The Irish must keep their promise. We cannot return to the Fatherland without the information. Tell me what to do. Tell me. I am your brother.

Sir Charles read on. So, that's what the Hitler Youth were after. And now he knew how they were going to get it. He pondered what to do.

Bert knocked and entered.

'I bring you a conundrum, sir.'

'Sounds like a cocktail.'

'It is Mr O'Neil, sir. He has returned from his game of golf. The gentleman, sir, is a changed person. He is smiling.'

'Maybe he won. Winning means everything to some people. Americans are very competitive. If it comes to war and they think we are winning they'll join us at the last moment and claim the victory as their own.'

'I don't know if the gentleman won or lost, sir. What I do know is that the golf clubs he loved so much and wouldn't let anyone touch are no longer precious to him.'

'The end of a love affair?'

'Yes, sir. I nearly dropped my salver when he gave me them to look after. "Park the clubs, Bert," he said, "and here's a pound note for your trouble." Then he asked for a coke, with a double rum on the rocks.'

'But he doesn't drink. You checked the clubs?'

'Of course, sir. The first thing I did, soon as I had a chance.'

'And?'

'Nothing wrong with them.'

'His Mashie-Niblick?'

'Full size. I got the impression, sir, when the gentleman gave me the bag to look after that he was telling me, "Snoop as much as you like old boy, you won't find anything".'

'And he was right?'

'No, sir, he was wrong. The golf bag he has given me to look after does not smell of The Hall.'

'The Hall smells?'

'Of lavender, sir. The golf bag should smell of lavender.'

'What does it smell of?'

'Carbolic soap and damp. It's been a long time somewhere like a hardware store. It smells the way things used to smell in the trenches.'

'You think it is not the bag he was so particular about letting no one touch?'

'I know it's not, sir. Her ladyship insists that all bedrooms, drawers and cupboards are "sweet" with little bags of lavender.'

'You know, I've never noticed.'

'It's familiarity, sir. When I visit my cousin in Jarrow … his house backs onto the railway, I'll say to him, "Billy, what's that noise?" when the coal train passes. He'll say, "What noise?" He's so used to it he doesn't hear it.'

16

At dinner the sole topic of conversation was, 'Will Britain and France honour their treaty with Poland.'

'You know,' said Weinberger, 'I don't feel hungry.'

'The situation?' said Sir Charles.

'As we both know, Charles, war is a terrible thing.' He looked at Harry who was looking at Marigold. 'Young men will die.'

'If it comes to war,' said Mancini, 'you won't have to be young to die. In this war you won't even have to wear a uniform. Look how many civilians the Nazis killed when they bombed Guernica.'

'Propaganda,' said O'Neil.

'You don't believe it happened?'

'In war all sides make things up.'

'Why are you drinking? I thought you were teetotal.'

'I won at golf. I'm celebrating.'

'When the Irish killed Pruney,' said Harry, 'I didn't feel like eating. I know how you feel, Jasper. It was Uncle Charles who restored my appetite. Uncle Charles is always right, isn't he, Aunt Elizabeth?'

'I wouldn't say that,' said Lady Elizabeth. 'If it wasn't for me, your uncle would smell. He only takes a bath when I remind him.'

'Talking of "smells",' said Sir Charles, 'can anyone tell me what The Hall smells of?'

'Baking bread,' said Weinberger.

'Lavender,' said Mancini.

'My room smells of lavender,' said Marigold.

'When I come to think about it,' said Weinberger, 'so does mine.'

'Yes,' said Macdonald, 'lavender. Very pleasant.'

'Bob?'

'British Imperialism.'

'How churlish,' said Mancini, 'for once in your life, O'Neil, can you not play the game?'

'"Play the game",' said O'Neil. 'You sound English. If it comes to war, Mancini, don't forget you are an American.'

'What do you mean by that?'

'You're an anglophile.'

'So?'

'You're in love with England. When a guy's in love he does stupid things.'

'And what might your love of Ireland make you do? Do you support the Irishmen who blew up the Assembly Rooms?'

'If we had not used violence against the British in our Revolution America would still be a colony.'

'Gentlemen,' said Sir Charles, 'If Ireland is a thorn in the flesh of England, Germany is a cancer. Let us concentrate on the greater danger.'

'Hitler's problem is that he's not married,' said Lady Elizabeth, 'A married Hitler would not have invaded Poland. His wife would have told him not to be so silly. I'm so pleased that Mr Roosevelt has a wife.'

'And girlfriends,' said Mancini.

'That's gossip,' said Marigold.

'I'm sure I don't know if Mario is right or wrong, but I hope he is right. If Mr Roosevelt has a wife and girlfriends, he will be the recipient of lots of feminine advice. I am sure if it comes to war all his lady friends will tell him to help our little island. Furthermore, Marigold and I do not wish to join you men for your port and cigars.'

'We have things to do,' said Marigold.

'A woman with a husband, don't you know, Charles, will always have things to do and not enough time in which to do them. Adieu.'

'What was all that about?' said Weinberger.

Sir Charles, who knew, just shrugged.

17

Fifteen minutes later Sir Charles prised himself out of a green leather armchair with wings.

'Gentlemen,' he said, 'I do apologise but I must leave you to enjoy the port and cigars without your host.' He gulped down a glass of port. 'I must also apologise to the port. That is not, definitely not, how port should be drunk. Not to overdramatize the situation, gentlemen, but I have to see to the defence of the realm. England is preparing for war. America is not. London, don't you know, is so much closer to Berlin than New York. Harry will do the honours. Noblesse oblige, Harry.'

'What if I have to join my squadron?'

'In the Great War, Harry, I found it best not to worry about what might happen. Be patient. Wait until what might happen happens.'

'Is there anything we can do to help, Charles?' said Weinberger.

'Yes, tell America to roll up her sleeves and help the country of her birth. Failure to help will be patricide.'

On his way to Mike's cottage Sir Charles wondered if he'd gone too far. His theatricality had been a way of reminding his guests of an unpleasant truth. He wanted them to be under no illusions about the seriousness of the situation. England could not defeat Germany without American help.

18

In the cottage Lady Elizabeth, Marigold, Mike, George and Jack were waiting for him; all were sitting round a roaring fire quite unsuitable for such a warm evening. The cottage's walls were thick. Only on the hottest of days was a fire not lit. In another room Mike's wife, Margaret, could be heard washing dishes.

'Ah, Charles,' said Lady Elizabeth, 'you are here. Good. Now tell me why I am here.'

The cottage's low ceilings made her feel claustrophobic. She was used to high ceilings. Through a door she could see a tin bath hanging on a wall. George and Jack had cats on their knees. She was not a lover of cats. Cats had fleas. George and Jack would bring fleas into The Hall. What would she do if the Americans started scratching?

'Mike,' said Sir Charles, 'have you told Jack what we want him to do?'

'He's willing to do it,' said Mike, 'aren't you, Jack?'

'If it hurts the Nazis, I will do it,' said Jack.

'It is not good to be vengeful, Jack,' said Lady Elizabeth, 'it will make you constipated.'

'You will give me more syrup of the fig. I like the taste.'

'Syrup of figs is a medicine. It is not to be quaffed the way men drink beer. Charles, what have you asked the child to do? And why are you involving myself and Marigold?'

'I am not a child,' said Jack. 'I want to do it.'

'Vengeance is a leech, Jack,' continued Lady Elizabeth. 'Some of the big ones I saw in India are capable of sucking every drop of blood out of your body.'

'Will my blood make the leeches constipated?'

'You must not let the nasty things you have seen steal your childhood; that is what, in my clumsy way, I'm trying to tell you, Jack. We brought you to The Hall to give you a second chance. We did not bring you here to murder Nazis.'

'Sometimes, Elizabeth,' said Sir Charles, 'events make us grow up rather more quickly than Nature intended. The Great War stole my adolescence. It killed many of my friends.'

Lady Elizabeth sighed.

'May I suggest you sit down, Lady Elizabeth,' said Mike. 'A few cat's hairs never hurt anyone's bottom.' He dusted a cushion. 'I'll get Margaret to make us all a cup of tea. Milk and whisky?'

'Where is your good lady?'

'In the kitchen.'

'She knows her place. I suppose I'd better shut up and learn mine. Charles … I'm listening. '

'Tomorrow morning at ten o'clock a member of the Hitler Youth called Gunther will collect a parcel from the railway station's left luggage office.'

'How do you know?' said Marigold.

'MI5 has its ways and means.'

'Ways and means not to be shared with your friends? Don't look so embarrassed, Charlie. I know the rules of the game.'

'If it comes to war there will be no rules. The rule book will be thrown out of the window.' He paused. 'When I think what might be about to happen my blood runs cold. Gunther's brother should be doing the collecting but, thanks to young Jack here, he's sick.'

'Mushroom poisoning?'

'Magic mushrooms. He is hallucinating.'

'What if he recovers?'

'There is a special ward in the hospital. It is out of bounds to the regular medical chaps. Crozier doesn't like it but can do nothing about it. All the poorly Hitler Youth are in it. Believe me, they are very comfortable. It is run by MI5. Until it suits us, Fritz will be kept as woozy as a weeping willow. Bad news about my chamber pot, though – the one Bert made Fritz wear like a hat. The medics had to smash it off the blighter's head.'

'Charles,' said Lady Elizabeth, 'I do hope it wasn't one of your treasures. I know how fond you are of your collection.'

'It was not the one used by Wellington after Waterloo, if that's what you mean.'

'Thank goodness for that. I hate it when you sulk.'

'Daddy collects fossilised dinosaur turds,' said Marigold.

'Does he really,' said Sir Charles, 'how very interesting. What he collects goes into what I collect, if you see what I mean. I wonder what Freud would make of that. I digress. When Gunther sallies forth to the railway station he will be, how should I put it? Interrupted. He will never reach the railway station.'

'Dear me,' said Lady Elizabeth, 'you are not going to kill him, are you?'

'No, Elizabeth, we are not going to kill him. This is England, not Nazi Germany. Big men will overpower him.'

'Are they the men pretending to repair the road, Grandfather?' said George. 'Yes.'

'When Jack and I got too close to them they told us to "bugger off".'

'George,' said Lady Elizabeth, 'I know you are quoting but I do not approve of swearing. Mike's cottage is not a quayside tavern.'

'One of them had a gun,' said Jack. 'I knew they weren't road menders. I told you, George, but you wouldn't believe me.'

'These people are on our side,' said Sir Charles.

'They are batting for us,' said Jack. 'I have used the proper English?'

'Yes, Jack, you have used the "proper English". When they apprehend Gunther, they will take him into their road menders' hut. Inside, a medic will give the young fanatic an injection powerful enough to knock out a horse. When he is comatose he will be searched.'

'You will find the left luggage ticket,' said Jack. 'You will give it to me. I will take it to the left luggage office; that's what Mike said I had to do, didn't you, Mike?'

Mike gave a thumbs up.

'I have hit the nail on the head?'

'Yes, Jack, you have hit the nail on the head. You hand it in and get what the Nazis want. In the meantime, an ambulance will take Gunther to hospital.'

'Another case of mushroom poisoning?' said Marigold.

'I'm afraid so; terrible thing, mushroom poisoning. We have a uniform for Jack … borrowed from one of the Nazis.'

'Not from one of the dead Nazis, I hope,' said Lady Elizabeth. 'You wouldn't let Jack wear a dead man's clothes, surely?'

'The uniform is from a sick Nazi. The uniforms belonging to the two dead Nazis were much too big.'

'Otherwise you would have used them?'

'Yes.'

'Charles …'

'Have you tried on the uniform, Jack?'

'Ja. The shirt fits, good. The trousers, they are too long.'

'So,' said Lady Elizabeth, 'that is why Marigold and I are here.'

'You want us to alter the Lederhosen, Charlie?' said Marigold.

'Not personally, of course, but you will know what to do much better than we ham fisted males. And, also, I want your help in dyeing Jack's hair. I want you to make him look Aryan. Can you make him blonde? I believe you use peroxide.'

'Charles, as you well know, I do not dye my hair. I have no need to. Even at my age I am still a natural brunette; not a grey hair in sight. I think of it as a gift from Nature, you know, like Mozart being able to play the harpsichord at the age of three.'

'Don't look at me,' said Marigold. 'I'm a natural blonde. What about your wife, Mike?'

'She wears a wig … alopecia.'

'Oh, sorry.'

'I know who will know about peroxide,' said Lady Elizabeth. 'The floozie at the post office.'

19

On his way back to The Hall, Sir Charles gave himself a pat on the back. He knew all about pride before a fall but the way in which he'd involved Elizabeth and Marigold in his scheme gave him a sense of a job well done. Wheels had been set in motion.

He thought his wife's calling Emily a 'floozie' excessive but, when spirits were running high, one tended to call a spade a spade, didn't one? He hoped that they would all arrive at the Post Office in one piece. When she'd driven off from Mike's cottage Elizabeth had put her foot down. Her passengers, Marigold, Jack and George had, he recalled, all been hanging on, as the expression goes, 'for dear life'.

His next problem was the Americans. He was weary of their chatter. Bloody fence sitters. If at all possible he wished to avoid them. His inclination was to sit in front of a good fire and smoke a pipe.

At The Hall's main entrance he was met by Bert holding a satchel. This had been left in the butler's safe pair of hands by a despatch rider on a motorbike.

Both watched the despatch rider set off down The Hall's drive at a speed which suggested urgency. When its rider went out of his way to run over a pheasant, Sir Charles and Bert were philosophical.

'One fewer for the guns, sir,' said Bert. 'He delivered this, sir.'

'From the Vicarage?'

'Yes, sir.'

'Where are the Americans?'

'The Billiard Room, sir. Mr Harry is playing them for money and promises.'

'Promises?'

'If he beats them they have to promise to make America help us to fight Hitler.'

'Who is winning?'

'The last time I popped in with another bottle of whisky, Mr Harry was, sir.'

'O'Neil with them?'

'Yes, sir, but not playing. He is drunk.'

'Drunk?'

'Yes, sir.'

'Not bad for a teetotaller, don't you think?'

'I did mention earlier, sir, that since the gentleman returned from playing golf, he's been, well, sir, a different person.'

'Golf does funny things to people, Bert.'

'Yes, sir.'

'Bert, I want to avoid the Americans.'

'Let Mr Harry take the strain, sir?'

'Exactly. You go first. If you see an American, cough. I want to get to my study unobserved.'

In the study Bert said, 'A home run, sir, is what I believe the Americans would call it.'

'Well done, Bert, we made it.'

Sir Charles pulled a chair close to the fire.

'Like being back in the trenches, sir, running around with our heads down.'

'But not as dangerous.'

'Whisky, sir?'

'And one for yourself, Bert.'

'Very kind, sir. I don't mind if I do.'

'Let's see what the Vicarage has sent us.'

Sir Charles opened the despatch bag.

'It's a report on O'Neil's golfing trip. He didn't know it, Bert, but from the moment he left The Hall he was watched … well, well, well, apparently he didn't play golf.'

20

Sir Charles locked the bedroom door, climbed into bed beside his wife.

'Why did you lock the door? You never do.'

'It's to keep the Americans out.'

'They are not so bad mannered that they wouldn't knock.'

'I know that; it's more of a gesture … a metaphor if you like.'

'You might have said goodnight to them. They were asking where you were.'

'To use one of their own terms, "I'm playing hard ball". I want them to know I'm upset. Hitler's invasion of Poland has upped the stakes. It's time for them to stop pussy-footing around.'

'O'Neil's so inebriated I doubt he's able to crawl never mind pussy-foot. He's had to be carried to bed. Not bad for a so-called teetotaller.'

'What do you think he did today?'

'He played golf.'

'Wrong. When he got off the train he went into Brown's Tea Rooms. You know the place. We went there once. You had a dirty cup. Instead of heading for the golf course he stayed there over an hour. He had a ham salad, chips and three cups of coffee.'

'You had him watched?'

'Of course. When he'd finished his meal he asked a member of staff if she would look after his golf bag for an hour. He tipped her half-a-crown. He wanted to go for a stroll. The bag was heavy. His excuse for not playing was that his partner had cancelled at the last minute.'

'What did he do?'

'What he said. He went for a stroll.'

'Did he meet anyone?'

'No, filling in time by all accounts. Bert thinks the golf bag O'Neil is now using is not the one with which he arrived. Bert tells me the fellow is not at all possessive about this bag.' Sir Charles leaned out of bed, opened a drawer in a bedside table. He sniffed. 'Lavender.'

'I'm pleased, Charles, that you're smoking has not interfered with your sense of smell. It is one of my foibles that bunches of dried lavender are placed in all The Hall's drawers and cupboards. Why do you think moths have not chewed holes in your woollies? Lavender. Have you never noticed? Men! There is something else you haven't noticed.'

'Is there?'

'I'm not wearing my nighty.'

'Is it my birthday?'

'If you want it to be.'

After they'd made love Lady Elizabeth said, 'I agree with Bert. If the bag was locked in the cupboard he says it was locked in it should smell of lavender.'

They pondered this anomaly. Failing to solve it, Sir Charles broached the subject of Jack's dyed hair. His wife had already told him the details. But, like a child who could never have a favourite story read to him too many times, he wanted to hear it again.

'Emily opened the door with nothing on but a dressing gown?'

'Yes.'

'And Sergeant Belt was upstairs. He was shouting ... "Tell them to bugger off"?'

'Yes.'

'You'd interrupted something?'

'Strip poker. Emily confided to Marigold. She'd not confide in me. She thinks Americans are broad minded.'

'And you are not?'

'My position demands I set a good example. Emily thinks I should be called the Virgin Mary, that my children were conceived without your help, Charles.'

'Really?'

'Yes, really.'

'And they were on to forfeits, you said?'

'Yes.'

'I wonder what he was going to make her do. Any ideas?'

'No.'

'But she dyed Jack's hair OK?'

'She knew exactly what to do. Tart!'

'But "tarts" have their uses, don't you think? And Jack looks the part? She's not overdone it, I hope, made him look too blonde? And he's happy with his new look?'

'Charles, do stop worrying. He looks the part.'

'And he and George are sleeping at Mike's tonight?'

'Yes. There are too many ways in and out of The Hall. Mike will make a good jailer.'

'You've changed your tune. I thought you considered Mike a bad influence.'

'He is good for some things and this is one of them. Any news of Freddy?'

'The medics in charge of the "special ward" are keeping an eye on him.'

'I do hope he's going to pull through. If anything should happen to him ... I wonder, would Dot sell their villa in France. If she did I'd miss going there, awfully.'

Saturday 2nd September 1939

1

Sunshine filled the big room. Under Bert's watchful eye Weinberger and Macdonald were helping themselves to The Hall's breakfast buffet.

'Bert reminds me of a totem-pole I know outside a drug store in Oklahoma,' said Weinberger. 'One of those with eyes that follow you around. Don't even think about nicking a spoon.'

'He carries a gun. It's in case of German paratroopers,' said Macdonald.

'The Brits are touchy as hell. Ever since we arrived The Hall's been more like the OK Corral than an English country house. Look out, here comes the President's eyes and ears.'

'What you boys whispering about?' said Marigold. 'Didn't your moms tell you it was bad manners to whisper? I hope you weren't talking about me.'

'We wouldn't do that, Marigold,' said Weinberger.

'Not much you wouldn't.'

'If it comes to war,' said Macdonald, 'America will need oil, that's Jasper's department and good guys, that's me, to keep an eye on businessmen like Jasper; make sure they don't overcharge.'

'I'd be a snake in the grass to profit from a war,' said Weinberger.

'You want me to mention your names to the President?'

'That's your call, Marigold.'

'We could bribe you,' said Weinberger.

'What with? I don't need money. Daddy's a millionaire. I have power. I am …'

'We know … the eyes and ears of the President of the United States of America,' said Macdonald.

'You sleep with the President?' said Weinberger.

'Jasper, you want to be bitten by a rattlesnake?'

'No, ma'am.'

'Then get down on your knees and beg my forgiveness, or do something useful like getting me a helping of kedgeree. Where's the boss, Bert?'

'Sir Charles is on manoeuvres.' He paused. 'Marigold.'

'I'm glad you remembered we are on first name terms, Bert. Makes it easier to share confidences, don't you think?' She winked.

'He mobilising the troops?' said Macdonald.

'Kedgeree for the eyes and ears of the President,' said Weinberger.

'Thank you, Jasper.'

'You will mention my company to the President? One good deed deserves another,' said Weinberger.

'Hi!' said Macdonald. 'I'm talking. Bert, Sir Charles, is he mobilising the troops?'

'Something like that, sir. Sir Charles is dressed for war, if that is what you mean. He is wearing army battle dress.'

'And where's O'Neil?'

'Mr O'Neil, sir, is in bed with a poorly head.'

'Hangover?'

'Yes, sir. When he wakes up the gentleman's bedroom will need cleaning.'

'Vomit?'

'Yes, sir.'

'Guys who can't take it shouldn't drink. And where's Mancini?'

'Mr Mancini, sir, refused breakfast. He wished to catch an early train to Newcastle. He told me he wished to see the sun rise over the Tyne Bridge. After the Rialto he said the Tyne Bridge was the most romantic in the world. He told me every year the boss man in Venice throws a gold ring into one of its canals. This is to show that Venice is wedded to the sea. He wanted to do the same from the Tyne Bridge but thought the wasting of a gold ring not a good idea. In lieu of this sacrifice he gave our head gardener a pound note to make a posy of roses?'

'You believed that bullshit, Bert?' said Weinberger.

'No, sir.'

'What's he up to?'

'There's a woman involved,' said Macdonald.

'You bet. The only bridge Mario would go out of his way to cross would be if it led to a brothel … sorry, Marigold, men's talk.'

'Marigold knows something we don't,' said Macdonald, 'she's smiling. Why are you smiling, Marigold? You know something we don't?'

'If I did I wouldn't tell you.'

'Discretion is not something I associate with women,' said Weinberger.

'Boys, even if you gave me a Chinese burn, I wouldn't tell you.'

'Is a discreet woman a dangerous woman?' said Macdonald.

'You mean,' said Weinberger, 'a chap tells a woman a secret only when he wants it spread around and when a discreet woman doesn't do this it upsets his plans?'

'Boys, you can needle me all you want, I ain't telling you nothing.'

'What you doing today?' said Macdonald. 'Can you tell us that or is that a secret? Hitler's invasion of Poland is playing hell with Charles's itinerary.'

'I'm off fishing with Mike and Harry. You want to come? Sample the good things this country has to offer before all hell breaks loose. Tell you what … you guys catch more fish than me and I'll tell you my secret.'

'You'd tell us anything,' said Weinberger.

'You'd make something up,' said Macdonald.

'And what do we have to do if we lose?'

'I'll think of something.'

'Bet you will … come on, Marigold, tell us your secret.'

'I love it when men are curious. If women's ankles were the only part of their anatomy forbidden to be seen in public, I wonder how many dollars you guys would pay for a peek.'

'Has the President seen your ankles?' said Weinberger.

'Jasper, that plate of kedgeree you brought me, you want it over your head?'

'No, ma'am.'

'In that case, shut it.'

'That's interesting,' said Macdonald, rising a smidge out of his chair to look out of a window. 'Lady Elizabeth and her grandson are chatting to one of the Hitler Youth; proper little Nazi he looks as well, all blonde hair and badges.'

'I'll bet he's a relative,' said Weinberger. 'The British Royal family are German. Sir Charles has blue blood in his veins. They are goose stepping. The Nazi is giving them the old Sieg Heil.'

'Maybe we've missed some announcement on the BBC,' said Macdonald, 'and Hitler has backed off Poland and the Brits and Krauts are all kiss and cuddle make up. Hi, is that your secret, Marigold?'

'If that was my secret the church bells would be ringing and they ain't, are they? What do you guys want to be … voyeurs or fishermen?'

Marigold was annoyed. It had all been agreed with Charles. Lizzie's task this morning was to dress Jack like a Nazi, then keep him out of sight. It made the task she'd been allocated, of getting Weinberger and Macdonald out from under Charlie's feet, more difficult. Get your countrymen out of the way, Charlie had said. Don't make it too obvious … what about taking them fishing? We don't want them in the way when MI5 take out Gunther, do we? You are family, Marigold. The old fox knew how to win her over. As for O'Neil … he was everyone's problem.

2

At nine-forty-five am an army field telephone rang inside an Anderson air-raid shelter. The shelter, one of thousands being put up throughout England in anticipation of the worst happening, was a few yards off The Hall's main drive. Bert, who was sitting inside waiting for the call, answered. 'Right-you-are.'

At The Hall's main entrance, Jack, dressed as a member of the Hitler Youth, sat in the back of a Rolls. Beside the car stood Sir Charles, Lady Elizabeth and George, holding Moses.

'Here comes Bert,' said George. 'Over here, Bert! Over here!'

'He knows where we are,' said Sir Charles, 'no need for that … over here, Bert!'

'Charles,' said Lady Elizabeth, 'you are getting excited.'

'No, I'm not … Bert?'

'It's on, sir. Lord Frederick's men have apprehended Gunther. A chloroform pad did for him.'

'And the left luggage ticket?'

'They have it, sir.'

'It's up to us now,' said Sir Charles. 'Hop in, Bert … put your foot down.'

'Good luck, Jack,' said Lady Elizabeth.

Before turning away to stop him seeing she was crying she blew him a kiss.

'Sieg Heil!' said George.

'Heil Hitler!' said Jack. 'And look after Moses.'

'I will.'

'What's going on?' said O'Neil.

'Mr O'Neil,' said Lady Elizabeth, 'what a fright you gave me.'

'What's a member of the Hitler Youth doing in your Rolls? Where is everyone?'

'We'll discuss your problem inside.'

'My problem?'

'Seeing things … we'll talk about it over a glass of sherry. What's the matter? George, please remove Moses from Mr O'Neil's head.'

3

Bert drove the Rolls to a road mender's hut. Parked beside it was a steamroller which, at intervals, breathed out steam and water vapour, rather like a spouting whale. There was a strong smell of tar and fried bacon. Lord Frederick's men knew how to look after themselves. An army ambulance was being loaded with a body on a stretcher.

'Gunther looks happy,' said Sir Charles. 'What have you given him, laughing gas?'

'It's the chloroform, sir,' said a big road mender. 'He'll be floppy for as long as we want him to be.'

'Here's the left luggage ticket, sir.'

'Thank you, Bunny,' said Sir Charles.

'Bit like being back at the old school, sir, don't you think? Pranks and high jinks after lights out. Ha! Ha!' He twirled his moustache.

'Here's the ticket, Jack,' said Sir Charles. 'You know what to do?'

Jack nodded.

'The Nazi's bicycle, sir,' said Bunny.

'Off you go,' said Sir Charles.

'Good luck,' said Bert.

'Remember, Lord Frederick's men are everywhere. What's the matter?'

'I can't ride a bicycle,' said Jack.

'What?'

4

'I never thought I'd see the day when I used a Rolls to carry a bicycle,' said Sir Charles.

'Funny things happen in times of conflict, sir,' said Bert.

'If war breaks out CB wants to use our Rolls-Royces as ambulances. Jack, how many languages do you speak?'

'Four.'

'But you can't ride a bike? If anyone asks why we are giving you a lift say it's because you've had a puncture. I've let down one of the bike's tyres. If anyone doubts our story they'll see the flat tyre. When we get to the railway station I don't know who might be watching; best to take no chances.'

5

'When the station opened in 1870, Bert,' said Sir Charles, 'this parking space was reserved for my great-grandfather. When a coal merchant tried to usurp it great-grand-pa-pa horse whipped the poor fellow. Not something one could get away with these days, what?'

'Things have changed, sir.'

'Jack, from now on you are not "Jack" you are "Gunther". You do not know me. I am the kind gentleman who helped you when you had a puncture. Bert, untie Gunther's bicycle. Meantimes I will affect a disinterested air.'

'Like you did when you knew I was hiding behind those bushes and you and Tom went to get a hose-pipe,' said Jack.

'Was my acting not very good?'

'I knew what you were going to do.'

'And I thought I was Lawrence Olivier. When Bert gives you your bike remember … you are, Gunther. You are a member of the Hitler Youth, give him a Nazi salute.'

6

In the W H Smith's outside the station Sir Charles browsed a copy of Country Life. An article on a Tudor mansion, the home of one of his wife's cousins, caught his eye. Too many show-offs in Elizabeth's family. And what he read wasn't true. They hated dogs.

A man with a white stick who'd just bought a newspaper had to be one of Freddy's men. No doubt the fellow was bored. How long had he been on duty? Still, boredom was no excuse for a fellow stepping out of role. It was like going off-piste, dangerous. Did he have to check the racing page? Now the chump was off again, tap-tapping his way to a seat. Fingers crossed that Jack was better at acting the part of a Nazi than this fellow was at acting the part of a blind man.

'Sir Charles!'

Who was hailing him? Of all the times to pick. He felt like shouting, 'not now. I'm on a secret mission, don't you know.'

'Sir Charles,' said Mr Crozier, 'what's going on in my hospital? That ward you had refurbished, it's not Bristol Fashion. The medics who run it are flying the skull and crossbones.'

'Lord Nelson would have approved.'

'Why are the Hitler Youth being looked after in there? Why are they not under my care?'

'I'm afraid I can't tell you that.'

'It's my hospital. I have a right to know. Are we living in a police state?'

'We are on the brink of war.'

'What's that to do with it?'

'New circumstances, new laws. You should know all about that.'

'Should I?'

'You have told me many times how you were Caesar's doctor. I do hope you are not forgetting how your patient from ancient history crossed the Rubicon and changed the laws of Rome.'

'Your uniform is making you aggressive, Sir Charles. You should not forget that when the military confront the Navy, the senior service always wins.'

'Sir!' shouted Bert.

Sir Charles turned, saw Jack struggling to push his bicycle while shouldering a rucksack. It looked heavy.

'A flat tyre?' said Crozier in German.

'Ja,' said Jack.

'You must allow me to help. That's my car over there. May I suggest you leave your bicycle here? I will drive you back to your campsite. Your bicycle will be quite safe. The English are so honest, ha! I'll bring you back with a repair kit. As a good Nazi you will be able to fix a flat tyre, ja?'

'Ja.'

'Give me the rucksack.'

'If you don't mind, Crozier, I'll look after the young man,' said Sir Charles. 'Bert ... '

'Sah!'

'Take this young man to the Rolls. We are giving him a lift.'

'Sah! Follow me, young'n. And none of your Heil Hitlers, if you don't mind.' He winked. 'Mr Crozier, sir, you've a spider on your starboard lapel.'

Sir Charles wheeled the bicycle, all wobbly because of its flat tyre, to the agent whose disguise was pretending to be a blind man.

'Look after this for me, will you,' said Sir Charles, 'there's a good chap.'

'Yes, sir. How'd you know I'm not what I'm supposed to be?'

7

On their way back to The Hall Sir Charles interrogated Jack.

'Well?'

'I handed in the ticket. The man behind the counter gave me this.' He patted the rucksack.

'No questions asked?'

Jack shook his head.

'Did you see anyone watching?'

'There was someone, I think, in a room at the back. The door was open.'

'A railwayman?'

'I don't know.'

'Uncle Charles, my legs feel wobbly. I'm thirsty. I really fancy a cup of tea.'

'Jack, my boy, you are becoming an Englishman. I wonder what's in the rucksack. It's awfully heavy.' Sir Charles poked a hand under its flap. 'Feels like sand. I wonder why the Irish would give the Hitler Youth a rucksack full of sand. Bert, on our way home, stop at the Vicarage. We'll give the rucksack to the boffins. They'll find its secrets, if it has any. Do you think Crozier was there by accident?'

'I was wondering that, sir. I set him a test, sir ... told him he'd a spider on his starboard lapel ... wanted to see which way he looked.'

'Did he pass the test?'

'No, sir.'

8

'You must wear a cap, I insist,' said Lady Elizabeth. 'In England all schoolboys wear caps. You do want to be English, don't you, Jack? Sir Charles would never dream of going hatless … though I have known him not dress for dinner.'

'Is it like a uniform?' said Jack. 'Like the Nazi uniform you made me wear this morning? When will I stop being blonde? I don't like looking like a Nazi.'

'Your hair will soon return to its normal colour. And please do not say you were "made" to wear the Nazi uniform … you volunteered. He volunteered, didn't he, Charles?'

'You did it for England,' said Sir Charles. 'Jack, you are a patriot.'

'When can I wear a bowler hat? If I wore a bowler hat I'd look English.'

'You'd look silly. The cap, please, on the head. George is wearing his cap.'

'He doesn't like wearing it.'

'Yes, he does … don't you, George?'

George shrugged. Jack had a lot to learn about how to handle English memsahibs. Why didn't he just wear the cap and take it off when Grandmother wasn't around?

'I'm waiting,' said Lady Elizabeth.

'What for?' said Sir Charles.

'Charles … '

With reluctance Jack placed the cap on his head.

'I am not being pernickety, Jack, but an English schoolboy's cap is not a yarmulke. The peak should be over your eyes, not pointing at the ceiling. Please adjust … thank you. It is meant to keep your head warm.'

'It's a hot day.'

'At Rorke's Drift, English soldiers wore red tunics.'

'I don't understand.'

'Jack's not getting your drift, Elizabeth.'

'Charles, please do not try to be clever. I've been married to you for a long time. You may not think it important that George and Jack should be properly dressed for their trip to Newcastle, but I do. Whatever will Rabbi Cohen think if they turn up not wearing caps?'

'Rabbi Cohen is broad minded. He has a cupboard full of yarmulkes. At least he'll have a drink with a chap … not like the Methodists in the village. I could never be a Methodist.'

'You may have forgotten, Charles, but I have not, that after they have visited the rabbi George and Jack are taking tea with my sister. Mildred would be appalled if the boys were improperly dressed. You know what a snob her maid is.'

'She should have married.'

'Who, Mildred or the maid?'

'Both of them.'

'Mildred has Labradors.'

'You'll like the Labradors, Jack.

'What about Mildred?'

'You'll like her too.'

'And the good news, boys, is … I'm driving you to the railway station. Sir Charles and the staff are too busy preparing for war to do any chauffeuring. I know what boys are like … as soon as my back's turned you'll have your ties off and your caps in your pockets. Well, you'll have to wait until your train's left the station.'

'You're not coming to Newcastle with us?' said Jack.

'No … that's the first time you've smiled today, Jack.'

'Do Labradors like ferrets?'

'Where is Moses?'

'Here.'

'You must leave the creature here.'

'I'm not going without him. Rabbi Cohen likes him. He'll be disappointed if he doesn't see Moses.'

'You have taken Moses before? Goodness me and I never knew. On a serious note, Jack, I think it a good idea that you wear your cap in case anyone thinks this English schoolboy looks too much like a certain member of the Hitler Youth who earlier collected a rucksack from a left luggage office. Sir Charles and I have discussed the matter. We do not know how many people are helping the Hitler Youth.'

'I can take Moses?'

'Be warned … Mildred's Labradors are carnivores.'

Lady Elizabeth drove Bashful round corners on two wheels.

'Are you stepping on the gas, Grandmother?' said George.

'Please do not talk American.'

'It means, you are going fast.'

'I know what it means.'

'What's Rorke's Drift?' said Jack.

By the time Lady Elizabeth dropped the boys off at the railway station and saw them to seats in a first-class compartment, Jack knew lots about the Zulu Wars, at least from the point of view of the British.

'Hold out your hands.' Into each of their palms she pressed a florin. 'That's for sweets.'

9

'Chron-ic-al! Eve'ing Chron-ic-al!'

It was simple. The more you shouted the more papers you sold. When he was selling, he never wore his prosthetic leg, it being an indisputable fact of the commercial life that a one legged man sold more newspapers than a man with two legs.

His ambition was to sell fruit and veg. Fruit and veg sellers weren't stuck with selling just one thing, they had variety, not like him, day-in, year-out, shouting the same thing … Chron-ic-al! Eve'ing Chron-ic-al! He wasn't a jealous sort of chap but he did envy Billy, the fruit and veg seller with one arm who traded from a barrow round the corner. Billy had lost his arm at Plug Street. Colonel Churchill himself had given him a glass of brandy or so Billy said; you never knew with Billy, though. Churchill, the war monger. What was going to happen?

'Chron-ic-al! Eve'ing Chron-ic-al!'

Tonight's headline … 'Getting ready for war'. What sort of headline was that? What were folk supposed to do? He was glad that if the worst happened he'd not have to fight; he'd done his bit … felt heart sorry for the poor buggers who'd have to do what he'd done in the Great War. That was another thing. Whoever had decided to call the last conflict between Germany and England 'Great', hadn't been a part of it. Great … it had been a bloody shambles.

Before 1914 he'd sold papers standing up … like a real man, a pile of them under an arm, handing them out to customers and taking payment fast as a machine. Now, with only one leg, the other being somewhere in France, he found standing for long periods painful. He had to use a crutch or sit on the chair he carried every day to his pitch.

He wouldn't call himself a pacifist, could never be a 'conchie' but, after what he'd seen, he was against war. Was Hitler mad? In the army he'd seen officers go mad. Too many of them didn't have a lot upstairs.

'Chron-ic-al! Eve'ing Chron-ic-al! Thank you, sir. Thank you, madam.'

Trade was brisk. Lots of people, all of them worried. Would he end up selling papers wearing a tin hat? Could you sell papers wearing a gas mask?

'Chron-ic-al! Eve'ing Chron-ic-al!'

Selling newspapers was like being an actor, wasn't it? You had to put on a show. On match days you wore a black and white scarf. It was expected.

Grey's Monument, across the road from his pitch. Why was it called a 'monument' and not a 'column'? It looked like Nelson's Column in London. It was every bit as high, maybe higher but probably not, everything being bigger in London. It should have been called Grey's Column like Nelson's Column was called, well, Nelson's Column.

The Monument or Column, or whatever you wanted to call it, was part of his life. Looking at it brought back memories. Before the war had taken off his leg he'd been to its top. A memory to treasure, that. For the price of a farthing you went through a door set into its pedestal. It was a little door. To get through it you had to bend double. Inside, stone steps spiralled upwards round a central stone column, like a staircase in a castle. Light came in through slits. It was dark but not so dark you couldn't see. When he and his pal had been going up, some lasses had been coming down. What fun they'd had passing each other. Later they'd all gone to the pictures, kissing and cuddling in the back row. Now, no lass would have him. Bloody war. Left right! Left right! Chest out! Toffee nosed officers. Spiteful corporals. Stuff the army. I want my leg back.

But you had to get on with it. What was it the song said? Wrap up your troubles in an old kit-bag. His pitch was a good one. He'd always be able to make a living. His ancestors had picked the spot. Grandfather had known a thing or two about selling. The pitch was hereditary. His father and his father before him had stood on this very spot shouting, 'Chron-ic-al! Eve'ing Chron-ic-al!'

The Duke of Northumberland inherited half of Northumberland and a castle, while he got a piece of pavement. Life wasn't fair. Nevertheless, he was as proud of his inheritance as no doubt the duke was of his.

Lots of others wanted the pitch. It was a good job he had family: two brothers – too young for the last war and hopefully too old for what might be about to happen – and five male cousins, all big lads. Everyone knew the rules; those who didn't had to be taught. The young copper who was watching him would have to be taught. You never knew with the police. They were like everybody else. Some were nice, some were bastards. An older copper had introduced them last week. Why was the kid, because that's what he was, all wet behind the ears, looking at him? Did he want his free paper? What was he looking at?

'Thank you, sir. Thank you, madam.'

The last customer, a fat wife with big thingies, annoyed him. She was one of those who had to have a look at the paper she'd bought, there and then. She was stopping other customers from getting to him to buy their Chronicles. Talk about blackouts! Billy had told him about customers who'd start eating an apple before they'd paid for it. Bugger that!

'Chron-ic-al! Eve'ing Chron-ic-al!'

As he put it to himself later, what happened next was as unexpected as an office offering to carry your kitbag.

The fat woman screamed. She slapped his face. What was he supposed to have done? What was the matter with her? Why was she knocking seven bells out of her skirt? In her frantic behaviour she seemed oblivious of the fact that she was pushing and shoving his customers all over the place. She pushed him.

'Hoy! I've only got one leg.'

When they fell on top of each other she landed on his stump. The pain he experienced made him scream oaths Tyneside men only use in the company of other men.

'Don't move, madam,' said the young policeman. 'I'll get him.'

'He's not going anywhere,' said the fat woman, I'm sitting on him. My husband is a solicitor. I wish to press charges. I am making a citizen's arrest.'

She rolled her weight.

'Missus, me leg.'

'It's not your legs I'm worried about, young man, it's your hands.'

'Get her off me, will you. Hire a crane if you have to.'

'Cheek! If you are after sympathy you won't get it from me. My husband lost an eye in the war.'

'Excuse me, madam,' said the policeman, 'this is delicate work.'

'It's like having a sticking plaster removed,' said the fat woman.

'Stay still.'

'It's clinging on.'

'Don't move.'

'Oh, my god, what is it?'

'Come you here, my little beauty, don't you go biting me, I'm a country boy. You bite me, I'll bite you. I've had my policeman's eye on you for quite a while. If you was human I'd be putting the bracelets on you; you running like that up the nice lady's skirt. What a story to tell the lads back at the station. My first arrest a ferret. Your collar tells me you are someone's pet.'

10

'Something wrong?' said Lady Elizabeth.

'That was Rabbi Cohen on the phone,' said Sir Charles. 'Wants to know where Jack and George are.'

'They haven't turned up?'

'No. They should have been there an hour ago. The Rabbi was in one of his Mount Sinai moods … very voluble; accused me of denying Jack access to his cultural heritage.'

'If they are not at the synagogue, where are they?'

'I'll phone Mildred and see if they are there. They might have gone trainspotting … George was telling me he only has one more 'streak' to spot, Mallard, I think it was, and he will have seen them all … the Labradors will be ever so disappointed. Mildred has told them to expect company. They are fond of George.'

11

The policeman looked at the disc attached to the collar round the ferret's neck.

'So,' he said at last, 'you're called Moses, are you? And what's this? You been used as a carrier pigeon?'

The policeman held the struggling ferret firmly and told it, 'You ain't going anywhere, my little beauty.'

The beast's efforts to be free made it difficult for him to undo the elastic band someone had used to tie a screwed-up piece of paper to its collar.

'If you were a drunk, my boy, I'd have you flat on your back by now,' he told the ferret.

On the scrap of paper he eventually managed to free, he read: HELP Prisoners in Monument Operation SOB Jack and George.

If this Jack and George, whoever they were, hadn't mentioned Operation SOB he'd have thought their asking for help a joke. Not many people knew about Operation Spies on Bikes. It was inside info. Everyone in the Force had been told to keep an eye on any Hitler Youth they saw, to be suspicious of anyone with an Irish accent. The inspector in charge had said, 'We're calling it Operation Spies on Bikes … Operation SOB.'

Prisoners in the Monument, eh? He looked across the road, pondered the Monument the way a man who knows nothing about car engines looks under the bonnet of a car. What to do?

'What does it say?' said the fat woman. 'Someone asking for help?'

'It's written in pencil,' mused the policeman, 'a soft pencil.'

'Who do you think you are, Sherlock Holmes?'

'Hoy!' said the newspaper seller. 'I can't sit down. You've broken my chair.'

'What are you going to do about it?' said the fat woman.

'You broke it,' said the newspaper seller.

'I wasn't talking to you,' said the fat woman, 'I was talking to the constable. What are you going to do about it? I am talking about the note, young man … the note.'

The policeman eased himself up and down on his toes.

'What are you going to do about it?'

'I'm going to ask you to move on, madam.'

'I beg your pardon?'

'Be a good lady and move on. You are in danger of causing an obstruction. This here ferret's the guilty party. May I suggest an apology to the gentleman with one leg?'

'I mean, come on, missus,' said the newspaper seller, keen to assert his rights now the law was on his side. 'Do I look the sort of bloke who'd put his hand up a lady's skirt?'

The look she gave him implied she thought him capable of anything, even murder.

The policeman coughed. He'd been warned about 'domestics'; how dealing with 'she's stealing coal out of my coalhouse' could lead to unpredictable consequences.

'That ferret sitting on your helmet makes you look ridiculous,' said the fat woman.

'I am adapting to circumstances, madam,' said the policeman, 'and so should you. Do be a good lady and move on.'

To show he meant business he took out his notebook and looked her in the eye while licking the end of a pencil; that did the trick. He chose to ignore her reminding him her husband was a solicitor.

It was with a sense of a job well done that he watched her disappear into the crowd. He'd not yet had the pleasure of being cross examined by a lawyer in a court of law. Older colleagues had told him stories about lawyers. 'They twist your words ... Make sure you know your off-side from your near-side ... They make you look stupid ... We don't like them and they don't like us.' His pals would enjoy hearing how he'd told off this fat wife who'd kept boasting that her husband was a solicitor.

'Notice anything funny going on at the Monument?' he asked the newspaper seller.

'There were two kids, about the time the first edition came out, posh kids they looked, Norfolk jackets, very well dressed. One of them had blonde hair.'

'What were they doing?'

'Playing, I don't know. If they hadn't been posh kids I might have thought they were teasing the Pied Piper, that's what the local kids do. He's a rat catcher, works for the council; lots of rats around here. They come up from the river at night, you know, head straight for the fruit and veg in the Grainger Market. He keeps his traps and poisons in the Monument, at weekends he's the ticket man for folk wanting to go to its top. There's a little door lets you inside.'

'How do you know this Pied Piper?'

'He's a customer.'

'Why do kids tease him?'

'Because he's Irish. The local lads know he's a rat catcher. That's why they call him the Pied Piper. When they follow him he shouts at them in Irish. A customer told me, "That's the Gaelic he's screaming." He laughs at them when they ask him what he's saying. When I come to think about it I've not seen him for the last few days. Hi! You don't think because he's Irish he's anything to do with bombing the Assembly Rooms?'

'Take the ferret. Don't lose him, he's evidence.'

'Hoy! I'm a newspaper seller not the bloody RSPCA.'

12

The policeman thought about what to do. If this Jack and George were prisoners inside the Monument who was holding them and why? Were they the two boys seen by the newspaper seller? Had someone locked them up for a joke? This Pied Piper fellow, for example. If the IRA was involved they might be armed. He had a truncheon. Operation SOB, he never thought he'd be involved in it. How did this Jack and George know about SOB? Telling his new pals back at the station that he'd arrested a ferret would be a laugh but, if he could tell them he'd foiled an IRA kidnap … he'd be a hero, straight up the ladder into CID.

On a trial for the police football team he'd been told he should learn to pass. The sergeant in charge of the team had started calling him 'Sticky Ball'.

'Learn to pass and we'll consider you,' he'd been told.

'I scored a goal.'

'You were lucky, son; take a telling … learn to pass.'

Should he investigate without telling anyone? Keep the ball to himself. Or, be a good team player, and report his findings to Pilgrim Street? The desk sergeant was the football coach. He could hear him, 'You should be on the beat, Sticky Ball; you're not due back for another thirty minutes.'

He was a big lad, a good six foot two inches. He drew his truncheon. He'd give the door at the bottom of the Monument a good banging; that's what he'd do. He'd let whoever might be in there know he wasn't pussy-footing around.

13

Even in the short time it had taken the policeman to cross the road to the Monument the newspaper seller realised that while it was true that a one legged man sold more newspapers than a man with two legs, a one legged man with a ferret on his shoulder sold even more.

'Thank you, sir.'

'Does it have a name?'

'Moses.'

'Funny name for a weasel.'

'It's a ferret.'

'Funny name for a ferret as well.'

'Chron-ic-al!'

'Thank you, madam.'

'What's it called?'

'Moses.'

'He'll keep your neck warm. I have a stole just like that … so, I should know.'

'Chron-ic-al! Read all about it!'

'Thank you, sir.'

'That ferret on your shoulder should be a parrot, with your crutch you could be Long John Silver … black humour, I'm afraid, but you have to keep smiling, don't you?'

'You read my mind, sir, keep smiling, that's what I say to myself every hour of every day I'm standing here selling the Chronicle … keep smiling.'

'Lose it in the war?'

'Somme.'

'What happened to your chair?'

'It's a long story.'

'At Ypres I lost half my arse. At least you can have a good shit; I can't.'

He watched the fellow limp away. There should be no more wars although the prospect of one about to happen did sell newspapers.

'Chron-ic-al!'

He wondered what ferrets ate. They put them down rabbit holes, didn't they? They were meat eaters … had to be with teeth like that. He knew a butcher in the Grainger Market. He'd have to keep the animal in the pink of health. It wouldn't go down well with the customers if it looked off colour. It didn't matter if he looked starved; a hungry-looking paper seller probably sold more newspapers than a seller who looked well fed. But an animal that looked uncared for, that was different. He'd get reported to the RSCPA. People were funny about animals. But would the cost of feeding the beast be more than the extra profit it brought in?

The gunshot made him jump.

'What's that?' said a customer.

'It's a car back-firing,' said another.

'It's a gun been fired,' said the newspaper seller. 'I should know, I've heard plenty.'

'Has the war started?'

All looked towards the Monument. Someone shouted that a policeman had been shot.

14

Sir Charles and CB were in Sir Charles's study discussing what to do with the Hitler Youth if Britain declared war on Germany.

'It helps make 'em soft,' said CB, dunking a ginger snap into a mug of tea.

'Damn,' said Sir Charles, who was doing the same, 'I've lost half my biscuit.'

'I've lost a wife and daughter.'

'You sound bitter.'

'I am.'

Sir Charles studied his neighbour. They'd always been acquaintances rather than friends. He sympathised with CB, of course he did, but, there was nothing he could do to reverse what had happened. You could not bring back the dead.

'If it comes to war,' said Sir Charles, 'I'll do my best to put in a word for you. I know it means a lot to you.'

'Thank you, Charles; getting a piece of the action will take my mind off things.'

'If it comes to war the Hitler Youth will be enemy aliens.'

'You will want them rounded up?'

'A job for the Territorials, don't you think, give 'em a taste of action.'

'I'd not call rounding up a few members of the Hitler Youth "action". Your refugee boy Jack has killed two of them already. Lots of 'em are sick. If they don't come quietly I'll let them know who is boss. War or no war, I'll keep an eye on them.'

'Good man, I know I can rely on you. May I borrow your spoon? Elizabeth is always telling me I dunk for too long.'

15

Bert handed Sir Charles a sealed envelope.

'From the Vicarage?'

'Yes, sir.'

'I see it's marked TOP SECRET,' said CB. 'Do you want me to disappear?'

'Of course not. You are on our side. Bert, more ginger snaps, please.'

'Dunking accident, sir?'

'Yes.'

Sir Charles broke the envelope's seal.

'It must be important, Charles, it's marked TOP SECRET,' said CB.

'MI5 mark everything TOP SECRET?'

'Oh.'

The envelope contained about twenty postcard-size black and white photographs. Someone had been photographing the masts. Most looked as if they'd been taken from a passing car – they were blurred. Others showed the towers in close-up detail. A telephoto lens? Had someone gained access to the site?

A note explained how a thirty-five millimetre film cassette had been found in the rucksack Jack had collected from the Left Luggage Office. 'It was in an oilskin bag hidden in sand. We nearly didn't spot it. You have foiled a plot, Charles. If the Nazis had gotten their hands on these snaps we'd have been sharing the secrets of the masts with Hitler. You'll get a gong for this, Charles. The Hitler Youth weren't coming to photograph the masts, they were coming to collect photographs of them taken by the IRA. What a lot we have to tell Freddy when he gets better.'

Sir Charles handed the note to CB.

'I say, thank you. I've never read anything marked "Top Secret" before. What's special about the masts?'

'I can't tell you.'

'What sort of gong will they give you? I don't suppose there's any chance of you letting me have a slice of the action? Between you and me, Charles, I'm desperate to win a gong.'

'Your ginger snaps, sir,' said Bert. 'And, sir, as soon as you are free, Lady Elizabeth wishes to have a word.'

16

'Charles, it's like coming back to a crossword clue after walking in the garden. The walk clears one's head, so to speak and one is suddenly able to get a clue that has stumped one for hours.'

'What are you on about?'

'The man struggling to carry four Gladstone bags. I recognised his face but couldn't place him.'

'But now you have?'

'He was the man driving the car with the smashed windscreen.'

'Where'd you see him?'

'At the railway station. It was the struggle he was having to carry the four Gladstone bags that made me notice him. Who needs four Gladstone bags?'

'A man with four Gladstone bags.'

'He got in the same compartment as Jack and George.'

'I do hope this chap didn't have a "funny" ear.'

Lady Elizabeth closed her eyes. When she reopened them she was full of fresh insights.

'When he put down the Gladstone bags to open the carriage door he twiddled with an earlobe. It seemed to me like a habit. You do the same with your wedding ring.'

'Do I?'

'Yes.'

'I never knew that.'

'Ditto the man with four Gladstone bags. I'm sure he was twiddling a minor deformity.'

'You should have told me this before. If you are right the man with the four Gladstone bags could be Doyle.'

'The man who tried to kill Marigold?'

'Yes.'

'Does he have a "funny" ear?'

'Yes.'

'Nobody told me that. This is what comes of you not telling me things. Freddy does the same to Dot. I think you men like having secrets. It makes you feel important. I'm sure it does.'

'How certain are you that this fellow you saw with four Gladstone bags is who you think he is?'

'It's him. I know it's him.'

'No news from Mildred?'

'I rang five minutes ago.'

'No sign of Jack and George?'

'No.'

'What about Rabbi Cohen?'

'I rang him while you were chatting with CB.'

'The boys are not with the Rabbi?'

'No. Charles, where are they? I nearly forgot, Rabbi Cohen apologised for shouting at you.'

'That was decent of him. I am going to assume that the man with four Gladstone bags was Doyle. I will telephone the Chief Constable. I've met him a few times at civil defence meetings. I have little confidence in the fellow. He is rather too full of his own importance. He takes bribes. And that, Elizabeth, is a secret. Don't ask me how I know.'

'MI5?'

'Yes. I'll pass on to him what you've told me. If he does his job properly every policeman in the area will be on the look-out for Jack and George. On the other hand, I'll put money on them having gone to the cinema.'

'I'll bet Jack knows this man Doyle has a funny ear.'

'I would not disagree with that assumption.'

'He's a terrible eavesdropper.'

'You think he recognised Doyle?'

'Yes, the ear would be the first clue. That would set him thinking.'

'And the second?'

'If he heard Doyle speak.'

'An Irish accent?'

'Yes.'

'Would Doyle recognise Jack? When he'd collected the rucksack he told me he thought someone was watching him from the back of the Left Luggage Office.'

'But that was when he was disguised as a member of the Hitler Youth.'

'Which is why we told him to wear his cap.'

'I do hope he didn't take it off after I left. With it on he looks like an English schoolboy.'

'Let us suppose Doyle is the man with four Gladstone bags and that the boys are suspicious: what would they do?'

'They'd follow him.'

'I agree … on the other hand they might be in a cinema eating sweets.'

'I gave them money for sweets.'

'There you are then. I'll ring the Chief Constable.'

17

The rookie policeman lay on his back. His pals from the station were bending over him. Why were they looking at him through frosted glass? Why was the sky as dark a blue as his policeman's uniform?

He waved at these vague shapes a bloodied piece of paper; they had to know about Jack and George.

'It's from Moses,' he said.

'What's he say?'

'He's delirious.'

'Don't try to talk, help is on its way.'

A sergeant began the job of moving the public back. The sooner the area was cordoned off the better.

'Back you go, madam.'

'I can see blood.'

'You'll see stars if you don't move back. Move along, sir, be a good chap, this ain't a peep show, you know.'

'I'm a journalist.'

'And I'm Errol Flynn.'

'No need to take that attitude. I'm only doing my job.'

'And I'm doing mine. I'll tell you once more ... move. I'm doing my best to keep you safe. You are in the line of fire.'

'Am I?"

'Yes.'

'Would you like a sweet?'

'No, I would not. What sort are they?'

'Black bullets.'

'Go on then, but don't think you can bribe me.'

'Here's my card. I've heard a rumour that the IRA are in the Monument.'

'Move!'

'I'm on my way.'

'And so is Christmas.'

Constables with drawn truncheons stood either side of the door leading into the Monument. The hole made in it by the bullet that had hit their colleague reminded them of the danger they were in. When they looked at it muscles in their faces twitched.

They were not armed with guns but they'd have-a-go at anyone who popped his head out of the door.

When would armed colleagues arrive? They needed back-up.

Other constables tended their wounded colleague. One made a pillow for him out of his policeman's jacket.

'Moses, the ferret ... name's ... on ... collar,' said the wounded constable.

'Don't talk, laddie.'

'He's going ... damn, where's that bloody ambulance?'

18

'I'll be there in one hour, thank you,' said Sir Charles. He put the phone down. 'Bert, tell Mike to get a Rolls ready.'

On the terrace Lady Elizabeth, Harry and the Americans, except Mancini, were drinking cocktails. O'Neil was drinking water. He kept looking at Lady Elizabeth. He knew he'd a bad hangover but, dammit, he HAD seen a Nazi sitting in the back of the Rolls Royce; well, he thought he had.

'You're one helluva fisher-girl, Marigold,' said Weinberger.

'Mike gave her the best "stretch",' said Macdonald.

'Sour grapes. I out-fished you, period,' said Marigold.

'Sure you did,' said Weinberger.

'Creep!'

'I like you, Marigold. You give it out but you as sure as hell can take it. What do you say, Harry?'

'Absolutely,' said Harry.

'Harry, you and me … we are supposed to speak the same language. How come I'm not getting your drift?'

'Quit the teasing, Jasper,' said Macdonald. 'The Brits need our support, not their legs pulling.'

'We did take a lot of fish out of that river.'

'Marigold took the most.'

'I know, I got the message, she won the bet. No secrets going to be whispered into Jasper's ear.'

'If you won, Marigold, that means we lost. What's our forfeit?'

'When you get back to the States tell your fellow Americans to support this little island.'

'Hell, we were gonna do that anyway, weren't we, Bob?' He winked. 'You having another glass of water? Why are you so damn quiet?'

'Gentlemen, I do apologise,' said Sir Charles, joining his guests on the terrace, 'I seem to be always doing this … '

'You gotta go and save the country again?' said Weinberger.

'Something like that.'

'What is it this time? Anderson Shelters? Pill-Boxes? It's serious, isn't it?'

'It is rather.'

'That's Brit speak for, "too bloody true it's serious".'

'Can we help?' said Macdonald.

'Very kind of you to offer but I rather think that on this occasion even your lending us a battleship would not help.'

'Two battleships?'

Sir Charles smiled. 'Elizabeth … '

In the drawing room away from their guests Sir Charles told his wife of the dreadful possibility that George and Jack just might have been kidnapped.

'You are not holding anything back?'

He shook his head.

'I'll look after the Americans. Do what you have to do. Come here.' She kissed him. 'Good luck.'

On the terrace she said, 'My husband is a workaholic. What the army would do without him … And the war hasn't started yet. Let's have lots to drink and tease Mr O'Neil.'

Before he left Sir Charles changed into uniform. Later, much to her annoyance, Lady Elizabeth found his evening suit lying on the floor of their dressing room. It was something he'd never done before. She hoped 'events' were not going to make him untidy. She'd spent years training him.

19

Sir Charles took charge of the siege. At a meeting of senior police officers he explained that their murdered colleague had not been delirious when he'd talked about a ferret called, Moses.

'The wee beastie belongs to a Jewish refugee my wife and I are looking after at The Hall.'

'Is he Jack or George?' said the Chief Constable.

'He's Jack.'

'Doesn't sound very Jewish to me.'

The tone of voice, the smirk exchanged with a fellow officer said it all. What had the Jews done to him? Was the oaf aware of his warped thinking? Probably not.

'And who is George? Another refugee … circumcised, is he?'

'He is my grandson.'

20

A police sergeant escorted Sir Charles to Grey's Monument. On their way they picked up Mike.

'My gamekeeper,' said Sir Charles.

'Mike,' said Mike, shaking hands with the Sergeant.

'Sergeant Small,' said Sergeant Small.

'Do they call you "Tiny"?'

Mike was a big man but the sergeant was a good two inches taller.

'They did in the army. Dear me, you've parked your Rolls-Royce in the space reserved for the Chief Constable, no wonder he's in a bad mood. Once drank out of his mug in the canteen, dear me, you'd think the end of the world had come.'

21

Sergeant Small guided Sir Charles and Mike to an abandoned tramcar.

'If we go up top, sir,' said Sergeant Small, 'we'll get a good view of things.'

'What am I looking for?'

'That little door, sir, over there … set into the Monument's pedestal. The stain on the pavement is our man's blood.'

'What happened?'

'A witness says she saw PC Brown knock on that door with his truncheon. She says he shouted, "Police, come out with your hands up, you are surrounded".'

'But he was by himself?'

'Yes, sir.'

'He had no back up?'

'That is correct, sir.'

'An act of bravado.'

'Poor lad took on more than he could chew. Whoever's in there shot, blind through the door. The bullet could have gone anywhere. He was unlucky. He was a good footballer. I coach the police team. His problem was he didn't want to pass. I'd started calling him "Sticky Ball". He didn't like that. He'd beat five or six men but in the end he was always brought down.'

'Like now?'

'Yes, sir.'

'It's easy to get carried away, to think we can do more than we are capable of.'

'Like when you charged that pill box full of Germans in France, sir?'

'You were there?'

'Yes, sir.'

'I don't recognise you.'

'You were Coldstream Guards, sir and an officer. I was a private … Northumberland Fusiliers. The men cheered you.'

'I got carried away.'

'You were brave, sir.'

'No, I was angry. What I did was foolhardy.'

'You were lucky, sir.'

'I know … which is why there will be no charging of the Monument … and there is definitely someone inside?'

'Yes, sir. The witness who came to the aid of PC Brown is certain that after the shooting the culprit did not scarper, probably believed what PC Brown had shouted.'

'That he was surrounded?'

'Yes, sir.'

'And since the shooting no communication has taken place with whoever is in there?'

'That is correct, sir.'

Sir Charles studied the scene. The absence of human activity. The tall fluted column, so high one had to fling back one's head to see the statue of Earl Grey on its top … but were George and Jack in there? The note delivered by Moses was typical of Jack. The lad was nothing if not resourceful. But were they in there? The shameful murder of PC Brown … appalling, quite appalling. A murmuration of starlings blackened the sky.

If Jack and George weren't in there, where were they? If they were inside, they were hostages. The shooter or shooters could … would use them to bargain their way out. Before he decided what to do he wanted proof they were in there. One thing was certain, whoever had fired the shot was trapped. A cornered animal was unpredictable. This worried Sir Charles. The possibility that George and Jack might be executed in cold blood was something he put to the back of his mind.

He recalled what the inside of the Monument looked like. At an anniversary dinner to celebrate one hundred years of Earl Grey's passing of the 1832 Reform Act, for which deed the good people of Newcastle had subscribed to have a statue of the Earl placed on top of a 135-foot column, Sir Charles, along with other VIPs, had been taken to its top where a door led out onto a two foot wide ledge, making it possible to walk all the way round the plinth upon which the statue of the good earl stood. Any fear of falling was all in the 'head' as the walkway was fenced in by high railings. Even so, Sir Charles remembered that shuffling round that 'bloody plinth', as he called it, had made his tummy do somersaults.

The meal in the Mansion House afterwards had been rather good … roast beef and Yorkshire Puddings, nothing fancy but very well done.

22

At the Police Station, Sir Charles wrote down the following.

Experienced Negotiator to be in charge of communicating with whoever is inside the Monument.

Armed police or the military to cover the door leading into the Monument.

Provide an army field telephone for the use of whoever is in there. How to deliver?

Observers to be positioned as high up as possible in all surrounding buildings. All to be issued with binoculars.

Army field telephones to be used to link all observers with a central command post.

A listening device to be inserted through one of the Column's ventilation slits.

A photographer with a telephoto lens to be ready to snap any activity at the door. If whoever is in there shows himself, a photograph might help identify him.

Explosive charges to be ready to blast open the door.

Find out who is responsible for the day to day running of the Monument. Is the door at its top kept open or locked? Does it have a lock?

No negotiations to start until all of the above is in place.

The command post to be the tramcar.

Until proven otherwise it will be assumed that George and Jack are hostages. Their safety is our first priority.

23

Before chairing a meeting to explain his plan Sir Charles telephoned the Home Office. He reminded the Home Secretary that Lord Frederick was in hospital.

'As I am "His Majesty's Eyes and Ears in the North" I propose to be in charge of Operation Spies on Bikes.'

'Charlie, do carry on, I'm far too busy signing bits of paper authorising the building of air raid shelters. You are lucky you caught me. I'm off to Number Ten … big meeting. You can guess about what.'

'I need your help.'

'So, it seems, does everyone else in England. What is it?'

'The Chief Constable … put him right, will you, there's a good fellow. Make sure he knows I'm pulling the shots … remind him which side his bread is buttered on.'

'I'll give him a tinkle … and, Charlie, good luck.'

24

Sir Charles ignored the Chief Constable's scowls; that's what people did when they'd been told off by his old pal, the Home Secretary.

To make matters worse he announced, knowing full well that he was being mischievous, 'No smoking, if you don't mind, gentlemen. I have asthma.'

This was a lie but like all the best lies it was a little bit true. As a child he had had asthma, but not now and would himself have enjoyed a pipe.

'Room's small and there are no windows.'

Men, in groups, were like dogs, they had to know who was boss. He took particular satisfaction in watching the Chief Constable return a cigarette to its packet.

'Plenty of time for Mistress Nicotine when we've solved our problem.'

He outlined his plan. They listened. They took notes.

'To conclude,' said Sir Charles, 'until it is proven otherwise we will assume that George and Jack are in there and that they are hostages. Our priority is for their safety. As soon as the boffins get a microphone inside the Monument and we can hear what whoever is in there is saying, we will know more about what and with whom we are dealing. If the boys are in there we want to get them out alive. If their captors are the IRA, then I fear they are in real danger. Yes?'

A policeman had put up his hand.

'Surely, sir, they wouldn't hurt two young lads?'

'You mean murder them in cold blood?'

'Aye, sir.' He stroked his chin. 'I suppose I do.'

'I don't know. I fear it is a possibility. I repeat, if they are in there, their safety is our number one priority.'

'And, if they are not in there,' someone shouted from the back row, 'we'll go in and get the bastard who shot Archie.'

'I suggest, gentlemen, that we now stand and pay our respects to PC Brown.'

25

Experts in the art of eavesdropping arrived at the Monument in an olive-green army staff car. They wore army uniform but did not look like soldiers, more like civilians wearing fancy dress. Their insignia showed them all to be Majors. An army lorry following behind carried their equipment. Its driver, a little chap with a bent cigarette hanging from his bottom lip, asked a policeman, 'Any chance of a cuppa, mate?'

'Jackson,' said one of the Majors, 'be a good chap and start unloading our stuff. It's to go in the tramcar, over there. That's going to be "home" for as long as this job takes.'

'There's the tramcar, Jackson,' said the policeman. 'At the double, Jackson, you heard what the nice man said.'

'What about giving him a hand?' said the Major. 'Some of those boxes are heavy.'

'I'm an officer of the law, sir, not a porter.'

'PC thirty-eight,' said Sergeant Small, 'give the soldier a hand. We're all in this together. Too young for the last bash, were you? You've a lot to learn. If you show willing I'll think about putting you on the football team.'

'I don't like football, Sarge.'

'That's not my fault, now, get lifting, that's an order.'

'I do believe I've found a coccinella septempunctata,' said the Major. He studied the ladybird he held in the palm of a hand. 'It has seven spots, look …'

The soldier and the policeman exchanged glances. They had found a common enemy, an upper class twit.

26

Less than fifteen yards from the Monument's bullet scarred door soldiers had built a redoubt made of sandbags. In it stood an army marksman and a civilian photographer.

'What you shooting with?' said the marksman.

'Contax, thirty-five mil, adapted to take a two hundred lens.'

'That like looking through binoculars?'

'If the shooter shows himself I'll be able to tell you if he needs a shave.'

'German camera?'

'Yes, rifle?'

'Mauser, telescopic sights.'

'German?'

'Yes … funny old world, isn't it? We like to use what Jerry makes but still can't be friends with him.'

'My wife's like that. She likes my photographs but doesn't like me being away from home to take them, which I have to, especially my artistic studies.'

'Artistic studies?'

'Nudes?'

'Women? You dirty old bugger … any samples?'

An army field telephone rang.

'Sir,' said the marksman.

'What's happening?' said the photographer.

'Fire engine's on its way. There it is now.'

'It's not ringing its bell,' said the photographer.

'It's not a fire,' said the marksman.

'What's it here for then?'

'Because it has a long ladder.'

'Ladder's not long enough to reach the top of the Monument … no ladder's long enough to do that.'

'Look through these.' The marksman handed the photographer binoculars. 'Can you see little slits every now and then up the side of the column?'

'Aye.'

'Someone's going to climb up a ladder and put a microphone through one of them, then the "listeners" in the tramcar …'

'The Command Post?'

'You catch on quick … will be able to hear what the nasty bugger who shot the copper is saying.'

'I once used a fire engine in one of my artistic studies. A woman wearing a fireman's helmet can be very erotic if you get the light right.'

The field telephone rang.

'Sir …'

'Testing, testing, testing. Abel, Baker, Charlie … one, two, three … '

27

'I haven't got eyes in my arse,' said the soldier walking backwards down the aisle between the seats on the tramcar's bottom deck, 'so watch your backs.'

He was unspooling cable. He'd done this all the way from the Monument, and was, by now, fed up. His back ached and he'd kill a cat for a cup of tea.

'You're just like a spider, Corky, spinning its web,' said a corporal. 'Bet you didn't go up that fire engine's ladder to put the microphone on the other end of that cable inside the Monument?'

'I'm a signaller, corporal, not a steeplejack.'

'If it comes to war, Corky, we're going to lose, and you know why, Corky? Cos we've got coppers what won't help unload a lorry and a signaller who won't climb ladders. It's called "demarcation", and it's got to stop. Give me the cable, donkey.'

'You said I was a spider before.'

'You are whatever I say you are, Corky.'

'Anyone got a brew going?'

'Shop doorway over there, the one selling bras … big urn on a paraffin stove. Army issue, ours, but the police are in charge of it. I've always said you can't keep flies off a turd. You'll have to ask nice.'

'Thanks, Corp.'

'You are going for tea, Corky, because we all want one.'

'How many?'

'Count.'

'One, two, three …'

'Do it in your head, Corky, not out loud like a five year old. When the boffins start listening to what's going on inside that Monument we'll need hush, now, piss off … milk and sugar for everyone.'

28

The tramcar's top deck gave Sir Charles the perfect vantage point. He could see the door sunk into the plinth upon which the column rested. His ad hoc command centre had been a good choice. Beside him stood Mike.

A member of the 'Eavesdropping' team informed them that quite soon they would be able to hear what was going on inside the Monument.

'We not only want to hear him off-the-record,' said Sir Charles, 'we want to know who is in there with him and we want to talk to him … find out who he is, what he wants.'

From their vantage point they watched an officer and a private soldier approach the Monument's door. One was carrying a field telephone, the other its connecting cable. The officer prodded the telephone towards the door with his swagger stick. If the killer fired 'blind' he would not be a target. When the telephone slid on a pool of the dead policeman's blood he stopped prodding.

'It's like offering a tiger a lump of raw meat,' said Mike.

'Now comes the tricky part,' said Sir Charles.

With an outstretched arm, his body out of the line of fire, the officer rapped on the door with his swagger stick. In the absence of people and traffic, the rapping sounded loud. Everyone waited. How would the murderer react? When no shots splintered the door, the officer delivered his message.

Sir Charles and Mike were too far away to hear what was said but knew the courier's brief. When he'd established that the person inside knew he was there and was prepared to listen the gist of his message was: The forces of law and order wish to parley. For that purpose an army field telephone is outside the door. It is for you to use. The choice is yours.

'Now we wait,' said Sir Charles.

29

Sir Charles knew the rules of the game; as a leader it was your job to look confident. A dithering fellow at the tiller, looking fretful and worried, was no good to anyone. It was for this reason he forced himself to stand still, to resist the temptation to run up and down the tramcar's stairs for no other reason than to be on the move. Being on the move calmed a chap; trouble was it rather gave the game away that a chap was worried.

'We'll soon know if they are in there,' said Mike.

'That will be a step in the right direction,' said Sir Charles. 'Then we'll know where we stand. Is that a newspaper seller I hear?'

To hear better and to give himself a legitimate reason to be on the move, he took himself down the tramcar's stairs and out onto its platform. If Jack and George were prisoners inside the Monument, what should he do? When should he inform Elizabeth and his daughter of the bad news? Apart from that newspaper seller shouting, 'Chron-ic-al! Eve'ing Chron-ic-al!' everything was so bloody quiet, no passing traffic, no pedestrians. The peace before the storm. Such a pity Hitler couldn't be cordoned off the way the forces of law and order had cordoned off the Monument.

'Interesting, Mike, don't you think, how normal life insists on carrying on … a chap selling newspapers while we bite our nails, a policeman dead … did he have family?'

'A wife, I believe. I heard some of his colleagues talking.'

'Poor woman … yet life carries on. A fellow selling newspapers, not a care in the world, while it is more than likely that my grandson and Jack are in mortal danger.'

'Reminds me of that farmer in France – didn't matter what Fritz fired at him, nothing stopped him milking his cows. Do you want me to tell the newspaper seller to shut up?'

'No, he gives me hope. It is the run of the mill things in life that are worth fighting for.'

'Sir!'

'Yes, sergeant, good news or bad?'

'The good news, sir, is that the microphone inside the Monument is operational. The Major doing the listening, sir, says reception's so good that if a spider wearing slippers went walkabout he'd hear it.'

'The bad news?'

'Three people inside, sir, definitely … a man, Irish accent and two young lads by the sound of them. If there's anyone else in there the Major says they're keeping awful quiet.'

'Thank you, Sergeant.'

'What now?' said Mike.

'We wait for the Irishman to take up our offer of the field telephone.'

'IRA?'

'It looks like it. We must get him to talk, Mike, we really must.'

'What if he doesn't take up our offer? What if he doesn't want to talk?'

'For the moment I am assuming that he will. A chap who does not wish to negotiate is capable of anything. We must get him to talk.'

30

'Your binoculars, Mike,' said Sir Charles.

'Not a good idea,' said Mike.

'Give them to me.'

What Sir Charles saw in close-up made him want to scream his regiment's battle cry and fling himself at the enemy. He saw George crawling out of the Monument's door, on a lead, like a dog.

His captor was not going to make himself a target for a marksman. But he did want the field telephone which meant he wanted to talk, which meant he wanted to negotiate, which meant he wanted to live. Despite the fellow's objectionable method of getting his hands on it, all in all, what was happening was a positive development. He must not be allowed to know that his wild shot through the door had killed a policeman. The thought of a noose round his neck might make him think he'd nothing to lose.

Would he make use of the field telephone? If he did, what would he want? The Negotiator was one of the boffins from the Vicarage. Sir Charles had spoken to him and thought him up to the job. A lot rested on that man's shoulders.

Sir Charles had wanted to take on the role himself. Mike had reminded him of his emotional involvement. 'Not a good idea.' His advice had been accepted.

George's face looked bruised, swollen … his hair, shiny, blood from a head wound? And where was Jack? Why had George been chosen to come out and pick up the field telephone? Was Jack, heaven forbid, in a worse physical condition? He was the bigger of the two, he'd pose a greater physical threat to his captor, be much more difficult to control. Jack knew from bitter personal experience how low his fellow men could stoop. He would know his captor was quite capable of executing him and George. He'd seen executions. To him killing someone in cold blood was not an abstract concept.

The note asking for help had been in Jack's handwriting. Sir Charles pondered what he knew of the lad's turbulent past. To survive rampaging Nazis lusting for Jewish blood, he'd broken the law of his ancestors and eaten pork. His sacrilege had enabled him to survive. He was a survivor; that was the point. When you fought back there was always a chance you might win.

Unable to watch more, Sir Charles handed Mike the binoculars.

'He's picked up the phone,' said Mike. 'He's taking it inside. He's been pulled in. The poor wee lad is exhausted.'

'You say he's been dragged in?'

'Yes.'

'The fellow doing the pulling will regret this.'

'He's inside now. God be with the wee fella … door's closing.'

The two big men, master and servant, used to sharing the dangers of the battlefield, companions for as long as they could remember, looked at each other. Words were superfluous. They both loved Jack and George with all their hearts and souls, though they would have been reluctant to admit this to anyone other than their wives. They were not given to showing their feelings. Anyone who did not know them might think them callous. They were men with the ability to stay calm under pressure. They'd been together in many a tight spot, never giving in, their ability to innovate and Lady Luck the reason they were both still alive. Without speaking they took the stairs down to the beating heart of the command centre.

Desks had been improvised by placing planks of wood across the tops of seats. On them boffins from the Vicarage had placed field telephones and other specialised pieces of equipment. The Negotiator, an army major, who would be responsible for talking to whoever was inside the Monument, had his arms folded, his head sunk into his chest. Like everyone else he was waiting for the Irishman to ring. Next to him sat the Eavesdropper, also a major. His headphones were plugged into a receiver joined by cable to the microphone inside the Monument. Other field telephones were connected to various observers, police headquarters and the marksman and photographer in the redoubt. The connecting cables spilled over seats, disappeared through windows and cluttered the car's central aisle. The Negotiator and Eavesdropper shook their heads to let Sir Charles know they had nothing to report.

31

Sir Charles knew a lot about sieges both in theory and in practice. In times of yore they'd gone on for months, even years. But for how long would this siege last? One day? Two days? Or would it be measured in hours? One thing was certain there would be nothing medieval about it. The Chief Constable was keen to use force. 'My lads are itching to get their hands on the bastard who shot Brown,' he'd explained. 'You see, Sir Charles, when one of our own gets hurt we do something about it.'

'Cup of tea, sir?' said Sergeant Small.

'Thank you, Sergeant.'

'Is the plan to ring him, sir?'

'I'd prefer him to take the initiative. On the other hand we can't wait for ever.'

'I understand, sir.'

'We've got to get the boys out safe. If they weren't in there I'd give your Chief Constable carte blanche.'

'I wouldn't do that, sir, he's liable to blow up the Monument and then our canny Newcastle wouldn't have its very own Nelson's Column.'

'Sledge hammer man, is he?'

'If you showed him a walnut he'd think steamroller.'

'That bad, not a negotiator?'

'No, sir.'

'Are you trying to tell me something?'

'In a roundabout way, sir, yes.'

'I will watch my back ... in the meantime we negotiate or at least try to. I wish the blighter would ring.'

'He's nothing to lose, sir, has he?'

'That is why I am so worried about the boys.'

'If we take him alive he'll swing for murdering Archie ... either way, he's a dead man.'

'By all accounts he did shoot blind. He wasn't aiming to kill anyone ... scare them perhaps, but not kill.'

'Manslaughter?'

'It's a possibility.'

'The Force wouldn't like that. The Big White Chief already hates lawyers.'

'If he doesn't swing for murdering your colleague ... which, by the way we are keeping him in the dark about ... we don't want him to think his position is utterly hopeless, the State may well take his life for his involvement in the murder of one of His Majesty's Secret Agents ... not to mention the bombing of the Assembly Rooms.'

'Is that what you are, sir, a secret agent?'

'I'm just an old man brought out of retirement to help make our dear England a safer place in which to live. My wife tells me I wouldn't hurt a spider.'

'I wouldn't like to cross you, sir, begging your pardon.'

'I will take that as a compliment … you make the tea?'

'Yes, sir.'

'It's very good.'

32

'Sir!' exclaimed the Eavesdropper. 'I've heard a click. It sounds to me that he might be going to give us a call.'

All eyes went to the Negotiator's telephone. It rang.

'It's him, sir,' said the Negotiator, 'he wants to talk.'

'At last,' said Mike, 'the fox has broken its cover.'

In planning for this eventuality Sir Charles had explained to his team, 'We don't want him to think we are so anxious that we are at his beck and call. He must not be allowed to forget that he's in a tight spot. Unless he's a psychopath, God forbid, and devoid of all feeling, his nerves will already be stretched to breaking point. We take every opportunity to squeeze him but not so hard that the pips squeak. We don't want to nudge him towards doing something silly. Judging his state of mind will be crucial if we are to get George and Jack out alive. Without hostages he's a busted flush. He must not be allowed to forget that.'

The Negotiator looked at the ringing phone. He counted the rings … one … two. The plan was to answer it on the fifth ring.

'He's shouting, sir,' said the Eavesdropper. 'He's shouting, "Holy Mary, Mother of God." He's very agitated.'

The Negotiator picked up the phone. 'Sorry to have kept you waiting, I was making a cup of tea … he's rung off, sir.'

'Did he speak?'

'Shouted at me in a foreign language, sir.'

'Gaelic?'

'Whatever the language, sir, it sounded like Anglo-Saxon to me, sir, if you take my drift, sir. Our Irishman is on a short fuse.'

'We'd better calm him down.'

'Shall I ring him, sir?'

'What's happening inside?'

While he strained to make sense of all he was hearing through the headphones clamped to his ears, the Eavesdropper handed Sir Charles a clipboard. 'Boy … Jack? Jack are you hurt? Heavy breathing … shouting. Someone being punched?'

'Ring him,' said Sir Charles.

'It's ringing,' said the Eavesdropper. 'He's telling Jack to answer it. I think Jack is hurt. He's giving Jack instructions. "You tell the Englishman … tell him … tell him if I don't get what I want, I'm going to blow your brains out. In the name of the Holy Virgin Mary I'm not joking. Tell them about the explosives. If I want to I can blow the Monument. I'm not scared to die for the cause. Answer it. If you don't you'll know what you'll get." He's shouting, sir. "Answer it! Answer it! Damn you." Jack, I think it's Jack, is screaming. Someone is being hit. The other boy … George, I think it's George, is shouting, "Stop it! Stop it!" The Irishman is repeating his demand. A revolver is being cocked. "If you put the gun down I'll do what you want." I think Jack is going to answer.'

At this point Sir Charles picked up a spare pair of headphones pre-jacked into the Eavesdropper's receiver. He closed his eyes and listened on one headphone.

'To whom am I talking?' said the Negotiator.

'Jack.'

'Go ahead, Jack, I am listening.'

'The man who is holding me and George prisoner has told me what to say.'

'Can you tell me his name?'

'I don't know his name. He says if you do not give him what he wants he will blow my brains out.'

'Do you believe him?'

'Yes. He says he can blow up the Monument.'

'What does he want?'

'I want food and water,' said a man's voice, a rough voice, a voice full of bravado, a bully's voice, 'and a car ... a car with a chauffeur to take me and the boys ... the boys with a gun to their heads, to Woolsington Aerodrome. Will you be understanding what I'm saying? You will fly me to Dublin. If you want the boys to live you will fly me to Dublin ... if you want them to live that's what you'll do. It seems to me that you and me ... both of us are in a corner ... what's your name?'

'William.'

'King Billy, eh? Trust the English to jump in with both feet. Your bosses should have picked someone with a good Irish name or told you to lie. If I'd been talking to a "Seamus", I might have dropped my guard. One up to myself, I'm thinking. Are you still there?'

'Yes.'

'You've not gone off to make a cup of tea?'

'No. Do you have a name? It's easier to talk to someone when you know their name.'

'You can call me Mr Ireland and don't forget the 'mister'. It would never do for you and me to get too friendly, now, would it?'

'I would like to be your friend.'

'Real friends don't want to put their friends in jail ... that's what you'd like to do to me, William ... you'd like to put me in a dark, damp cell and leave me there to rot. Have you the gallows ready for me? What's your rank?'

'Negotiator.'

'Army or civilian?'

'Army.'

'Pips or stripes?'

'Pips but they are honorary. I don't have to have my hair cut short.'

'Special forces? Surveillance?'

'Maybe.'

'Oxford or Cambridge?'

'Both actually and yourself, IRA?'

'Maybe … but you wear a soldier's uniform?'

'Yes, and I part my hair down the middle.'

'William, if I met you on a dark night in Dublin wearing that uniform, I'd kill you … do you understand? I'd kill you. I'm a soldier and you, King Billy, are my enemy.'

'I understand your point of view, Mr Ireland, I really do. You said before that in your opinion both of us were in, and I quote, "tight spots". What did you mean by that? I don't feel like that.'

'Jack and George are in "tight spots". Would you like to swap places with them? Soldiers I execute with a bullet … I make them kneel, get them to look down, that's the best way … the quickest way. Now, William, I hope you are listening … are you listening, William?'

'I'm listening.'

'I'm going to explain to you why you are in a "tight spot". Your "tight spot", William, is finding out if I'm bluffing when I say, if I don't get what I want I will kill the boys. You see I know who they are. They didn't want to tell me, but I persuaded them … you want to know how I persuaded them?'

'Only if you want to tell me.'

'If I told you, you'd be sick … if you were sick you might stop listening, so I won't tell you … except they didn't enjoy it. They were too well dressed to be anything but toffs … live at The Hall, don't they? And George, well, he's a VIP, isn't he? Grandson of some English milord called Sir Charles, isn't he? Couldn't shut the cripple up about his ancestors … probably has relatives with a big house in the Pale, an Anglo-Irish family with blood on their hands. Are you hearing the bitterness in my voice? I hope so. You see, I wasn't bluffing when I said I knew who my hostages are … get it into your arrogant English skull that I'm not a bluffer, that I mean what I say. And next time I ring you'll be answering straight away … don't be playing silly buggers with me. Jack will be the first to die … one bullet, bang! George, what a very English name … after your king? But not my king … George, I'll keep to last. He's important, isn't he? I'll be looking out for the victuals. No funny stuff. No poison. George and Jack will be eating first.'

'He's rung off, sir,' said the Negotiator.

Sir Charles nodded. The inside of the Monument echoed sound. He kept listening because he wanted to hear his grandson's voice. He heard sniffles, sighs, the shuffling noises people make when they are uncomfortable, for example when they are stuck in a seat in an overcrowded railway carriage and want to move but are unable to do so. Then … a scream, an animal cry from the Irishman. The only other time Sir Charles had heard such a poignant bellow had been from a condemned man, a private soldier, in the hours before he'd been shot at dawn, for lack of moral fibre. The Irishman knew he was in serious trouble, no doubt about that. Sir Charles pressed the headphone to his ear. The Eavesdropper signed to everyone to be quiet. The Irishman was talking to George and Jack. 'I have a son in Ireland. He's close enough the same age as you lads … I don't want to but, I'll kill you if I have to. I will make you famous. Would you like to be famous? You will go down in history as martyrs. They gave their lives that all the people of Ireland might have their liberty. He lives with his mother in Belfast … my little Sean. His mother's English … me, of all people, marrying an English colleen but she looks Irish … black hair and blue eyes, dark as blue sky reflected in bog water … I'll kill you if I have to. No Englishman is going to put a noose round my neck. I'll die for the cause … you see if I'm not prepared to … damn you, why did you have to … what was that?'

What had frightened the fellow? Sir Charles looked towards the Monument; all was still and quiet. Perhaps the Irishman's imagination was beginning to get the better of him. Perhaps a shaft of light had made a shadow on a wall that looked like a noose. Perhaps Jack had been playing shadow puppets. It was the sort of thing he'd do.

The Irishman's soliloquy had provided Sir Charles and his team with valuable information. He had a son called Sean, did he? A family home in Belfast. In the meantime, arrangements were put in place to give the fellow the victuals he'd demanded. The aeroplane he'd asked for was another matter; nevertheless, preliminary steps were taken to make one available.

33

'Sergeant Small,' said Sir Charles.

'Sir?'

'Grateful if you will tell the constable over yonder to let that soldier into the cordon sanitaire. The one with the bicycle. By the looks of him he's a despatch rider ... might have something important for me.'

'At the double, sir.'

The despatch rider approached the tramcar pushing a red bicycle of the sort used by employees of the GPO for delivering telegrams.

'I don't think you need a crash helmet and goggles to ride a push bike, son,' said Sergeant Small; 'you taking the piss?'

The despatch rider was very young, very thin and not very tall. Sergeant Small knew the type well. He sighed. He was dealing with a Tyneside Cork.

'What's your name, soldier?' said Sir Charles.

'Bell, sir.'

'What's the problem, Bell?'

'The policeman, him over there, the fat one, doesn't believe I borrowed it.' He looked at the bike. 'As if me, an army despatch rider would steal a pedal bike. I ask you, sir, would a millionaire bend his back to pick up a penny? Course he wouldn't. It just wouldn't happen, sir, would it?'

'Sergeant Small?'

'A matter of opinion, sir.'

'How long have you been in the army, Bell?'

'Three weeks, sir.'

'You want to do your bit, eh?'

'I like riding motorbikes, sir.'

'Is that why you joined?'

'Yes, sir.'

'And the army has given you a pedal bike?'

'I had a motorbike until a few hours ago, sir. I was delivering top secret documents to this posh place called The Hall ... had to use a map to find it. No good using the signposts, they're all pointing the wrong way ... that's in case we're invaded, it's to confuse the enemy. I'll tell you this, sir, it confused me.'

'What did you make of this place ... what did you say it was called?'

'The Hall, sir ... lovely gardens, sir. The posh geezer what owns it grows melons.'

'Who told you that? Never mind,' said Sir Charles. 'Were you made welcome?'

'Oh aye, Cook give's a mug of tea and a pasty and a bloke with a broken nose give's a clip round the ear 'cos I didn't call him sir.'

'Was he the Lord of the Manor?'

'Nar, one of the flunkies … said he'd been in the army and that I should keep my bad manners for the Germans and my good manners for God fearing Englishmen like himself. Then, when I did call him sir, he said I was saying it the wrong way. "You say sar! In the army," he said.'

'I still do not understand what this has to do with you losing your motorbike.'

'I didn't lose it, sir, it was taken off me by an officer. I was obeying orders, sir. It was just after I'd left The Hall, he flagged me down. If I hadn't stopped I'd have killed him. Despatch riders don't hang about, sir. I was on full throttle. When I stopped I took a lot of rubber off my back tyre. He said he was commandeering my motorbike because he needed it to chase Nazis. I asked him if Hitler had landed paratroopers. He said the Nazi he was after was riding a bicycle and was a member of the Hitler Youth. He ordered me to take him to this army place called the Vicarage. He rode pillion. He was very proper about his commandeering, sir. At the Vicarage he got me a travel warrant to get the train back to Newcastle.'

'The officer who commandeered your motorbike, did he have a name?'

'An officer at the Vicarage, sir, called him CB. When I gets back to my barracks in Newcastle, sir, there's a flap on. I'm told to take this despatch to Grey's Monument, something about a siege. It's two miles away. Nobody would listen when I said my motorbike had been commandeered. What am I supposed to do? Walk. "Is it urgent?" I asks. "Too bloody true it is," I was told. So, that's when I did a deal with the telegraph lad. The way I look at it, sir, is, we both work for the government, only difference is, his enemies are dogs while mine might soon be the whole bloody German army. Do you think it will come to war, sir?'

'Yes.'

'Bloody hell, sir, I didn't think you'd say that.'

'What have you got for me that's so urgent?'

He handed Sir Charles a pouch.

'Thank you and, by the by, I think it would be a good idea if you returned the bicycle to its owner. He's over there, if I'm not mistaken, waving a golf club. He looks angry. I do believe if it wasn't for the policeman restraining him he'd be over here doing goodness knows what damage to your good self.'

'Threatening a member of His Majesty's Armed Forces I'd call that, sir. You're a policeman, sergeant, you should lock him up … the Wild Animals Act of 1823. He's looked in the golf bag, that's why he's angry. "While I borrow your bike," I told him, "you play with the golf clubs." That was the deal.'

'Are you a golfer?'

'Used to caddy for the toffs, sir.'

'But you have, from what you have just said, a set of clubs.'

'Found them, sir, didn't I? Strangest thing I ever saw, apart that is from the chicken with two heads at the Town Moor Fair last year … cost me a penny to get in. The showman said, "That's cheap, laddie, it's only half-pence a head." I didn't laugh … showmen can talk, can't they? They've got the gift of the gab, haven't they? I was walking to the railway station, looking at my travel warrant as if it wasn't real. It's not far on a motorbike but a long way on Shank's Pony. It was hot. I needed a rest. I'm young and fit but I'm not in-de-fat-ig-able.'

'And you didn't want to get back to your barracks too early?' said Mike.

'Aye, maybe, sir, but I was knackered. Anyways, there I was sat under this tree, a nice shady spot, Garden of Eden, you might say, when this car stops. Bloke, gentleman, I mean, sir, gets out ... he didn't see me but I saw him ... starts to act shifty, like to make sure no one's watching what he's up to ... opens the car's boot and pulls out a golf bag with a little hat on its top to stop the clubs falling out. I knew he was up to no good because he wasn't on a golf course, was he? He keeps looking round ... his neck didn't need oiling, I'll tell you that. I flatten meself into the ground, 'cos I'm curious what he's up to. Then, what's he go and do? He goes and flings the golf bag ... full of clubs as well, mind, not empty, over a hedge, jumps back into the car and off he goes, leaving me scratching my head like when I had baby eczema. I had a helluva job climbing the hedge, but I remembered that story about Robert the Bruce and the spider, so I didn't give up. When I got the bag I thought, finders, keepers. I carried it all the way to the railway station. How a camel manages to carry its humps, I don't know. Station Master ... didn't like him, don't know why, kept touching the bag; "hands off," I said. Couldn't keep his hands off it. I thought if he's like that with a golf bag, heaven help his missus. Then I got to thinking, funny, I thought, one bloke wants to get rid of the golf bag and, now, this geezer is all interested in it. He'd have taken it off me, if I'd let him. I told him straight, "This belongs to an officer, it's more than my life's worth to let it out of my sight." I don't think he believed me but then the Newcastle train came in and I was off. It was back in the barracks that I found out what the telegram lad's found out.'

'And what might that be?' said Sir Charles.

'The clubs in the bag are for midgets, aren't they? Or kids? No good for playing golf. The heads on them are the right size but their handles have been sawn off, making them half size ... vandalism as bad as when me dad painted the netty seat and didn't tell me mother afore she'd sat down.'

'Where is the golf bag now?' said Sir Charles.

'With the telegram lad. He's over there. He's a good runner, I'll give him that, and me, pedalling hard all the way.'

'Describe the man who threw the golf bag over the hedge.'

'Tall, white hair, a toff, begging your pardon, sir ... well to do, dark suit, collar and tie and, he was wearing white leather gloves ... driving gloves, maybe. He might have been a doctor.'

'Why do you say that?'

'There was a sticker on the car's windscreen ... Doctor on Call.'

'What sort of car was it?'

'A Bentley ... I told you he was posh.'

Sir Charles took from his wallet a creased black and white photograph. It showed a group standing in front of the village's Cottage Hospital. Sir Charles was in its middle, smiling. His operation for haemorrhoids had been successful. He was being discharged.

'Do you recognise him?'

'That's him.'

'He threw the golf bag over the hedge?'

'No, he's the one what commandeered my motorbike.'

Sir Charles had forgotten that CB had muscled his way into the group photograph. The bandage made his hand look enormous. He'd been having warts removed.

'Do you recognise anyone else?'

'Course I do … that's him there.'

'He threw the golf bag over the hedge?'

'Yes.'

'Are you sure … it is very important that you are certain?'

'The army doc said I've twenty-twenty vision. "You should have wings", he told me "and a curved beak for a nose … you can see as good as an eagle, you can" … of course I'm certain.'

'Bell, if you'd been the telegram boy I'd have given you a ten-bob note but, as you are in uniform, and so am I, I can't.'

'Oh.'

'However, your good work will not go unrewarded. Mike, go with Bell, and get the golf bag. Bell, I want you to take the bag to the Vicarage. If the boffins there can't unravel its mysteries, no one can. Sergeant Small, the police have motorcycles; get Private Bell one.'

34

The despatch rider's pouch contained photographs taken by the photographer in the redoubt. All but one were images of George collecting the field telephone. The odd one out was an enlargement of a small area. Its magnification made it fuzzy. It showed a side view of the Irishman's head. The image was good enough to hint at an ear with a deformity.

When Bell took the golf bag to the Vicarage he could take this photograph to The Hall, show it to Marigold. If she identified the grainy image as Doyle then they would have a positive identification of the man with whom they were dealing. Some fast motorbike riding would be called for.

'How powerful are police motorbikes, sir?' said Private Bell.

'The sooner you pick up the golf bag the sooner you'll find out,' said Mike.

If this bloke Mike hadn't been so big and tweedy and a henchman of that posh officer, he'd have told him where to stuff the golf bag. All in all, he was beginning to wish he'd never seen the damn thing. What was so special about it? The bloke who'd thrown it away hadn't thought much of it, otherwise he wouldn't have slung it, would he? He remembered a story he'd read in a newspaper about a bloke who'd bought a painting for a pound and sold it to a museum for thousands. Maybe the toff who'd thrown it away didn't know how much it was worth, but the posh officer did. In the meantime, muggins was a beast of burden.

'I'd carry it myself,' said Mike, 'but I'm older than you and I've a bad leg.'

'Any more excuses?'

'Yes, I was shot yesterday.'

'Go on … '

'Ricochet.'

'What's it like being shot?'

'If Hitler doesn't behave himself you might find out.'

Private Bell heard what he thought were a lot of motorbikes back-firing. From experience Mike knew they were gunshots.

'What's that?' said Private Bell.

'Jesus Christ!' said Mike, 'Follow me and don't drop the bag.'

'Bloody hell.'

They ran to the tramcar bent double. As they did so they heard more gunshots.

'I've been hit,' said Private Bell to no one in particular in the tramcar, which was just as well because no one was paying him any attention. 'I've been hit.' He dropped the golf bag and stared at a scratch on the back of his hand.

'Good job there's not eggs in there,' said a soldier, 'and keep your head down.'

35

If Sir Charles's vital functions had been hooked up to sensors they'd have set off bleepers. The police had tried to storm their way in, on whose orders?

'I did try to warn you, sir,' said Sergeant Bell.

Two constables dragged a fallen colleague to safety. The contents of a food hamper littered the Monument's base. Sir Charles 'read' the situation. The supplying of the Irishman with food and water had given someone the idea to go in and sort things out. The person responsible had placed George and Jack in terrible danger. Sir Charles's preparations to expect the unexpected had all been centred on the unpredictability of the 'enemy' not on 'friends'.

What was happening inside the Monument? The Eavesdropper, sitting on the very edge of his seat, hands tamped to the earphones he was wearing, was trying to find out. When Mike entered, Sir Charles, eavesdropping on a single ear phone, held up a hand to show he was listening, that he needed all his concentration to find out how the Irishman was reacting to this botched attempt to winkle him out.

'I've been hit,' said Private Bell. 'Hoy, I've been wounded.'

'Shut up,' said Mike, 'it's only a scratch.'

'I don't feel well.'

'Sit down and put your head between your legs.'

'I want to see a medic.'

'You'll see the back of my hand if you don't shut up. People are trying to find out what's going on inside that Monument and, to do that, they need quiet … here, take my handkerchief, use it as a bandage. There are two young lads in there in a lot more danger than a scratch on the hand … and stop muttering, it is only a scratch.'

36

Sergeant Small, despatched by Sir Charles to find out who had ordered the storming of the Monument, returned from his mission looking glum.

'It was the Chief Constable, sir. It's all gone badly wrong … no hostages freed and the Irishman is still safe inside his bolt hole. Another constable dead and one badly wounded.'

'I've been shot as well,' said Private Bell.

'It's a flesh wound,' said Mike, 'nothing serious.'

'But you can still ride a motorbike, Bell?' said Sir Charles.

'I'll do my best, sir.'

'Good man. Sergeant Small, the police motorbike I ordered you to get for Bell …'

'The Chief Constable wasn't keen, sir.'

'After the mess your boss has made of things I don't think he's in a position to deny me anything. Get back to him and don't pull your punches … tell him to expect a phone call from the Home Secretary. Bell, you like to ride fast?'

'Yes, sir.'

'And run over pheasants?'

'Eh?'

'Never mind. Take the golf bag to the Vicarage and this to The Hall,' handing him the envelope containing the photographs.

On the front of the envelope he'd written: FOR THE ATTENTION OF MARIGOLD STRIKER. Marigold, is the man in the photo Doyle? 'Bell, you are to wait for a reply. Tell Cook to feed you … eat in the saddle if you have to but get back here ASAP.'

'I wouldn't like to tell that cook what to do, sir.'

'Tell her Sir Charles said you had to ask.'

'And who's he?'

'He owns The Hall.'

'Are you Sir Charles?'

'Yes, I am.'

'Bloody hell. I'll do my best, sir.'

'I know you will. One more thing before you go.' Sir Charles removed from the envelope those photographs showing George being used as a human retriever. 'I don't want Elizabeth seeing those. Sergeant Small, get Bell the most powerful motorbike you can find.'

37

Sir Charles read the Eavesdropper's log. Since the attempted storming of the Monument the Irishman had done a lot of shouting. He'd threatened to kill the boys, told them he'd a mind to blow out their brains. He'd shouted abuse at King George. He'd said five Hail Marys. Many times he'd warned the boys not to try anything. On this aspect of his behaviour the Eavesdropper had made the comment: 'Suggests he sees the boys as a threat, that though they may be bruised and browbeaten they are not subdued, they still have fight in them or at least he thinks they have.' He has ordered them up the stairs. 'If I can't see you I'll be less likely to kill you. Without you two I'm a dead man. And don't think you can get out of the door at the top, it's locked and I have the key. If I'm trapped then so are you … don't doubt me, you fine young English gentlemen, I'll take you with me, if I have to.'

The Chief Constable's frontal attack had made dialogue with the Irishman a thousand times more difficult.

'Shall I ring him, sir?' said the Negotiator.

'What's he doing?' said Sir Charles.

'Showing signs of calming down,' said the Eavesdropper. He checked his log. 'The time between his outbursts is getting longer. He's been quiet for the last ten minutes.'

Sir Charles looked through the tramcar's windows. Soon it would be dark. It was going to be a long night. The tweeting of thousands of roosting starlings made him think himself in some kind of urban aviary. The only other sound to be heard in this cut off part of the city, put in limbo by the dire events taking place inside the Monument, was the plaintive cry of the newspaper seller. The chap with the lungs of an opera singer.

Food spilt in the aftermath of the abortive attack provided pigeons with a banquet. A generator arrived to power portable lights.

How sad and solemn the scene looked. Streets were built for traffic, people and bustle. If anything should happen to George and Jack he'd never forgive himself.

The Irishman had used his fists on them, had he, the bastard. The problem was that no one, not himself or the Irishman, was in control of events. A condemned man, for that's what the Irishman was, could not be counted on to behave in a rational manner.

'Shall I ring him, sir?'

'Is he still quiet?'

'Yes, sir. What he's doing I don't know … nothing that makes a noise anyway. The boys are quiet too, apart from the odd sniffle.'

A tummy rumble told Sir Charles he'd not eaten. He looked at his watch. Had the siege been going on for as long as that? If he was feeling peckish what must the boys and the Irishman be feeling? If only the Chief Constable had obeyed orders they'd now be talking to someone who'd had a good meal. It was much easier talking to a chap who'd dined well … thirst would be their problem.

'It's of vital importance that we get him to talk,' said Sir Charles. 'We must get him to trust us. If only the boys weren't in there.'

'But they are,' said Mike.

'Your Chief Constable has a lot to answer for, Sergeant Small.'

'I wouldn't like to be in his shoes, sir.'

'Nor would I, if anything happens to the boys.'

'You are very fond of your grandson, sir?'

'Yes, I am … ring him.'

Through the earphone he'd used before, Sir Charles joined the Eavesdropper in being able to hear what was going on inside the Monument.

He heard the field telephone ring. With each unanswered ring the tension in the tramcar increased. Sir Charles was aware of pressing the headphone he was holding too hard against his ear, that its Bakelite was becoming slippery with his sweat. What was going on in there? All he could hear was the field telephone ringing and ringing. It rang with an echo like a bell being rung in a cave. Someone coughed. It sounded like a boy. It seemed to him that the person doing the coughing was doing so in order to draw attention to himself as you might in a shop when a shop assistant has failed to notice that you are waiting to be served.

'Please, sir.'

It was Jack's voice. Sir Charles's heart broke into a gallop. 'Go on, you are doing the right thing. You are not being aggressive, you are showing the vile fellow good manners which, though he does not deserve them, is the right thing to do if you don't want him to kill you. You sound calm and under control. You are a brave lad, Jack.'

'Please, sir, the phone is ringing. Please, sir, the phone is ringing.'

'Let them wait,' said the Irishman.

'Maybe they want to give us food. I'm hungry and thirsty and so is my friend George.'

'I'm thirsty as well … thirsty and hungry for a free Ireland.'

'Shall I answer it, sir?'

'Touch it and I'll kill you … back up the stairs and out of my way … go on, do as you are told unless you want a bullet in your head.'

The noise he heard through the headphone made Sir Charles wince.

'He's firing through the door,' said Mike, 'he's hit the redoubt. I can see sand trickling out of a sandbag … the bastard.'

'He's reloading,' said the Eavesdropper. 'I wonder how much ammunition he has … how many weapons.'

'I'll answer the phone when I'm ready,' said the Irishman, 'do you hear? When I'm ready. Do you hear me? Answer me, damn you, answer me.'

'Yes, sir,' said Jack.

'Yes, sir,' said George.

'They made me wait, now I'm going to make them wait … I'm going to make them sweat.'

'Let's give him time to calm down,' said Sir Charles. 'At the moment I fear he's a stick of dynamite with a lit fuse. If he's not rung within the next thirty minutes we'll ring him … give him five rings. If he still refuses to answer give him five rings every fifteen minutes. If he's anything about him he'll see the pattern … make him think he's in control because he knows what to expect.'

38

While they waited for something to happen, Sir Charles and Mike mulled over the problem of how to rescue the boys. By now it was dark. Lights on tripods lit up the bullet scarred door at the bottom of the Monument. Every so often, more by reflex than conscious intent, the two men picked up binoculars and studied it. The magnified image seemed only to magnify the problem.

'I wonder what decision the Cabinet has reached over Hitler's invasion of Poland,' said Sir Charles. 'For us, the siege has rather put international events on the back burner. It will soon be Sunday, a new day.'

'Sunday, the third of September, 1939,' said Mike. 'Do you think we are saying goodbye to the last day of peace between England and Germany?'

'I do. Halifax will be dithering, but Chamberlain has backbone … more than most people think.'

'If we could talk to Jack and George without the Irishman knowing that would give us a tremendous advantage.'

'What do you suggest? Give them their own field telephone.'

'We have to do something.'

'We are, we are being patient … anything happening inside?'

'Quiet as the grave, sir,' said the Eavesdropper. 'Sorry, sir, that was inappropriate.'

'He'll be exhausted,' said Mike, 'after the attack to winkle him out by force of arms he'll be licking his wounds. He's a fox gone to earth.'

'Time to let him know, I think,' said Sir Charles, 'that the hounds know where he is. It's imperative that we get him to talk to us. Give him five rings. It will cheer up the boys.'

'It's ringing, sir,' said the Eavesdropper.

Sir Charles picked up a headphone and joined in the listening. After the fifth ring the Irishman screamed. In a strange sort of way he knew how the fellow felt, for he too wanted to scream. He had it in him to scream louder than the Irishman. His heart ached for the boys but especially for his beloved grandson. The unpredictability of all that had so far happened, scared him. In a gesture of despair he knew to be unworthy of a leader, he buried his head in his hands, concern for his grandson and Jack overwhelming him.

'We'll get them out safe,' said Mike, 'I know we will. The Irishman's like that big stag I'm after. I've missed him twice but I'll get him. You know why? Because he'll make a mistake.'

'He already has,' said Sergeant Small. 'He's told us that his wife lives in Northern Ireland and the name of his child. If your American friend, sir, identifies him as the man Doyle, some good old fashioned police work will track down his family. I've taken the liberty, sir, of making a few phone calls. There's not many IRA men the Ulster police know nothing about. What I'm going to suggest, sir, is not the Queensbury Rules but I think you'll agree with me, sir, we are not dealing with a gentleman, are we?'

Harry's unexpected appearance in the tramcar stopped the good sergeant from explaining more of what he had in mind.

'Aunt Elizabeth sent me,' said Harry. 'She wants to know what's going on and so do I. Don't blame the despatch rider for telling us more than he was supposed to … Cook's bread and butter made him blab like a brook.'

The news that Elizabeth knew of the danger facing George and Jack made Sir Charles aware that another burden had been placed on his shoulders.

'I suppose the "Babbling Brook" played the wounded soldier?' said Mike.

'He did mention a few times that he'd been wounded. He's a good chap, though, gave me a lift here on the back of his motorbike … damn scary. The last time I was that scared was when you, Uncle Charles, and Mike made me retrieve my shotgun from the Tyne, remember? Marigold told me to tell you that the man in the photograph is Doyle. This is from the boffins at the Vicarage.'

Sir Charles opened the envelope. What he read made him smile. So, that was the secret of the golf bag.

39

The banshee wail of an air raid siren.

'I keep forgetting about Hitler,' said Sir Charles.

'It's not the real thing, sir,' said Sergeant Small. 'We had one last night. It's to get folk used to knowing what to do when the Germans start dropping bombs.'

'I'm a fighter pilot,' said Harry; 'the RAF will stop them doing that.'

'If it comes to war, sir, I wish you all the luck in the world.'

'Thank you.'

'Switch off those lights,' shouted an angry voice. 'You're the Bull's Eye on the bloody dartboard.'

'ARP,' said Sergeant Small.

'I'll bet he has a little moustache, just like Hitler's,' said Mike.

'As a matter of fact, sir, he does. Do you know him?'

'I know the type.'

'It's dark,' said Harry, stating the obvious.

'It won't be when your eyes get used to it,' said Sir Charles. 'In the trenches I used to read Shakespeare by moonlight. I must admit that my familiarity with the text did help. And tonight we have a moon. Has the siren upset Doyle?'

'All quiet, sir,' said the Eavesdropper.

'The number of burglaries will go up, you mark my words,' said Sergeant Small. 'Blackouts is like giving thieves a ration card. Tyneside Corks are hard enough to keep down when you can see them, never mind when you can't. The sales of black Balaclavas will go through the roof, you mark my words.'

'Without its lights the city is more like what I'm used to,' said Mike. 'It's like this when you lot are in bed and I'm out chasing poachers. The Monument's column could be a tree, couldn't it? Black shapes ... it doesn't do to have imagination when you're out at night in a forest. Let your dog roam free, but, if you want to stay sane, keep a leash on your imagination. Don't you think the shape of that building over there looks like the Duke of Wellington? It won't look like that in the morning, in the full light of day. I'd love to get my hands on the Irishman.'

'Have you been at the herbal?' said Sir Charles.

'My hip flask was lonely; would you like to pat it on the head?'

'No, I would not.'

'Quite right too.'

'Shall I ring him, sir?' said the Negotiator. 'It's time.'

A shaded candle lit the tramcar.

'This is what it must have been like in olden times,' said Sir Charles, 'all flickering shadows.'

'He's quiet, sir,' said the Eavesdropper.

'Ring him.'

'It's ringing, sir.'

'Pick up the phone, Doyle … sooner or later you are going to have to talk to us.'

'He's had five rings, sir,' said the Negotiator, 'shall I keep trying, sir?'

'We stick to the plan.'

The Eavesdropper held up his hand for quiet. What had he heard? Sir Charles picked up a headphone.

'You,' said Doyle, 'come here, hands in your pockets. We wouldn't want you using your paws on myself, would we? Kneel … kneel, damn you … that's right, on your knees, as if you're in a church praying that the good Lord will forgive your English sins. They say he's a forgiving God but I doubt he'll ever forgive the English … they've sinned so much there's no room left in Hell … damn them! Damn them! Pick up the phone, go on, your English friends want to talk, I'm going to give them something to talk about, pick up the phone … do it!'

'I don't know what to do.'

It was Jack.

'This is what you do.'

The phone in the tramcar rang. The Negotiator picked it up.

'Is there anybody there?' said Doyle, 'or are you still making your cup of tea, like last time? The English and their cups of tea. Your king is not my king. I'm not a terrorist, I'm a soldier. The rules of the Geneva Convention apply to me. You can't put a noose round my neck. I'm a soldier fighting to free his country from an occupying force. When the Germans invade then you English will know what it's like to be occupied. You will know how we Irish have suffered for centuries. Has the war started? Are you still there? Yes, you are, I can hear your breathing … worried, are you? Scared what I might do? I've explosives enough to blow this Monument into a thousand pieces. Am I still talking to, William? To King Billy?'

'Yes.'

'Jack, be a good little English schoolboy and tell King Billy how many guns I have.'

'He has two guns.'

'Tell him where they are pointing.'

'At my head.'

'Do you know about guns, William?'

'A little.'

'The modest English … would you be knowing, Billy, the difference between a Webley and a Luger?'

'Yes. Would you like me to arrange for you a supply of food and drink?'

'Like last time … use it as bait to get your hands on me and put a bullet in the back of my head.'

'The boys will be thirsty.'

'I'm thirsty and it's doing my head in … what a choice, die of thirst or take a glass of water off the mighty English and let them put a noose round your neck. I'll take the parched tongue before the broken neck.'

'It doesn't have to be like that. I give you my word that you will be allowed to access food and water without in any way being threatened.'

'Are you listening, Billy? I hope you are. In the Wembley there is one bullet … which chamber? Tell Billy what I'm doing, Jack … tell him!'

'He's pressing the gun into the back of my head … you're hurting me.'

'If you hear a bang, Jack will be dead. If you hear nothing he will have been lucky.'

Sir Charles exchanged glances with the Negotiator.

'What's happening?' said Mike.

'I've cocked the Webley. Jack, tell Billy what I've done.'

'He's cocked the Webley.'

'I can't hear you … say it louder, louder.'

'He's cocked the Webley.'

'My finger is on the trigger … tell them, Jack, tell them.'

'His finger is on the trigger.'

'Put the phone down, Jack.'

'He's rung off,' said the Negotiator.

'What the hell's going on?' said Mike. 'What's the bastard doing? Charles, you'd best sit down before you fall down. What's he doing? He's not killed the boys?'

'It's alright, sir,' said the Eavesdropper, 'he's telling Jack to stand up. I think the lad is safe, at least for the moment.'

'Did he pull the trigger?' said Sir Charles.

'I heard a click but, who knows where the gun was pointing or if it was loaded.'

'I believe it was loaded and that he was pointing it at Jack's head. It is my opinion, gentlemen, that Doyle is capable of cold blooded murder.'

'For Christ's sake will someone please tell me what's going on?' said Mike.

After the explanation Sir Charles said, 'If you don't mind, Mike, I rather think I will take up your offer of a dram. I think we all need a fortifier. Gentlemen, if you think it will help, help yourselves. My gamekeeper is a generous fellow when it comes to buying his round, and his hip flask, as you can see, is not the diminutive vessel one associates with that name.'

40

'That's the All Clear,' said Sergeant Small.

'What a bloody awful noise,' said Mike.

'Get used to it,' said Sir Charles.

The street lights came back on. Once again the generator throbbed life into the portable lights shining on the Monument's door.

'Chron-ic-al! Chron-ic-al!'

'Does he never stop?' said Sir Charles.

'The newspaper seller is one of our best informers, sir,' said Sergeant Small. 'He's a wooden leg, lost his real one in the Great War.'

'I wonder if a man with a wooden leg is able to shout louder than a man with two legs,' said Harry, 'you know, as a sort of compensation.'

'Harry, I hope you never find out,' said Sir Charles.

'He's a good chap, the very best type of Tyneside Cork,' said Sergeant Small.

'The siren is like a switch, don't you think?' said Harry. 'The first time it sounds it switches the lights off, the second time it switches them back on.'

'I wish we had a switch like that for Doyle,' said Sir Charles.

'Something that could switch him off forever,' said Mike, 'like a bullet. If we could persuade him to open the door, a marksman might get a shot in … the photographer did.'

'If the marksman missed, what might he do to the boys?' said Sir Charles. 'We are dealing with a fellow who is prepared to die for the cause in which he believes. He is a fanatic. I've been told I am fanatical about growing melons. Jack teases my gardener by putting snails on my prize plants. How I would miss his teasing if anything happened to him. I did a deal with him, you know? I negotiated with him. He liked being humoured and I liked humouring him. I fear there will be no negotiating with Doyle.'

'Sir,' said Sergeant Small, 'before Mr Harry arrived I was about to tell you … if we can get Doyle to talk and listen, we can, in a manner of speaking, blackmail him. Police colleagues in Northern Ireland have given me the name of Doyle's wife, the name of the street and the number of the house in which she lives. We know a lot about Doyle. If he threatens to kill the boys, we threaten to kill his wife and child.'

'He would know we were bluffing. He would never believe that HMG would sanction the murder of an innocent woman and her child.'

'He would, sir, if we told him the Loyalists were involved … tit-for-tat killings are commonplace in Northern Ireland. We could tell him that the Loyalists are holding his wife and child prisoner. He has two hostages but, so do we, in a manner of speaking.'

'We want to save the boys and I for one am not fussy about the means we use,' said Mike.

'I will bear what you have said in mind, Sergeant,' said Sir Charles. 'How long since his theatricalities with Jack?'

'Two hours, sir.'

'And in between times we've rang him every fifteen minutes?'

'Yes, sir.'

'I suggest we wait at least an hour until we try again; unless, that is, he does something stupid. He will realise that we have changed our tactics. He will wonder why. Sooner or later he will have to talk.'

'Or, he kills himself and takes the boys with him,' said Mike.

'Just as well he can't see how helpless we all look, damn him.'

In the ensuing silence Mike put a hand on Sir Charles's shoulder. 'Charlie,' he whispered,' you look close to falling down. It's time to delegate ... go for a walk, get a breath of air; trust your team. Teams win battles, not individuals, you know that.'

41

'I'll come with you, Uncle Charles,' said Harry 'to keep an eye on you.'

'Is that what your aunt told you to do?'

'Yes, I'm obeying orders, don't you know.'

They walked towards the perimeter of the cordon.

'In confidence, Harry, my anger at what this man Doyle is doing to Jack and dear George is making it hard for me to think straight. What we need is a plan that will give us a better than fifty-fifty chance of getting them out alive. How can you trust a man who plays Russian roulette with the life of a child? You can't, you just can't.'

'How will it end, Uncle?'

'I don't know, real life is not fiction. In a book one can find out if the hero lives or dies by peeking at the last page.'

'I suppose that not knowing what is going to happen next is what makes real life exciting.'

'Under the present circumstances I'd be happy to know exactly what is going to happen next and do without the excitement.'

'If it comes to war who will win?'

'We will.'

'On our own?'

'Good heavens, no.'

'With the help of the Americans?'

'Yes. How are my American guests?'

'All they talk about is Hitler and Poland, oh and Mario.'

'Interesting, don't you think, how, in the midst of an international crisis, when bombs might soon be raining down on their heads, people still find time to gossip. Is Mario still absent without leave?'

'Yes. I overheard Weinberger calling him a philanderer. O'Neil said it was because Mario was more Italian than American and what could you expect from someone who was an ice cream seller. It turns out that O'Neil has a chip on his shoulder about ice cream sellers. Weinberger reminded him of it. O'Neil's father was cuckolded by one. Every time the father was away on business the ice cream seller's cart stayed all night outside the O'Neil family's home. After the divorce O'Neil was sent to a Catholic boarding school. His hatred of ice cream sellers is Freudian, Uncle. He blames them for the break-up of the family home.'

'Let's get something to eat. I know just the place. Apropos of what we have been talking about you will find it interesting. By the by, in my absence what have the Hitler Youth been doing?'

'CB's keeping an eye on them. He's hounding them as if war's already been declared.'

'Any more died?'

'No.'

'Pity, don't you think?'

'Yes.'

'You see, Harry, even the prospect of war is making us brutal … making us want young men dead … terrible, terrible. God knows what we'll be like when the real thing starts.' They passed through the cordon. 'That's better, back to what a street should be like. A bit of noise and bustle cheers a chap up, don't you think?'

A uniformed member of the policeman protection service followed them. This had been Sergeant Small's idea. 'To protect you from journalists, sir,' he'd said.

They followed an agreed route. If Doyle made a move a runner would be despatched to find them. If, God forbid, they heard gunshots, well, they'd run back without the need to be told.

'It reminds me of that painting by Breughel,' said Sir Charles. 'In the painting I'm thinking of, Icarus is shown falling out of a clear blue sky, yet, life goes on as normal … I mean, a chap with a pair of wings strapped to his back, falling out of the sky, is not normal … yet, this ploughman in the painting goes on ploughing.'

From across the road a familiar voice shouted, 'Sir Charles! Sir Charles!'

Crozier came over to join Sir Charles and Harry at the speed of a brisk walk.

'Oh, hello … Crozier,' said Sir Charles, 'I didn't see you, rather too deep in thought, I fear.'

'A lot on your mind, shipmate. I've heard rumours. The gunmen responsible for blowing up the Assembly Rooms are trapped inside Grey's Monument and they have hostages.'

'Chinese whispers. It's only one member of the IRA.'

'We know who he is,' said Harry.

'You have a name?'

'We have.'

'But you can't tell me. Hush, hush, is it? The Secret Service's very own Hippocratic Oath.'

'His name is Doyle,' said Sir Charles.

'I've never heard of the fellow.'

'Is there any reason why you should?'

'Of course not.'

Two crease lines running from Crozier's nostrils to the corners of his mouth twitched. He was lying.

'I was thinking, perhaps, you knew Doyle in one of your previous lives?'

'Not that I recollect. Sir Charles, you are beginning to sound like an interrogator.'

'I apologise. I am rather worn down … a little too much on edge. How is Lord Nelson?'

'Your wounded colleague is still confused. Blows to the head … their consequences are unpredictable. He keeps telling me he's a secret agent. I keep telling him I'm Alexander the Great who, as a matter of fact, I knew quite well. He had haemorrhoids, Sir Charles, just like you, not many people know that. As a medical man, Sir Charles, I feel it's my duty to tell you …you look awful. Do you need pills to keep you going?'

'A cup of tea and a sit down is all I need to put me right.'

'If Uncle Charles looks poorly it's because he's worried. Doyle is holding George and Jack hostage inside Grey's Monument.'

'Your grandson and the Jewish boy … I'm sorry. If there's anything I can do … I have pills in my bag. I was on my way home when I heard about the siege.'

'And you thought you might be able to help?' said Sir Charles.

'I confess to curiosity. I was among the crowd being kept at bay by the police when I spotted you.'

'But you do not confess to knowing Doyle either in this life or in a previous existence?'

'I have told you, Sir Charles, the name means nothing to me. If you will excuse me, I have a train to catch.'

'Port or starboard?'

'I beg your pardon?'

'I am indulging your whim for all things nautical … which side of the road for the Central Station?'

'I'll stick to the port side.'

Sir Charles and Harry watched him disappear into the night.

'He's on the starboard side,' said Harry.

'I know.'

'But he's ex-Royal Navy.'

'The place I have in mind for a bite to eat is down here … what the?'

Harry's quick reaction stopped Sir Charles tripping over the lead.

'Sorry, sir,' said the newspaper seller. 'Damn you, Moses, come here, you are going to get me into trouble you are. Not everyone is as fond of ferrets as what I am.'

Moses! The sight of the beast made Sir Charles smile.

The ferret was free, ditto, George and Jack were free. The silliness of the syllogism irritated him.

'No need to apologise,' Sir Charles told the newspaper seller, 'Moses and I are old friends; aren't we, Moses?'

'I can see he's fond of you, sir.'

In all the hurly-burly the wee beasty had been forgotten.

'How'd you come by him?'

Here we go, thought the newspaper seller. The bloke doing the asking was an officer, high ranking as well, those pips on his shoulder weren't bird shite. He knew the type.

Preparatory to telling his story he did his best to show the respect his class took as their right. He stood to attention; not easy though when you only have one leg and are balancing on a crutch.

Sir Charles listened without once interrupting. This impressed the newspaper seller. Maybe the cove wasn't as bad as most of his type.

'So,' said Sir Charles, 'the "fat wife" who fell on your stump, was she alright?'

'Never thought of that, sir.'

'Quite; look here, my good fellow, my nephew and I are going for a brew at Garibaldi's Gelato Emporium. "Gee-Gees", you know it?'

Every Geordie knew 'Gee-Gees'. London had Harrods, Newcastle had 'Gee-Gees'.

Bully for you, thought the newspaper seller, it's alright for some, but changed his tune when Sir Charles added, 'I want you to join us and bring the ferret.'

'Me, sir?'

'That's what I said and the ferret. I'm fond of Moses. I can see that he likes you. Come along, we've not got all day.'

42

'Here we are,' said Sir Charles. 'Where's my "minder"?'

'Here I am, sir, the regulation four paces behind the job.'

'Job?'

'It's what we in Police Protection call whatever it is we have been called upon to look after, sir.'

'I'm a "job", am I?'

'Yes, sir … more than that to your loved ones, I hopes, but that's what you are to me.'

'The "Job" will send you out a cup of tea and a sandwich.'

'Very kind, sir, milk and two sugars, heaped spoons.'

'If Sergeant Small should send a runner for me, you know where I am.'

'Yes, sir. If I may make so bold, sir, I'll have a ham sandwich. I was at this very same Italian ice cream parlour this morning in pursuance of a domestic … nasty business … fight between an American gentleman and Gina, everyone knows Gina. She'd kicked him in the groin area, sir, if you takes my meaning. Wink. Wink. Some men never learn. So I knows the ham's good. It's off the bone, just the way my missus does it … and it's a nice night, not too hot, not too cold, for sentry duty, if you takes my meaning, sir?'

Sir Charles, Harry and the newspaper seller, with Moses on his lap, sat on form seats in a booth with a table.

'My treat,' said Sir Charles.

''You are going to take Moses off me, aren't you?' said the newspaper seller.

'Moses is Jack's pet,' said Sir Charles. 'It will be for him to decide. You have explained how he came into your possession. Without your involvement we might never have known that George and Jack were being held hostage; for that, I thank you and give you my hand.'

'Thank you, sir. Did the policeman who took the note off me get hurt? I've heard so many rumours.'

'The shot killed him.'

'That's sad, sir; like me, sir, you'll have seen too many dead. I recognised you, sir, soon as I saw you. You were an officer in my old regiment. Never thought I'd share a table with an officer.'

'You led the singing when we marched.'

'That's right, sir. Now I sing Chron-ic-al.'

'Are you coping?'

'You mean the leg, sir, what I haven't got?'

'Yes, damned hard lines.'

'The old lie,' said Harry, taking his eyes off the menu to look at the newspaper seller's wooden leg, 'Dulce et decorum est Pro patria mori.'

'What'll you be having?' said Sir Charles.

'Not what the young man's just said, sir. I've had enough of foreign to last me for the rest of my natural. If you don't mind, sir, I'll have an ice cream.'

'What a good idea … and let's ask to have that syrupy stuff squirted on the top like we had when we were children and knew nothing about war.'

'I'll have a Knickerbocker Glory, Uncle,' said Harry.

'Glory,' said Sir Charles, 'the glory of war, of fighting for a cause in which you believe … a load of rubbish.'

'Amen to that, sir, there's no glory in losing a leg … it's bloody awful. You won't believe this, sir, but it itches. How can something you don't have itch?'

'How do you scratch it?' said Harry.

'I shuts me eyes and pretends.'

'Harry, be a good chap, go and order three Knickerbocker Glories, tea and a ham sandwich for my bodyguard and a tub of ice cream for Moses. He's very well behaved for a ferret.'

Harry did not think it quite the thing for him to be fetching and carrying for his social inferiors, but Uncle Charles was the boss and this newspaper seller chap, well, the poor chap was missing a leg. To add to his simmering sense of being put upon he couldn't find a waitress. Was there a bell he could ring? He wondered how such places stayed open. They did not deserve business. It would never happen at his college.

In search of someone who would take his order, he lifted a flap at the end of the counter and made for a door with a porthole window marked 'Staff Only'.

Looking through the porthole, before knocking, he saw a chap lying on his back with a woman riding him as if he was a horse and she was its jockey. The chap had his hands clasped behind his head, the way chaps do when, on a sunny day, they are lying on their backs on a grassy bank, watching clouds sail overhead.

The woman had long black hair. When she moved up and down Harry saw she was not wearing knickers.

'Is anyone serving?' said Sir Charles. 'What's happening?'

'Someone will be coming soon,' said Harry.

'And about time too. Moses is starving. He's very well behaved for a ferret.'

43

To bring the meeting to order Sir Charles tapped a Knickerbocker Glory glass with a spoon.

'My beautiful, beautiful Gina,' said Mancini, blowing kisses to the buxom brunette polishing glasses behind the counter. 'She loves me … ain't I the lucky guy?'

'I'm sure she does,' said Sir Charles.

'I know she does,' said Harry.

'What's that supposed to mean?' said Mario.

'Mario,' said Sir Charles, 'less than a three minute walk from here, two boys are in danger of losing their lives. I've explained to you what has been happening.'

'What do you want?'

'I want your help.'

'You Brits always want help … where's my cheque book? Sorry, Charles, I'm behaving badly. What do you want?'

'I want you to talk to O'Neil.'

'Why?'

'I think you know why.'

'Enlighten me.'

'I think you know why O'Neil came on this trip to The Hall.'

'To further US-UK relations in the event of Mr Hitler doing something stupid.'

'No. Do I have to spell it out?'

'Yes. What is it I'm supposed to know and how do you know I'm supposed to know it? Love you, Gina.'

Sir Charles sighed. 'I don't normally give away my sources, but do you know who Harry's aunt is?'

'Nope.'

'Tell him, Harry.'

'She's your aunt? There's nothing happens in Washington that she doesn't know about. She tipped you off, eh? Before I start talking I want to know how much you know.'

'Do you know how he brought the money in?'

'No.'

'But you thought that's what he might be doing?'

'Yes.'

'Did it not occur to you that he was sticky with his golf bag?'

'Some golfers love their clubs more than their wives. When golf gets into a guy's tubes he goes kinda crazy.'

'I have O'Neil's golf bag.'

'He won't like that.'

'He doesn't know. The bag I sent to the Vicarage for examination ... you look puzzled.'

'The Vicarage?'

'An old manse taken over by the army. It's next door to our cottage hospital. As I was saying the golf bag I sent to the Vicarage is the one he brought with him from the States. His co-conspirators have provided him with a replacement. Bert's sense of smell gave us the clue that a switch had taken place. Do you know who his accomplices are?'

'The IRA.'

'Just so. I have been informed that the original golf bag has a false bottom.' Sir Charles produced an American twenty dollar note. 'Do you know where this came from?'

'The golf bag, I guess.'

'The recipients of O'Neil's largesse were so keen to get their hands on the booty that they left it behind. O'Neil is an IRA courier, isn't he? He's supplying them with money to buy arms?'

'We suspected him.'

'We?'

'I think you know who the "we" is.'

'Tell me.'

'You want to take my fingerprints?'

'Not necessary, we are batting on the same side.'

'I don't play cricket.'

'Captured spies are not usually treated to a Knickerbocker Glory. Come along, Mario, there's a good chap, spill the beans.'

'You knew I was here, didn't you? It was not by chance that you picked this emporium to take refreshment.'

'Mario, you have had a "eureka" moment.'

'How'd you know I was here?'

'I've already revealed to you one of my sources; to reveal another would be foolhardy. When you get back to The Hall you will have much to discuss with Marigold. You and she, I believe, are working on the same case.'

'Charles, is there anything you don't know?'

'If it comes to war I don't know if America will help England.'

'Nor do I, and, you know what? I don't think anybody does.'

'How were you recruited?'

'That's a National Security issue, but I'll tell you anyway. Marigold and I were in the right place at the right time, or, depending on your point of view, in the wrong place at the wrong time. When the CIA had suspicions about O'Neil and knew I was of the party visiting your good self, they asked me to help. My brief was to keep an eye on the guy and report back. They didn't give me a shooter, just a notebook and a pencil.'

'And Marigold?'

'Our agents knew about Doyle's contacts with high ranking Nazis. Marigold was coming to Newcastle and so was Doyle. She was told to book a passage on the Nord and, same as me, keep an eye on a guy.'

'Only our agent almost got her killed.'

'Did he blow her cover?' said Harry.

'She's pretty certain Doyle had no idea she was spying on him. She was a dumb American blonde. Your guy wanted to use her as a carrier pigeon, that's all.'

'Marigold's not dumb,' said Harry, 'she's a professor of history.'

'OK, so she knows in 1492 Columbus sailed the ocean blue.'

'It takes a lot more than that to be a history professor.'

'You in love with her, Harry? Harry, you are going red. You want me to give you an introduction? I won't charge. I'll debit it to Anglo-American relations. Gina has a sister.'

'Has she really?'

'You like chocolate, Harry?'

'Yes.'

'Me too.'

Sir Charles coughed.

'That's your uncle smacking my hand. Harry, stop leading me astray. I'm paying attention, Charles. What do you want me to do? But, remember, I'm a professor of economics, not a professional spy. I mean, hi, don't ask me to shoot anyone. I'm more of an ice cream seller than a professional assassin. I've a PhD in Supply and Demand Theory. I know nothing about invisible ink. I believe you use lemon juice.'

'You "supply" and Gina "demands",' said the newspaper seller.

'You got it … hi, some of the smartest guys I know sell newspapers. Moses, eh. Does he bite? The guy who led the Jews out of Egypt. So, the boys used the ferret as a postman. Why don't you use him to deliver a message to them? Quattro cappuccini, Gina.'

'You know,' said Sir Charles, 'I think that's a very good idea.'

'You like cappuccino?'

'I meant your idea of using Moses to send the boys a message.'

'American know-how, Charles. No problem too big for an American to solve. Gina, go heavy with the chocolate. It's going to be a long night. I don't know about you, Charles, but making "love" makes me hungry. You find that, Harry? Sor-ry, I'm forgetting, you're English. Chaps don't talk about things like that. It's bad form. Charles, as the African elephant said, I'm all ears, give me my marching orders.'

Mario promised to be a good American boy, to toe the line, to follow Charles's instructions to the letter. Sir Charles was sceptical. Why couldn't the fellow behave like an Englishman? And all those kisses he kept throwing at Gina, really, it was too much, but, then again, he was an American.

'So,' said Mario, 'you want me and Harry to go to this army base you call the Vicarage, collect the phoney golf bag and use it to spook O'Neil. I am to involve Marigold in the subterfuge?'

'Of course.'

'In a shoot,' said Harry, 'as you well know, sir, beaters are used to make the birds fly.'

'And my job is to make O'Neil fly?'

'If you can get him to confess he's an IRA courier and knows Doyle, he might be prepared to talk some sense into the Irishman.'

44

The newspaper seller drained the dregs of the cappuccinos into a saucer for Moses.

'It was like this in the trenches,' said Sir Charles; 'after a spell of leave your stomach churned when you had to go back.'

'Mario, comma here,' said Gina. 'You are definitely not-a married a-man?'

'Gina, if the sun is cold, I'm a married man but, if it is hot, I am not.'

'You are a poet.'

'And you, my beautiful Gina, are bella, bella.'

'Mario, love of my life, you are not a poet you are a liar … that mark on your finger where the married a-man wears his wedding ring, it betrays you. It is the stigmata. Do you think Gina is stupid? But, I forgive you. You know why I forgive you?' To Sir Charles, Harry and the newspaper seller, 'Do you know why I forgive him? I forgive him because he satisfies me. He is a wonderful lover. Comma here, Mario, comma close to Gina … close your eyes.' She tweaked his nose. 'Kiss me.'

'Ouch!'

'Baby.'

'Do I not get a kiss?' said the newspaper seller.

'I kiss you on the lips, why? Because you are a war hero. My kisses ease pain. They are better than the horse embrocation. Mario, this young man is a war hero, he gives his leg for his country. I love warriors. What did you give your country? When were you a soldier?'

'I thought about it.'

'You think before you make-a love? No, you do it. And stop a-rubbing your nose. When this a-business is finished you will need comforting. Gina will comfort you. My hero with one leg I give you free ice cream all the time but not a tutti-fruity. A tutti is too much. You spoil a-man you put ideas in his head.'

45

On their way back to the tramcar Sir Charles told the newspaper seller, 'I want you on my staff. You are fond of Moses?'

'I am, sir.'

'And he is fond of you?'

'He is, sir. I'd not be overstating the case, sir, to say, sir, that on both sides, it was love at first sight.'

'Your job will be to look after him.'

'Am I back in the army, sir?'

'Yes. By the by, what's your name?'

'Me pals call me Chronicle, sir.'

Everyone in the tramcar made a fuss of Moses.

'Don't get him excited,' said Chronicle, 'he's on active service. Before a chap goes over the top he needs time to reflect.'

'Anything happened?' said Sir Charles.

'All quiet, sir,' said the Eavesdropper.

'A cup of tea, I think, before you, my dear Harry and Mario, drive back to The Hall. You will take the Rolls. It's parked in the police station. Tea, Sergeant Small?'

'There's always a brew on, sir.'

'I've just had a cappuccino,' said Mario.

'Among other things,' said Harry.

'Mario, my dear chap,' said Sir Charles, 'this is England. Our HGVs run on diesel, our cars on petrol and ourselves on tea. What would Assam do with its tea if we English were to turn our backs on the leaf?'

Sir Charles cupped his mug. Its utilitarian enamel made him smile. It reminded him of Elizabeth's attempt to protect The Hall's bone china. In this situation enamel mugs were appropriate. A flare of anger made him swear that when the bombs started falling he'd drink out of The Hall's finest Worcester all the time. Hitler was not going to destroy his way of life.

'Why won't this Doyle talk to you?' said Mario.

'He's a fanatic; fanatics see things in black and white. There's no room for compromise.'

'Football fans are like that,' said Chronicle. 'Newcastle's colours are black and white. The toon's fans are fanatics. It makes them not see things what other people see, like fouls. In the back lane where I used to live there was this girl; she turned men into fanatics. She had big front teeth, one eye and Apache Head; at least that's what some of the lads called it. The poor lass had bald patches. In the cowboy pictures the Apaches always scalped the white man. You're an American, Mr Mario – is that true?'

'Chronicle, I'm from Boston, I've never seen a Red Indian in my life.'

'Anyway, this girl always had lots of boyfriends.'

'Maybe she was like the sweet shop owner who, when his scales showed the correct weight, always dropped another sweet into the bag,' said Sir Charles, 'if you take my meaning.'

'I do, sir, I do.'

'Very delicately put, Charles,' said Mario.

'I am a diplomat. Now, gentlemen, finish your tea and, as they said in times of yore, let battle commence. Mario, the golf bag with the false bottom is your secret weapon; collect it from the Vicarage; use it to scare the living daylights out of O'Neil.

'Harry, tell the Intelligence chaps at the Vicarage I want to know why Crozier does not know his port from his starboard. Damn it, I can't believe the fellow might not be a full shilling. He's poked obscene instruments up my backside. How more trusting of a chap can one be?

'Tell Marigold everything; tell your aunt as much as she needs to know. I do not want her worrying. The boys are in terrible danger. Thanks to Mario, we have a plan. Moses led the Jews out of Egypt – can our Moses help us rescue Jack and George? Mike, hand over the keys to the Rolls. Put your foot down, Harry. Drive like Mike.'

Sunday 3rd of September 1939

1

For those involved in the siege, Sir Charles arranged a watch system of two hours on and two hours off.

In the redoubt the photographer and the marksman spun a coin to decide who should be first to go without sleep. When the Photographer lost, he tried to bribe the marksman.

'You let me get some shut-eye and I'll give you some samples.'

'What of?'

'"What the Butler Saw."'

'Those machines you put a penny in on the ends of piers and turn a handle while you look through a viewer and someone picks your back pocket? I'll have my shut-eye if you don't mind, thank you very much. You lost, mate. It was a fair toss. You watch until two. I sleep until two.'

In the tramcar the Eavesdropper whispered to Sir Charles that all was quiet inside the Monument. The Interrogator snored.

'He's gone to earth,' said Mike. 'I've had many a fox do that to me.'

'Is it true, sir, that when they do that they eat their young?' said Sergeant Small.

'Only if they are not too busy shitting themselves.'

'The fellow's under a lot of pressure,' said Sir Charles.

'Don't start feeling sorry for him.'

'It is for dear George and Jack that I fret. The longer this goes on the greater the chance that Doyle will try something desperate. If only he'd talk to us. We must get him to trust us …to talk to us. I wonder what he's thinking… perhaps we should contact Mr Freud and ask his advice.'

'Who's Mr Freud, sir?' said Chronicle.

'He's a kind of scientist who looks into people's minds.'

'Like a mind reader, is he? I wonder if he'll ever come to the Empire. I once saw a Memory Man there. He wasn't top of the bill, but he should have been.'

'I'll tell you what Doyle is thinking,' said Mike, 'he's thinking about the hangman's noose. His collar will be feeling tight, you have my word on that.'

'If he won't answer the phone, post him a letter under the door. When the rent man knocks and I don't answer, that's what he does,' said Chronicle.

'A note under the door,' said Sir Charles.

'It's worth a try, sir,' said Sergeant Small. 'I've known hardened villains what can hardly read come out with their hands up when you post them a billy-do, especially if you draw a hanging man under your signature.'

'I'll deliver the note,' said Mike.

'No, you will not. You have a bad leg. I will be the postman.'

Sir Charles addressed the note to 'Mr Doyle'. It was a polite note, a one step at a time note, a food for thought note, no provocation, fatherly in tone. It offered food and water, promised that if this offer of goodwill was accepted that there would be no repeat of the attempt to storm the Monument. Also mentioned were the names of Doyle's family and the address of the street in which they lived. The inclusion of this information would give Doyle something to chew on. Before he left to deliver the note, Sir Charles checked with the Eavesdropper.

'All quiet, sir.'

He approached the tiny door from the side. If Doyle went berserk and started shooting blind, he would not be in the line of fire. Portable arc lights lit the scene. The door looked like a pepper pot. He bent down and skimmed the note through the gap between its bottom and thresh bar. The way he did this, with an assured flick of the wrist, reminded him of skimming pebbles across water to see how many times they'd bounce.

It would be dark inside the Monument. Had Doyle been able to see or hear the delivery? He looked over to the tramcar. The Eavesdropper gave him the signal that all was still quiet. In that case the time had come to waken the Irishman up.

His patience all but exhausted Sir Charles rapped on the door with his swagger stick.

'Mr Doyle,' he said, 'I know you can hear me. I have delivered you a note. I beg you to read it.'

The shot through the door and the fellow's oaths confirmed Sir Charles's opinion that with this chap negotiation was pointless.

Back in the tramcar he told his team, 'We give him time to read the note. We stick to our plan of ringing every fifteen minutes. We keep monitoring him.'

'Sir,' said the Eavesdropper, 'he's reading the letter … he's reading it out loud. He's screaming the names of his wife and child. I think he's going mad, sir.'

'He's not doing anything to the boys?'

'Don't think so, sir. He's screaming and crying. He's smashing something against a wall.'

'I repeat, we stick to our plan, regular as clockwork we ring him every fifteen minutes. Our regularity will make him think we have no other option but to negotiate. If we think he means to harm the boys, only then, do we go in with guns blazing. If he'd only talk, ask us for something we could give him … a repeat of his request for a car and an aeroplane to fly him to Ireland.'

'The Chief Constable wouldn't be happy seeing him fly off to Dublin, sir,' said Sergeant Small.

'Nor would I, nor would any of us … as for your Chief Constable the least said about him the better.'

'Do you think O'Neil might be able to get him to talk?' said Mike.

'Before that can happen we have to get O'Neil to admit he's an IRA courier.'

'Marigold and Mario will make him talk.'

'I would like to think that if O'Neil knew the lives of two children were at stake, he'd co-operate without someone having to twist his arm. And don't forget, Marigold and Mario are Americans and so is O'Neil. He is one of their own. They may prefer to deal with him in a way that we might find less than satisfactory. I don't know.'

'O'Neil might be a hard nut to crack. He might be as fanatical as Doyle.'

'He might indeed. Time, I think, to use our secret weapon.'

'Moses,' said Chronicle, 'wake up.'

Sir Charles tied round the ferret's neck a strip of black and white checked material cut from a scarf.

'When George sees the Northumbrian tartan,' said Sir Charles, 'he'll know help is on its way.'

'And when he reads our message, he'll know what to do when the balloon goes up,' said Mike.

2

'Still no answer, sir,' said the Eavesdropper. 'I can hear the phone ringing … no chatter from anyone.'

'All of them will be exhausted,' said Mike. 'Once, in the trenches, I slept through a bombardment.'

'Keep trying,' said Sir Charles, 'we stick to the routine … keep casting the fly. Maybe our persistence will be rewarded.'

'Remember that day on the Tweed? We cast flies all day and caught nothing.'

'Which is why, gentlemen, I am ordering the start of phase one of, "Operation Slugs on Melons" … Mike.'

Mike wound up a field telephone. Into its handset, without explanation, clearly expecting those he was ringing to know what he was talking about, he said, 'Slugs on melons. I repeat, "Slugs on melons".'

'Chronicle, prepare Moses for action,' said Sir Charles, 'check the message he is carrying is secure. Unless Doyle does something stupid between now and sunrise, Moses goes in at first light. All we need is enough light for the boys to read our note.'

'What if Moses doesn't find Jack and George?' said Mike.

'He's Jack's pet. They went everywhere together. The lad was kind to the beast. Once he is inside the Monument I am certain he will seek out Jack. If he doesn't and if, for whatever reason, the boys don't get our message, we put everything on hold. We accept that once again Dole has the upper hand.'

3

'When I say, push, lads,' said the corporal in charge, 'I bloody well mean push. Push!'

Ever so slowly, at least at first, the fire engine began to move.

'This is how they built the pyramids,' said one of the pushers, 'bloody slave labour. Why don't they use its engine? That's what I want to know … bloody slave labour.'

'Walters, come here,' said the corporal.

'You want me to stop pushing, Corporal?'

'I want you where you can smell my breath. Walters, you are a Geordie Snot Gobbler. What are you, Walters?'

'A Geordie Snot Gobbler, Corporal.'

'I'll tell you why we are not using the fire engine's engine … it's because we don't want this geezer Doyle to know we're going to use its ladder to rescue those young heroes held hostage, against their will, in the Monument. Now, if you don't mind and it's not too much trouble, get back to building the pyramids afore Corporal Pharaoh, here, turns nasty and tears up your weekend pass. And keep your mouth shut otherwise we might as well use the bloody engine … the bloody noise you're making. You're a disgrace to the British Army, Walters.'

'Yes, Corporal.'

At one hundred and thirty-five feet the monument's railed platform was beyond the reach of any ladder. The plan was to use the fire engine's turntable ladder as a stepping stone.

The fireman in charge kept the ladder just off the column. This was to enable the marine, tasked with getting to the top, to see the railings at which he'd be aiming his grappling iron. The ladder, so much thinner at its tip than at its base, now fully extended, resting against nothing, swayed.

Sir Charles had personally picked the officer for the job. Hamish was the best of the best: came from a good family, fit, a crack shot, an experienced mountaineer, a little mad and blessed with a sense of adventure that had led him to climb Ben Nevis, in winter, in a kilt and without wearing underpants.

At the top of the ladder, as if perched on the end of a wobbly fishing rod, Hamish swung the grappling iron.

'He's like one of those cowboys in the pictures,' said the marksman, 'when they swing their lassos over their heads.'

'Bet he doesn't do it first try,' said the Photographer.

'How much?'

'A bob.'

'Put your money on top of that ammunition box.'

'I haven't got a bob on me.'

'Bugger that … if you lose you'll be wanting to give me one of your dirty pictures. You're a joke, you are.'

'Look!'

The grappling iron soared.

'It's over the railings.'

'It won't hold.'

'It will.'

'How much?'

'Piss off.'

'He's done it; good job you didn't take my bet. If you had I'd be short of a bob.'

'I did.'

'No, you didn't.'

'My god, he's fallen off the ladder.'

'No, he hasn't. He's climbing up the rope … go on, lad, you can do it. Where's my camera? Your blathering's made me forget my profession.'

4

From the ledge at the top of the Monument Hamish let down a rope to a waiting fireman. To this thin rope a fireman tied a much heavier rope. Hand over hand Hamish now pulled this rope to the top.

When both its ends were secure – one end to the railings at the top of the monument, the other to a ratchet bolted to the fire engine – two firemen began to work a long steel pole backwards and forwards.

Ever so slowly the rope began to tighten, rising from the ground like one of those barrage balloons floating over Armstrong's gun factory.

When its tension was judged to be correct a fireman gave Hamish a thumbs up.

To test the boys' escape route, Hamish sent down a message on a hook. 'Can you send me up a cup of tea? What a pity gravity only works one way!'

Sir Charles did his best to restrain his optimism. He was an old campaigner and knew everything there was to know about the cup and the lip. Still, it was a good start. If George and Jack were to be got out alive they needed luck by the bucketful.

Another piece of the jigsaw was in place. At a given signal Hamish would blow the door connecting the outside platform to the Monument's internal stairs. The boys would run up those stairs, dash out onto the platform, slide down the rope and be back at The Hall in time for tea. That was the plan. Sir Charles was too aware of what could go wrong. But for the life of him he could not think of an alternative.

In the redoubt a team of five heavily armed soldiers joined the photographer and the marksman. When they were given the signal, it would be their job to blow open the door set into the base of the Monument.

5

In the trenches this was the time you blew your whistle and led your men over the top. The time when you committed yourself. He'd read the message tied to Moses' collar without the aid of a candle. If he could do that, then so could Jack and George; no good sending a message to them when it was dark. He prayed the beast loved Jack enough to make it want to go straight to him. This was the part of the plan over which he had no control. He wasn't a gambling man. He'd watched friends in Monte Carlo take the most enormous risks. Their gambling had been voluntary, done for the hell of it. He was gambling with lives, not money. He had no choice. Dawn was exciting the starlings. His mouth was dry.

For the umpteenth time he re-read the note attached to Moses's collar. 'GEORGE JACK When you get this note shout, "Slugs on Melons". We will hear you. Never mind how, just shout. When the air raid sounds you must RUN up the stairs to the top of the Monument. And I mean RUN. Good luck, Egghead.' He stroked the ferret's back. 'He's very well behaved for a ferret.'

'I've used fisherman's knots,' said Mike; 'it won't come off. Luggage labels are indestructible.'

Before sending Moses on his mission Sir Charles looked at the Eavesdropper. 'All quiet, sir, nothing happening.'

'I've been ringing as per orders, sir,' said the Negotiator.

'The line is working, sir,' said the Eavesdropper. 'I've heard it ring.'

'But he's not answered?'

'No, sir.'

'He's not screamed or shouted?'

'No, sir.'

Sir Charles made up his mind. 'Are you ready, Chronicle?'

'I am, sir.'

'Good man. You're in charge of the beast. He likes you. I can tell. I'll let you do the honours. He's used to you handling him. Best to keep the wee chap as calm as possible. You know what to do?'

'I take Moses to the soldier over there. He climbs the ladder, not the big ladder, but the ladder off the small fire engine.'

'That's right, the one we used to access the vent slit through which we inserted the Eavesdropper's microphone.'

'I give Moses to the soldier. He climbs the ladder, puts Moses, with his message for George and Jack, through the slit.'

'And then we all cross our fingers,' said Sir Charles. 'If only animals could talk. Off you go, Chronicle. Good luck.'

6

Moses had been gone more than half an hour. What the hell was the ferret doing? The Eavesdropper, hands clapped to the earphones straddling his head, kept letting Sir Charles know that nothing was happening. Then …

'Sir, I can hear the boys.'

'Have they got the message?'

'Too early to say, sir.' The Eavesdropper concentrated, fell into his habit of placing a finger gently against each earphone. 'They're whispering, sir. Something's happening in there that's giving them something to talk about. It's not Doyle … no sound coming from him. Jack's whispering, "Hello" … Moses has found them, sir.'

Sir Charles picked up the spare head set, heard Jack say, 'Moses, you've come back.'

It's up to you, Jack. Take the lead, Jack. Read the note. Can you not see it? Show it to George. George, do you not see the Northumbrian tartan. It is your tartan. Talk. Tell me that you know what to do. That you've read the note. Say the code. Tell me that you are able to do all that the plan asks; that you are not tied up, that you are free and able to climb the stairs; reach the door at the top and you will be safe. Please, read the note.

'Say the code,' said Sir Charles, 'say it … say it. Dear God, say it.'

'Give them time,' said Mike; 'it's a lot for them to take in. They are not in the best shape.'

Why was Doyle shouting? He'd a vile mouth. What was happening inside that hell hole? Had Moses bitten Doyle? If only he could see what was happening. Say the code, lads. Shout it out. Scream it out. Whisper it, but just say it. A lot of banging. What was Doyle doing now?

'He's done that before, sir,' said the Eavesdropper. 'I don't think he's hitting the boys, more like lashing out at walls or anything else that's in his way.'

'He's very angry.'

'He is that, sir.'

Jack's voice, 'Are you going to kill us?'

'I might.'

'Have you not made up your mind?'

'Shut up! Shut up!'

'Slugs on melons.' George's voice.

'What was that? I've told you, shut up. Kids, you're driving me mad.'

'Slugs on melons.' … George's voice … shouting.

'Slugs on melons.' … Jack's voice … shouting.

'Slugs on melons … slugs on melons.' … George and Jack together … shouting … shouting.

'Damn you both. I will kill you … up the stairs out of my way or I will … I don't trust you two … slugs on melons … you're mad … all the English are mad … out of my way, up the stairs, you're not going to take Doyle by surprise.'

'Give the signal,' said Sir Charles.

7

Into a cloudless morning sky Mike fired a flare. Before it had reached its zenith the soldiers in the redoubt were running towards their objective.

As they did so, the Photographer gave the marksman a thumbs up, as if to say, 'The Irishman's had it now … wouldn't like to be in his shoes.'

On cue an air raid siren began to wail. In the tramcar the Eavesdropper told Sir Charles, 'They're on their way to the top, sir. I can hear them. They've heard the siren, sir, and are on their way. They know what to do. What a racket … wouldn't like to get in their way, sir.'

From the top of the Monument … Bang!

'He's blown the door,' said Sir Charles. He checked through binoculars. 'Hamish is going in.'

'They're still running up the stairs, sir,' said the Eavesdropper. 'I can't hear Doyle giving chase. They must be well on their way, sir.'

'One hundred and sixty-four steps to freedom,' said Sir Charles.

Mike confirmed that the soldiers from the redoubt were about to 'blow' the bottom door.

'Doyle won't know what's hit him.'

8

The explosion lifted the tramcar off its rails, sent a Gladstone bag, Thwack! Into the redoubt.

'Bloody hell!' said the marksman. 'Where's my tin hat?'

'The silly bugger's gone and blown himself up,' said the photographer, 'or someone's dropped a lighted fag in a box of bangers.'

'Hi! That's my hat, give it here. I'm the soldier, you're the photographer.'

'I'll buy it off you.'

'You've got no money, you haven't even a bob.'

'I have now, look … '

Pieces of paper, as if the column was a tree shedding its leaves, were falling all around them.

'It's snowing …' said the Photographer.

'Money …' said the Marksman.

In between smaller explosions, powerful enough to make them duck but insufficiently scary to rein in their acquisitiveness, the two men went at the floating dollar bills the way seagulls go at fish and chips.

9

Clouds of black smoke puffed out of the Monument's top and bottom doors, as if someone inside the column was working overtime on a pair of enormous bellows. Smaller puffs of smoke, creeping out from its air vents, gave it lots of little legs; making it look like a vertical millipede.

'I can't hear them, sir ... nothing ... sorry, sir,' said the Eavesdropper.

'The explosion's destroyed the microphone,' said Mike, 'that's why.'

Everyone in the tramcar had been cut by flying glass; through binoculars Sir Charles scanned the top of the Monument.

'I think I can see them ... damn the smoke; one large figure and two small ones. I think ... can't see ... too much smoke. Did you see them, Mike?'

Mike shook his head.

'Sergeant Small?'

'I'm afraid not, sir. What's all them floaters? It's like being at a wedding when folk throw confetti?'

Samples floated through the tramcar's shattered windows.

'Dollar bills,' said Sir Charles, 'I'll be damned.'

'Would that be the money, sir, the American courier was giving the Irish bombers?'

'I do indeed think that's what it is.'

'Speaking as an officer of the law, sir, we'll have a job getting it back, sir. If this courier bloke had given them pound notes it would be "Mrs Mulligan's washing", all over again.'

'I beg your pardon?'

'A local case, sir, happened a long time ago. Mrs Mulligan hung out her washing. It was purloined.'

'What's that to do with this?'

'In the Force, sir, when something is purloined and never seen again, it's "Mrs Mulligan's washing". Say "Mrs Mulligan's washing" to a bobby, sir, and he'll nod his head, knowing at once that you mean: "It's no good bothering, waste of police time." By now, any notes falling outside the cordon will be stuffed in bras and knickers, underpants and unsavoury places I'd rather not think about. Do you take my drift, sir?'

'I do indeed, Sergeant. Can anyone see the boys?'

Flashes of gunfire penetrated the smoke. Where were they coming from? Who was pulling the trigger? Who was the target? Whoosh! Bang! What the hell had Doyle stored in the column? For many minutes after the main explosion there were mini explosions.

10

Lady Elizabeth rose early; bad 'vibes' were stopping her sleeping. In the Great War she knew Charles had been hurt because of a pain in her arm.

George and Jack were in danger, Harry had told her. The vibes she was getting made her 'feel' something awful was happening to them. Why didn't Charles ring? No one in Newcastle would answer her calls. Did they not know she was the daughter of a duke?

In the reading of tea leaves Phyllis was nonpareil.

'Cups or mugs?' said Lady Elizabeth.

'Mugs, milady,' said Phyllis.'

'They are best?'

'More room to swirl, milady.'

'I understand. Shall I pour?'

'Begging your ladyship's pardon, I'll pour. You see, it's my parlour, so I'd best be Mother. When I bakes a cake I follow a recipe. It might be in my head or in a book, but I follows it. When I read the "leaves" I follows a recipe. A full cup, milady, or a half?'

'What does the recipe say?'

'Follow your inclines,' said Phyllis.

'That's allowed?'

'Under the circumstances …'

'A full cup?'

'A good choice, milady. More leaves, you see.'

'Does it matter where we pour the tea?'

'I have my lucky basin. It belonged to my mother and her mother before that; family lore says it was touched by Merlin, but I don't believe that.'

'I seem to remember it is important to drink the tea.'

'Not all of it, you don't, milady, just enough for the "leaves" to read your fingerprints. You remember, milady, when I read the "leaves" for the groom and the boot boy? I told the groom he should stay away from water and the boot boy he was going to fall in love.'

'But the groom fell in love and the boot boy drowned and you couldn't understand how you'd got it the wrong way round.'

'They'd switched cups, milady, hadn't they? Trying to be clever, they were, you see. They weren't serious about the "leaves". They weren't believers. You and me, milady, knows the power of the "leaves". "Leaves" is the kitchen's crystal ball.'

'It's nice tea. Earl Grey?'

'Yes, milady. I always finds the "Earl" gives a good window into the future.'

'George and Jack are prisoners inside Grey's Monument. Earl Grey's the earl who invented the blend. I wonder if that's an omen. One more sip. I've had no breakfast.'

'Worrying about George and Jack, milady?'

'Yes.'

'Worry never was good for appetites, nor for cooks. If people don't eat they don't need cooks, milady, and, if that happened, I'd be doing goodness knows what. Vibes?'

'Yes.'

'Good or bad, milady?'

'Mixed, but more good than bad.'

'Pour the tea into the basin, milady … slowly does it, we wants lots of leaves left in the mug. Leaves is words left by the "Great Mystery" for us to read.'

Phyllis took the mug.

'What do you see?'

'The globe in Sir Charles's study.'

'Not a column?'

'No.'

'That's disappointing.'

'The globe is on fire.'

Marigold joined them without knocking.

'Found you at last; I've been searching for you to tell you the news. Lizzie, your Prime Minister has been on the radio, Great Britain is at war with Germany.'

11

No longer having the strength to play the part of the leader who never shows weakness, Sir Charles sat in the tramcar with his head in his hands.

A crunching of feet stamping to attention on broken glass made him look up.

'The boys are safe, sir,' said Hamish, 'battered and bruised but …'

Mike and Sergeant Small caught him before he fell.

'Medic!' shouted Mike.

'It's for you, sir,' said a soldier handing Sir Charles a field telephone.

'Are you free to punt the pill?'

'Freddy, no, I'm not. I'm on a field telephone in a tramcar opposite Grey's Monument. While you've been out of action a lot has happened.'

'I know all about it. Are the boys safe?'

'Yes.'

'Splendid. Splendid. Wonderful, wonderful news.'

'You sound awfully chirpy for a chap recovering from a bash on the head.'

'It was never as bad as you thought. When Jack hit me and I ended up in hospital being looked after by that man, Crozier, I played dead Indian. A chap has to make use of the cards he's dealt. We've had our eyes on him for quite some time.'

'You never told me … the fellow operated on me for haemorrhoids.'

'I know, I know … just because the chap is an IRA sleeper doesn't mean he's not a good doctor. He tried to keep me dopey. When you told him I was as important as Lord Nelson, you made me a target, old boy. A nurse working in the "special wing" made sure the tablets he prescribed were harmless. She's an MI5 operative, like yourself, fluent in German. You might know her, she's Lord D's eldest.'

'Pamela?'

'The very same.'

'Pleased we're keeping things in the family.'

'It's the only way to run a tight ship.'

'Where's Crozier now?'

'In a police station. He was about to give me an injection when he was arrested.'

'A lethal dose?'

'That's what I wondered. Three big chaps wearing white coats took him away. When he knew the game was up he started name dropping. Told them he knew Julius Caesar and Alexander the Great.'

'Do you think he's mad?'

'Aren't all fanatics? The Pied Piper is in a coma. The knock on the head he received from Marigold was a lot more serious than mine. The chap in charge of your local railway station is missing. By the by, now that war's been declared … '

'Freddy, what did you say?'

'Now that war's been declared …'

'When?'

'You don't know? Chamberlain was on the radio, oh, fifteen minutes ago. There's talk of bringing Winston back into the government.'

'That's a step in the right direction.'

'By the by, CB's rounding up the Hitler Youth … can't have young Nazis wandering all over the place, spoiling our green and pleasant land, goodness knows what damage they might do. They are now enemy aliens. It's official.'

'What do you know about O'Neil?'

'Can't lock him up. He's an American.'

Sir Charles confided his new knowledge.

'MI5 didn't know about that.'

'At last there is something I know that you don't.'

'Never mind that, how are we going to deal with him? The Americans look after their own, you know.'

'Which is why I'm leaving Marigold and Mancini to deal with him. He's their problem.'

'Charlie, I'll have to go. The Hitler Youth are attacking the hospital.'

Before the line went dead, Sir Charles heard an explosion and small arms fire.

'Sergeant Small …'

'Sir?'

'I need a car, now.'

'What's happening?' said Mike.

'The Hitler Youth are attacking the hospital.'

12

Mike drove Sir Charles back to the Vicarage in the Chief Constable's car. En route they passed an army lorry full of soldiers.

'I wonder where they're going?' said Mike.

'Same place as us, I'll bet. Heaven help us. Did you see what they were armed with?'

'Pitch forks, 'said Mike. 'If they think the Hitler Youth can be harvested like hay they are in for a shock.'

'Faster, Mike, faster.'

A mile from the hospital the army had set up a road block.

'At least they have rifles,' said Sir Charles.

Two soldiers approached the car. When they saw Sir Charles's army uniform and rank, they came to attention.

'Stand easy,' said Sir Charles. 'What the hell is going on? Why the road block?'

'It's the Hitler Youth, sir. Once they knew we was at war with them they turned nasty.'

'Very nasty, sir,' said the other soldier.

'What have they done?'

'They've attacked the hospital and the Vicarage, sir.'

'It's the mushroom poisoning, sir. They're after revenge.'

'The devils are in groups, sir. They've stolen cars. The ones we've captured have rubbed mud on their faces, proper little camouflage experts, they are.'

'They're making for the coast, sir.'

'The masts at Boulmer?'

'Yes, sir, that's what the officer said.'

'Who's in charge?'

'CB, sir. I mean Major Clarkson-Ball, sir, begging your pardon, sir. The Nazis are armed, sir. They are in no mood for taking prisoners.'

'We've heard a rumour, sir, that they've killed the major.'

'Are they a second front, sir?'

'People are saying Hitler sent them here to guard a landing ground for paratroopers.'

'Rubbish. Give me your rifle.'

'It's not loaded, sir, no ammo for it in the armoury.'

As they sped off Sir Charles said, 'Clearly, England is not prepared for war. If a couple of dozen teenage Nazis can cause this much mayhem, God help our chaps when they come up against panzers.'

'The German is a good soldier,' said Mike. 'He's well trained and well led.'

'Hitler's taught them to jump over six foot walls and not give a bugger. This is going to be a long war, Mike. Heaven help Germany if she loses. If they thought the Versailles Treaty was too harsh a punishment the penalties imposed on them for a second defeat will demand they be left destitute.'

'Heaven help us if they win.'

'America would never allow that to happen.'

'I wonder if the Nazis have killed CB.'

'We'll soon find out.'

13

At the Cottage Hospital windows had been broken. A wheelchair lay on its side. A Wolsey saloon car was on top of a flower bed, its doors open, as if its occupants had left in a hurry. What with unseasonal storms and the Hitler Youth, the lupines were having a rough time.

Two nurses, all white starch and efficiency, were bandaging a wounded soldier. He looked as if he'd live. Broken glass all over the place. In their time in France both men had seen a lot worse.

Had the Hitler Youth attacked The Hall? Where was Freddy?

'Charlie!' A booming voice.

'Freddy!'

'How'd you like the uniform? No time to change, you see. It's the uniform of a patient. In the Guards you wear a red tunic, in the Cottage Hospital you wear this flimsy thing that barely covers the vitals. The Nazis paid us a visit to collect their pals still alive after the mushroom poisoning scare … funny business that. They've killed CB, you know. His motorbike's up the road. By the by, The Hall's safe. As soon as this show started I sent up a platoon to look after Elizabeth and the Americans. It would be a blot on the escutcheon, if the Hitler Youth killed HMG's American guests.'

'It might have provided them with a casus belli.'

'They'll need a kick up the arse before they help us in this war. They'll know what life is about if they ever have to run an Empire.'

'What happened to CB?'

'Funny business. We chaps were paying our respects to Pruney, the hearse was taking her home, support CB in his hour of need, you know. I nearly didn't join the line-up … not dressed for the job but, knowing CB, I reasoned the more the merrier, no levity intended, but you take my drift. When he sees me, the head of MI5, bowing his head, I'm thinking, it'll give him a boost … status, Charlie, status, the pecking order meant a lot to CB. It would do you no harm, Charles, to take a leaf out of his book.

'The hearse taking the poor gal back home … CB wanted her "home" before the burial … the hearse was just about to leave when the Nazis arrived … bad timing but CB always was unlucky … they attacked us with grenades … all hell broke loose. Those of their pals recovering from mushroom poisoning joined them … chaos, absolute bedlam … that's when they commandeered the hearse. To get as many of their own in … well, they removed … to call a spade, a spade, they chucked Pruney out. The coffin broke open. Terrible, terrible, I never knew she'd lost her head … there was no holding CB back, went after the hearse on a motorbike … blown up by a stick grenade. He's all over the place. See those crows on the roof … I've a pretty good idea what they're dining off … terrible … terrible.

'The Nazis are all over the place, damn them. It's guerrilla warfare, Charlie
… a shameful incident at the post office. The Nazis blew up its switchboard
… destroyed our communications … all the lines are down. We found the
postmistress and her fancy man, starkers, under a bed. He was tying his Long
Johns to a curtain pole, thought the war had started and wanted to surrender.
If German paratroopers ever do land, Charlie, we're done for. If London's not to
be the next Warsaw, someone's going to have to put a bit of backbone into our
people.'

14

The gates to The Hall were closed.

'We never close the gates,' said Sir Charles. 'Mike, toot the horn.'

A bell-cheeked soldier appeared from behind a bush eating a pie.

'What … you want?'

Mike got out of the car.

'What do you want?'

'Open the gates.'

He looked at the police car.

'Police, are you? There's a war going on, mister. Its soldiers what fight wars, not Bobbies in plain clothes.'

Sir Charles got out of the car. At the sight of the latter's uniform the soldier snapped to attention.

'Open up,' said Sir Charles.

'Yes, sir, oh, who goes there?'

'I live here, damn you; open up.'

15

Bert answered the door holding a Webley. In the lounge the Americans were drinking whisky.

'Charles,' said Lady Elizabeth, 'where are the boys?'

'Safe and well in Newcastle's Royal Victoria Infirmary. When I was told our hospital was under attack, I'd to put them on the back burner.'

'We've had the most frightful scare ... dreadful, dreadful news about CB, an unlucky family. If his stud business comes up for sale, Charles, we might take a look at it?'

'If the price is right and Hitler hasn't bombed it and us to smithereens.'

'The army has been wonderful. Freddy sent them to guard me. He's out of hospital, you know.'

'I know.'

'Excuse me ... '

Lady Elizabeth ran out of the room, sobbing.

'Excuse me,' said Sir Charles.

In the privacy of their bedroom husband and wife embraced.

'I've been so worried, Charles. What must the Americans think of me, dashing out like that?'

'I think they will understand.'

'I didn't want to break down in front of everyone.'

'You didn't.'

'My reputation is safe?' She tried to smile.

'Yes.'

'And, the boys, they really are safe?'

'Yes.'

'I want them home.'

'As soon as the telephones are working I'll ring the Infirmary. When you see them, you must be brave. Doyle has used his fists on them.'

'They are bruised?'

'Yes, I've been told they look as if they've been in a fight which, god bless them, they have ... a very one-sided fight. Now, bring me up to date ... what news about O'Neil? As far as I could tell, when Mike and I barged in downstairs, he was the only one not carrying a weapon. As usual he did not seem part of the company.'

'He's worried.'

'The golf bag?'

'Yes.'

'Mario has used our secret weapon?'

'As far as I can tell all the Americans are out to get him. If he was an English gentleman Marigold told me she'd give him a loaded pistol and tell him to go for a walk in the woods.'

'But he's not an English gentleman, is he?'

'No, he is not; he's a banker ... an American banker. Bert removed the bag that did not smell of lavender and replaced it with the bag with the false bottom. The one discarded by Crozier. I find it impossible to believe he's not on our side. Charles, you were under his knife ... what damage might he have done you? When the switch had taken place Marigold challenged O'Neil to a knock-about game of golf. When he removed a club and found it short you could tell he was taken aback.'

'What's his story?'

'He claims never to have seen them. Marigold needled him so much, he stormed off; since then he's been in the leper colony. Mario is an awful tease. Every time he sees O'Neil he pretends to pot a golf ball, Angus just looks at him and Jasper puts a pretend gun to his head and pulls the trigger. Charles, they've sent him to Coventry. It's awful. It's been like this since Harry and Mario came back from Newcastle yesterday evening with the bad news about the boys ... Charles, I was so worried, you might have rung.'

'Not so easy, my dear, in the midst of all that was going on ... anyway, I reasoned that you'd know no news is good news.'

'When you were away I threatened to scream at the next person to give me that piece of advice.'

'Sorry.' He squeezed her hand; she squeezed back. 'Are you up to re-joining the party?'

'For a little while I was forgetting I'm the daughter of a duke; of course I'm ready.'

'As soon as Freddy has rounded up those young Nazis he'll be knocking on our door demanding to be fed. I'd better tell Phyllis to expect him. By the way, how close to The Hall did the Nazis get?'

'Marigold was the hero. She dropped a Nazi through a mullion ... shot a grenade out of his hand like a trick shooter. She'd make Harry a wonderful wife.'

16

George and Jack arrived back at The Hall in an ambulance, accompanied by a nurse who told Lady Elizabeth, 'They are walking wounded, milady. Please do not smother them with kisses and cuddles. They are bruised. Too much physical affection will result in more bruising and we don't want that, do we? Come along, boys, you are home now.'

Word that George and Jack were back spread. Before they were out of the ambulance the original welcoming party of Sir Charles, Lady Elizabeth and Bert was swelled by the Americans and every member of The Hall's staff.

Phyllis cried. Bert offered her his handkerchief. A scullery maid, the emotion of the occasion making her forget her lowly position, shouted, 'Three cheers for George and Jack.' Bert led the cheering.

'It's your turn now, Bert,' said Phyllis.

Bert dabbed his eyes.

George and Jack saw smiling faces, heard cheering; knew they were home, that they were no longer in danger. They did not want to be hailed as heroes, they wanted to lie down in a nice warm bed with clean sheets smelling of lavender. They'd run out of adrenalin. They were exhausted.

The best they could give in reply to such a warm welcome were wan smiles and feeble waves.

'Moses!' shouted the scullery maid, 'we want Moses.'

'Moses!' came the cry from the well-wishers, pretty well in chorus.

The sound of his name made the ferret move from an inside pocket in Jack's Norfolk to one of his guardian's armpits where he enjoyed being squeezed like a bagpipe.

'Bed!' said the nurse who'd come with the boys in the ambulance.

She was a tall woman with blonde hair and ice-blue eyes like a husky's. Her nurse's uniform with its starched headpiece, as big as the spinnaker on Freddy's yacht, thought Sir Charles, made it impossible for her not to be obeyed.

Sooner than those wishing them well would have wished, the boys were put to bed. Phyllis was disappointed but understood why they'd not eaten any of the goodies she'd prepared for them.

After the euphoria engendered by George and Jack's escape the adults returned to the topic of war. When would the German bombers come?

'I'm worried about how I'm going to get home,' said Mancini. 'I have a wife and children back in the States.'

'The Nazis wouldn't dare torpedo a ship flying the Stars and Stripes. Hitler would be mad to declare war on the States,' said Weinberger.

'What if he is mad?' said Sir Charles.

17

Sir Charles took the call in his study.

'Are you free to punt the pill?' asked the familiar voice.

'Give me time to check the weather.'

Sir Charles pressed the button.

'Go ahead, Freddy, I'm on the scrambler.'

'As you will have gathered, Charlie, communications have been restored. My apologies to Elizabeth, but I won't be able to make it tonight; there's a flap on. The Hitler Youth are proving more difficult to catch than a swarm of bees. The blighters are popping up all over the place. They've wiped out the men I put in place to stop them reaching the masts ... captured one of our machine guns, damn them. They've been firing at my men from the back of the hearse they commandeered. I've had to order armoured cars from Fenham Barracks ... all very embarrassing. You should be OK at The Hall. The Nazis are after the masts. The ones we've captured are wild as rattlesnakes ... waste of time being nice to them. The boys?'

'Sound asleep in bed.'

'Best place for them after what they've been through ... and the Americans?'

'Packing.'

'The rats are leaving the sinking ship?'

'They won't be going home on a ship flying the Red Ensign, that's for sure. All our ships will be targets. From the way they are talking I don't think they'd feel safe crossing the Atlantic in a battleship.'

'What's your feelings about the Americans declaring war on Germany?'

'America will sit on the fence for as long as it can.'

'Charlie, between you and me, I'm worried. If a few dozen adolescent Nazis can cause this much damage, I don't give much for our chances when the slogging starts. It'll be 1914 all over again. My heart goes out to the men who will have to do what we did.'

'CB was looking forward to the war.'

'Silly fool. I know it's bad form to criticise the dead but only a fool or a madman would look forward to a war.'

'He wanted me to put in a word for him, fancied himself leading a battalion over the top. I tried to tell him he was too old, that he was a part-time soldier, that his German equivalents were young, full-time professionals but ... will you recommend him for a gong?'

'Letter's in the post, as they say; government publicity will mythologise his charging the hearse on a motorbike. It will make him a hero. What's happening to O'Neil?'

'Denies everything … terrible atmosphere when he's around. He's dining in his room tonight. Marigold will be informing the President of our suspicions. What happens after that is a matter for the Americans. He's a big name in the States. His crime would not be good publicity. Personally, I don't bloody care what happens to him, I have enough problems of my own. Now that CB's with the angels Elizabeth wants to know who will be in charge of our local civil defence. Her concern is the unresolved problem of how many stretchers will fit into the back of one of our Rolls-Royces when the cars' rear seats have been removed.'

'Charlie, I'll have to go. I can hear shooting.'

'The Hitler Youth?'

'Sounds like them.'

18

To clear his head, Sir Charles walked to Mike's cottage. He found the gamekeeper skinning a rabbit.

'Let's go into the shed,' said Mike, 'I've a couple of bottles hidden.'

Later, when the two men were deep in their cups, Harry joined them.

'Look who's here … come and join us,' said Mike. 'Sorry I can't offer you a drink … the cellar's dry, you see.' To prove his point he turned an empty bottle upside down. 'You wouldn't happen, by any chance, just happen to be carrying a hip flask, would you?'

'No, I would not.'

'Bad form coming into a mess empty handed, isn't that right, Charlie?'

'Very bad form.'

'It's called etiquette, Master Harry.'

'I think you should call me, "sir". I am an officer and a gentleman, you are a gamekeeper, an employee. Uncle Charles …'

'You'll always be Master Harry to me.'

The gamekeeper stood up. At well over six foot and, after a lifetime of hard manual labour, as tough and branchy as a mature oak, he made the teenager look weedy. He pointed an accusing finger at the young man's Norfolk. 'Tut! Tut! You been dribbling, Harry? What's that?'

When Harry looked down, Mike whipped up his finger.

'Howzat!'

Harry waited for Mike and Uncle Charles to stop laughing. Old men. Juvenile humour. At the same time he was annoyed that he'd fallen for the trick.

'Has Elizabeth sent you to spy on me?' said Sir Charles.

'I've come to say goodbye, Uncle Charles. A telegram's come to say I'm to report to my squadron. I'm leaving now.'

Sir Charles looked at Mike, Mike looked at Sir Charles; this was serious.

'Give me your hand, sir,' said Mike.

'Damn you, Mike, I think I like it best when you call me Master Harry.'

'That's my boy! What's that?'

Harry looked down. Mike shook his head.

'Good luck, Master Harry.'

'Thank you and thank you for making me retrieve my gun from the river. A lesson for me to stay alert in combat … don't fall for silly tricks.'

'I'll walk back with you to The Hall,' said Sir Charles.

'Watch out for the Hitler Youth,' said Mike.

'Freddy has them in the bag.'

Before going round a corner and out of Mike's line of sight, Harry paused and turned. After a few seconds of stand-off, Mike came to attention and saluted. Harry saluted back.

19

They lay in bed, side by side, on their backs, holding hands.

'When will the bombs start falling?' said Lady Elizabeth.

'As of now, I don't think even Hitler could answer that question,' said Sir Charles. 'I suspect our declaration of war may have taken him by surprise. He is not as ready for war as he'd like to be.'

'But more ready than we are?'

'While we have been reading P G Wodehouse, they have been burning the midnight oil with von Clausewitz. The German is a hard nut to crack. He is a formidable opponent. The determination of the Hitler Youth to fight to the last man, or should I say "boy", scares me. They believe in the Third Reich. It is a cause for which they are prepared to die. Our lads will not be going into battle against soldiers but against fanatics. The fanatic does not fear death; the soldier does. CB was fanatical when he charged the hearse. He's going to get a medal, you know, so Freddy tells me.'

'The VC? He was jealous of your VC.'

'I would have given the silly chump mine if I'd thought it would have stopped my nightmares.'

'Charles, don't talk like that. It is your medal … you should be proud of it.'

'Well, I'm not. When we were seeing Harry off I was tempted to shoot him in the foot … tell him, you're wounded, old boy, no fighting for you … stay at home and be safe.'

'Harry's a patriot. I'm proud of him. Someone has to stand up to Hitler.'

'Quite right, my dear.'

'You don't sound as if you meant that.'

'I do and I don't. I don't want Harry to get hurt.'

'Will Jack and George be prosecuted?'

'For poisoning the Hitler Youth? I don't think they meant to kill, I really don't. But, whether they did or didn't, no longer matters. Now that we are at war with Germany, no investigation will take place. The police will not be involved. I suspect that by the time this conflict comes to an end the incident will be forgotten … anyway the Germans stole the mushrooms. It was their own fault. In the coming conflict hundreds, probably hundreds of thousands will die. Both sides will commit atrocities. Things will be done that will make us hang our heads in shame. Battles will make the names of towns no one has ever heard of, household names. If battles had not been fought in their fields no one would have heard of Agincourt and Waterloo.'

'I do hope The Hall never achieves fame that way.'

'If it does I think we may assume that we will be dead.'

'We'd die fighting?'

'I'd dynamite the place before I'd let the Germans have it.'

'I've told Phyllis to prepare an early breakfast. The Americans are determined on an early start. They want to get to their embassy in London before it's bombed to smithereens. I shall miss Marigold but be pleased to see the back of O'Neil. If he is an IRA courier he deserves to be shot.'

'Best to let the Americans deal with their own. If we are to win this war we must keep them sweet.'

'You know, lying here reminds me of Papa when Mother died. He would not accept that she was dead. Do you remember how cross he got with you when you tried to make him face the truth?'

'Threatened to have me put in the looney bin.'

'I cannot believe it is all going to start again … Great Britain at war with Germany … Charles, tell me it isn't true.'

Monday 4th September 1939

1

Mike drove the first Rolls-Royce. Billy, a stable boy who wished to work with 'petrol' rather than 'manure', sat, full of self-importance, behind the wheel of the second Rolls. They stopped in line, one behind the other, in front of The Hall's front door; making, for the time they were there, a taxi rank. The Americans were going home.

'Under normal circumstances,' said Sir Charles, looking forlorn, 'we'd have had all the staff out to see you chaps and Marigold on your way … a regular guard of honour for you to inspect, but, sadly, circumstances are not normal.'

'The staff,' explained Lady Elizabeth, 'are on a civil defence course. When they come back to doing what we pay them to do they will know all about how to put out an incendiary bomb.' She dabbed a tearful eye. 'When you "guys" … I am trying to sound American; when you "guys" are sipping your cocktails in Manhattan, I do hope, perhaps between sips, you will spare a thought for the people who gave you Democracy and you, Marigold, for your ancestors.'

'Lizzie,' said Marigold, putting her arm round the older woman, 'I'm on your side. I'm batting for you … now I'm sounding like a Limey. The President, he's on your side, I know he is.'

'So, what's stopping him declaring war on Germany?'

'Politics,' said Mancini, 'and people who eat more than five Hershey Bars a day.'

He nodded at O'Neil who was taking big nervous bites out of one. The fellow's nerves weren't looking good.

As had become his habit he'd chosen to stand apart from Sir Charles and his guests. His self-imposed isolation suited everyone, just fine.

'Bert,' said O'Neil, wiping his mouth with the back of a hand, in a manner Lady Elizabeth later described as 'vulgar, 'put my bags in the Rolls to be driven by the young man; put them on the back seat … spread them out.'

'That will leave no room for the other gentlemen, sir.'

'That's the idea.'

'Yes, sir.'

'Bert … '

'Thank you, sir. That is most kind.'

'The door, Bert, open the door. I didn't tip you to stand idle.'

'Of course not, sir.'

In the Rolls O'Neil looked like a man in a condemned cell.

'What will happen to him?' said Sir Charles.

'He has powerful friends,' said Macdonald.

'If he becomes an embarrassment he might just cease to exist,' said Weinberger.

'That is the sort of thing the Nazis would do,' said Lady Elizabeth. 'Surely we are fighting this war to stop things like that happening.'

'No phaeton, Charles?' said Mancini.

'Now that war's been declared I don't feel up to making romantic gestures. I dread what is about to happen … such a sunny day, yet I feel shivery. When I close my eyes I see the faces of the friends I lost in the Great War. How many will I lose in the coming conflict? Will dear Harry come through safe and sound? Nobody knows. Despite the weather, I don't think any of us feels "sunny", do we?'

'Don't let the Nazis depress you,' said Weinberger.

'If they do, they'll have won without having fired a shot,' said Mancini.

'I thought the Great War would be the last war,' said Sir Charles. 'It seems unbelievable that we're once again going over the top … madness … madness.'

'Too much whisky last night,' advised Macdonald, in a friendly attempt to pass over his host's melancholia; 'the electric soup's not for everyone.'

Bert held open the door of the Rolls Mike was driving.

'Bert, you big slab of English oak, gimme a kiss,' said Marigold. She proffered a cheek.

'Do as you are told, Bert,' said Sir Charles.

'Charlie, I do believe my breach of etiquette has made you smile. Thank goodness something has cheered you up.'

'It's not normal procedure, sir,' said Bert.

'Bert, dear thing, after this war is over the English class system will be as dead as the dodo … dooks will marry cooks and earls will have to sell their pearls.'

'I certainly hope not,' said Lady Elizabeth.

'Put your peck here, Bert, I'm waiting.'

Bert obliged.

'Thank you, Bert … a present for you. Among my many talents I'm a pretty good pickpocket … this is from O'Neil's pocket.'

'A Hershey Bar,' said Bert,' thank you, milady.'

'Bert, I'm an American. I'm not a "milady".'

'Thank you, Marigold.'

'That's better … chin up, you guys, next stop the White House. Bert, the door, please, the front door. I wish to sit beside Mike.'

'Thank you, Bert,' said Mancini.

'Thank you, sir.'

Bert knew the value of the tip without looking. Very nice. He loved Americans.

'Thank you, Bert,' said Macdonald.

'Thank you, sir.'

The note slipped into his palm felt handsome.

'Thank you, Bert,' said Weinberger.

'Thank YOU, sir.'

2

'Give them lots of waves,' said Sir Charles, 'make them feel we've really enjoyed having them.'

'Bon voyage!' shouted Lady Elizabeth. 'Safe journey back to the land of milk and honey.'

'You know,' said Sir Charles, 'I'm standing in front of my own house, I'm master of all I survey, yet I feel threatened. It's as if the Americans are fleeing, rather than leaving.'

'I know, it's as if one has been jilted.'

'Left standing at the altar. My dear, we are at the start of a long journey. How will it end?'

'I know you'll think me silly but this morning I took my tea cup to Phyllis.'

'When you left the breakfast table at speed clutching your tea cup, opinion was divided as to whether you were going to be sick or tear a strip off a servant. Weinberger said, "Someone's in for it." I, of course, had my suspicions.'

'But you kept them to yourself?'

'Of course, I don't want people thinking I'm married to a pagan. There are some things a gentleman doesn't talk about in public. Sex is one and the other is that your wife reads tea leaves.'

'Charles, you have your whisky, I have my tea leaves. I think that's fair. Anyway, you'll never guess what Phyllis saw in the "leaves" … a swastika, one of its legs was broken.'

'That means?'

'We are going to win the war.'

'I hope you're right. What would the Americans think if they knew we Brits were reading tea leaves to see into the future? With their love of technology and "can do" attitude I think they'd shudder. We can only win this war with their help. Marigold's on our side, I know. Unless O'Neil is a double agent, he's definitely against us.'

'Climbing into the Rolls like that … did he say "thank you"? Goodbye? You'd think him being a banker he'd have better manners.'

'I wouldn't.'

'Did you notice that in the Rolls he was eating one of those chocolate bars Marigold gave Bert?'

'Hershey Bars, milady,' said Bert.

'I do hope he doesn't make a mess inside the Rolls. I dislike finding chocolate on upholstery.'

'It's like watching the last lifeboat pull away from the Titanic. Yes, Bert, what is it?'

'It's Tom, sir, he wants a word … says it's urgent. I made him wait until the Americans had gone.'

'Where is he?'

'I'm here, sir,' said Tom. 'You won't like what I'm going to tell you, sir … it's the melons, sir.'

'Jack up to his old tricks, is he? After what he's been through, Tom, he can do what he likes. As far as I'm concerned he has carte blanche. I'm just so pleased that he and George are alive and, if they still have enough pluck in them to put snails on my melons, well, so be it.'

'It's worse than that, sir. I think it best, if you've the time, sir, to come and see for yourself.'

3

In the greenhouse Sir Charles held his nose.

'See what I mean, sir.'

'The boys didn't do this,' said Sir Charles.

'That's what I thought, sir.'

'Any ideas?'

'The Hitler Youth, sir. Everything was fine when I shut the door and put the melons to bed last night. You knows, sir, I always tells them, goodnight. Someone slept here last night … maybe more than one, and they was hungry, that's why they've eaten all the melons.'

'Did they have to use the place as a toilet?'

'I'll soon have that out of the way, sir, but, we'll have to wait another year for a crop of melons.'

'What's that?'

'A bandage, sir.'

'It looks bloody.'

The explosion, albeit a long way off, made Sir Charles duck.

'Get down, Tom! Get down!'

The gardener obeyed. He'd never been to war. For the life of him he couldn't see why Sir Charles was lying on the floor.

A few seconds later, Sir Charles reached the same opinion.

'Sorry about that, Tom–' standing up and dusting himself down– 'but that was a German stick grenade going off … thought I was back in the trenches. The only reason I'm here now to pay your wages is that in the Great War I learnt very early on to keep my head down. Now, if you'll excuse me, I'm off to find out what the hell is going on.'

He ran. The Hitler Youth, it had to be ... how everyone had underestimated them. How many were they? So much for Freddy saying they were all in the bag.

The tooting of a car's horn made him stop. From a mass of shrubbery a Rolls-Royce had appeared, like a black butterfly from a chrysalis.

4

He caught up with the car at The Hall's front door where he found Marigold holding a handkerchief to a bruised cheek. Beside her, Mancini, Weinberger and Macdonald were sitting on the ground, looking pale and shaky.

As if someone had pressed a button for room service, Bert appeared with a tray of drinks and Lady Elizabeth with a bottle of sal-volatile.

'Bert,' said Weinberger, 'I love you. Hell, I'm lucky to be alive.'

'Death to Hitler,' said Mancini.

'I'll drink to that,' said Macdonald. 'It's a long time since I've been under fire … opens the bowels and scares the shit out of you.'

Mike sat behind the Rolls' steering wheel, unable to move, as if in a catatonic state; his knuckles glowed white; his staring gaze, held by something only he could see.

Sir Charles waited. After many seconds, Mike said, 'After all their tries to get me in the Great War, this time they nearly did.'

'But,' said Sir Charles, 'they didn't. Are you hurt?'

'No.'

'Let go of the wheel … that's an order.'

'Bugger your orders. I'll let go when I want to.'

'Where's the other car, the one driven by Billy?'

'It stopped … I didn't. I recognised the station master. He wasn't wearing his railway uniform but I knew him … standing in the middle of the road, holding up his hand like a copper on traffic duty. I've sharp eyes. I spotted one of the Hitler Youth hiding behind a bush. I put my foot down. The young Nazi threw a grenade. It was close, Charlie. I came back cross-country.'

'The Rolls Billy was driving stopped, you say?'

'That's what I said.'

'I suspect O'Neil has had dealings with the station master. I wonder if Billy was told to stop.'

'By O'Neil?'

'It's a possibility. I think the station master and the member of the Hitler Youth you saw, spent the night in my melon house. They've trashed everything, used the place as a toilet, sacrilege. I think one of them is injured. They left behind a blood stained rag.'

5

Sir Charles telephoned Freddy, explained all that had happened.

'Send reinforcements, soldiers armed with rifles, please, not pitchforks. Freddy, I'll have to go, someone's taking pot-shots at my home.'

At the front of The Hall, Sir Charles found the Americans lying on the ground. He took charge.

'Everyone inside. Bert, guard the door. Elizabeth, women to the cellars.'

'I'm not going in a cellar,' said Marigold. 'Give me a gun. I can shoot. Charlie, I know you mean well but we survived yesterday without you.'

'History doesn't repeat itself.'

'Give me a gun. Lizzie, which way to the gun room?'

'Where are the boys?' said Lady Elizabeth. 'Where are the boys? Charles, they are out there … find them.'

'They could be anywhere on the estate.'

'Find them … we have to find them.'

'I'll get the dogs,' said Mike, 'they'll find them.'

'Marigold, you stay here and guard the house,' said Sir Charles, 'I'll go with Mike. But first to the gun room.'

6

Two black Labradors sniffed a pair of George's shoes.

'Find!' said Mike. 'Find!'

The dogs led Mike and Sir Charles to the kitchen.

'What's all that shooting and banging?' said Phyllis. 'They're not at it again, are they, the young Nazis? It was Miss Marigold what saved us yesterday. That girl deserves a medal.'

'Have you seen George and Jack?'

'I fed them "extras" this morning, sir … you know what growing boys are like. When I saw their bruises I screamed. I wanted to make them butter poultices but they would have none of it, said they looked worse than they were. To show them I loved them I gave Moses a bit of butter. Making a friend of someone's friend, I always say, pleases everybody. The little biter liked the butter but he's the hero, sir, isn't he? At least that's what I've heard. We can't give him a medal but we can give him butter. The boys ate sausages outside.'

'Show me.'

'Is it safe to open the door?'

'Yes.'

'They sat there, sir, see all those shavings, sir? They're from Jack's arrows. He borrowed one of my kitchen knives to sharpen their ends. I hadn't the heart to say no, after what they've been through they need a bit of spoiling … an extra spoonful of sugar never hurt a pan of gooseberries, an old saying but none the worse for that.'

'Do you know where they were going?'

'George was excited because he said Jack was going to make him a bow.'

The dogs sniffed the shavings.

'Find!' said Mike. 'Find!'

7

'Are you certain they have the scent?' said Sir Charles.

'Trust me. Find! Find! Good Girl! Good Boy! Jack and George are lads; lads don't walk in straight lines, they wander, especially when they're looking for something,' said Mike.

'What are they after?'

'If what Phyllis told us is true, they're looking for a piece of wood to make George a bow … see how the dogs keep going over to bushes and trees where there's saplings; look, there, someone, and not long ago at that, snapped off a branch.'

'How's the leg? You seem to be limping.'

'Sore. Damn Nazis … when that grenade went off, I'll admit this to you, Charlie, but to no one else, I almost lost control … thought I was back in the trenches.'

'I was in the melon house when I heard it … like you, knew at once what it was, flung myself on the greenhouse's floor. I think Tom thought I was mad. Our nerves are not what they used to be. That is why I am so worried about the boys. They have not yet learned to keep their heads down.'

'If we see an adder, we leave it alone …'

'If Jack and George see one they will pick it up. They have the curiosity of kittens, which is why they were unable to resist going into the Monument.'

'You mean, if they see the Hitler Youth they won't run away?'

'They may retreat but, as soon as they are able, they will go onto the attack. Jack is feral.'

'I hope we are wasting our time.'

'So do I; nothing would please me more than to be told the two imps are back at The Hall, all safe and sound, tucking into one of Phyllis's apple pies. Freddy is sending a platoon over. They'll scour the area … best if we keep well behind the dogs; if any of the Hitler Youth are hiding I want to see them before they see me. I've no wish to go down in history as the grandee who was shot in his own garden.'

'Find! Find!' said Mike.

His urgings increased the dogs' enthusiasm. It was what they'd been trained to do. It was what they were good at. They knew that when they found what Mike was looking for they'd get pats on the head, maybe even a biscuit. Their velvet noses searched the ground at an astonishing speed.

A line drawn through a scatter graph, little x's marking the dogs' various excursions into dead ends, would have early hinted at their final destination – the campsite set up by the Nazis at the bottom of the Meadow Field.

As soon as they were close to it the dogs began to bark. In anticipation of he knew not what, Sir Charles closed the shotgun he was carrying. Mike unslung his Mauser.

The dogs' interest, however, was not in the tents the Nazis had left behind but in a nearby clump of rhododendron bushes.

'Don't shoot, sir! Don't shoot! It's me.'

'Come out with your hands up,' said Mike.

'It's me, sir,' said Billy.

Sir Charles and Mike lowered their weapons. The dogs stopped barking. Had they found what they were supposed to be looking for?

They were confused. This human had the wrong smell.

8

'The Nazi who shot Mr O'Neil, sir, went that way. I saw him. He was chasing Jack. Jack was shouting at him, in German, I think it was German. I don't know what he was saying but the German did and he didn't like what he was hearing. It was the flag that did it though, sir.'

'The flag?'

'Jack was waving it at the Nazi.'

'The Union Jack?'

'No, sir … a white flag with, sort of blue triangles on it.'

'The Star of David,' said Mike.

'Jack's goading the Nazi,' said Sir Charles. 'Any sign of George?'

'I think I might have seen him at the top of the hill, sir, but I'm not sure.'

'Jack's leading the Nazi into a trap … I know he is,' said Sir Charles.

'Sir,' said Billy, 'why am I shaking? I want it to stop but it won't.'

'You're in shock, Billy; your body is reminding you that you are lucky to be alive.'

'Will it stop, sir?'

'Yes … it will stop. You said the Nazi shot Mr O'Neil …'

'Mr O'Neil told me to stop the car, sir. I did as I was told … then, everything happened fast … there was an explosion … a big blonde Nazi pulled me out of the car. He was going to shoot me but Mr O'Neil shouted, "No!" When they were arguing that's when I said, "Billy, I'm out of here."'

'You ran?'

'Leapt into the bracken, sir … funny what you can do when you have to. Did I do right, sir?'

'Yes, Billy, you did right.'

'He fired at me, sir. But he wasn't even close. When I knew they weren't going to follow me I doubled back. I've been spying on them ever since, sir … they couldn't see me but I could see them … and hear them. Bad tempered fellows, all of them. They tried to start the car, sir, but it wouldn't. When you find it, sir, you'll see there's lots of little holes in its bonnet.'

'Shrapnel damage from the grenade,' said Mike.

'When the car wouldn't start I don't think they knew what to do. The man who'd stood in the middle of the road to stop the cars … I think him and Mr O'Neil knew each other; they put their heads together. The Nazi didn't like that … he kept walking up to them and shouting, in German, I suppose it was. It was Mr O'Neil's chocolate bar that did for him, sir. The gentleman was eating one when we left The Hall, sir and through the car's mirror I seen him start a second. The Nazi said he was hungry and wanted the chocolate bar. He said he was sick of eating melons. Well, sir, one thing led to another. I couldn't believe my eyes when the Nazi shot him. I mean, sir, you don't shoot someone for a chocolate bar, do you, sir? I mean, sir, what's the world coming to? When they set off walking I followed them. Mr O'Neil wasn't going anywhere. He was flat on his back staring at the sky.'

'You followed them here, to the camp?'

'Yes, sir.'

'Where are they now?'

'As I told you, sir, the Nazi went charging up the hill there, after Jack, who was waving this flag as if he was leading the Charge of the Light Brigade. The man who put up his hand to stop the cars, sir, he's in that tent over there.'

Sir Charles and Mike turned fast, guns at the ready.

'Don't worry, sir, he's dead. Do you mind if I sit down, sir? I'm not used to seeing dead bodies and getting blown up.'

9

Sir Charles and Mike looked up the hill. Jack's den was at its top. They knew it well. When they'd been young, it had been their den. From where they were standing it was hidden by trees. What were Jack and George up to? Where were they? Had the Nazi caught them? One thing for sure, they were not sitting in The Hall, snug and safe in an attic making Spitfire aeroplanes out of balsa wood.

'Show us the body,' said Sir Charles.

'I don't want to see that horrible sight again unless I have to,' said Billy.

'You are sure he's dead?'

'If he's not, sir, he should be on the stage. He's doing a lot of staring and not a lot of blinking, oh, and there's a lot of blood.'

At the entrance to the tent Sir Charles told Billy that it was fine for him to stay outside.

'You can have the dogs for company,' said Mike. 'If there's anything out there, they'll tell you. Don't watch the trees, watch the dogs.'

In the tent Sir Charles and Mike found the station master with an arrow through his neck.

'Jack's handiwork,' said Mike.

'He's dead alright,' said Sir Charles.

'Lost a lot of blood … look what's on the arrow's tip.'

Sir Charles and Mike bent down to take a closer look. The arrow had entered one side of the station master's neck and come out the other.

'A straightened fish hook,' said Sir Charles.

'Sharp as a razor,' said Mike.

'Jack's an ingenious fellow, I'll give him that.'

Outside the tent they asked Billy if he'd seen what had happened.

'I was a good way behind the murderers, sir. I mean, I didn't want them to know I was following them. I mean, sir, him that's lying in there and the Nazi are killers. When I think about it, I'm lucky to be here. No wonder I can't stop shaking. It was Mr O'Neil who saved me. He wouldn't think of offering me a bite of his chocolate bar, but he did save my life … takes all sorts. All I saw, sir, was Master Jack running up the hill and doing what I told you before and the Nazi going after him.'

'And maybe George, in the distance?'

'Yes, sir.'

Mike took the dogs into the tent. He let them sniff.

'Find! Find!'

Much to his surprise they left the tent by a cut in its back wall. By the time he re-joined Sir Charles and Billy they were way up the hill, this time following a scent as straight as the flight of the arrow which had felled the station master.

10

'Billy, you go back to The Hall,' said Sir Charles. 'If it's any comfort to you, the army is on its way; report to Bert, tell him what's happened … off you go.'

'What about the Nazi, sir?'

'Mike and I are quite capable of dealing with him and, as I said before, the army is on its way.'

'Before you go,' said Mike, 'how is the Nazi armed? Rifle? Pistol?'

'He's a pistol with him, sir, definitely, and a rucksack full of those bombs on sticks.'

'Potato-mashers, are you sure?'

'Yes, sir. Before he set off after Jack I watched him take two of them out of the rucksack he was carrying. He put them round his neck and carried them like my sister sometimes carries her skipping ropes, the ones with the big wooden handles.'

An explosion, some way up the hill, made Sir Charles, Mike and Billy fling themselves to the ground.

'Off you go, Billy,' said Sir Charles.

'Is it safe to get up, sir?'

'He wasn't aiming at us … go the long way round, good luck and keep your head down.'

Billy ran off, bent double and at the double.

'Let's move to get a better view,' said Sir Charles. 'I want to be able to see the top of the hill. I want to see Jack's den.'

'You think, if the boys are anywhere they'll be in there?'

'If they are teasing the Nazi they'll need a bolt hole, somewhere they can run to and hide. The den you and I used to play in when we were lads is impregnable. I can't hear the dogs.'

'He's killed them.'

'Damn him!'

'I'll go first.'

Mike crawled into an area of bracken as large as a football field. Sir Charles followed. His knees ached, his back ached. He was no longer a young man. Was that blood he could see, seeping through Mike's breeks? His man's leg wound had had no time to rest. How long would it take Billy to reach The Hall and raise the alarm? How far off was Freddy with his platoon of soldiers? He indicated to Mike that before they took a peek, they should camouflage themselves. A Nazi armed with a rucksack full of 'potato-mashers' was a formidable opponent.

They stuck fronds of bracken into their shirt collars and into the peeks of their tweed caps. They spat into handfuls of soil; this 'disgusting mixture' as Lady

Elizabeth would have called it, they smeared across their foreheads and with little circular motions, rubbed it onto their cheeks, like women applying rouge.

When they raised their heads above the bracken, they were not going to pop up, like two white balloons, on a shooting range. From a pocket in his Norfolk, Mike took out a telescope. Sir Charles looked at his watch. They'd been hiding in the bracken for five minutes. During that time nothing had happened. The lack of a response from the Nazi suggested he did not know they were there. All they could hear was birdsong. How many times had it been like that in the Great War? Then, suddenly … Woosh! The chap beside you was in bits and pieces. They knew the arbitrariness of war, how coming to a halt at a certain spot, for no particular reason, other than perhaps to swat an irritating fly, while a comrade walked on, could save your life or lead to its end.

Sir Charles raised five fingers. Mike nodded. Sir Charles mimed one … two … three … four. At number five Mike raised his head above the bracken. No shots … nothing. But where was the Nazi? Was he closer to the bottom of the hill or the top? Through his telescope Mike scanned the hillside. When he lowered himself back down he said, 'He's killed the dogs. I've seen them or, what's left of them.'

'Do you think he knows we are here?'

'If he doesn't he damn well soon will.'

'He must know the dogs are with someone.'

Mike broke cover again but this time for less than a second before bobbing back down again.

'I've seen him.'

'Did he see you?'

'No, he'd his back to me. He's at the top of the hill, close to Jack's den. I'll take another look.'

Sir Charles also risked a peek, saw a distant shape moving towards the rocky outcrop hiding Jack's den. If it was the Nazi, and Mike armed with his telescope assured him it was, and the Nazi was armed only with a pistol and grenades, then, they were out of his range of fire. The Nazi, on the other hand, was not out of their range.

'Give me your shoulder, Charlie,' said Mike. 'It's a long shot, uphill, best if I rest on something.'

Both men stood up. Mike laid the rifle's barrel on Sir Charles's shoulder. Sir Charles, in anticipation of the noise the exploding cartridge would make, averted his head.

Through the rifle's telescopic sights Mike saw that the fanatic was on his knees, pulling at something sticking out of a clump of gorse.

11

Inside the cave George said, 'He's got hold of it … he won't let go.'

Jack put down the bow he was nursing and took hold of the sapling George was trying to stop the Nazi pulling through the fissure. On its end was a Star of David flag.

'It is a red rag to a bull,' said George.

'It is the flag of the country we Jews will build in Palestine. It is not a "red rag".'

George knew that now was not the time to explain that saying something was a 'red rag to a bull' was an English saying which meant you were making someone angry.

'Keep poking it out,' said Jack. 'I want to make him mad.'

The two boys were playing with the Nazi as a cat plays with a mouse. So far the Nazi had been an obliging mouse. He'd reacted as Jack had predicted. It did not occur to them that the 'mouse' might turn into a 'cat'. Jack shouted, in German, that Hitler was piece of snot.

'We give one hard tug, then let go,' said Jack.

'He's strong,' said George.

'Let go.'

In anticipation of what he thought would happen next Jack fitted an arrow to his bow; at its tip a straightened fish hook. He took aim. The cave grew dark. The Nazi must be looking through the fissure. He was stealing their light in the same way that the rest of his race had stolen Poland. Jack saw the hint of a moist, wet eye, an oyster in a red socket. He let the arrow fly.

12

'How obliging,' said Mike, 'he's standing up … damn, he's fallen down.'

Sir Charles looked through the telescope. The fellow was lying on his side. What was he doing?

'He's flinging a grenade at the den, damn him,' said Mike.

The exploding grenade made a noise all too familiar to Sir Charles and Mike and a little black cloud, which quickly disappeared.

In the ensuing quiet both men scanned the top of the hill; Sir Charles through Mike's telescope and Mike through his rifle's telescopic sights.

'I can see him,' said Sir Charles, 'he's lying down. You know, I do believe he might be injured.'

The two men took the hill at a pace they knew they could sustain. It would get them to the top quicker than running. Nor did they take the most direct route. They took advantage of trees and bushes to give them cover. The Nazi wasn't moving but that did not mean he was dead. Every so often they stopped to look at him. He was lying on his side with his back to them. 'Potato-Masher' grenades had spilled out of his haversack. Of most concern was the fact that in an outstretched hand he was holding a grenade. If he wasn't dead and threw it when they came within range, they'd be in mortal danger.

As a precautionary measure against this eventuality they split up. If the Nazi did 'come to life' he might take one but not two good Englishmen with him to Valhalla.

Sir Charles was taking the 'safety' of his shotgun when Mike shouted, 'He's dead … look.'

Moses was making a meal of the Nazi's ear. If the fellow didn't move when that was happening to him then he must be dead.

13

The Nazi had an arrow sticking out of an eye. Moses was enjoying licking blood coming from the wound.

'Nazi black pudding,' said Mike. To make sure the young man really was dead, he kicked him hard. Only then did he remove the 'potato-Masher' grenade, which, even in death the fanatic appeared to be on the point of throwing.

'It's Gunther,' said Sir Charles. 'I wonder if he's happy knowing that he died for a cause in which he believed?'

'God help us when we start fighting adult Nazis,' said Mike. He looked at the 'potato-masher'. 'I wish the top brass would arrange to put handles on our grenades. If they did we'd be able to throw a lot further. In close combat a yard or two makes all the difference.'

Sir Charles pushed aside a clump of gorse. He saw the fissure in the rock, an opening barely wide enough to take a chap's fist.

'George … Jack,' he shouted, 'can you hear me? You can come out now.'

'We can't,' said Jack.

'Grandfather, we're trapped,' said George. 'The Nazi has blown up our way out.'

Sir Charles moved closer to the fissure. 'Can you see me?'

'Yes,' said Jack. 'Is the Nazi dead? Did I get him?'

'Would it please you if I told you he has an arrow sticking out of an eye?'

'Yes … George, I got him.'

'That's super.'

'Boys, are you still there? What are you doing?'

'We're shaking hands,' said Jack. 'He tried to kill us but we killed him. We are the victors and he is the loser.'

'The sooner you two are returned to civilisation the better. For once in your lives do as you are told. I want you to watch your heads.'

'Why?' said Jack.

'I am going to open an entrance in the roof.'

'There's only one way in,' said Jack. 'It is my cave, I should know.'

'Do as you are told. George, put your hands on top of your head; tell Jack to do the same.'

'Yes, Grandfather.'

Sir Charles and Mike walked around the side of the outcrop and onto its top.

'It must be fifty years since we blocked the chimney,' said Mike.

'And now, two wars later, we are going to unblock it.'

14

The wooden plug, large as a dustbin lid, was hidden by heather. To anyone who did not suspect its existence, it was invisible. Sir Charles and Mike had made it with the help of Mike's father; that good man had understood their dream of having an impregnable den. When the chimney was blocked they would be safe from attackers showering them with red hot coals. At the time Sir Charles had been reading Ivanhoe.

Sir Charles' knuckle tapped the wood.

'Did you hear that?' he shouted through a gap where the plug was not a good fit.

Two voices shouted, 'Yes.'

Despite their best efforts the plug did not wish to move.

'We need a lever,' said Sir Charles. 'Speaking of which, here comes help.'

Soldiers, armed with pitchforks, were jumping out of a lorry. Lord Frederick, dressed in hairy tweeds but armed with a shotgun, led them upwards and onwards.

At his Lordship's approach Mike doffed his cap.

'Freddy, good to see,' said Sir Charles, 'though you are rather coming to close the stable door after the horse has bolted.'

'Is Harold dead?'

'Ah!' said Sir Charles, 'got your drift … the young Nazi with the arrow in his eye, yes, he's dead. What we need is a crowbar.'

'Could do with a snifter myself. What's in it? I've heard of a "screwdriver" but not a "crowbar" … American, I'll bet. These days everything that's new is American.'

Sir Charles explained

'Sergeant, back to the lorry for a crowbar, at the double.'

A few minutes later the sergeant returned with a five foot long steel pole.

'Just the job,' said Sir Charles. 'Mike and I will do the honours.'

'You should learn to delegate, Charlie. No reason why you should get your hands dirty, but I know I'm wasting my breath.'

The leverage made possible by the pole popped the plug. Sir Charles and Mike looked down into their old den; that lovely smell of peat and heather; the perfume of their youth.

Two bruised faces, but still more white than black and blue, looked back up at them. The light flooding into the cave made George and Jack blink.

Jack was first to recover his composure.

'You said you didn't know about the cave,' he said, 'but you did know.'

'It was a white lie,' said Sir Charles.

'It's a good job we did know,' said Mike, 'otherwise you two might have been buried alive. Bloody hell …'

The sight of the low flying German plane poleaxed them.

'The cheeky sod's waving at us,' said Mike.

'He's doing reconnaissance,' said Sir Charles. 'But how the hell did he get through? Where's Harry and his Spitfire?'

The soldiers scattered, threw themselves under bushes. Lord Frederick blasted the Nazi plane with his shotgun, a pointless gesture he knew, but, by god, it did make him feel good.

'What's happening?' shouted Jack. 'That's a German aeroplane. I know by the sound of its engine. I have heard that sound many times in Germany.'

Sir Charles looked down into the cave and saw that Jack was fitting an arrow to his bow. George had his hands on his hips as if ready to give the German a good dressing down.

'I'm going to get a rope,' said Sir Charles. 'Freddy, we need a rope.'

'Sergeant, back to the lorry, at the double. We need a rope.'

'Shall I get one with a noose in it, sir, ready for the German if he crash lands?'

'If he gets home,' said Lord Frederick, 'that fellow will be the toast of his mess. "I made the British army run like rabbits", that sort of thing. He'll be drinking schnapps on the back of his foray across the North Sea for the rest of his life.'

Thursday 7ᵗʰ September 1939

1

'Are you free to punt the pill?' asked the familiar voice.

'Give me time to check the weather,' said Sir Charles. He pressed the red button. 'Go ahead, Freddy, I'm on the scrambler.'

Over lunch Sir Charles told his wife, 'While you were out learning how to bandage a wound, Freddy rang. Don't look so alarmed.'

'When Freddy rings it means trouble. Why are we using the Royal Worcester and not the tin mugs?'

'We are using the Worcester to put up two fingers to Hitler.'

'Don't be rude, Charles. You have been tainted by the Americans.'

'At least they've gone.'

'Thank goodness for that, though I did like Marigold. Harry was quite smitten … wouldn't it be ever so nice if they were to form an attachment, don't you think?'

'Harry was the reason Freddy phoned. He was using the scrambler to stop anyone earwigging that Harry's going to give us an air show this afternoon. He's flying a Spitfire down from Scotland … going to fly low over The Hall, fifteen hundred hours, raise everyone's spirits. Show the people that when Hitler's Luftwaffe attack we have the wherewithal to give the blighters a bloody nose. The boys will enjoy it, which reminds me, I promised to arrange for Jack to have a ride in Harry's kite; he won't have forgotten … memory like an elephant. Where are they by the way?'

'At the Big Lake.'

'Fishing?'

'Yes, they were excited.'

'About fishing?'

'Yes.'

'That pleases me very much.'

'Why?'

'Do you remember that storm, the day Freddy rang to tell us about the Hitler Youth? How it flattened the flowers? How the next day was warm and sunny? How the plants picked themselves up, kind of shook off the rain the way dogs shake off water after a swim? After the "storm" of events the boys have been through, the fact that they are excited about a fishing trip tells me that, like the plants, they have come through … that is why I'm pleased.'

'Have you come through?'

'I am, my dear, the worse for wear.'

'It was nice of Jack to give Moses to the newspaper seller. Why are you smiling?'

'When I took George and Jack into town to say thank you to Chronicle the ferret Jack handed over to that good man wasn't Moses.'

'Jack still has the horrid little beast?'

'Yes. I'm afraid we will still have to be on our guard. The ferret we gave Chronicle was a substitute provided by Mike. Jack regards Moses as his lucky mascot.'

'To avoid misfortune one should be practical and not rely on lucky mascots.'

'Like reading tea leaves?'

Lady Elizabeth looked at her husband, took a deep breath and said, 'You have a point. CB's funeral was sad.'

Sir Charles nodded. 'It seems longer than yesterday.'

'A father and daughter, one grave, two bodies. The vicar was nice but he did keep casting glances at Emily.'

'Sergeant Belt won't like that. If the sergeant and the vicar come to blows over her, who will do the quelling? I was pestered by one of CB's cousins.'

'You told me.'

'All the CBs must come from the same stable. This chap's been to London to see about a command … wants to do his bit. Only some chap called Montgomery told him he was too old, that the TAs were amateurs and that the Germans were professionals. He's rather fuming. He wants me to write a letter to the General Staff complaining about his treatment. I don't know who this Montgomery chap is, but I have to say that I think he's right. The silly fellow told me he was all packed for the off, had his cricket bat strapped to his kit bag. No German officer would take a cricket bat to war.'

'Charles, you know as well as I do that Germans don't play cricket.'

'I want everyone out,' Sir Charles told Bert, 'on the front lawn. Here's a box of Union Jacks. I want everyone to have one.'

'Everyone, sir? Phyllis won't be happy, sir, to leave her kitchen at this time in the afternoon and stand on the front lawn waving a flag.'

'Leave Phyllis to me. Elizabeth, be a dear, go down to the kitchen, tell Cook what she is going to see. In the coming months all of us will have our noses put out of joint. It's something we'd better get used to.'

They heard the Spitfire before they saw it.

'That's thunder,' said Phyllis looking for clouds in the blue sky.

'That's not thunder, Phyllis,' said Bert, taking the liberty of linking arms with the cook, 'that's a Spitfire.'

Out of nowhere, on the stage of the sky, a great actor appeared. When it dived low over The Hall, Sir Charles cheered and shouted as loud as anyone. Later he locked himself in his study and wept.

CPSIA information can be obtained
at www.ICGtesting.com
Printed in the USA
BVHW032307160419
PP9843900001B/8/P